SF Books by Vaughn Heppner:

DOOM STAR SERIES
Star Soldier
Bio Weapon
Battle Pod
Cyborg Assault
Planet Wrecker
Star Fortress

EXTINCTION WARS SERIES
Assault Troopers
Planet Strike

INVASION AMERICA SERIES
Invasion: Alaska
Invasion: California
Invasion: Colorado
Invasion: New York

OTHER SF NOVELS
Alien Honor
Accelerated
Strotium-90
I, Weapon

Visit www.Vaughnheppner.com for more information.

Planet Strike

(Extinction Wars)

by
Vaughn Heppner

Copyright © 2014 by the author.

ISBN-13: 978-1496094155
ISBN-10: 1496094158
BISAC: Fiction / Science Fiction / Military

I remember the day the aliens struck back at us. They didn't like it that some of their combat slaves had killed their overlords and stolen a high-grade battlejumper.

We were in Earth orbit. It had taken us twelve days to get here from the Sigma Draconis star system. The "we," by the way, was one hundred and sixty-eight assault troopers, *former* assault troopers. We were free men now, looking down at our radioactive world.

The last humans lived in several dozen, city-sized space freighters: zoo specimens, I suppose. Most of the aliens thought of us as beasts. I'd come back to save humanity, to give us a fresh start. Thanks to yours truly, we had a military space vessel all our own. It wasn't much, but it was a start, the kernel to my plan.

I should have known the aliens of the Jelk Corporation couldn't let our rebellion stand. They had a grudge against us, which was symmetrical, because I had a granddaddy load of resentment against them.

I wore coveralls and boots when the aliens made their first attempt, a stealth attack we should have foreseen, but we didn't. I floated before an observation port in our battlejumper. My gut seethed because I had a terrible decision to make, one with no good answers. I'd come here to mentally wrestle with the issues, not fight to the death.

The clock showed three o'clock ship time. I floated because the grav-plates were down again, as engineers tinkered with the main system. We were still trying to figure out all the angles concerning the alien tech, and it was taking longer than I liked.

Our battlejumper orbited Earth about three hundred and sixty miles above England. I remember because of the wispy clouds high above the shallow cratered lake where London used to be. Like most of the great cities of Earth, London had been obliterated, leaving nothing but a radioactive pool of cobalt-colored water. I was looking at a dead world and it made me angry.

I could faintly see my face in the inner glass of the observation port. In the reflection, I saw a man floating toward me. I'd told the others I needed to be alone to think. They understood the importance of the decision. So what was the man doing here?

I turned around, and I realized I didn't recognize him. That should have given me a clue about what was going to happen.

He looked ordinary enough, a little under six feet with dark hair, a round face and slightly protruding frog's eyes. He wore an engineer's coveralls and seemed to be having trouble in zero gravity. He carted a toolkit in one hand and pulled himself along a rail with the other, showing the grace of a seal humping across ice.

"Commander Creed?" he asked, in a stilted way.

Something about his speech, about him, felt wrong. On general principle, I drew my laser pistol, aiming it at his head.

"Do not be alarmed," he said.

The way he spoke… Something jarred in me, turning my spine cold. "You're not human," I said. "You're an android."

Instead of answering, he pulled the toolkit closer to his chest, unlatching it with a snap.

I'd learned bitter lessons this past year. They had turned me into a paranoid killer. *Shoot first; ask questions later.* That sounded like good advice about now.

I aimed between his eyes and listened to my trigger click as I pulled it. To my shock, no laser beamed from the pistol's orifice. I clicked the trigger several more times and came up just as empty. Either my gun was defective, which I doubted, or… The android had something in the toolkit that shorted electronics. What else made sense?

2

Without any change of expression, the android told me, "Shah Claath sends you greetings, beast." Then he reached into the kit.

His words caused a small shock at the base of my skull. Then fury erupted in my heart. I'd never be anyone's slave again, certainly not the little red-skinned Rumpelstiltskin of a Jelk named Claath. If my laser didn't work—

I grabbed a float rail and pulled myself toward the android. As I moved, I let go of the useless pistol and slid my Bowie knife from its sheath.

I'd kept a blade on my person ever since my stint in prison as a youth. In those days, it had been a shiv with a cloth handle. The Bowie was bigger and better than that. It was my baby, a razor-sharp instrument of high-grade steel.

As I flew in the zero G, I noticed the android snapping something together in the toolkit. Was it a gun? If he'd already had it pieced together, I wouldn't have had a chance. He must have figured he'd have enough time so he'd left it unassembled. And this way, if someone had looked inside the toolbox too soon, he wouldn't have suspected the android. Very clever.

I grabbed the float rail two more times, giving myself greater velocity. I had to get to him before he assembled his weapon.

He pulled out a long-barreled gun with an oversized chamber in front of the trigger. He raised it, and his eyes widened.

I was there. I stabbed. His head shifted impossibly fast so the steel hissed against his cheek, making a hairline scratch but nothing more. Since I was speeding by, I didn't have time for another stab. Instead, with my other hand, as he turned to fire at me, I grabbed the barrel of the gun. The tip of the iron sights dug into my palm. I yanked the weapon out of his grip.

I laughed in an ugly way and twisted my body so my feet aimed in the direction I traveled. Sometimes my Jelk-induced training came in handy. Reaching a bulkhead, I used my legs to absorb the shock and brought myself to a stop about forty feet from him. I lined up the long-barreled gun and pulled the trigger. The weapon hissed, and it shivered slightly each time a

3

thin sliver sped from the tube. They stitched against his coveralls, shredding the synthetic material. Unfortunately, they crumpled against the android's toughened skin, failing to penetrate and do damage.

I could solve that. I switched targets, aiming for his eyes. They'd have to be soft enough, right? He lowered his head, taking the slivers against the hardened skull. Then he latched onto a float rail with his left hand, grabbed the toolbox-handle with his right and hurled the thing at me.

The box opened all the way and tools floated out. They still sped at me, coming like a cloud of meteors. I crossed my arms over my head and endured the box, wrenches and power drills. Something knocked my hand hard enough so the gun tumbled out of reach.

My forearms ached and cuts lacerated the skin. I looked up in time to see the android sailing at me. I leaped out of the way, barely in time. Open-palmed, he clanged a magnetized left hand against the wall. His right fist smashed against the bulkhead where I'd been. With a metallic screech, a section of wall folded and broke like tinfoil, with his forearm sinking halfway in. Circuitry behind the wall sparked and made crackling sounds.

Damn. He was stronger than I was, because I sure couldn't punch through metal like that. The thing was deadly, a killer.

I sailed in the zero G and bounced off a bulkhead like a ballerina, having nearly perfect body control. I'm not trying to brag. I'm just telling it like it was. The Jelk had trained me to combat perfection and I was going to use it now to stay alive. In those seconds, I realized I couldn't give the android time to go for the floating gun, so I sailed straight back at him. You don't win a fight by defending, but by going over to the assault. I had a feeling I had to take him down quickly, as his presence indicated other problems.

I reached him as he pulled his fist out of the wall, with driblets of insulation foam drifting from his wrist. With one hand behind his head, anchoring me, I stabbed the Bowie, thrusting the blade into his right eye.

That should have finished it. Instead, he shook his head and reached up for me. Despite my surprise, I pushed off and spun

4

away, twisting free of the grabbing fingers. He ripped my coveralls, though.

I watched as I floated away, waiting for the thing to die. Black gunk like oil dribbled out of the ruptured eye-socket, staining his nose and dripping into his mouth. To my surprise, he reached up, grabbed the bone handle and slid the Bowie out of his skull. The blade came out slowly and black-stained. How could he do that? He had pain sensors, right?

As if reading my thoughts, he grinned with oily teeth. "I do not keep my brain where you keep yours," he said.

I felt a terrible sense of deja vu. Claath had said something similar once, but concerning his heart. That he kept it in a different place where I kept mine.

The android lowered himself as if doing heavy squats. Sure, he must have magnetized his feet. He was getting ready to sail up at me.

I waited tensely. I'd have to time my reaction perfectly.

He jumped at me. I flew away from him but not fast enough. He grabbed an ankle with a bone-crushing grip, stopping my momentum. How much mass did this thing have? I used my free foot to hammer at his face. Once, twice, three times I struck, smashing the nose and breaking teeth with the heel of my boot.

He released me, trying to grab my kicking foot with both hands. My final kick came in faster and catapulted me away from him. I struck the floor, pushed off, shoved against a wall and reached the floating toolbox. Welded inside it was a small black container. I felt it buzz until I flipped a switch, turning it off. This must have been the device shorting the electronics in my laser pistol.

He stared at me with his good eye. I peered back at him for a frozen moment. He leaped. I leaped. We both went in different directions, trying to reach different objects. He touched the sliver-firing gun as my hand curled around the laser pistol. We each swiveled around. One of his thin projectiles stitched into my side. It hurt like a son of a bitch. I fired a fraction slower so I could aim, and I melted enough of his weapon to render it inoperative.

5

"Surrender," I said. "We'll reprogram you so you can work for us. You'll get to live that way."

He hurled the useless weapon, launching it like a missile. I'd expected him to say something first, so I almost failed to dodge in time. I could feel the thing lift my hair in its passage. At that speed, the melted gun would have killed me if it had struck my head.

I couldn't give him any more chances, so I fired the laser in a continuous beam. It put the smell of ooze in the air. Even as he magnetized his feet again, I used the laser like a giant scalpel and sliced his head free of the torso.

That didn't stop him, though. He jumped as his feet demagnetized, and he sailed at me. The head remained floating where it had been, gently turning.

The surreal spectacle slowed my reactions, although I ducked the grasping hands by flattening onto the deck plates. Then I leaped away. I had to put an end to this now. Maybe more were coming. Maybe androids attacked all over the battlejumper, hunting us down one by one. The vessel was huge, as I've said earlier. There were still areas we hadn't checked in detail. Could they have hidden there like vampires waiting for night to fall?

After two more bounces, I reached the drifting head. I burned out the remaining eye, blinding it. I figured the torso had a wireless connection to the head.

Still, the body kept attacking, following in my general direction. Did it use sound, smell or radar to locate me?

My pistol's battery indicator blinked red. I didn't have enough juice left to burn through the armored chest chassis. I imagined that's where it kept its AI. What was my goal anyway? It would be good to capture the mind, to interrogate or download it, find out what the thing knew. No. I had to disable it and find out if there were more like it aboard.

The torso sailed at me. I jumped at it. We collided. It grabbed flesh, and its fingers crushed with heightened strength.

I had an idea; and it came from an ugly expression I'd heard in prison from angry cons: "I'm going to rip off your head and piss down your neck." The android no longer had a head. It had a gaping opening in its torso there instead. I shoved the gun barrel into its neck. Instead of pissing, I used the remaining juice and beamed the laser into the body cavity.

Seconds later, the fingers relaxed their grip as the construct convulsed. I hadn't been able to burn through the chest chassis to the brain. Just like on a tank, though, the armor had been less thick above.

My ribs ached and the flesh felt pulped where it had held me. I checked my side where I'd been shot. My fingers came away bloody, but it could have been worse.

I jumped to the android's weapon. I'd never seen the design before: black, with a flat top. Breaking the gun open—it was the barrel that had melted—I discovered it had a gas cartridge. Yeah, I remembered hearing it hiss. The gas propelled a spring, ejecting a sliver. The weapon lacked electric impulses of any kind. Thus, the device in the toolbox hadn't shorted it. Tricky android.

I stuck the defective gun in my belt for further study later and remembered I'd left my communicator in my room. I'd wanted to be alone to think. Given what had just happened, that had been a stupid idea.

I swore, and I leaped for the hatch down the corridor. The android had originated from somewhere. The way I saw it, two possibilities existed. Either he had flown through space to the battlejumper, gaining entry from the outer hull, or there was a secret compartment in the vessel where he'd hidden for who knew how long. That would mean something had activated the android. At least that seemed like the most logical explanation. If he came from space, wouldn't that imply an enemy force was in the solar system? But if he'd been a sleeper aboard ship, my questions were two: first, were there more like him aboard? Second, what had woken him?

In some manner, the battlejumper was under attack. I swore again, opening the hatch. Was it already too late for us?

Why couldn't the damn aliens leave us alone? What had we ever done to them? One way or another, I was going to make them wish they'd never heard of me or of Earth.

-2-

For a time, I float traveled through empty curving corridors, straining to reach the others. I risked slamming against bulkheads when I made sharp turns because I sailed so fast.

The battlejumper was huge, a true space ark never meant to enter a planet's atmosphere or gravity field. It could hold tens of thousands of individuals and masses of equipment. Counting our engineers and techs, there were only a little over two hundred humans aboard. A pittance, really, less the number of curators it would have taken to keep the vessel a clean museum piece. To make matters worse, I had gone a long way into the uninhabited areas to ensure I could think alone, without interruption.

In case you're wondering about my big decision, it was this. We had three defective freighters. Nothing anyone did could get the grav-mechanisms working again on those three. That's how the Jelk had landed them in the first place. Without the gravity nullifiers, the huge scows could have never endured the Earth's Gs without breaking apart. If they remained broken, it meant none of the three freighters could lift off planet, and that stranded half a million humans.

The battlejumper had three working assault boats and a few air-cars. When the warship had been in top condition, there had been one hundred assault boats launching from the shuttle bays at a time. With a measly three boats, it would take us *weeks* to transport that many people to the other freighters already in orbit. In my estimation, we didn't have weeks. As I traveled

8

through the haunted corridors, I wondered if we even had a few days left.

Time was a huge problem. If I couldn't transport the half a million souls to the freighters, did I stick around as the techs tried to fix the grav-plates? Or did I write off those half a million humans in order to take the rest to a safe place? Yeah, I realized our situation called for hardhearted, no nonsense thinking. What was the most logical answer? I wanted to bring humanity back from extinction. If I saved too few people, maybe we'd simply die off like old dinosaurs because we lacked enough genetic diversity.

I'd racked my brain for an answer, arguing pros and cons both ways. Now the android assassin had showed up, ending the debate for the moment.

I gulped, and my heart beat faster. Three dead... I squinted. They were engineers by their coveralls and toolkits: red ones with black handgrips. Their toolboxes opened into levels. The men, their kits and tools floated in the middle of the corridor.

Using a rail, I slowed down until I reached the corpses. Blood globules drifted around them, while their faces had frozen in painful grimaces. A quick examination showed me tiny and multiple puncture wounds in their chests and necks. None wore communicators or smartphones. Androids must have taken them.

I nodded to myself.

I hadn't seen any comm-equipment on the one I'd slain. That implied different androids had killed these three. It told me the battlejumper was definitely under assault.

No, no, wait a minute, a colder part of myself said. My android could have easily killed these three and stashed the comm-equipment elsewhere. Yet if that was true—that he'd killed the engineers—had he broken apart his spring-firing gun after finishing them?

Hmm. The truth was I still lacked enough data to make a concrete conclusion.

As I wondered about my next move, I felt an aching sensation like a cold or flu. It felt as if the sickness was in my bones. I shivered, and I glanced at the damp spot on my coveralls. The sliver from the spring-gun had gone in just under my bottom left rib and out my back. Why should that make me ache? Had the splinter projectile contained a toxin?

While rubbing the material of one of the dead men, I realized I had to ignore the ache for now. I had to warn the crew. There might be more androids posing as engineers, moving through the ship and slaughtering us one by one or three by three.

I resumed traveling, listening for odd sounds. I didn't want to run into another assassin just yet. I needed a weapon first.

The interior battlejumper made plenty of its own noises, such as long creaks of shifting metal. It reminded me of a whale, this one a creature of the void. Pumps cycled air and they caused a constant thrum. Finally, recyclers occasionally hummed into life, always ending with a rattle like a smoker's hack.

I'd gotten used to the noises. Now they seemed alien again as I sought to hear something different. The flu-like pain became worse as I pulled myself along, and I shivered more often.

Finally, I reached an emergency comm-panel some of our techs had installed. I expected to find it wrecked, but it looked good. I pressed a button, and loud static came out of the speaker. I tried it again and got the same result.

My stomach twisted in concern. Was everything I'd fought for this past year going to be a waste of time? Had I gained freedom only to have it snatched away from me? Ever since the Lokhars—

I forgot. You might not have heard about them. The Lokhars were the first aliens, the ones who dropped the thermonuclear warheads and sprayed the bio-terminator on Earth. They were like upright tigers, seven feet tall with thick chests, dangling arms and retractable claws in their fingertips. They were also militarists, the Spartans of space. They'd gotten wind of the Jelk idea of using humans as ground pounders. To end run the idea, to make sure they didn't get our kind of competition, the Lokhars visited the Earth first. I hated the tigers. Their day was coming, believe you me.

Back then, during the first alien visit, my dad Jack went up to greet their ship. He went in a shuttle. The Lokhars used a laser on the craft, killing Mad Jack Creed.

What's the point of my telling you this? Instead of fearing the aliens—Lokhars, Jelk, whoever—I wanted to bust their heads. I wanted to get even. So despite the fear of another alien attack, there was also anger and rage, the primitive desire for retribution of the worst kind.

Thinking dark thoughts, I resumed my journey. The reward came five minutes later.

I heard rapid-fire talk down the corridor, like computers with voices who only spoke that way when humans weren't around to hear. I knew that androids sometimes communicated like that. Maybe just as bad, the voices headed my way.

I retreated until I reached an empty compartment, opening its hatch and closing it behind me with a minimum of sound. Floating near the top, I kept peering out the round glass window in the hatch. Finally, I saw three androids float past. They carried rifles and wore cyber-armor: mechanical skin, molded to fit them.

The sight jarred me. That was combat weaponry, not just an assassin's tool. Well, now I knew. The battlejumper was under a full-blown enemy stealth assault. I hadn't heard any klaxons wailing due to hull breaches. That was telling.

I had to use my wits. So what did I know? My android killer had given me greetings from Claath. That implied…what exactly? I expect it meant someone had sent a radio signal, or some kind of signal, activating the androids. Had they been in hidden storage areas as I'd first suspected? That made the most sense. But if someone had sent a signal, that would have to mean at least one alien vessel had reached our solar system, and that meant they knew where we'd taken the battlejumper.

Yet if all that were true, why hadn't I heard from anyone else yet? Why hadn't a ship-wide alert gone out? Was I alone, the last human left on an empty vessel?

I need my armor and a gun, a real one.

Exiting the dark compartment, I floated stealthily through the corridors. I felt naked and defenseless, hating the sensation.

The next ten minutes were among my worst. Not only did I feel rotten and weak, but I also had no idea what the situation was with the rest of my troopers. I couldn't afford to lose a single soldier.

Sweat dripped off my face as I finally entered my room. A groan escaped me. The chamber was a mess, with cushions, bed sheets and junk floating everywhere. Androids must have been here, and they had tossed it, looking for something. Did that mean they'd taken my armor and weapons?

I jumped to the closet, hitting it harder than I wanted, rebounding and drifting away. For twenty seconds, I flailed uselessly. Eventually, I floated to a wall and shoved off. This time I grabbed the closet handle, anchoring myself. I opened the thing and knew a vast sense of relief as I spied the heat unit. The green light was on, indicating that it still worked. I drew out the unit, lifting the lid. I found it there, and pulled it out: a hefty black blob. I pushed it onto the floor where it quivered in anticipation. Taking off my shoes and my clothes, I stepped naked onto the blob. The substance oozed onto my legs, coating my flesh. It felt warm, a comfortable sensation.

This was second skin, symbiotic alien armor, genetically engineered for human use. Alive after a fashion, it could heal itself at times. The outer surface would harden and it allowed the wearer to operate in a vacuum, in outer space. The skin also amplified human strength. At times, it secreted a battle drug into our system. It must have done that now, giving me something to counteract the toxin.

The familiar symbiotic skin rushed up my thighs, over my belly button and didn't stop until it reached my chin. I put on my helmet and grabbed the gun in the closet. The androids should have disabled it. That was a mistake on their part. I checked the battery pack. It had a bar symbol on it, with the green all the way to the + sign on top. The laser rifle had a full charge. We had taken to calling it a Bahnkouv assault rifle. Dmitri had told us about an experimental Russian laser, the design headed by a Dr. Bahnkouv. I liked the name because it was human.

As the aching feeling receded, righteous fury boiled in me. I would attack with my Bahnkouv. I would kill. I would—I shook my head.

The armor was doing that, or some of it, at least. The symbiotic skin had been engineered to prompt soldiers to attack head-on in a storm assault. That meant the suit often turned a trooper into nearly a berserker warrior. How else could a man psyche himself up into attacking blazing weaponry?

At this point, outwitting the androids was the key. I had to save troopers and the battlejumper, not just win a firefight.

Did the androids monitor my helmet's radio frequency? I had to risk transmitting. I chinned the command channel. Before I could send out a signal, I received one.

"There are too many," Rollo was saying to someone. "They're driving us away from the armory."

"You must fight through," N7 said. "Unless we—"

Rapidly spoken chatter—enemy androids—broke onto the channel. Did they do that to disrupt our communications or were they directing each other on the same frequency? Probably the first reason. That showed me more than ever they had originated on our vessel. They must have been monitoring us for some time to know the right frequency to use.

With a grimace, I leaped out of my room. On my helmet's HUD display, I pinpointed N7's location in the battlejumper's control room. Rollo was closer, several corridors over, in fact.

"Okay, you bastards," I muttered to myself. I leaped with power, with feral, suited strength. I was a space-assault trooper again, with vengeance thrumming in my brain. My neuro-fibers gave me heightened speed. The bio-suit amplified my muscles—

I heard laser fire before I actually saw it, a high whiny noise. Cyber-armored humanoids also clanked down the halls like automatons. It told me they used magnetized boots in the zero G.

I unlatched a grenade from my belt, twisted the setting and peered around a corner. The androids had gotten cocky. They hadn't left a rearguard. Three of them in a staggered formation moved purposefully away from me, with their rifles beaming.

13

Farther away on the other side of the androids, I heard men shouting, my friends. I recalibrated the grenade's setting to something lower. Rollo's comment earlier meant they were unarmored. I didn't want to kill my friends with too high a blast.

I hurled the grenade and ducked back around the corner. A terrific flash and a loud *crump* told me the grenade ignited. Instantly, I darted back into the corridor. One android drifted. One was missing an arm. The last one had torn cyber-armor on its back and swiveled toward me. Blasting with heavy laser fire, I beamed through its visor. Then I remembered my original attacker. I switched targeting to the chest and burned him down with several seconds of concentrated fire.

Then it was over. I'd killed the three androids.

"Rollo," I shouted.

"Creed?" he yelled. "Is that you? The androids told us you were dead."

"Hurry here. We have to get to the armory."

"Creed, Starkien warships are coming through the jump point. N7 counted at least five beamships near Neptune."

I closed my eyes in pain. We needed time to get every freighter in orbit, and time to escape from here and hide in a lonely star system. If I couldn't win free from Earth, human life might cease to exist.

By what Rollo said, it appeared as if Starkien contractors had come after us. I hated the technocratic baboons. That's what Starkiens looked like: furry monkey-creatures with bulging foreheads so you knew they were clever. Just like all the other aliens, they thought that humans were animals.

I'd worked with Starkiens before. In their case, contractors really meant they were nomadic pirates for hire. Had the Starkiens signaled sleepers hidden on our battlejumper? If true, that meant the Starkiens worked under Jelk backing, and that likely meant Claath.

"Hurry up!" I roared. "We have to clear the androids off our battlejumper. We have to get ready to face the Starkiens."

Rollo appeared at the other end of the corridor. Three other troopers followed him, one with a bandaged and broken arm. My friend used to be long and lanky. Steroid-68 had turned him into a muscled gorilla with thick deltoids. He had an angry red laser burn on his cheek, looking like Indian war paint. How close had I come to losing my best friend?

"Come on," I said. "We have to get to the armory. We need to get you boys suited up."

"How are we going to beat five Starkien beamships?" Rollo asked, as pain flashed across his face. The laser burn must hurt. "We're screwed, Creed. Everything we worked for—it's over."

"Not yet," I snarled. The pain had apparently made him pessimistic. "Now hurry up. We don't have all day."

I took point. As we traveled through the metallic corridors, I noticed the flu feeling again. It pulsated in my bones, attempting to steal my strength and dull my wits. The suit tried to counteract it. I could feel each drug entering me. The toxin must be more powerful than the suit's ability to handle, though.

That made me paranoid. If the android poison was too strong, the symbiotic skin could be dampening the symptoms even as the toxin killed me. I had to get to sickbay and get treated. First, however, I had to clear my battlejumper of android sleepers.

"Creed," Rollo whispered.

"What's wrong?" I asked in a low voice. I had my visor open so I could hear him.

"There's something just up the corridor," Rollo whispered. "Can't you hear it?"

I must have been sicker than I realized. No, I hadn't noticed anything. Now I did. From around the corner, metal scraped against metal and I heard a purr that could only mean a flamer, a portable piece of heavy weaponry that fired heated plasma.

"We know you are near," an android called. "We see you on our scanner. Surrender; you cannot reach the armory and it is useless for you to die."

"How did you get on my ship?" I shouted.

"The battlejumper belongs to the Jelk Corporation," the android said. "It is the property of Shah Claath, your owner. You must return it."

"Is that what you are, property?"

16

"Why do you labor against reality? You know the answer to your question."

"Do I?"

"If you are Creed, know that we will accept your surrender. Shah Claath is eager to regain you in prime condition."

"The thing's trying to trick us," Rollo said.

I motioned Rollo to give me his jacket. Once he did, I balled it up. Then I whispered, "Get back, and await my signal."

Rollo retreated to the others.

"Have you come to the logical conclusion?" the android asked. "Are you ready to submit?

"You promise me you'll take my surrender?" I asked.

"You have our word," the android said. "Claath will be most pleased."

"All right," I said. "Don't shoot. I'm coming in."

I edged toward the T-shaped corner and hurled the jacket. I saw a flash of silver buttons just before the jacket disappeared into the other corridor. Almost immediately, the flamer whirred with sound and made a belching noise. The superheated plasma boiled through the corridor, no doubt burning the jacket in a second.

I'd already backed up. The expanded plasma passed me. I felt the wash of heat through my suit and helmet. Luckily, I'd already shut the visor, or I might have sucked down superheated air.

As soon as the ball of plasma passed, I pulled myself around the corner and fired, aiming at the tripod-mounted flamer. It would take the mechanism at least another thirty seconds to recharge for a second shot.

"I see him," an android said.

"Fire!" the leader told him.

My suit absorbed their laser fire for less than three seconds. At the end of that time, my beam broke into the flamer's armored core. The heavy weapon exploded with the building plasma charge.

I ducked behind my corner.

17

An orange glow like a new sun told me the plasma expanded. It made sizzling noises, meaning it ate corridor steel and androids.

Portable plasma cannons were like old-time flamethrowers from WWII. Both were nasty, terrifying weapons. They each devoured enemy soldiers. The problem with both weapons was their vulnerability to enemy fire. If a bullet hit a flamethrower's tank back in the day, it could end in a fiery death for everyone nearby. The same thing had happened here to the sleepers.

Finally, the glow died down like a setting sun.

"Be careful as you pass the area," I told the others. "Everything is hot and could burn you if you touch it."

"Don't worry about us," Rollo said.

We passed the melted androids and the metallic sopping walls. I saw beads of molten metal dripping like tears. One of the troopers shouted in pain then as a floating piece of red-hot plasma sizzled against his calf muscle.

Another turn in the corridor brought us to the front of the armory. I opened the vault and in a matter of minutes, I had five suited troopers, not just one.

"What's next?" Rollo asked, as he sealed a helmet over his head.

I'd been mulling that over; the answer depended on several factors. How many androids were on our ship and where did they attack? And where were the rest of my people?

"N7, can you hear me?" I said through my helmet's comm-unit.

I got high-speed chatter for an answer, and that told me all I needed to know. The enemy still blocked our communications.

"We stick together," I told the others. "We're a hunter-killer team."

"Which way do we go?" Rollo asked.

What would I do if I were a Starkien contractor? If I could wake sleeper units on an enemy vessel, I'd go for life support first and the engine second, disabling it. But in order to do their task…yeah, they had to keep the troopers away from their suits. The best way to do that would be to kill them.

"We're heading for our main quarters," I said. I meant where the majority of the troopers slept and practiced.

On the way there, we slew three more androids. Then we hit another concentration of them, and it devolved into a firefight.

These androids had more mass and strength than we did and they had tougher skin than the training models used on us a year ago. Even so, the androids couldn't compete against a suited trooper. That was only logical. Otherwise, Claath would have built androids and used them for his soldiers for hire. He had come to Earth for a reason. One of them clearly was that humans made excellent ground pounders, individual soldiers with a Bahnkouv and grenade.

We proved that during the next few minutes.

"Lucy is hit," Rollo said, meaning the trooper who had burned her calf earlier. Her left shoulder smoked from concentrated enemy laser fire.

"Get behind us," I told her.

She didn't want to do that, as Lucy was in the grip of battle fury. But she obeyed because she belonged to the toughest, best-trained outfit in the galaxy: the last of us out of many thousands. There had been something like twenty-three thousand human troopers in the beginning. One hundred and sixty-eight had made it back to Earth: the lucky, the mean, the tough and the royal bastards that nothing but atomic weaponry could take down.

"I'm done playing around," I said, a minute later and after a particularly nasty laser exchange with the androids. The bright beams had put little purple splotches in my vision. "Cover me." I wanted to take out these androids *now*.

"Creed, wait," Rollo said.

No. We didn't have any more time to wait. Starkien beamships were near Neptune. How much time did that give us here on Earth? Several days, hours, I don't know. What I did know was that we had to kill these androids yesterday.

I clicked a grenade onto the highest setting and hurled it at the final clump of androids in the game room. We'd managed to drive them into there. They hid behind metal boxes, gaming equipment and lifting machines.

19

Two androids leaned out, beaming the grenade as it sailed at them. *Thank you, you piles of automated crap.* I shot one through the neck, a direct hit with a heavy laser. The other one darted behind the gym equipment.

A third took a shot at me as I sailed into the room. The laser smoked against my symbiotic armor. Then I was down behind a metal box. My armor squirmed, and it secreted an oozing black substance that acted like a scab. Given time, the suit would heal. I slithered along the floor, and tossed another grenade. None of the androids saw it, and the capsule sailed past the gym equipment before going nova. That meant I took damage, but not as much as the closer enemies did.

"At your two o'clock," Rollo said.

My turn came to beam a grenade, which I did from my back while shooting from the hip. An android decided for a fancy play, slithering out to meet me. He died. I leaped up toward the ceiling and caught another one trying the same thing on the floor. I beamed him in the back.

Then Rollo charged into the room, followed by Hanks.

We took out the rest of the stubborn constructs, and we burned the carcasses for good measure.

That freed ten troopers holed up in the other room. They'd had several laser pistols, and had held off the androids just long enough for us to get here.

"Escort them to the armory," I told Rollo. "Once they're suited, head for life support. My guess is more androids are on their way there."

"How many of those things are loose on our battlejumper?" Rollo asked.

"Too many," I said.

"Claath should have used them when we first stormed aboard in Sigma Draconis and grabbed the battlejumper," Rollo said. "He might have stopped us that way."

"He was too busy at the time." I meant with Jennifer. A cold feeling knotted my gut. Jennifer was on the battlejumper somewhere.

Jen was my girl, an Earth orphan, her parents picked up during WWII during a Jelk observation run. She'd grown up as a tame human on an alien world. Trained as a nurse, she had come back to help process millions of men and women through neuro-fiber surgery. The Lokhar nukes and bio-terminator meant she'd only helped with a few thousand surgeries. In any case, she'd held Claath at gunpoint after we'd teleported onto the battlejumper at Sigma Draconis.

Maybe that's why the androids had remained hidden until now. Claath hadn't been able to release them against us. In a way, I wish he had done so back then. We could have killed them all then, as long as they wouldn't have tipped the scales against us twenty-one days ago.

"Go," I told Rollo.

"What are you going to do?" he asked.

"Hanks, you're coming with me. We need everyone suited and armed," I told Rollo. "Now no more jawing. We all have work to do."

Rollo saluted, a lazy, two-fingered thing, and left with the others. Hanks and I traveled in a different direction.

During the next twenty minutes, the two of us freed fifty more troopers, killing eight androids in the process. The alien chatter had grown less on the helmet channel. It told me the number of androids had become considerably fewer.

"What's happening in space, N7?" I asked. "Give me a status report."

Our android was in the control room.

"There's something else coming out of the Neptune jump point," he said from the bridge.

I checked my HUD map. I saw five suited trooper teams now, moving through the vessel. We'd lost ten people so far, most of those techs picked off the various freighters.

"Can you fire our battlejumper laser at the Starkien warships?" I asked N7.

"Fire the laser all the way to Neptune?" he asked.

I recalled the Sigma Draconis battle. The Jelk battlejumpers and Starkien beamships had taken on a Lokhar guardian fleet. During the battle, I'd seen how Jelk heavy lasers had outranged the Lokhar primary beams. I figured we had that same advantage here against the Starkien vessels. The only problem was that we had a single working beam and they had brought five of their warships…well, at least five.

I wanted to be in the control room with N7. It surprised me the androids hadn't already hit the place. Yeah, I saw N7's point about range. Neptune was an insane distance. I didn't know about any alien weapons system other than missiles that could reach so far. Clearly, our laser couldn't.

"I'm heading for you," I told N7.

"I've managed to finally bring up the interior battlejumper schematic," he told me.

"I thought that was being jammed."

"It was," N7 said. "I rerouted and now I have a full interior map."

"Excellent."

"I'm transmitting to you," N7 said.

My helmet uploaded through the link and I studied the situation on my HUD. According to this, five android teams remained. We'd gotten half of them, and there were more suited troopers every minute.

Okay. Good. The enemy had played a surprise. They had bought themselves some time with it, but that was all. They hadn't murdered very many of us and so far, they hadn't been able to dismantle the battlejumper. On our side, we'd eliminated half the androids and gained full control of the battlejumper—or would very soon.

I better recalled ship laser distances from what I'd seen during the Sigma Draconis Battle. We should be able to target and hit Starkien beamships something on the order of ten million kilometers away. The Starkiens had much smaller vessels. Their beams could only reach a million or so kilometers. That was still far, but not against a Jelk heavy laser.

We could win this fight…provided our primary laser didn't burn out and provided we got all the sleepers aboard our ship.

I should have realized there was a third enemy option. Yeah, I should have realized it even as I hurried to the control room.

-4-

I floated onto the bridge. There were various stations built on a main dais in the center of the chamber. They were like a Stonehenge ring, although on a smaller scale. The lower floor circled the dais. One part of the wall down there held a giant screen, the main one. Presently, troopers manned the stations, along with one of the new engineers and N7.

He was an android, an N-series, heavy-G mining type with advanced upgrades and a bio-brain. N7 had thrown in his lot with us during the storming of the Lokhar Planetary Defense Station. The android had proven invaluable to our gaining freedom and he had become my friend.

N7 was strong, although not steel-wall punching powerful, looked like a blond-haired choirboy and knew far more about Jelk technology than any of us did. He was the reason why our engineers and techs had learned anything useful.

As I entered, I saw Earth below on half the main screen. Morning dawned in the Sahara Desert in North Africa. The other side of the split-screen showed Neptune, 4.5 billion kilometers away, and the five blue dots indicating the Starkien beamships. The actual jump point was a small yellow dot near the gas giant. As I entered, another blue dot exited the jump point. Clearly, the Starkiens still had more warships coming.

I wasn't as interested in the baboons at the moment. There were three red dots on Earth, showing where the last freighters rested. The other barges had already climbed into orbit.

"I see you've spotted the enemy flotilla," I said. "But I doubt any radio signal came from them to us to wake up the sleepers."

"Agreed," N7 said.

"You do?"

"Logic dictates there should be a source point somewhat closer."

"Have you been scanning for that source point?" I asked.

"Indeed," N7 said. "I sent Bey and Hodges onto the other side of Earth, patching through their instrumentation to us. So far, I have not detected any anomalies."

Bey and Hodges each commanded a space freighter. Originally, Claath had left the people in each vessel to their own devices. They hadn't been able to lift off then. It had made the places prison houses, with the toughest and most cunning climbing to the top. Few of the freighters had practiced democracy, but the law of tooth and claw instead. Murad Bey was a Turk and Rex Hodges had once been a tackle for the Dallas Cowboys. I had left them in control of each of their ships for now, since we didn't have time for anything else.

"What about the Moon?" I asked N7. "Is anything suspicious going on there?"

"There are no anomalies near Luna," N7 said, "although someone could be hiding on the dark side."

"What do you believe about the androids? Did they gain entrance from space or were they sleepers aboard ship?"

"Probabilities and logic indicate the stealth teams originated on the battlejumper," N7 said.

"Obviously then, somebody woke them to coincide with the appearance of the Starkien flotilla."

"I congratulate you," N7 said. "That is the most logical conclusion."

"Then you believe like me that someone is out there closer to us than Neptune?" I said.

"I have already indicated as much."

Making a fist, I tapped it against my chin. A Starkien flotilla, android stealth teams…what else had Claath thrown against us? This all must have originated with him. No one else among the Jelk would care enough. Still, the last time I'd seen

Claath, he'd turned into a ball of energy, burning through bulkheads and floating away into space. He'd done that to escape me—I'd tied him to chair and tortured him for answers. He'd still been humanoid, flesh and blood then. Could he operate like a ball of energy, communicating with regular people? Or had Claath been forced to turn back into a flesh and blood creature? It seemed like a crazy question, but there was too much about interstellar space that had turned out to be just plain weird.

"How far out could a signal have originated to reach the sleepers?" I asked.

"Far?" N7 asked.

"Reasonably," I said, "taking into consideration that this was a military operation."

"That would depend on the sophistication of the message."

"We—"

"A moment, please," N7 said. He tapped his board, checking it, and said, "I have detected an anomaly in Mars orbit."

"Put it on the screen," I said.

He complied, saying, "I am amplifying the image and giving the anomaly a blue color."

Earth and Neptune disappeared from the split-screen. Now Mars appeared, and like a mole peering out of its hole, the blue image showed on the far left edge of the Red Planet, practically in the atmosphere.

"I am increasing magnification," N7 said.

Mars grew so we only saw a portion of the planet. The anomaly likewise gained size, and I saw it had a shark shape, although minus any dorsal fin. Instead, there was a rotating dish up there.

"Is that a Starkien vessel?" I asked.

"It would appear so: a cutter class, a scout."

"That clinches it," I said.

"The logical course is to destroy the scout," N7 said. "I suggest we launch a missile and prepare to leave the solar system now."

"With three freighters still stuck down on the planet?" I asked.

"The majority of something is better than nothing," N7 pointed out.

I frowned and rubbed my forehead, which was sweaty and hot. What should I do? To cut and run, and leave those half a million people to the Jelk Corporation...

"Launch the missile," I said. "And launch several drones farther out toward Neptune. If we decide to head to Jupiter, we're going to want to give the Starkiens something to think about."

The solar system had three known jump points: one near Jupiter, another near Neptune and the last far beyond Pluto. Each jump point led through its own route and came out into vastly different star system.

"I am launching the first missile," N7 said, as he tapped his board.

We didn't feel anything. The battlejumper dwarfed the missiles, although they were bigger than the old cruise ship Queen Mary.

"How many drones should I launch toward Neptune?" N7 asked. "Our supply is limited."

"Good question," I said. "We don't want to fire the drones yet if we're not heading for the Jupiter jump point."

"I suggest that we must escape the solar system while the opportunity presents itself," N7 said. "We must therefore begin now. The Starkiens block the Neptune jump point, so we must either try for Jupiter or Pluto."

"Do you think the Starkiens or the Jelk will have warships waiting at the other end of either of those two routes?" I asked.

"Unlikely, but possible," N7 said.

I tapped my chin again, thinking. The distances involved in our solar system were huge. Light took approximately eight minutes, seventeen seconds to leave the Sun and reach Earth. Battlejumper teleoptics were many times more powerful than the Hubble telescope had been. They showed us the Starkien flotilla near Neptune. That information was already many hours old, the speed light took traveling from Neptune to Earth: something over four hours, if I remembered correctly. The same thing had occurred with the Mars scout, but within a much smaller timeframe, mere minutes instead of hours.

"It would appear the Jupiter jump point makes the most sense," I said, "given that we would begin running now."

"Affirmative," N7 said.

"The battlejumper could get there much faster than our freighters," I said. After mulling that over, I told N7, "Contact the freighter leaders. See how long it will take each of their ships to get ready for steady acceleration."

N7 and several other crewmembers began working on that, hailing the vessels. As they did, Rollo entered the bridge. His visor was open, the helmet framing his face and laser burn. He looked concerned.

"I found something you might want to see," Rollo told me. "We tore it off one of the androids, a commander model, I believe."

"What do you have?" I asked.

Rollo dug a small silvery object out of a belt pouch. The thing was about the width of my thumbnail, with the thickness of a smartphone.

"The android was shredded junk after we were through with it," Rollo said. "This thing seemed out of place. I thought it might be important, so I checked it."

"Interesting," I said, without touching the tiny object. "What do you suppose it is?"

"I already know. Are you ready for it?"

I glanced at him, curious now, and nodded.

Rollo pinched the thing so his fingernails whitened, and the tiny device seemed to flicker. A closer examination showed me that it glowed on one end. Then a hazy light or a projection emanated from it. The projection spread outward several feet until a holo-image of Claath's head appeared. The head was normal-sized for a Jelk, meaning as big as a seven-year-old's.

Claath had blood-colored skin and narrow features. And he had dark, extremely intelligent eyes. When he opened his mouth, one could see pointy teeth like a piranha. The worst was the voice.

"If you're watching this," the image said in Claath's arrogant manner, "I must assume the androids failed. I would call that a pity, except I will take immeasurable pleasure in capturing you. The indignities you have heaped upon my person have burned the desire for retribution deep into my psyche. You are doomed, Creed-beast. The entire resources of the Jelk Corporation will be turned against you and your pitiful species. You might have endured if you had remained faithful to your contract. Now, your ingratitude has sealed your fate and that of your kind."

I wanted to punch Claath in the face. I wanted to figure out a way to kill the Jelk. I'd tried once, and as I've said, he turned into a ball of energy, burning through bulkheads to escape into space. Now the little prick was threatening me again. That seemed like a pretty fast turnaround, which was daunting.

"Know this, Creed-beast," the image of Claath said, "Jelk never fail. Savor your last few hours or days of life. By now, you must realize that your worst fears are descending upon you: the utter extinction of humanity. That is the dreadful cost for laying hands upon my sacred person."

The holo-image smiled nastily and the eyes seemed to shine with ruthlessness.

"The next time you see me, beast, I will be standing over your prone form as my servant withdrawals your intestines from your bowels. It will be a brutal end for a savage creature I should have destroyed the first time I laid eyes upon you."

The image flickered and abruptly withdrew into the silvery object as a genie turned to smoke pours back into its bottle.

I glanced at Rollo.

"I've been with you for years," he said. "And there's something I've always been wondering. It doesn't matter if we're on Earth or in space. You have a knack for making people angry."

"*Molon labe*," I said, speaking Greek.

"What's that mean?"

"You ever hear about the Battle of Thermopylae?" I asked.

"Of course," Rollo said. "That's where the three hundred Spartans stood off the Persian army for a couple of days."

"Actually, it was about six thousand Greeks holding the Middle Gate pass through the mountains," I said. "The Persians finally found a Greek goat herder to tell them about a secret path to get behind the blocking force. King Leonidas of the Spartans sent most of the force to try to block them, but was too late. Seven hundred Thebans and others stood with the three hundred Spartans at the Middle Gate. The others soon surrendered, though, the seven hundred, I mean. The main army got away to fight another day."

"Okay," Rollo said. "But what does any of that have to do with *molon labe*?"

"The Persians surrounded the three hundred Spartans and told them to surrender their weapons." Despite our predicament here, I grinned, thinking about King Leonidas and his three hundred battered hoplites. I loved the story. Maybe I loved it more now because I could relate to it better than ever. Those had been men, those Spartans, soldiers to the very last.

"What's wrong now?" Rollo asked. "Why are you grinning like that?"

"The Spartans were known for giving laconic answers," I said. "Laconic means 'brief' or 'terse.' *Molon labe* was probably their shortest answer ever given. It meant, 'come and take.' Can you imagine that? Thousands of enemy surrounded them, demanding their surrender, and they said, 'Come and take,' like giving the Persians the finger."

"What did the Persians say to that?" Rollo asked.

"Something like, 'Our arrows will fly so thickly that they will block the sun.' The Spartans answered a second time, saying, 'Good. We'll fight in the shade then.'"

Rollo smiled ruefully so only his upper teeth showed.

"*Molon labe* also meant something else, too," I said. "You know how some in the U.S. Government wanted to grab all our guns?"

"I do," Rollo said.

"Well, people had begun writing molon labe on blogs and stuff. It meant the same thing, 'Come and take.' The idea being, if the government sends its agents, they're going to have to kill us first before we surrender our guns to anyone. In other words, we're going to fight to the death for our freedom, even against government tyrants."

"And that's our answer to the Jelk?" Rollo asked.

"That's right," I said. "We're going to stand like men to the very end. Only I'm planning to change the outcome of the story, at least compared to the Spartans. I plan on winning, not losing. I'm going to kill our Persian king."

"That would be a good trick," Rollo said.

Yeah. It would, especially since the Starkiens had already found us.

I studied the main screen. It showed the jump point near Neptune. The point wavered. It meant yet another ship was coming through, maybe more.

"What kind of vessels are the Starkiens bringing in now?" I asked. "Are they more beamships?"

N7 made adjustments on his panel and brought up a zoom image. The regular Starkien ships were as big as city blocks. It made them much smaller than the battlejumper. That was important in a space battle. A lesser engine generated reduced wattages compared to a big one. A smaller ship also had lesser mirrors and coils, meaning a much weaker laser.

"This is interesting," N7 said.

"What is it?" I asked. "Show me."

N7 indicated the screen. A vessel exited the jump point. It had a different kind of geometric design.

"That doesn't look like a Starkien ship," I said.

"It is not," N7 said.

"It doesn't look like a Jelk vessel, either."

"I will save you time as you attempt conjectures. It is a Lokhar military missile."

"I knew it looked familiar," I said. "What kind of missile?"

"A teleportation bomb such as we saw in Sigma Draconis," N7 said, "but a bigger version than the one we used reaching the battlejumper."

Teleportation bomb—the idea put a cold lump in my chest. As the name implied, the thing teleported across distances. It meant one couldn't shoot it down as easily as it approached, because one minute it was far and the next it materialized right next to you. Then: *kaboom!* It was a tricky bit of business.

"What's the range of those things?" I asked. "How far can one teleport?"

"An interesting question," N7 said. "I will check the data banks."

"Did the Starkiens pick those up after the battle at Sigma Draconis?" I asked.

"We did during the battle," N7 said. "Why couldn't they do the same thing afterward?"

I nodded. That made sense.

As I waited for N7 to find the missile's range, I started feeling even worse than before. My bones felt as if they pulsated with pain. I gutted it out, even as sweat pooled under my collar. My stomach began roiling and twisting.

The main hatch opened, and Jen floated in. She was beautiful, with a sweet face. I particularly loved her warm hands. A healer by nature, she was the heart I lacked. Maybe that's what attracted me so deeply to her.

"Hey," I said.

Normally, she smiled. Fear and worry showed on her face now. It put red splotches on her cheeks. "Look at him," she said. "What's wrong with you people? Can't you see he's sick?"

"What?" I said. "I'm fine."

"No you're not," she said. "Ella brought me the gun, the one that fires biodegradable toxins."

"The sliver?" I asked, as I began to shake.

"Rollo, help me," Jen said. "We have to get him into the healing tank now. He must be dying. The toxins are killing him."

"N7, have you come up with the distance yet?" I asked.

Our android said something that I didn't fully catch. I might have asked him a second time. I'm not sure. A klaxon began to wail. It startled me. I opened my mouth to demand to know what was going on. Then I must have passed out, because I remembered nothing after that.

5

I must have been dreaming as I floated unconscious in the healing tank. Did the dream come because of the toxins or from the drugs Jen injected into my system?

I don't know.

The dream seemed to have something to do with one of our missions, one we'd fought as assault troopers for the corporation.

Claath had wanted something called the Altair Object, a piece of Forerunner equipment. The structure turned out to be massive, many kilometers long and wide, a torus or donut with a black hole in the center. The object had been in the middle of an asteroid maze, protected by the Lokhar Fifth Legion. They manned the many asteroids and the laser domes and missile pits on them.

The Starkiens had brought us near the maze. Androids like N7 piloted our boats from them and we burst out on attack sleds. Our task had been to kill the Lokhar legionaries on the asteroids. Once done, big ships could clear the space junk. The reason Claath hadn't used massive nukes to simply blow the asteroids out of the way, I guess, was to make sure nothing harmed the artifact and because we fought on holy ground or in holy space.

In essence, we assaulted a giant space shrine.

We lost half our assault troopers hitting the asteroids, but we made the tigers flee. Until then, everyone had thought the religious fanatics invincible when faced as ground-pounders.

Did I mention the Forerunner object had religious implications for the aliens concerning the Creator? Crazy, huh? But it was the truth. I imagine Creator meant God or God to the aliens. Who would have expected loads of extraterrestrials to be zealots for God?

In any case, I remember as if it happened yesterday. The Lokhar legionaries fled from us, fleeing in single ships and with thruster-packs, heading for the Altair Object. I guess Claath and the others called it that because this all took place in the Altair star system.

As I've said, a maze of asteroids orbited the Forerunner artifact. In this case, *forerunner* meant those who had come before, the First Ones, in other words. As the defeated Lokhars raced to the torus with the black hole in the center, it began to glow like the Holy Grail.

That freaked me out at the time. It freaked out all of us. Then it got worse. The giant artifact became ghostly faint and then disappeared, taking the nearest Lokhars with it to some unknown destination.

We killed the remaining tigers. Well, the assault troopers didn't. We retreated and let the Starkiens butcher them with nuclear-tipped torpedoes. Those put nice colorful explosions on the screens like big pieces of popcorn. Since the holy object had done a bunk, the baboons could employ heavy weapons without worrying about harming the artifact.

I didn't dream of the battle, as might be expected. No. I dreamt of the Forerunner artifact, where it had gone. The dream felt all too real.

I floated alone in space far enough away from the object that the thing looked small. I knew it was the artifact because of the strange glow. That's exactly how it'd been at the end of the Altair battle. I almost swear I could hear angels singing.

I didn't want to be out here in space like this. In the dream, I drifted in my assault trooper gear, wondering how to get back to my ship. I twisted around and saw that the battlejumper was a pile of wreckage. I was stranded, adrift in space.

Swallowing in the dry throat, I looked at the object again. I realized I had to reach it, although I didn't know why. I used a thruster pack and headed that way. Long before I made it to the artifact, I passed drifting Lokhar legionaries. Once, I happened to spy a tiger face. Horror twisted the features. The tiger had died petrified. I realized then all the Lokhars were dead.

I took my thumb off the thruster pack control. I wanted to leave this area of space. As I floated toward the artifact, I noticed a swirl of dark matter behind it. Something waited in the swirling particles, something evil and old beyond reckoning.

Nothing had told me, but I knew it to be evil because that was the way with dreams. I twisted around, looking for stars. I couldn't see any, and that seemed impossible. There had to be stars.

This is important, I told myself. *You're seeing this for a reason.*

What reason? I licked my lips, trying to gin up courage. My suited thumb hovered over the thruster control, but I couldn't force myself to continue traveling closer.

I had a hard interior debate with myself. I needed to check this out. That was the truth. So I finally pressed down my thumb. Instead of feeling the pack push against me, light blinded my eyes, horribly bright light. What did that signify?

"Creed, darling," a sweet voice said to me.

Terror coursed through my body. Was that the Creator? Did He speak to me? I felt grossly unworthy for this.

"Creed, you must wake up. It's time."

Huh? Wake up?

"Help me, Rollo. Help me lift him out of the tank."

I heard liquid slosh and then I felt a stab of cold on my bare shoulders. Someone tore a mask off my face and I breathed canned ship air once more. A whiff of my girlfriend's perfume finally broke the dream-spell.

I opened my eyes to medical banks, cots, tubes, hypos and Rollo helping me toward a length of bed with white sheets. I left a trail of puddles on the deck plates.

Jen toweled me off before pushing me down and pulling covers up to my chin. The sheets were smooth and clean. Then I recalled the dream.

"The object," I said, weakly.

"Rest," Jen said, smiling tenderly.

"What happened...?"

"You were very ill," she said. "You should have come straight to sickbay after getting shot." She frowned. "If the android had pumped more slivers into you..."

"The thing almost killed me?"

"Yes," she said, with a warm hand against my cheek.

I wanted to ask her something important. Instead, my eyelids closed and I slept.

My lids snapped open a few minutes later. Well, I thought it was a few minutes. It turned out being three hours.

"What happened?" I said, my voice sounding raspy as if I gargled sandpaper.

Jen turned around. She stood beside a table, inspecting something I couldn't see. She smiled. It put dimples in her cheeks. She came around the table and walked to me.

The grav-plates were working then. Good. We could employ hard maneuvering if we had to.

Jen sat on the edge of the bed and put her hand on my forehead. "You're not hot anymore," she said.

"There were klaxons before," I said.

"Which ones?" she asked. "There's been several emergencies."

"On the bridge before I went down. What's been going on?"

"You almost died," she said.

"I mean with the ship."

"Oh." She turned away and picked up a communicator, clicking it on. "Rollo, he's awake."

In a few seconds, Rollo towered over the bed. "You okay, buddy?" he asked.

I flexed my left hand and glanced questioningly at Jen.

"Your body is still healing," she said. "You might feel lightheaded for a day or two. You should rest."

I flung off the covers and sat up. She was right, though. I felt dizzy. I closed my eyes, but that didn't help the pain in my mind.

"Did you get the scout?" I asked, meaning the one at Mars.

"You haven't been out that long," Rollo said. "Our missile is still accelerating at it. N7 believes the scout will remain behind Mars instead of trying to make a run for it. That means the missile will have to decelerate before it can swing around the planet to make the attack."

"That's smart on the scout's part," I said. I scowled. "There was a klaxon before while I was still on the bridge. What happened? Did the Starkiens use one of the teleportation missiles on us?"

"Not yet," Rollo said. "According to N7, the missiles have a similar range to our main laser, about ten million kilometers. They can possibly teleport farther, but the mechanisms become more unstable the farther they try to materialize. If they become too unstable, they reappear scrambled and useless."

"So why did the alarm sound?" I asked.

Rollo frowned, putting lines in his forehead. He used to have a long thin face. Now it was puffier due to the steroids. "Oh yeah, we spotted a second scout."

"Another Starkien vessel?"

Rollo nodded.

I cursed. How many scouts did the baboons have sprinkled throughout the solar system? Perhaps as importantly, how long had the scouts been here?

"You need to relax," Jen said. "You shouldn't get yourself excited. Your body needs time to fully recover."

I glanced at her. I loved Jen, but… No, no, never mind. I'm not going to say anything negative about her. She was a good person, a healer, in love with a killer. The innocent rabbit living with the wolf: sometimes I wondered how we could make a go of it for the long haul.

"The second scout was near the Jupiter jump-point," Rollo said. "It darted into it and left the solar system."

That was even worse. I lurched to my feet, and swayed as if drunk. A warm hand steadied me.

"Creed," Jen said.

"The Starkiens not only know we're here," I said. "They've obviously gone for reinforcements, and down a different jump route than the one they used coming here."

"Yep," Rollo said. "That about sums it up."

"We have to leave Earth," I said.

Rollo nodded.

"But does this mean we should head for the Pluto portal?" I asked. "If we do, we're going to have to face the beamships and their teleport bombs."

"That's the consensus."

I mulled that over before asking, "Are any of the last three freighters in orbit yet?"

"Nothing has changed with them," Rollo said. "In my opinion, they're grounded forever."

I muttered to myself like an old man hating a new idea.

"By the way," Rollo said, "Diana has been trying to get hold of you. It sounds urgent."

"Who's Diana?" Jen asked.

Rollo answered for me. "She's a freighter leader, one of those still grounded on Earth. Creed talked to her before he left on our first corporation mission. She liked what Creed said and has been organizing her people for prolonged resistance."

"Against the Jelk?" asked Jen.

"Yep," Rollo said. "She's one of Creed's strongest supporters."

Jen glanced at me, and she wasn't smiling.

I ignored her for now. I had enough problems to deal with. I didn't want to bring jealously into this.

"There's something else," Rollo said.

I heard it in his voice. This was why he'd been waiting around for me to wake up.

"Let me get dressed first," I said.

"You should rest," Jen told me for the umpteenth time.

"I can't rest, darling," I said. "This is go-time, but I appreciate your concern."

"You're risking a relapse," she said.

I laughed, and I pulled her to me and kissed her on the lips. Then I gave her a good squeeze. She felt great.

"Thanks," I whispered in her ear. "I'm really glad I have someone around who worries about me. Now I have to do my part and keep you safe."

She hugged me and looked up into my eyes. I could see her fear and worry, but she nodded.

I grabbed her butt and gave it a squeeze. Since the first moment I laid eyes I her, I knew I wanted her beside me.

"What were you working on at the table?" I asked.

"The ammunition," she said.

"What ammunition?"

"The one shot into you."

"That's a good idea." I put on the rest of my clothes and tested walking. I could feel the dizziness threaten my equilibrium, but less than earlier.

"You have something to show me?" I asked Rollo.

"Outside, yeah," he said.

I got the feeling he didn't want Jen to see or hear about it. So I asked, "You've been searching the ship like I said?"

"That's right," Rollo said.

"Let's go."

We left sickbay and walked down the corridor until we turned a corner. Then I stopped, leaning against a bulkhead as I faced him. Maybe Jen was right.

"What do you have?" I asked.

Rollo handed me a cardboard-thin tablet, small like a smartphone with a tiny keyboard.

"What's this?" I asked.

"I showed it to N7," Rollo said. "He's believes it's a long-range communication device. The thing's memory has a list of operable and inoperable battlejumper weapons systems."

I'd been turning the device over in my hands, tapping it with a fingernail. It was made of a light metallic alloy.

I looked up. "One of the android assassins had this?"

"That's right."

"What's does N7 think?"

"That the android sent periodic updates to the Starkiens with it," Rollo said.

"Thus, they know we have a crippled battlejumper."

"Yeah," Rollo said in a Western drawl, as if he had a toothpick dangling in his mouth. "We're not going to be able to bluff them."

"Who said anything about that?" I asked.

"I'm just saying."

"Wait a minute," I said, eyeing him "It's more than that. If they know we're crippled, maybe they really will try to capture us."

"There's that too," Rollo said. "Despite the trick the android with the flamer tried to pull, I think Claath really does want you back. Maybe he wants us all back. I helped you torture him. It makes me nervous thinking about falling into his hands. I think we have to run for it, Creed. It's crazy for a busted battlejumper to try to take on seven beamships and however many teleportation missiles the Starkiens have."

"You want to run?"

"Hard, fast and far," Rollo said.

"What about the three freighters on the planet?"

"This is a hard luck story all the way around," he said, no longer looking me in the eye. "We have to save what we can."

I studied the android device. I'd had plans earlier to give the freighters some weapons: old Earth nuclear missiles modified for space. A couple of MX missiles or SS-20s would give the freighters close-range punch. The missiles would be like shotguns, good for giving a hard wallop of a blast to anyone who came too close.

The Starkiens—or the corporation—wasn't giving us time for anything tricky, though. Claath had done the right thing from his perspective. The longer he took hunting us down, the more we could learn and the tougher we would become.

"I don't know about cutting and running, Rollo. That's half a million people we're talking about. You want to just leave them for the aliens?"

"No. I want to survive. I want the human race to survive. We've already lost most of it. What's a few more?"

"Are you serious?"

He looked at me and looked away again. "This is a messed up universe. Yeah, I want to save them. This is a fight to the finish. But we have to have a chance for victory if we're going to go toe to toe with the enemy."

"Who said anything about that?" I asked.

"What's your plan then?"

"It's pretty simple," I said. "We outdistance the Starkiens with our primary laser. That means we shoot them down before they can close with us to hurt the battlejumper."

"They have those teleportation missiles. Those might trump our laser."

I recalled the battle of Sigma Draconis all too well. The Jelk lasers had taken a heavy toll of the Lokhar guardian fleet. They had sent the teleportation missiles, which blinked out and appeared before the battlejumpers. The atomic explosions had taken their toll of the Jelk vessels.

"We have to rig something up for that," I said. "If we know what they're going to do—" I snapped my fingers. "Maybe we can build a mine field with old nukes from Earth."

"How would that work?" Rollo asked.

I was thinking on my feet, off the cuff. "It would be easy," I said. "We put detonators on those old warheads and salt them in layers before us, up to whatever N7 figures is the Lokhar warhead blast radius. When a Lokhar T-missile materializes— boom—we blow it apart before it can ignite."

Rollo scratched the back of his head. "Huh. That could work."

"That forces the Starkiens to bore in at us," I said. "While they do, we laser them as I first suggested. Ergo, we win the fight."

"Provided our weapon lasts long enough," Rollo said.

"We're going to have to work overtime to get ready," I said. "During that time, we have to get those three freighters into orbit."

"The techs have been over them. Nothing works on those old scows."

"Let's change up the idea... Okay. Maybe we need to take grav-plates out of orbital freighters and reinstall them in the bad ones. That at least gets the freighters into space."

"You're just guessing," Rollo said. "You should talk this over this with N7, see what he says."

I recalled the dream of the Forerunner artifact. Claath had wanted it very badly. I wondered why he did. I also wondered why I'd dreamed about it and thought about it now. Was my subconscious trying to tell me something?

"How much time did N7 say before the Starkiens are in range of our laser?" I asked.

"The Starkiens aren't killing themselves to reach us. At their present rate of acceleration: four days."

"That includes time for deceleration?" I asked.

"Yep," Rollo said.

Crazy alien tech. It had taken mankind in the Apollo days that long to reach the Moon. Grav-plates and powerful acceleration made a ton of difference.

"We don't have much time," I said, as I ran my fingernails against my cheek. "I need to pick up extra techs from the orbital freighters and bring them down onto Earth. And we have to collect nuclear warheads. Oh, and we need to rip out some grav-plates."

"Are there any thermonuclear weapons left down there?" Rollo asked. "Didn't we fire them all off the day the Earth died?"

"We're going to find out," I said. "Come on. We have to hurry."

6

I piloted our least damaged assault boat, plunging through the atmosphere, heading for Baja, California. Intense colors swirled around us, red, orange and purple. As they swirled, our boat rattled and lurched one way and then the other. There were powerful winds outside.

It reminded me of the day the aliens first landed, when I attacked them with Rollo beside me while carrying an M-14. We'd been in Antarctica during the end of the world. Penguins had already started dying in their tens of thousands.

I'd wanted to go out with a bang that day, and I'd wanted to hurt the world-killers. I still wanted to hurt them, but I'd changed my mind about going out with a bang. This was for human survival, not revenge.

"You might want to slow down," Rollo said.

We wore our symbiotic armor as a precaution, and I took us down as if we were on a combat run.

"Dying won't aid us," Rollo said, while hanging onto the straps crisscrossing his torso.

We plunged down into a dead world. In a little over a year, the bio-terminator had killed even the tiniest spores. Mars probably had more life than Earth did now.

I had a plan for that. We'd accomplished step one: freedom. Step two had been gaining our own space ships. Check. Most of the vessels were junkers, though, and low on fuel. Our battlejumper needed massive repairs, as it had taken heavy damage during the Sigma Draconis fight and later with our teleportation attack. We lacked funds to pay for alien dockside repairs and we lacked goods to barter for it. Step three would be getting funds or goods. I planned to do that the old-fashioned way, by stealing them. Or in our instance, through Viking raids against alien worlds.

Problem: I only had two hundred troopers—well, a few less actually. Solution: the freighters held millions of Earthers. I could recruit more and train them. Problem: I didn't have time for training just yet. Another problem: the leaders in the freighters controlled their people and wouldn't want to give them up. If they did give them up, they might try to slip their own people into my little army.

"Hang on," I said. I banked the assault boat sharply, plunging even faster.

"Are you crazy?" Rollo shouted.

The vessel shook and rattled more than before. The glass covers over my gauges vibrated, making them seem to jiggle. All the motion helped me collect my thoughts, helped me to focus.

As I said before, most of the freighters ran along tooth and claw rules. The leader was a ruthless bitch or son of a bitch, and kept a vicious pack of henchmen nearby. He or she kept order like a prison lord. That meant many people aboard the freighters likely hated the leader. It also meant the best recruits, the toughest people, already worked for the boss man or woman. I didn't want a Trojan horse among my assault troopers. The troopers were my political strength, the reason I ran the show instead of someone else.

Still, many of the have-nots in the freighters were likely just as tough as the henchmen. The survivors had been in the out of way places like Antarctica, the Arctic, Greenland, submarines and military outposts. Far more men than women had survived. With training and neuro-fiber implants—

Question: could Jen and the other nurses do the surgery on any volunteers? I sighed. My laundry list of things to do seemed never-ending.

Soon, I was too busy piloting the boat through vicious cyclones to do much thinking. The Lokhar thermonuclear devices and especially their planet wreckers had changed the weather patterns for the worse.

Like the best plans, mine was straightforward. Ella and Dmitri commanded the majority of the assault troopers. They presently scoured the battlejumper, hunting for more hidden sleepers.

We'd beaten the android stealth assault. Unfortunately, we'd lost too many badly needed techs and a handful of troopers. It meant we were down to one hundred and fifty-one effectives.

I'd visited ten orbital freighters collecting techs and grav-plates before heading down to Earth. They were my payload, and they would go to work on Diana's freighter in Baja. I didn't plan to talk to her, though. I was too busy for that.

Another assault boat had collected techs and brought them to the battlejumper. They helped with repairs. Our battered vessel's shield was still down. By shield, I meant an electromagnetic screen. The Starkien beamships had those. We had some hull armor, some hull and lots of useless, empty ship to destroy before any blast or beam reached the engines. None of that would matter if our laser outranged theirs for the entire fight, demolishing them before they could fire.

Let me make this sweet and short. Rollo complained about my piloting until we landed near Diana's freighter. He went outside, escorting the shaken techs to a hatch. Fifty-five brilliant men and women entered the grounded scow, ready for some hard repair work.

Soon, a forklift and suited driver appeared. She carried the grav-plates to an engine bay. It took five trips before the hatch shut for good. By that time, Rollo had returned to the boat. After the scrubbing and decontamination, he sat down beside me, took off his helmet and gave me a look.

I had ignored my comm-unit the entire time he'd been in the freighter.

"Diana wants to talk to you in person," he said.

I shook my head.

"Why won't you see her?" he asked. "Is it because of Jennifer?"

I revved the engines instead of answering. A minute later, we lifted, heading for the first missile silo in what used to be near Minot, North Dakota.

***

Working overtime and after the first twenty-four hours, while powered on stimulants, we hauled eleven nuclear warheads aboard our boat. It took three trips down and up to get them onto the battlejumper. There, techs attached the warheads to Jelk ejectors. We could fire them from torpedo tubes, laying down a pattern. It meant we could create an operable minefield in an hour or so, by launching the ejectors and easing the warheads into place.

So far, the fifty-five extra techs hadn't had any luck with the grounded freighters.

I had a short talk via screen with the chief engineer on Diana's scow. I was in the battlejumper control room, staring at a small monitor in my station. A crazy zigzag kept slashing through the screen, but I tried to ignore it. Reception was never good with those down on Earth. The chief tech was from India or from what had once been India. She'd been to school in Germany and knew her stuff. She also had the darkest eyes I'd ever seen. I think her name was Gupta.

"I am surprised this freighter made it down to Earth," Gupta told me. "The electronics are in shambles and the seals…" She shook her head. "I need a week, Commander, maybe more before this thing will fly again."

"You don't have a week," I said. "You have a day."

She took her time answering. "I watched American shows while I went to school," she said, "the old space adventures. This isn't anything like them. When I say a week, that is exactly what I mean. Don't expect a miracle because you say we need it."

"But I do need it."

Gupta's dark eyes flashed angrily. "With all due respect, Commander, I'm tired, my people are exhausted—"

"We all are," I said, cutting her off. "Now listen carefully. Get the job done now or give it someone who can."

Gupta wasn't backing down. Like most of the survivors, she was made of stern stuff. "N7 could not make this ship fly any faster."

"Do you *want* me to relieve you of command?"

With both hands, Gupta rubbed her face. I knew I pushed her. Sometimes you had to set the bar too high. That way people strove diligently to reach it. If that burned her out, we failed anyway. But by not pushing, we failed. So, one had to demand the impossible in impossible situations.

She took her hands away from her face. "Do not relive me. I am the best at this you have. I listened to N7 when he made his explanations, not just pretended to listen. You do realize that—"

"I realize bloodthirsty aliens are bearing down on Earth," I said. "I don't want to leave anyone behind. I'm counting on you. Those people in the freighters are counting on you. Take chances if you have to. Risk."

"Maybe you are right."

"You know I am," I said. "Creed, out."

As Gupta's image flickered and disappeared, I rubbed the back of my neck. It had a kink in it that wouldn't go away.

"You push them too hard," N7 said.

As we stood at our stations, various engineers crawled here and there: fixing panels and adding various pieces of new instrumentation.

I'd had enough resistance today, and just like Gupta, I was tired. "What would you know about being pushed?" I asked. "You're an android, not a man."

N7 raised his eyebrows. "You are upset at my words? That is an indication you are exhausted. I suggest you rest."

"Yeah? Is that what you suggest? And how do I manage such a trick? I'm too wound up to sleep."

"All the more reason for you to relax," N7 said.

It was my turn to rub my eyes. Being in charge was different. Before, Claath had kept his thumb on us and particularly on me. I knew how to react to that. It was my natural heritage, I suppose. I'd been to prison as a youngster and disliked authority. The only thumb pressing down on me now was the pressure of the Starkien flotilla. They had passed Jupiter's orbital path, still building up velocity as they came toward Earth.

"There's an incoming message for you, Commander," Ella said.

I don't remember if I've told you about Ella. She used to be a Russian scientist. Now she was an assault trooper. Despite the steroid-68, Ella was still thin, with a pretty face, dark hair hanging to her cheeks and a mind like a razor. She liked things you could cut and weigh—using the scientific approach. I didn't know much about her previous life. I knew I could count on her when the chips were down. Right now, that's all I needed to know.

"Put it on the main screen," I said.

Ella did, and I found myself staring at the Starkien commander, Naga Gobo. As N7 had once told me, Naga was his name and Gobo was his rank. It meant *lord of ships*.

A regular Starkien was the size of a baboon and looked as furry and as ugly. Naga sported two long canines at the end of his wrinkled muzzle. He must have weighed sixty or seventy pounds and had a mane like a lion. His had white streaks in it. I don't know what that meant about his actual age, just that he was old for a Starkien.

Naga Gobo sat on a dais with raised controls around him. Others moved behind the dais. I knew the place stank because Starkiens did. When I'd met them in person before on a beamship, the chamber had smelled like a filthy zoo cage. Naga Gobo seemed to be what he looked like, the dominant male of a high-tech baboon pack. Instead of clothes, he wore a harness around his body, with various tools or weapons hanging from it. Instead of a handkerchief in a breast pocket, he had a silver tube with a black ball on the end dangling there.

"I wish to speak to Creed-beast," Naga said on the screen.

He fit perfectly into Jelk Corporation thinking, having a low opinion about humans. I let the insult pass for now. The time would come to teach him differently.

"I'm Commander Creed," I said, stepping off the control deck onto the lower plates.

"Is this subterfuge?" he asked.

"Explain yourself," I said.

He stiffened at my tone, saying, "You all look alike to me. How do I know it is really Creed-beast I address?"

"I do not understand," Ella whispered behind my back. "How can we be communicating instantaneously with him?

He's near Jupiter. His radio waves should take an hour to get here and our reply an hour to return."

"That is an intelligent question for an animal," Naga said from the screen. "You should put her in charge."

"Just a minute," I said. I motioned for N7 to mute sound. Once he did, I asked, "What's the answer to Ella's question?"

"It would appear he is using Lokhar teleportation communications," N7 said. "I have heard of the technique, and am surprised to realize it is factual, not fiction."

"What are you talking about?" I asked.

"It is complicated in theory," N7 said. "Do you wish me to explain the details?"

"No. I think I understand. They teleport the radio waves at us and somehow teleport our replies back to their ship."

"That is crudely stated," N7 said, "and it is not altogether accurate. Still, I suppose it is close enough to the truth for an operating understanding."

"Wonderful," I muttered, before scowling at Naga Gobo. He kept calling us animals and beasts. I'd never liked that while I'd been a corporation slave and I sure didn't like it now that I was free. "I'm getting tired of their arrogance," I said. "It's going to be a pleasure killing them."

"We must negotiate if we can," N7 said. "Or we must at least attempt it. They outnumber our ships and surely have greater firepower."

"Once they get in close, you mean," I said.

"Correct," N7 said.

"I don't know. Do you really believe negotiating is worth the effort?"

"I would not have said it otherwise," N7 said.

"Sure," I said. "I'll keep that in mind. Unmute the baboon."

N7 did so, causing a beep to sound from the screen.

I took a wider stance and put my hands on my hips, letting them rest on my belt. "So you're Naga Gobo, huh? Last time I saw you, you looked more impressive. Maybe it's because we met in person aboard your flagship." I smiled. "I imagine Claath is pretty pissed off at you Starkiens about now."

Naga glanced at something to the side on his vessel, something we couldn't see, before regarding me again. "Your voice modulation matches with our records. You are the loathsome creature I seek. I have a list of complaints against you."

"I have a list of my own concerning you."

Naga hooted to someone off screen. Then he wrinkled his snout and learned toward me. "You are in the inferior position, Earthbeast. Therefore, you are advised to watch your tongue."

"Inferior, huh? Is that why I'm standing in a corporation battlejumper?"

"You state one of the chief items on my list: that of robber. You must return the stolen property in as good as condition as the day you lifted the vessel. Secondly—"

"Secondly," I said, speaking louder. "If you pass Mars' orbital path, I can no longer guarantee your safety or the safety of your little band of beamships."

Naga Gobo blinked at me like a kicked dog. "You dare to threaten a representative of the Jelk Corporation?"

"Third, if you so much as scratch the paint on my freighters," I said, "I will hold you personally responsible for the damage. Since monetary rewards mean little to me, I will recoup the losses with my knife." I drew it, showing him the Bowie. "With this blade, I will personally peel off your skin and nail it to my bedroom floor. Every time I think of you, I'll wipe my feet on the fur."

Naga Gobo stared into my eyes. His became bloodshot as his mane stiffened. Slowly, he opened his muzzle and then he began to shriek with rage. Like some zoo specimen, he pounded the dais before him, hooting, screaming and jumping about.

"You have excited him," Ella said. "Was that your intention?"

I shrugged in order to maintain my pose. She'd nailed it, though. In a fight, it was often a good idea to enrage your opponent so he made foolish decisions. Besides, I was tired of him calling me an animal. If they wanted a beast, they were going to get one, but not in the manner that they imagined.

The shrieks and hoots finally died down until Naga Gobo panted. His eyes were red rimmed and evil looking. "I will purchase you from Shah Claath. Then, human, I will make your life miserable and painful. You will long for death and—"

"I'm tired of your jabber," I said. "Do you have a message for me or not?"

He glared, panting faster, with saliva dripping from his fangs. Finally, he stirred, and said, "Surrender your ship at once."

"Come and take," I said.

"You cannot defeat my beamships."

"Saying it doesn't make it true."

"Only a fool would speak as you do."

"Is that what you truly believe?" I asked. "You think it's impossible for us to win? Well, that will make our victory that much more impressive."

"If you trust in Jelk technology, know that I have the codes to interrupt your ship's interior functions. Just as the androids slaughtered your crews, so shall your failsafe bring you to grief at the worst possible moment."

"Is he so simple that he gives away their plan?" Ella whispered.

I didn't respond. I just watched the agitated Starkien. This was getting more interesting by the moment.

Naga looked away. It appeared as if someone addressed him too quietly for us to hear the words. Finally, the Starkien stared at me again. "If you feel I've given you valuable information, you are quite wrong."

"No doubt you're right," I said.

"Your damaged vessel doesn't have a hope against us."

"I'll try to explain this simply so you and your crew can understand," I said. "We were down and out about twenty-three days ago, so-called animals stranded on a planetary defense station. All we owed were the weapons in our hands and our wits. With that, we took Claath's own warship. Have you considered the implications carefully? Do you wonder why the little Jelk hasn't come to take us himself? In case you can't figure it out, I'll help you. It's because he's frightened of us— and for good reason."

"Your boasts are absurd," Naga Gobo said. "Claath doesn't come because he hasn't yet regained—"

A Starkien voice shrieked from the background, sounding like a crazy high school librarian. Naga Gobo turned toward the voice. A flurry of words passed between them. Finally, the *lord of ships* faced me again, looking chastened.

"You have animal cunning," Naga said in a low voice. "I will grant you that. You have also achieved a notable feat. I refer to your capture of the Jelk battlejumper. I congratulate you on your valor."

This was an odd twist, the compliment. What did it mean and why did he try it? I decided to play along and see what happened.

"I accept the honor you give me," I said. "Because of your change of attitude, I will reevaluate mine toward Starkiens. Yes, you are a free people. It is a noble thing to be free."

Naga's eyebrows thundered; and he leaned closer yet toward the screen. "You are a shifty creature—being, a shifty being," he said.

"Yeah, it's been said."

"A moment," Naga Gobo said. He muted his sound and jumped off the dais. Soon, four Starkiens sat in a group. They pounded the floor with the flats of their hands, jabbering at each other.

"May I interject a thought, Commander?" Ella asked as we waited.

"Of course," I said.

"They have the appearance and possibly the mannerisms of beasts. But it would be good to remember that they're driving starships with the capability to destroy us."

"Your point?" I asked.

"Don't underestimate them."

"I don't plan to," I said.

In time, Naga Gobo climbed back onto his dais. The sound returned and he stroked his mane as he regarded me.

"Let us speak as warriors," the Starkien said.

I waited.

"Do you agree to that?" he asked.

"I greet you, Naga Gobo, a warrior chief of the Starkiens."

It took him a moment, and then Naga said, "I greet you, Commander Creed, an assault trooper of the Jelk Corporation."

I let that pass. He wasn't trying to insult me now. At least I didn't think so.

"*You* know I have the codes to your battlejumper," Naga said. "*I* know that most of your systems are already damaged beyond repair. Yet you achieved an amazing feat back in Sigma Draconis when you captured the ship. Perhaps Shah Claath does not recognize the daring and the courage your actions took. We of the Starkiens appreciate it. Because of that, we will make you an offer."

"I'm listening."

"Surrender your battlejumper and your assault troopers. We will let the freighters go. Clearly, many are in working order. Perhaps they can find a home elsewhere, or perhaps they can take up a Starkien-like existence."

"Without warships to guard them?" I asked.

"Having guardian craft would be better," he said. "But surely my offer is superior to their destruction or capture."

"I am not convinced you can destroy us."

"Come, come," Naga Gobo said. "Our advantages trump yours."

"I suspect that's true. But we are free and you're planning to make us slaves. Free men do not easily accept the slave collar."

"Not even to save your race?"

"A moment, please," I said.

"It is granted," Naga Gobo said.

I turned to N7. With the press of his forefinger and an audible click, the android muted the speaker.

"Does he make the offer in good faith?" I asked N7.

"It is difficult to tell," he said. "The Starkiens are known to keep their oaths. I imagine it depends on whether or not he truly believes you're people."

"A man's word doesn't mean anything if given to an Indian, eh?" I asked.

"I do not understand your reference," N7 said.

"It happened several hundred years ago when the Europeans came to the New World," I said "That's the only Earth analogy I can think of to help guide me here."

"I don't trust him," Ella said.

52

"No," I said. "But if our sacrifice can buy humanity life…"

Ella looked away.

"I advise you to reject the offer," N7 said. "Without military protection, the people in the freighters will not long remain free."

I inhaled through my nostrils. "Give me sound," I said.

Naga Gobo looked up.

"It is time for warriors to fight," I told him.

"You refuse to surrender?"

"Do you?" I asked.

He appeared perplexed. "I do not understand your words," he said.

"Will you surrender to us?" I asked.

"That is a ridiculous proposal."

"There's my answer."

He stared at me for a few more seconds. "You cannot win," he said. "You believe your position strong enough to fend us off, but that is because you do not understand the full situation."

"Go ahead then," I said, "explain it to me. I'm listening."

A different Starkien muttered off-screen.

Naga Gobo deflated. "You were given the chance," he said. "You must remember that. It is now on your head."

"You're in my solar system," I said. "Don't think you're going to escape it alive. I tried to offer you safety, but you have rejected me. Remember that."

"Foul creature," he muttered, and Naga Gobo made a sharp gesture. A second later, the connection broke, and the Starkien beamships continued their path toward Earth.

7

The next two days became a blur of activity.

During it, N7 monitored our missile's approach to the Red Planet. The Starkien scout finally made a run for it, blasting away from the far side of Mars with hard acceleration as our missile ended its first braking schedule.

Waiting until our missile had expended most of its fuel was a good idea. At least, that must have been the scout crew's thinking.

The scout accelerated for the braking flotilla. Naga Gobo had reached the inward edge of the Asteroid Belt and needed to rid himself of excess velocity. Like a hound chasing a burglar, our missile increased acceleration for the scout. The missile would no longer have to swing around Mars to try to catch the enemy by surprise. This was a matter of velocity, a race. Could the scout reach the flotilla in time for the beamships to destroy the missile with their million-kilometer range?

Naga Gobo made another communication's appearance. After a preliminary greeting, he said, "Let our conversation be brief."

I'd only slept a few hours these past days. My eyelids felt like sandpaper every time I blinked. The good thing was that one of the downed freighters had lifted off world. It joined the other freighters behind Earth—behind the planet in relation to the approaching flotilla. Diana still demanded to speak to me. Her scow remained on the poisoned surface.

"I'm listening," I told the Starkien.

"The scout is innocent," Naga Gobo said. "The crew merely observed you. Why destroy it needlessly?"

I laughed before I could control myself.

"You mock me?" Naga asked, bristling, with red showing around the whites of his eyes.

He was trying to save his scout. That was reasonable enough, I suppose. "Hold up, chief," I said. "There's no mockery intended. I just don't believe you're asking me this."

"You accuse me of lies?"

"That's not what I meant. But now that I think about it, yeah. I do accuse you of lying."

"How dare you insult me of—?"

"Hey!" I shouted.

Naga Gobo blinked in surprise.

"Killer androids attacked my personnel on the battlejumper," I said. "One of the things even carried a message from Claath, telling it to me. I'm wondering who activated the hidden killers. We found their sleeper tubes, by the way. We even found a few extra ones that failed to wake up, destroying the things before they changed their minds. Do you know what we found? The sleepers had activation features built into their skulls. Who turned them on by beaming a long-distance message? I'm guessing it was someone in the scout."

"The scout crew beamed a message, I admit," Naga Gobo said. "They were go-betweens, innocents."

"No. In my book, sending the message that activated killers was like launching a missile. Instead of a metal tube, this missile came in radio waves. That means the scout crew is longer innocent bystanders. They drew blood. Now, they're going to have to pay the ultimate price for failing."

"Heed me, Creed-beast."

"So we're back to insults, are we?"

Naga Gobo shook his head. "I will drop all pretenses. You are an animal. Thus, it isn't an insult to speak the truth. Did you build the battlejumper? No, you stole it. Have you risen into space technology through your own intellectual efforts? No. You—"

"I get your point. Maybe it's time you understood mine. If you kill humans, we come and kill you."

"Heed me, beast. If you cannot show mercy to our scout, I will not show mercy to your freighters once I demolish the battlejumper."

"I never expected any mercy from you anyway," I said.

"It does not have to be this way," Naga Gobo said.

"A moment, Commander," N7 said. "May I speak with you?"

I turned to N7, finally nodding.

N7 muted the screen. "Commander," he said, "I would accept his offer. Show the scout mercy so your freighters may survive."

"That's a screwy deal and you should know it. He's telling me I can't hit our attackers or he's going to commit genocide against us. That shows he doesn't have a conscience. Therefore, why should I believe him when he promises something?"

"You spoke of genocide," N7 said. "You should accept his promise because the returns are so high and you give so little in return."

"You're missing the point," I said. "He doesn't get to decide when I can kill his boys or not. Anyone who comes at me with a knife in hand, especially a blade wet with human blood, I kill. There are no deals unless he backs off."

"Offer him that," Rollo said.

"Good idea," I said. "N7, put him back on."

"Have you finally come to your senses?" Naga Gobo asked me.

"I'll tell you what," I said. "Turn your flotilla around and don't come back, and I'll let your scout live. Do we have a deal?"

Naga Gobo didn't respond immediately. "I am under contract," he finally said. "I must gather Claath's stolen property and return it to him. I must finish what I began."

"The scout crew's blood is on your head then."

With a snarl, Naga Gobo made a motion. The connection ended.

Two hours and thirty-three minutes later, our missile's warhead exploded. The thermonuclear charge sped along targeting rods before annihilating them, beaming gamma and

X-rays at the fleeing scout ship. Shortly thereafter, the small craft disintegrated.

"First blood," Rollo said.

"Second," I told him. "The android assassins took first blood."

"First ship death then," Rollo said.

"Yeah," I said. "It is that."

"Commander," N7 said. "I suggest you sleep to regain your stamina. My analysis suggests the battle will not begin for another sixteen hours."

I felt strung-out like a paranoid addict awake for seventy-two hours. My eyelids kept drooping on their own account. It wouldn't help us if I couldn't think straight.

The freighters gathered behind Earth, getting ready to make a run for the Sun. From there they would slingshot to the Pluto portal. I didn't give them high odds for long-term survival if we failed to defeat the Starkiens. But at least they had odds. That was better than dying right off the bat.

I left the bridge, staggered down the corridors and collapsed in my bunk. I went down hard and slept a solid twelve hours. When I got up, I felt worse than ever. Was that an aftereffect of the toxins? I don't know.

I searched out Jennifer, and we spent an hour together. It might be the last time we'd ever have with each other.

Later, I went to our makeshift gym and ran a few kilometers, working up a sweat. I showered afterward and ate a big meal. I was finally starting to feel better. On impulse, I put on symbiotic armor and grabbed my Bahnkouv, my laser rifle, making sure it was fully charged. Only then did I head to the bridge.

The second-to-last grounded freighter lifted from Greenland and joined the others in time for the initial acceleration. It was just us now in the battlejumper and Diana and her people down in Baja, California. That was insane. Earth had become a desolate planet. If we beat the Starkiens, could I really turn the world back into a paradise?

Like everyone else, I used to bitch about lousy TV shows, poor fast food and the rain. Before the Lokhars showed up, we Earthers had killed each other in wars, mugged those richer than us and insulted one other for a thousand different and usually petty reasons. Wasn't that funny? I missed the old Earth. I missed the teeming cities, the fierce political debates, the yelling, the honking…everything that made us human.

In an angry frame of mind, I walked into the control room. The aliens had stolen all that from us. Now they wanted to take the table scraps, too. You know the saying: *over my dead body.*

"Let's get the show on the road," I said. "N7, I have no doubt you've been analyzing their attack run."

"I have," he said.

"Let's spread out our mine field then."

I watched the main screen. The ejectors used hydrogen propellant. That meant they were cold, not hot, and harder to spot by enemy scanners.

We had one battlejumper, with three assault boats ready as escape pods. Our laser could reach ten million kilometers. For good measure, we had a dozen missiles left, the big ones like we'd used on the scout. I hadn't seen any reason to launch them at the beamships. The Starkiens would just laser them. No. I was saving the missiles for a better opportunity.

On the big screen, I watched the enemy flotilla approach. Naga Gobo had seven beamships. They came in a cluster, four leading and three following. By the orange glows around them, each had an electromagnetic field. The beamships protected three Lokhar teleport missiles behind them. Well, they were liberated ones anyway, no longer Lokhar property.

"Any surprises so far?" I asked N7.

"The teleport missiles are unsettling," he said.

"Tell me why again?"

"It is an unstable technology," N7 said. "The Starkiens are a nomadic race. They are therefore cautious and conservative. It is unlike them to take a technological risk."

"Claath must have ordered it."

"I do not accept that," N7 said. "The Starkiens are contractors. They do not accept orders they do not like."

"So the missiles are unstable," I said. "So what?"

"Perhaps the Starkiens will program one wrong, and the missile will reappear among them instead of materializing near us. That would cause grave devastation to the beamships."

"They need something to beat our laser," I said. "The T-missiles are it."

"They already have something," N7 said, "their shields."

"Something more than that, I mean."

"You appear to be correct," N7 said. "I refer to fact of the T-missiles. But I am not convinced we have the entire answer as to why the Starkiens are using them."

"What are your suggestions?" I asked.

"None other than what we are already doing," he said.

"Sure," I said to myself. "Great."

Time slowed down. It always does when you want it to speed up. The freighters began their play, accelerating at full throttle for the Sun. I wondered if we'd ever see any of them again. A bad feeling came over me.

I walked away from my station and stood before the main screen. Putting my hands behind my back, I stared at the stars. With the battlejumper, I stood between survival and the apocalypse. It made my gut clench, and I hoped I was making the right decisions.

"Creator," I whispered. "If you're listening, I ask for a fighting chance. Don't let the Starkiens wipe out the human race. Give us another play at life."

I stood there for several minutes, and finally returned to my station. There was nothing to do now but wait. The Starkiens didn't launch any missiles and neither did we.

"The enemy flotilla is thirteen million kilometers away," N7 reported twenty minutes later. "I suggest we run the engines at three quarters capacity and begin to warm our laser coils."

"Do it," I said.

Soon, the interior ship thrum increased substantially. I felt the vibration under my feet and the noise grew until a loud and sustained whine made my spine uncomfortable. It took gobs of power to make the laser kill at ten million kilometers.

"Targeting," I said, "are you ready?"

"Affirmative," Ella said.

"Do we know which one is Naga Gobo's vessel?" I asked.

"Negative," Ella said.

"Which ship sent the message?" I asked.

"It may not be that simple," Ella said. "He may have moved to a different beamship."

"N7?" I asked.

The choirboy android tapped a finger against his console. "That seems like a reasonable precaution," he said.

"Yeah, and maybe Naga Gobo didn't take it," I said. "Aim at the ship that communicated with us. Let's make him earn his survival."

Time passed.

"Eleven million kilometers," N7 said.

The Starkien flotilla bored in toward Earth. It would appear they planned to do their heavy braking once in their own laser range of one million kilometers. At their present rate, they would flash past the planet and us.

"Do you think they mean to chase down the freighters?" I asked.

"We have not found any more scouts," N7 said. "I do not believe they know of the freighter maneuver yet. The Earth still blocks the Starkien sight of them."

"The enemy could have guessed our intent," I said.

"It is possible," N7 said.

"Great," I whispered.

"They're almost in range," Ella said.

"Get ready," I said. "And make sure you destroy the first ship before you start on the next. Better that we utterly destroy them ship by ship than that we damage all of them but leave them intact."

The next few minutes dragged as if I were a child again sitting beside the Christmas tree, waiting for my parents to wake up so I could open the gifts. Would our laser hold long enough for us to burn through seven shields and seven armored hulls?

"Ten point one million kilometers," N7 said.

"Fire," I said. "Let's do this."

Ella touched the targeting screen and a new noise burst into existence. Power rushed through the coils, energizing the giant laser cannon. The whine was low-pitched at first. It rose rapidly throughout the ship. Then a huge ray of concentrated killing light stabbed into the void.

The enemy wasn't in range yet. It didn't matter. He would be when the light reached its targeting point. Light travels at 300,000 kilometers per second. That was roughly a little over three seconds per one million kilometers. The tip of our laser would reach ten million kilometers in a little over thirty seconds, half a minute. Ella targeted where the enemy beamship would be in that time. It called for fantastic targeting capabilities. It would have been far beyond Twenty-first century human tech, but it was within the parameters of Jelk battle gear.

The obvious question no doubt rears its brainy head. Why not jink, move in random patterns to throw off enemy targeting. The answer was equally pointy headed. Because at the velocity the Starkiens came, jinking caused too much G-force stresses to the vessel itself, never mind the crew within.

I had to wait more than a minute for Ella to yell, "Hit! We're burning through the electromagnetic field." Thirty seconds to reach the target and thirty more seconds—roughly speaking—for our teleoptics to see what was happening. The first beamship's shield turned from an orange glow to a deeper red color. Starkien generators likely pumped power to their electromagnetic field, attempting to hold. Our laser put energy—heat—on it. Some of the power bled away from the point of impact, discoloring the enemy shield in a wave pattern. Where the beam burned, the shield turned from red to black.

Here was the question, a simple formula really. How much energy would it take to burn through a shield, the hull behind it and destroy the beamship? The answer would tell us if we had a chance or not. If we did have a chance, our engineers would have to make sure our laser could beam for the entire battle.

Ever since Naga Gobo's boast our techs had worked, putting in new battlejumper codes and rerouting many of the systems. If he could jam us with a computer virus, we had to know and then foil it beforehand.

The minutes ticked by. The Starkiens kept coming, and the first enemy shield finally overloaded. Our sword of light stabbed the beamship's hull, melting the outer alloys and digging deeper, deeper—

A silent explosion heralded the first Starkien vessel's destruction. Like a slow-motion grenade, it burst apart with glaring, flaring light behind it. Sections of hull parted. Water, globs of bubbling steel, plastics, fiery fabrics and pieces of flesh and shattered Starkien bone fragments blew outward from the central mass. Radioactive gamma and X-rays also smashed against the nearest Starkien vessels. Those beamships' shields glowed red with overload.

"That's beautiful," I whispered. "The beamships are like bombs in the middle of their formation. The baboons have kept them too close together in order to shield the T-missiles."

"The laser, sir," Ella said.

I went cold inside. "I hope you're not going to tell me it's overheating."

"No, sir," she said. "I'm retargeting for the next beamship."

"Commander," N7 said. "I have run the computations. If we can continue to destroy them at this rate, we will win the battle."

I shouted triumphantly as if I'd won a jackpot on a Las Vegas slot machine. Rollo and a few others also roared.

"We can do this, people," I said. "We can beat the aliens at their own game."

I should have known better than to jinx us.

"Commander," N7 said. "One of the Lokhar teleportation missiles is appearing."

I balled my right-hand fingers into a fist and struck my console. "Get ready to ignite the nearest warhead," I said.

On the main screen, I saw the Lokhar missile, a big bad thing of hostile intent. The missile sped toward us. Soon it got close, well within one hundred thousand kilometers of our battlejumper. That was sharp teleportation targeting.

"What's happening?" I asked N7.

"Our nearest warhead doesn't respond," the android said. "I suspect the T-missile—"

Before N7 could finish his sentence, the teleportation bomb activated. The thermonuclear reaction beat ours to the punch. It went nova, turning into incandescent light.

I shielded my eyes. I needn't have bothered. Our teleoptic equipment automatically filtered out harmful light.

"It's huge," Rollo said.

"Two hundred thousand megatons," N7 reported.

"Get ready for impact," I said.

Heat, radiation and a powerful electromagnetic pulse sped toward us. As they did, the combination swept over the other Earth warheads we'd painfully put into position as an atomic minefield.

"The blast is neutralizing our warheads," N7 reported.

Then it reached us. Temperatures soared on the outer hull. The EMP hit our hardened electronics. The bridge lights flickered. Sparks flew from Rollo's station.

I kept striking my console. Damn, damn, damn, why couldn't we have beaten the T-missile to the punch and blown it apart?

"Well?" I asked. "Are we finished? Did they win?"

Ella looked up, her features unreadable. "The laser is still operational, Commander. Our team retracted the main cannon behind an armored bulkhead. We put it away before the T-missile blew."

"How long until we're ready to fire the laser again?" I asked.

"Five minutes," she said.

"That's not good enough," I said. "Make it three."

The lights stopped flickering and came back on as strong as ever.

"Damage report," I said. "I have to know if we're still in the battle."

"Commander," N7 said. "I've run an analysis. The T-bomb materialized too far for full effectiveness against us."

"You mean they made a mistake?" I asked.

"Yes, Commander," N7 said.

"They won't next time," I said. "Do we have any ejectors left with warheads?"

"Two," N7 said.

"Get one of them out there."

N7 attempted to relay the message to the torpedo crew. He looked up at me. "Commander, the tubes are blocked, destroyed."

I couldn't believe this. Everything had been working a few minutes ago. "How long until the tubes are operational?" I asked.

"Not until the battle is over," N7 said.

"What? No. Tell the crew to haul an ejector to a shuttle bay. They can launch it manually."

Our N-series android stared at me. "That is an excellent suggestion."

"Tell them to hurry," I said. "If the Starkiens are smart, they'll launch another of those things now and finish us for good."

A minute later, that's exactly what happened.

"The laser is almost ready for firing, Commander," Ella told me.

"N7, do we still have a margin for error?" I asked.

"It is one tenth as large as previously," N7 said.

After he spoke, I saw wavering space on the main screen. I knew what it meant. We'd just witnessed it a few minutes earlier. As before, a teleportation missile materialized in close range.

"Ella," I said, "can you retarget the laser at the T-missile?"

"Not fast enough," she said.

With impotent rage, I watched the teleportation missile solidify. This one didn't have the same velocity as the approaching beamships. That should have been impossible. How had the T-missile managed such a trick? I didn't know.

Seconds ticked by. The T-missile had not only materialized, but it sped toward us.

"How come it hasn't ignited yet?" I asked.

"I'm picking up life readings," N7 said.

"Come again," I said.

"Commander?" N7 asked. He hadn't been built on Earth. He still didn't know all our idioms.

"What are you talking about?" I asked. "What life-readings? Where are they coming from?"

The android frowned. He even had a line in his forehead, a thick one. "The life-readings are coming from the T-missile," N7 said.

"Say again," I told him.

Before N7 could manage, the T-missile burst apart. It didn't do so as before with a thermonuclear explosion. The missile parts flew away as if ejected by magnetic force. Smaller pieces like interior pellets began to brake, causing long fusion tails to burn at us.

"What are those pellets?" I asked.

"I'm analyzing, Commander," N7 said.

"Ella, get the laser back online *now*. Quit hiding it behind the armored bulkhead."

"That's what I'm doing, Commander," she said. "It's almost ready."

"N7," I said, "I'm still waiting for an answer. What in the hell are those things."

The pellet-shapes burst apart as the T-missile had, through the power of magnetic force. In the pellets' place were several thousand individual soldiers. At least, those sure looked like soldiers in heavy powered armor.

"Is what I'm seeing real?" I asked.

"I do not understand this," N7 said. "The readings make no sense."

"Tell it to me anyway," I said.

N7 looked up from his board. He looked as confused as the android ever did. While his face was humanlike, the mobility of his features lacked our range of differences.

"I'm tracking Lokhar life-readings," N7 said.

"As in: Lokhar legionaries?" I asked, dumbfounded.

"Yes," N7 said.

"Tigers?" I asked, as if that would clarify the situation.

"Yes, Commander," N7 said. "Those are Lokhar legionaries flying toward our battlejumper. It is my belief they are attempting a storm assault."

"Why are the tigers aiding the Starkiens?" I asked. "I thought Lokhars hated the pirates."

"They do," N7 said. "I find this inexplicable."

I stared at the main screen. Is this what it had been like on D-Day for the Germans, staring into the sky and seeing thousands of Allied paratroopers coming down on their heads?

This didn't make any sense at all.

-8-

"Listen up," I snarled. "I see Lokhars coming for our battlejumper. I don't know why they're so far out from us, but we're going to use that against them and take the tigers down hard."

As I spoke, another T-missile materialized in close range. We'd spotted three of them coming through the jump point near Neptune. Therefore, this seemed like the last one we'd have to deal with. It reacted as the second missile, spilling more braking pellet-shaped craft, which in turn put more Lokhar power-armored legionaries into space.

"How many of them are you counting, N7?" I asked.

"Five thousand," he said. "This is an entire legion."

"Perfect," I said. "How are the ejectors coming? Have they launched one yet from a shuttle bay?"

"You're going to blow a nuclear warhead among the enemy?" Ella asked.

"You're reading my mind," I said. "I want your laser back on target. We have more beamships to kill if we're going to win the fight. N7, tell them to launch the second ejector. It's possible the tigers have anti-missile tech." I drummed my fingers on the console, debating whether to use some of the regular Jelk missiles I'd saved. If the legionaries reached us...

We launched three more missiles, the big Jelk ones. If we lost the battlejumper, I'd never need those missiles anyway.

The minutes flashed past. Soon, our ship-killing laser burned into the void. It seemed like the spotlight of Death Search: a grim, interplanetary game. Just as good, I watched our first ejector accelerate toward the cloud of approaching Lokhars.

"This seems reckless and senseless on their part," I said. "Do you think the Jelk captured the Lokhar soldiers at Sigma Draconis and have forced them into service?"

"I do not deem that as likely," N7 said. "Lokhars are notorious and well-known for fighting to the death. They would never surrender to Jelk."

"Just like they fought to the death in the Altair system?" I asked. "If I recall correctly, Lokhar legionaries fled from us like wet hens."

"The Altair episode still does not compute with me," N7 said.

"No," I told him. "You should say, 'it doesn't make sense.' To say it doesn't compute makes you sound like a computer. You may not be human, but you're no computer."

Finally, our laser began torching the second Starkien shield. At the same time, an ejector approached the Lokhar mass of soldiery. I was feeling hopeful again. But some of those legionaries must have been carrying semi-portables: infantry heavy beam weapons. Rays flashed in the darkness, hitting our warhead.

"Should I ignite the ejector?" N7 asked.

"It's still too close to our battlejumper," I said. "The blast will hurt us."

"You must decide quickly, Commander."

The enemy's semi-portables burned against ejector armor, chewing into the heavy plating. More rays appeared, adding their help. The legionaries that fired the lasers no longer came at our vessel. Their individual mass was practically non-existent compared to the beam wattage, which acted like a propellant, pushing the shooters away from us.

"Do it," I said. "Explode the first warhead."

"It's too late, Commander," N7 said, as red from his panel flashed against his face. "The Lokhars destroyed it."

I came to an immediate decision. "Accelerate the three Jelk missiles. Let those reach the legionaries first as decoys. We can't allow those warheads to explode this near the battlejumper anyway. We have to get our Earth nuke among

67

them if we're going to save ourselves. The Jelk missiles will simply take all of us down."

After N7 made the adjustments, he came upon a startling discovery.

"You'd better look at this, Commander," N7 said.

"What now?" I asked.

"There is another vessel coming through the Neptune jump point."

"More Starkiens?" I asked.

"Negative," N7 said. "It is a Lokhar dreadnought."

The words didn't register right away. Maybe because of my confusion, my head swiveled away from the main screen so I faced our android. "What did you say?"

"I'm magnifying the image," N7 said. "You should see this for yourself."

I regarded the main screen again. I couldn't believe what I saw. The dreadnought looked exactly like the monstrous vessel that had attempted to wipe out the human race a little over a year ago. It seemed as big as Rhode Island or a large asteroid. This one had fins like a '57 Chevy, but it was a metal construct: a thing aliens had built.

"That just came through the Neptune jump point?" I asked.

"The image is over four hours old," N7 said. "Otherwise, that is affirmative."

I didn't know what to think or say.

"Commander," Ella said. "That's the same jump point the Starkiens used to reach our solar system."

She was right. That was weird. "Is the dreadnought hunting down the Starkiens for taking Lokhar soldiers?" I asked.

"I believe we should hail the dreadnought." N7 said. "They should have the superior Lokhar comm-tech, allowing near-instantaneous communication. Speaking with them might clarify many things."

I walked off the command deck toward the main screen. What was going on? What had happened at Sigma Draconis after we'd left?

"What are you going to do about the approaching legionaries?" Rollo asked. "They're going to board us soon if we do nothing. They've already managed to take down one of the Jelk missiles, and they're beaming the other two."

"This changes nothing," I said. "We're still going to blow up the legionaries."

"A Lokhar dreadnought is coming," N7 said. "We cannot defeat such a vessel. It may be unwise to kill so many Lokhar legionaries within their visual range."

I whirled around toward the others. "Blow them up!" I shouted. "The Lokhars destroyed our planet and most of our race. We're going to kill them because of that. Ella, detonate the Earth warhead. Do it now before they destroy the last ejector!"

The color drained from Ella's face. Her mouth opened, maybe to speak. She was a scientist first. Maybe I asked her to do more than she was capable. It was one thing to fire a laser at an enemy vessel. That was impersonal. You destroyed a machine. You could block the idea of killing all those people aboard. With the tigers coming at us individually, there was no way to fool yourself about what you were doing.

I dashed onto the command deck, shouldering Ella aside.

"Commander," N7 said. "The dreadnought captain is hailing us. He wishes to discuss terms for our surrender."

"I'll give him terms," I said, and I tapped the red image on the board.

The legionaries coming in their individual thousands used semi-portables and rifle lasers to disable the last of the three Jelk missiles. Now a mass of beams shot toward the final ejector.

I ground my teeth together in frustration. Was it already too late? Lokhar legionaries were considered some of the finest fighting soldiers in this arm of the Milky Way Galaxy. They must have trained for such a tactic as I used against them.

Then, outside the battlejumper, the nuclear warhead originally constructed to detonate against Chinese or Russians blew up against the alien world-killers.

I sagged in relief. That was the first reaction. The second was to grin like a manic: fiercely glad to destroy alien bastards. I wanted to take down the entire race of Lokhars if I could.

They'd tried to annihilate us. I would destroy them whenever I had the chance.

The thermonuclear blast lacked the punch of the first T-missile or our own Jelk warheads. On the other hand, it ignited closer to our ship than the first alien warhead had. Even so, the battlejumper's laser survived the explosion and so did we. The Lokhars legionaries coming for us—not so much.

The front mass of them disappeared in a fireball of atomic annihilation. It was beautiful. Others farther away blew backward, carried by the wave front of flying particles. Many of the powered armor suits melted away, exposing tiger flesh. I imagine that those who kept their suits intact boiled like lobsters in a pot. Others looked like machine-gun victims, their suits riddled by speeding particles.

My grin continued to widen like little Red Riding Hood's wolf. Did that make me despicable? Maybe it did. I was a soldier, an assault trooper. The Jelk had trained me to kill. I was doing my job. If I did my job well enough, the human race survived. If I fouled up or got soft, we died. So if I happened to enjoy my job, well, that's the breaks. I'm the one who had to live with it. I'm the one who stood in the breach for mankind. If you feel you can judge me, go ahead. If I have nightmares sometimes because of the things I've done…

No, forget it. I'm not apologizing to anyone. At least not yet, I'm not. I killed the incoming legionaries because I did my job for keeps.

"Commander," N7 said. "The dreadnought captain wants to speak with you."

"Tell him I'm busy." I tapped Ella's board, and I brought up the far-range teleoptics. I did it in time to witness our laser burning through the second Starkien shield. Soon, the second beamship exploded, and this one seemed to damage a third vessel.

"We're doing it," Rollo said. "We're killing them."

I raised my right eyebrow questioningly at Ella. Quietly, she returned to her station as I moved aside.

"The Lokhar captain demands your attention," N7 said. "He is very insistent."

I took a deep breath. "What's his dreadnought doing?" I asked.

"Accelerating for Earth," N7 said.

"What's his flight time look like?"

"He had a greater initial velocity upon entering the solar system. He should be here in a day. Of course, it depends if he plans on braking or if he will chase down our fleeing freighters."

I had to reach out and steady myself. It hit me then what had happened. The Lokhars were back in the solar system. I became lightheaded and felt like vomiting. The Lokhar dreadnought was returning to Earth. Had the captain come back to finish what he'd started a little over a year ago?

I checked the others. Rollo looked pale, and his right eye twitched. It did that sometimes when he became frightened. Not that he'd ever admit to the fright and not that I'd ever call him on it.

Well, I couldn't worry about the dreadnought now. We fought the Starkiens. One battle at a time, right? Hmm. Now that the baboons were out of T-missiles, we could beat them, the flotilla of theirs anyway. There was no way I could destroy the tiger dreadnought. If I recalled correctly, the Lokhars didn't have too many of those. Was that the same ship that had polished off my old man?

I shook my head. None of the dreadnought questions mattered. The Starkiens...

"The tigers have never spoken to us before," Ella said. "To finally talk to them would make this an historic moment."

I scowled. That's why Mad Jack Creed had gone up in his shuttle that day. During their first visit to our solar system, the Lokhars had acted like the Sphinx, silent and inscrutable. We'd desperately wanted them to communicate with us. They ignored every plea and brought about Armageddon.

"This is an opportunity for us to study them," Ella said. "You must speak to the Lokhars, Creed. What can you lose?"

"Keep targeting the Starkiens," I growled. "Finish them."

"I understand your single-mindedness," Ella said. "But you must broaden your approach this time. We lack data, and we will be dealing with the Lokhars shortly—if we survive the Starkiens."

I watched our laser stab a baboon shield. Maybe I could do two things at once. The dreadnought would be here soon enough. Our scientist had a point.

"All right," I told N7. "Open a channel with the tiger. Let's see what he has to say."

"Naga Gobo also wishes to speak with you," N7 said.

"Forget him," I said. "He's dead to me, and good riddance."

"Maybe he wishes an alliance against the Lokhars," Ella said. "Shouldn't we pursue all options?"

"No," I said. "Naga Gobo had his chance. He played his last card and found himself with a losing hand. The way I see it, he reaps the reward of gambling and failing. Like candles in the dark, we're blowing them out one by one."

"But—" Ella said.

"You know we can't afford to do anything less or we risk the battlejumper. Besides, his beamships won't make any difference against the Lokhars. An alliance with him is meaningless."

"I'm putting the Lokhar captain's image onto the main screen," N7 said.

I ran my fingers through my hair. I was going to do what my dad had tried to do and failed: talk to the Lokhars.

On the main screen, the latest beamship with its blackening shield disappeared from view. A proud Lokhar military officer stood in its place. A large flag with zigzagging lightning bolts wavered ever so slowly behind him. It reminded me of the times the President of the United States used to address the nation.

The Lokhar was taller than we were, I knew, a little over seven feet tall. He was broad shouldered and muscular. There were subtle differences to his face so he didn't look exactly like a bipedal tiger. For one thing, the braincase was larger and the features more narrow. His eyes were yellow, with tiny slits in them. The uniform was black and orange, with golden braid and shoulder tabs. He wore medals, and carried a large blaster on his hip. The cap stood higher than a human would have it, and had a crest on the front of crossed blasters, with a tiger's clawed paw in the background. Well, instead of paws, it had fingers, or a cross between fingers and paws. The Lokhars were clearly into fancy dress uniforms. That was interesting right there.

The jaws moved but no sound came. Like a bad old Japanese movie, the voice was out of sequence with the lips. The tiger must be using a translator. I'd spoken with corporation Saurians who had done the same thing. At first it was disorienting, but I quickly became used to it.

"I wish to address the battlejumper's commanding officer," the Lokhar said in a deep voice.

I put my right hand on my chest. "That would be me," I said.

The Lokhar studied me intently. "Do you possess a name of office?"

"I'm Commander Creed."

The Lokhar cocked his head. "That is the office's designation?"

"Commander is my title. Creed is my name."

"I comprehend. I am—" The Lokhar turned sharply to his left. He blinked his eyes several times. The fur around his face stiffened. When he regarded me again, his eyes seemed to shine with rage.

"How do you do that?" Rollo asked me. "In less than a minute the tiger already hates your guts. That's got to be a record."

"You detonated an atomic warhead amongst the 121st Legion," the tiger said. "You vaporized my men."

"Oh boy," Rollo said.

"Those were yours?" I asked. "I'm sorry. I thought they were renegades who had hired out to the Starkiens. I thought you'd be glad for what I did."

The tiger worked his jaws for several seconds and his shoulders hunched as he lifted his arms. He was the picture of a Lokhar ready to pounce and rend to death.

"You are barbarian swine," the tiger spat in feline fury. "Not only did you butcher them, now you attach degradation to noble warriors who died for the Lokhar Pride."

73

"Pride?" I whispered.

"You humans call it 'empire,'" N7 said. "A Lokhar calls it 'pride.'"

"Oh," I said.

"The Starkien scum would never command Pride legionaries," the tiger spat at me. "Soldiers of the Race possess honor and loyalty. On oath to the Creator, they serve the Jade League and protect this quadrant of the galaxy. Needlessly murdering them is a barbaric offense of the first order. Besmirching their holy honor is a crime beyond words."

"So sue me," I said. Genocide against humanity was no big deal to them, but if one singed a few tigers, they became a holy terror. I was sick of the double standard.

"The Starkiens are attacking us and then teleport missiles appeared nearby, disgorging legionaries for a storm assault," I said. "The facts spoke for themselves: the Lokhars worked for the Starkiens."

"Do you lack all objectivity?" the tiger asked. "The Lokhars do not hire themselves to Starkiens. I have forced Naga Gobo to do my bidding."

I don't know if my mouth dropped open. Probably I looked like a fish out of water, making futile gasping motions. My worldview took several seconds to readjust. In a moment the floor became the ceiling. Yeah, okay, I was beginning to see it. This had been a tiger operation from the beginning, not a Jelk or Starkien show.

"So...you're saying the Lokhars reversed the military decision at Sigma Draconis?" I asked.

"Barbarian swine, we all but destroyed the Jelk's devilish offensive thrust. They paid a bitter price for their infamy, even if they gained the information they sought."

"Hold on a minute," I said. "I have to think this through."

N7 muted the screen, even though the tiger lord continued to move his jaws, to rail at me, no doubt.

"What do you make of this?" I asked N7.

"I believe the Lokhar," N7 said, "as that would explain how Naga Gobo acquired the T-missiles and legionaries."

I nodded. Check. That made sense in this screwy part of the universe.

"It means Lokhar reinforcements must have appeared after our departure from Sigma Draconis," N7 said. "More from the Lokhar's words I cannot glean."

"What do you think the Jelk sought in Sigma Draconis?" I asked.

"The Lokhar says they sought information."

"I got that," I said. "What kind of information?"

"I do not know," N7 said.

"Perhaps you should ask Naga Gobo," Ella suggested.

"You really want those baboons to survive, don't you?" I asked.

"I abhor senseless slaughter," she said, "especially when we can gather useful information instead."

I faced the screen. Ella had her points, but I had mine, too. N7 reconnected audio. I wanted to shout at the tiger. I wanted to laugh in his face. The situation demanded cool thinking, however. The invincible dreadnought changed everything.

"I am unfamiliar with you space races," I said. "I don't know your customs or legends. Lokhars fight hard. I know that much." *And you dirty bastards nuke worlds.* "I don't know why you've hailed us, but—"

"I originally called to demand your surrender," the tiger said.

I snorted.

"Now I am reconsidering withdrawing the offer," he said.

I didn't want to jump to conclusions. But had the destruction of the 121st Legion frightened him? The Lokhar didn't act frightened. Why would he withdraw the demand to surrender then?

"For such barbarity," the tiger said, "I desire your deaths, not your capture."

Oh. "Wait a minute," I said. "You call us barbaric? You're the ones who attacked an unarmed planet. You sprayed a bio-terminator on a defenseless people: mine. I'd say that's barbarity of the first order."

"You state inaccuracies," the Lokhar said.

"What? Your people *didn't* launch nuclear missiles at us?"

"Of course I did."

"*You* did it?" I asked, with fury making my voice shake.

I noticed N7 switched to a split-screen. On one-half, I watched another Starkien beamship explode. On the other, the tiger spoke to me.

"I stand proudly by my military record," the Lokhar told me. "I have acted honorably throughout."

"You're kidding, right?"

"You are an insufferable creature who spews insults and slurs," the tiger said. "I am the High Lord Admiral of Dreadnought *Indomitable*. I never joke or kid as you suggest. I am a Lokhar of intense gravity and seriousness."

"I'm sure you are," I said, licking my dry lips. I needed to get a handle on the tiger. I couldn't see what he wanted. Maybe to destroy the last of us, to finish what he'd started.

"Why did your tigers—why did your legionaries attempt to storm my battlejumper?" I asked.

"You cannot be that dense. The reason is obvious."

"Hey, listen to me," I said, finally deciding how I was going to do this. "I'm Commander Creed. We don't use fancy titles like you Lokhars because we're too serious-minded. I am the highest-ranked human in the solar system. You will address me with honor and decorum—with gravity—or I'm ending this dialogue right here and now."

The Lokhar glared, and if it was possible, he stood straighter and more stiffly. I finally noticed a teal-colored medal pinned to his uniform. It glittered with a harsh inner light.

"I don't know your protocols," I said. "I don't pretend to know how you think."

"Barbarian," he muttered.

"That's another thing. You will not call me a barbarian or swine. If you do, I will begin using the same terminology regarding you."

"You would not dare," he said.

"I laughed. "Sure I would dare. I have nothing to lose."

He stared at me, and he opened his mouth, only to close it. "The Jade League is at war with the Jelk Corporation. We desire an enemy battlejumper."

"And that's why you tried to storm mine?"

It looked as if he grinded his back teeth together in frustration. "You will surrender the battlejumper to me," he said. "You will do so at once."

I almost told him, "Come and take." But I had to think of the fleeing freighters and their precious cargoes.

"Are you trying to tell me that in all the years of fighting the corporation, you've never captured a battlejumper?"

The admiral turned his head and appeared to watch an unseen screen. He soon regarded me again. "You will cease at once your attack upon the Starkien beamships."

"I don't think so."

"We are parleying," he said, as if pointing out a key argument. "Your continued attack is a dishonorable—"

"Hold it right there," I said. "Let's get something straight. I can see you're big into honor. But you Lokhars destroyed a defenseless planet. That doesn't strike me as honorable, but…as the opposite," I said.

"Cease attacking the beamships or the parley ends."

"Nope," I said. "Naga Gobo activated androids on my ship. The assassins slew some of my crew, my people. He's going to pay for that with blood. Ever since your cowardly assault on my world, I've vowed to make aliens pay ten thousand-fold for every human death."

"If Naga Gobo released stealth androids on your battlejumper, he did so against my direct orders."

"I guess you have less control of your hirelings than you think," I said.

The admiral snarled with frustration so bits of spit flew.

"The Lokhar could be lying to us," Ella said.

"I do not lie," the tiger said. "To suggest otherwise is to besmirch my honor."

"What honor?" I asked. "You destroyed an unarmed world, mine."

"My assault on Earth followed the conventions of war," he said. "You will immediately cease these slurs upon my military conduct."

"That's some honor code you Lokhars have managed to invent. That's all I have to say."

"I hear you speak, but I do not understand your meaning."

"How many times do I have to say it?" I asked. "You dropped nuclear bombs on a defenseless world. What's honorable about that?"

"You are mistaken," the tiger said. "Your world was massively armed. Large quantities of missiles lofted to attack us. Perhaps you mean to say that your weaponry was antiquated and feeble. That does not mean you were unarmed."

I figured the British during the colonial era must have used the same logic when using a Maxim machine gun on spear-armed natives in the Congo. A spear against a bullet would have had a better chance than Earth did against a Lokhar dreadnought.

"Commander," N7 said. "Naga Gobo begs an audience with you."

"High Lord Admiral," I said, "I'm going to consider your offer of surrender."

"You do not know the terms yet."

"I want to talk about the concept with my crew."

The admiral's head jerked back. "But you told me you were the highest ranked, the commander."

"I am," I said.

"Then your words strike me as pretense. Give the order and your inferiors will follow."

"We don't play the game the same way you do. Commander Creed out." I turned around. "Cut the connection."

N7 did so.

"Put up Naga Gobo," I said, while glancing at Ella.

"He has three ships left," Ella said. "I should inform you that our laser is overheating."

"Take it offline for a moment," I said. "Let them think we're going to do this their way."

"We are not?" N7 asked.

"I think our days of doing anything are just about over," I said. "Therefore, I plan to kill as many of these aliens as I can."

"Thank you, Commander Creed," Naga Gobo said, as he appeared on the big screen. He looked worried and fearful. "I would like to offer my abject surrender to you."

"Okay," I said. "Drop your shields."

The baboon blinked at me. "Commander, you have not yet accepted my surrender."

"Consider it done," I said.

"Yes...of course, Commander. But what assurances do I have that you will not continue to fire on our ships?"

"None," I said.

"But—"

"Drop your shields or I'm going to think you're just buying yourself time to get within your beamships' range."

"No, no," he said, "I assure you that it not my intent. I desire life. I—"

"Did you hire yourself to the Lokhars?" I asked.

He stared at me for just a moment. "Yes, of course," he said.

"Did the Lokhars defeat the Jelk fleet at Sigma Draconis?"

Naga Gobo tugged at his mane, and his manner became shifty. "That is prized information," he said.

"Forget about your games or about stalling," I said. "Either tell me what I want to know or I'll know you're up to your old Starkien tricks."

"A Lokhar mobile fleet arrived several hours after your departure from Sigma Draconis," Naga Gobo said.

"Did Dreadnought *Indomitable* show up with them?"

"No."

"No?" I asked. "Are you sure?"

Naga Gobo appeared perplexed. "The Lokhars do not normally use their dreadnoughts in fleet actions."

"What are you talking about?" I asked.

"The dreadnoughts are survey vessels."

"Meaning what?" I asked.

"Exploratory ships," he said. "They are the offensive arm against the Jelk."

I massaged my forehead, wondering what the baboon meant. I felt out of my depth, as if there were mysteries swirling around me of which I had no knowledge.

"Did the three Jelk commanders escape from Sigma Draconis or did the Lokhars kill them?" I asked.

"All three Jelk escaped. They always do."

"Naga Gobo's remaining vessels will be within beamship range in twenty-nine minutes," N7 said quietly.

Without turning around, I nodded. "What do the Lokhars want?" I asked that baboon.

"I assume you mean here in your solar system," Naga Gobo said.

"Exactly," I said.

Naga Gobo shook his head. "I do not know. I merely know they hired us to make an assault so they could launch their legionaries and capture your battlejumper. Lokhars do not confide in Starkiens."

"What was your hiring price?" I asked.

Naga Gobo tried to look imposing, but he couldn't pull it off. "They captured the majority of my fleet in Sigma Draconis. If they can capture your battlejumper, they will free my fleet."

"And if you fail?"

"They will destroy the ships and the Starkiens in them."

"You're not really going to surrender to me, are you, Naga Gobo?"

"I am. I swear it."

"The rest of your fleet in Sigma Draconis will die if you surrender to me."

"And I will live," he said.

"No... I don't believe you're that venal."

"Commander, I implore you to listen closely," Naga Gobo said. "The Lokhars want to capture you, all of you. I do not believe they mean to kill the last humans. Isn't that excellent news? Knowing it, you should be merciful toward the Starkiens. We used to be allies after all."

"What's really going on here?" I asked. "Your actions make me believe you're not telling me everything."

Naga Gobo hesitated, giving me time to think.

"One of the killer androids you released gave me greetings from Claath," I said. "How did it know to do that? How did you gain Jelk codes if Claath didn't give them to you?"

"It must have been a prerecorded message," Naga Gobo said.

I laughed. Did he think I was stupid?

"The laser is ready," Ella said.

I glanced at her. A green light on her panel shined against her face, highlighting her cheeks

"I think you're right," she said quietly. "I believe he's trying to deceive us so his beamships can get within range of our ship."

"Turn him off," I said.

"No, wait!" Naga Gobo shouted. But N7 broke the connection.

I faced my command crew. "Does anyone have any suggestions?"

"From what I know," N7 said, "I find it incredible the Lokhars used Starkiens. Their loathing for the pirates is well known. Yet it doesn't seem that Naga Gobo is lying about everything. Why otherwise did his flotilla possess teleporting missiles and the 121st Lokhar Legion? The dreadnought admiral corroborates his story about an ultimate Lokhar victory at Sigma Draconis."

"All this," I said, waving my hand, "seems like a pretty elaborate ploy just to capture our battlejumper."

"I notice that originally Naga Gobo wanted to find our commander," Ella said. "I think he wanted to find out if you were here."

"Me?" I asked. "Why me specifically?"

"Maybe the why would give us the reason for the ploy," Ella said.

"I don't know," I said. "With the dreadnought here, I think the Lokhars mean to finish their task of eliminating humanity. I think we're doomed, and I think running is out. The question for us is this: how do we want to end our lives?"

"Go down in a blaze of glory?" Rollo asked in a rough voice.

"I don't see what else there is," I said.

"Then keep bargaining," Ella said. "If we're going to die, if humanity is the verge of extinction, then engaging in futile acts of martial valor does nothing other than assuaging your soldier egos."

"I concur with Ella," N7 said.

I glanced at Rollo.

The massive trooper shrugged. "It doesn't matter to me," Rollo said. "I just want to make sure we're not captured and tortured. After that, I want to kill as many aliens as I can."

"Okay," I said. "It's one thing bargaining with the Lokhar admiral. He seems honorable in his own way. The Starkiens—I don't trust them at all. They're going to be in range soon. I say take them out and see what the admiral has to offer."

"That's incredibly harsh," Ella said, "but I don't see an alternative."

"Sometimes you gotta do what you gotta do," I said.

"I agree with you," Rollo said. "Kill the Starkiens. They mean to kill us."

"They are sly," N7 said. "Destroying them is the most prudent course of action."

"I don't trust them," Ella said. "But shouldn't we continue to bargain while we have an opportunity. Who knows what new data we might receive?"

I exhaled sharply, took several steps and said, "Bring the laser back online. Let's clear out the beamships. Once they're gone, I'll talk to the admiral. If the Lokhars really hate the Starkiens that badly, I don't think the admiral will lose any sleep with the pirates' deaths."

-9-

I never did talk to Naga Gobo again. At my orders, we destroyed the last three beamships. Soon, the Starkien flotilla was gone, a smear of space debris in our lonely universe.

Silence fell upon the control room as Ella took the laser offline.

I wanted to tell them we'd done the right thing. Could we have trusted the slippery Starkiens? Really trusted them? What could we have done differently? The Starkiens couldn't have brought the beamships to a halt before reaching the million-kilometer mark. Nor could I have allowed the flotilla to veer away. They could have gone after the freighters then. No. They had entered the solar system and killed humans. Whether the Starkiens did that under duress or not...they had lied to me all down the line. The fate of the freighters was too important to gamble with if I didn't have to. Instead of gambling, I killed every last one of the alien enemy.

Still, it was one thing to blaze with rage in the middle of a battle, quite another once you realize that your actions had slain thousands of sentient beings. Maybe I could hide behind my medals like the Lokhar High Admiral. Instead of honor as my excuse, I used human survival.

I don't know. What's the point of hand-wringing hindsight? I gave the orders and the Starkiens were dead. I had to live with that. Were the Cherokees right, though? Did a man own a conscience, and every time he went against it, did he wear it down a little bit more?

I'm guessing so. I felt hollow inside when I should have felt ecstatic. Maybe I hadn't fully turned into a coldblooded butcher yet. I had to give it time.

"You had to do it," Rollo said from his station.

Ella's head snapped up. "No. Do not put it all on his shoulders. We did it. We all did it."

"I'm not sorry we did," Rollo said. "We had to. We all know that. So why are we feeling bad about it?"

"Because we're human," I said.

"You're the history buff," Rollo said. "You gotta know there were plenty of killers in the past who didn't give a damn about something like this. This was our job, folks. If we'd failed...ah...I don't know. Commander, permission to leave the bridge."

"Where are you going?" I asked.

"I want to get drunk," Rollo said. He tugged at his collar, which was tight around his thickly muscled neck. "I think I earned that," he added.

"You did," I said, "but not just yet. We have a bigger crisis afoot. Our laser will do no more against the dreadnought than my dad's radio beam did a year ago. N7. Put the Lokhar vessel on the main screen."

The massive dreadnought appeared against the backdrop of stars.

"I don't understand," Ella said. "How can it be so big?"

"Is that a serious question?" N7 asked. "They used large construction techniques and—"

"I understand that part," our Russian scientist said. "Think of what it takes to build a warship hundreds of kilometers in depth and width. Think of the sheer mass. It must be like moving a very large asteroid." Ella shook her head. "Are there millions of Lokhars in there? Do you know, N7?"

"I have no idea," the android said.

"A legion of lost Lokhars—" Ella stopped speaking before adding, "That's a pinprick compared to how many must be in that ship."

"What did Naga Gobo say?" I asked. "The Lokhars don't use the dreadnoughts in fleet actions, but in exploratory adventures. That seems backward to me. They should us those things in battle and send smaller ships out as scouts."

"There is logic to your words," N7 said. "That implies a mystery concerning the dreadnoughts."

One of the engineers entered the control room with a tray of steaming cups of coffee. He put one in a holder near N7's panel. The android snipped. He liked his coffee scalding hot and black. It always seemed to me as if N7 drank oil. He was an android, not a human. Why did I have to keep telling myself that?

"Okay," I said. "We've taken care of the first threat. We don't have to worry about the Starkiens anymore. Now we have to figure a way to deflect the dreadnought. There's no way our freighters can beat *Indomitable* to the Sun—not unless the tigers begin braking."

"We can do nothing to deflect the dreadnought," N7 said.

"I don't accept that," I said.

"You would have surprised me if you did," N7 said, finishing his coffee, handing the cup back to the engineer and taking another. "I am curious what you suggest we do. We do not possess any T-missiles this time to invade within the targeted vessel."

"Maybe we don't need T-missiles," Rollo said. "Let's pack the assault boats and follow the battlejumper as it rams the dreadnought. Whoosh, we fly inside and take control."

Ella laughed sourly. "We have approximately one hundred and fifty assault troopers left. Can that number defeat tens of millions of legionaries?"

"No," I said. "At this point, all we have left is our honeyed tongues. We have to talk our way out of trouble."

"The Lokhars strike me as creatures of action," Ella said.

I clapped my hands together and pointed at her. "Not only are they creatures of actions, but they appear to admire honor and courage. Rollo, tell the engine techs to get ready for propulsion."

"What are you planning?" N7 asked.

"Do any of you happen to know the story of David and Goliath?" I asked.

I received blank looks of incomprehension.

"It's in the Old Testament," I said. "A giant named Goliath from an army of Philistines threatened the ancient Israelites. He was like a Homeric champion, as in Achilles and Hector of Troy. Goliath boasted of his skills and demanded King Saul sent out a champion to face him. Whoever won the fight, the other side's host would have to surrender. As you can imagine, the Israelites quaked in their sandals, dreading the idea of facing the warrior giant. Finally, a young shepherd boy around sixteen or seventeen showed up. He told the others God would help him defeat the giant. David used a sling and ran out to fight the hardened warrior. He asked for God's help and twirled the sling, hitting old Goliath in the forehead. The giant fell, and David used the champion's own sword against him, chopping off the Philistine's head."

"And that's what we're going to do to the Lokhar dreadnought?" Rollo asked dubiously.

"No," I said. "I don't see that we even have a sling-stone of a chance fighting them. But we can show courage by charging the Lokhars."

"What does that achieve?" N7 asked.

"Not a whole heck of a lot," I admitted. "But at least it will feel better than cowering in fear." I glanced around the control room. "This is it, though. I'm not going to order you to your certain death. If you want to use an assault boat to go down to Earth and join Diana, that's your choice."

"Commander," N7 said. "The Lokhar admiral is calling. Do you want to speak with him?"

"Of course," I said. "Put him on."

The same tiger as before regarded me. The same time lag of lip and sound gave the conversation a surreal feeling.

"You destroyed the Starkiens," he said.

"They were my enemy."

His yellow eyes seemed to glow. "I have recordings of the battle of Sigma Draconis. During my voyage here, I have watched them. I know you, Commander Creed. I am aware of your bloodthirstiness toward my people."

"Do you think I might have a reason for that?" I asked softly.

"I am uninterested in your reasons," he said. "Here are my terms. You must leave the battlejumper, you and every one of your personnel. I do not care where the rest of your people go, but you must come to me."

"Go on," I said, feeling a knot tightening in my chest. "Tell me the rest."

"I give the orders," he said. "You are in no position to order me to speak."

"That's true to a point," I said. "I do have one card I can still play."

"That is incorrect. You have nothing."

"I can destroy the battlejumper, blow it up."

His eyes widened. "No! You must not do that."

That was an interesting reaction. "Admiral—"

"High Lord Admiral," he said promptly.

"High Lord Admiral," I said. "You haven't yet given me a reason why I should comply with your request."

"I give orders, not requests."

"I'm not under your orders. I don't fear your threats. That makes it a request. If you want the battlejumper, then I'm inclined to destroy it."

"If you do," he said, "I will slay every human in the solar system."

"So what?" I said. "You're already going to do that."

"Incorrect," he said. "My orders call for me to pick up every human here, not kill them."

The knot in my chest twisted into something cold and hard. What kind of vile experiments did the Lokhars wish to perform on the last humans? I had a feeling I would be doing everyone a favor by destroying the battlejumper. Better a dead man than a shrieking tortured man soon to be dead.

"What is your reason for wanting to pick us up?" I asked.

"I am not in the habit of explaining my actions to inferiors," he said.

I was already tired of the arrogant admiral and found it impossible to control my every reaction. "Well, you'd better start getting in the habit pretty quick," I told him. "Otherwise, you're going to lose the battlejumper."

"You are obstinate and unreasonable. I do not understand why you wish to die."

"I don't wish it," I said. "But I'd rather pass honorably in battle than face torture at Lokhar hands."

He stiffened and his left hand-paw opened and closed spasmodically. I noticed the tips of his claws appearing and disappearing. "Have a care, Earthling, how you address a High Lord Admiral of the Pride."

Why did aliens always act so strangely? "I'm curious," I said. "Could you explain what I said that just made you so angry?"

He glared at me, finally saying, "We of the Pride do not torture anyone. We slay honorably in battle and treat our prisoners with dignity. However, you will not be prisoners."

"What will we be?"

"Detainees for a time," he said.

"And then?"

He seemed to become uncomfortable. "It will depend on several factors."

"So...you're saying you want me to come to you? Is it to discuss terms?"

"*Indomitable* will soon be in orbit around Earth," he said, ignoring my question. "Then you can come to us. Then you *must* come to us and formerly surrender."

"I'm supposed to surrender to the Lokhar who personally murdered my father?"

A voice broke in on his side, and a second Lokhar quite unlike the admiral appeared. This tiger was taller and thinner, with a different type of uniform. He spoke rapidly with hisses and snarls.

The admiral raised a heavy paw as if to strike the new Lokhar. That one stiffened, as if waiting for the blow to fall. Finally, the admiral lowered his arm.

With a stiff bow, the taller Lokhar retreated out of view.

The admiral cleared his throat and turned to me. "I am..." He snarled quietly, as if to himself. Then he looked up, glaring into the screen. "The Alien Contact Officer has...informed me of, ah, forgotten protocol. You will not officially surrender. Instead, we will—"

The admiral snarled with obvious frustration. He pointed a clawed finger at me. "You will board my ship, Commander Creed or your humans will perish. If you are so foolish as to reject this offer—"

"No," I said. "I'm going to come. If this is a setup, it's well done on your part. Still, getting to see you squirm, in person no less…I wouldn't miss that for the world."

The admiral glared a moment longer before the connection ended.

"Are you crazy?" Rollo asked. "You plan to go onto his dreadnought?"

"There's something weird going on," I said. "And we really don't have many options left. Besides, I want to understand these tigers. They've killed our planet but we've beaten them in battle each time as assault troopers. The Alien Contact Officer interests me. And I'm curious about the dreadnought being an exploratory vessel."

"What about us?" Ella asked. "What should we do?"

That was a good question. "I think the rest of you should head down to Earth," I said. "Join Diana in her freighter. If this is a trick and the Lokhars mean to torture us, better that just one go than all of us."

"I will join you," N7 said.

"Me, too," Rollo said. "I'm not going to let you do this alone. I didn't the first time. Why would I now?"

"I will also come with you," Ella said. "I might see connections you would miss."

"While I appreciate the offers," I said, "this time I'm going alone."

"That's madness," Rollo said. "You need at least one of us with you. Two are better than one."

He had a point. One man by himself usually didn't act as bravely as two men would. The reason was easy to understand. If someone you knew watched your actions, it helped stiffen your spine. As a youngster in prison, I wanted to be like a leopard or hawk, a creature who stalked through live independent and alone. I since came to understand that man was social. He needed the company of his own kind. He wasn't a leopard and seldom did well if completely isolated.

"You have a point," I told Rollo. "N7, you will come with me. I want you others to stick together somewhere on Earth. If you don't hear from me after several hours, then take the assault boats and go as deep as you can in an ocean or lake. Maybe a few of you can survive Lokhar treachery."

"I don't see how playing submarine will help us if the Lokhars kill everyone else," Rollo said.

"I'll tell you how," I said. "You wait a week, lift off afterward, take the assault boats through a jump point and go to a planet with starships. Board one, capture it and then—I don't know, give the aliens hell for as long as you can."

Rollo snorted, shaking his head.

"You are the most bloodthirsty, one-tracked man I know," Ella said.

Before I could reply, Rollo asked, "Are you sure about this, Creed?"

"No, despite what Ella believes, I'm as uncertain as can be. This mess…" I squinted at the screen, watching the approaching monstrosity from the stars. "Ever since they hit Earth the first time, I've wanted to get onto the Lokhar killer. This is my chance. If I'm lucky, who knows, maybe I can plant my Bowie knife in that big admiral bastard's chest. Give him my piece of tin, so to speak, as his reward for what he did to my dad."

There was more arguing, and it took another thirteen hours before *Indomitable* reached Earth. But I was crossing my Rubicon.

For those of you who slept through history class, the Rubicon was the name of the stream Julius Caesar splashed across before starting the Roman Civil War. The senators had told him to stay out of Italy with his legions, but J.C. didn't like to listen to others. He waded across and had his run of victories against Pompey and company. In the end, though, all the war gained Caesar was a legend and a chest full of senatorial daggers as he choked to death on his own blood. I had no idea what crossing my Rubicon would win me. I just hoped I could be courageous no matter what happened next.

-10-

Everyone left the battlejumper, but not before the engineers rigged the vessel to self-destruct. I gave Ella the trigger device: it looked like an old gym locker, the kind you dialed back and forth. Her trigger had a four-sequence number. The self-destruct would give her, and maybe me, one last bargaining chip with the admiral.

The others rode two assault boats and various air-cars down to Earth. I watched them fade into the distance, with central Africa in the background. The last I saw were dark pinpricks against the most beautiful planet in the galaxy. Maybe Diana could use them...provided the Lokhars told the truth and weren't here on an extermination mission.

Yet if the aliens told the truth and the Starkiens really had been working for them, why had the android assassin first shot me with toxins?

I sat up in my control chair—I took the last assault boat out to meet the Lokhars. Most of the androids had used lasers against us. Against me, the plastic killer had used drug-laced needles. Did that mean the android hadn't been trying to kill me, but capture my butt?

Naga Gobo said he was supposed to bring me back as a captive. Why would the Lokhars want me that badly? Did they see me as a war criminal and want me before a people's tribunal? If that were true, why bring a dreadnought to capture me? Surely, the vessel had vast operating costs. What were the Lokhars looking or exploring for, using something so massive?

Was the sought item so dangerous that they actually needed a ship of such size?

"There," N7 said, "Dreadnought *Indomitable*."

The asteroid-sized ship must have dumped gravity waves. On our screen, I could see it brake into a stationary position, but I didn't see a long exhaust tail. So how was it doing that?

While nervously chewing on a lip, I engaged the boat's thrusters. Both N7 and I were pressed against our padded chairs as the assault boat headed toward destiny.

Our N-series android didn't wear symbiotic armor. The stuff didn't take to his kind. He wore cyber-armor, the mechanical skin molded to fit him. Our helmets were nearly identical, though.

"I think Rollo's right," I said. "This is the craziest thing I've ever done."

"Negative," N7 said. "That would be using the teleportation bomb to appear inside the battlejumper. I still find myself amazed we are alive. Perhaps that is the reason the admiral wishes to capture you. The Lokhars are a conservative military race. You used one of their weapons in an interesting way. Learning about the new tactic might be worth the price of bringing *Indomitable* to Earth."

"That's an interesting thought. But I don't think that's it."

"Neither do I," N7 admitted. "Their actions are most perplexing."

It nearly took a half hour for us to journey to them. Finally, we slowed our velocity, and soon the monstrous dreadnought came in visual range.

I swallowed hard staring out the viewing port. *Indomitable* brought back painful memories. It looked too much as it had a year ago in orbit around our world. How wise was it to head in to meet the arrogant dick of a tiger admiral who had blown away my dad and my world?

"Interesting," N7 said, as he leaned forward in examination.

He didn't have to point. I saw it. The dreadnought had taken damage, heavy pounding. The part we'd seen through our teleoptics hadn't shown the shredded side of the vessel. Now, as we brought the assault boat in for a landing, I saw jagged rents in the armored hull. It took a moment for that to register. The rents were kilometers in width, and sometimes, places glowed in there and then quit glowing.

"Have they been in a battle?" I asked.

"It would appear so," N7 said.

"Did someone mange to get nuclear warheads close enough?"

"I do not know," he said.

"Wonder what the other guy looks like?" I asked.

"A prudent question," N7 said. "Yes, that would reveal much if we knew."

I couldn't help but grin. Seeing the giant vessel damaged felt good. Someone had hurt them at least. I would have liked to shake their hand or tentacle and buy them a beer.

A Lokhar hailed us on the comm-unit. He appeared to be a functionary to guide us to the correct portal.

"Perhaps I should pilot us in," N7 said. "You have much on your mind and need to maintain a high energy level."

That sounded like good advice, so I took it. I'd thought about wearing my symbiotic armor to the historic meeting. If the tigers planned to capture me, I'd fight to the death. But if that were true—the capturing—why was I coming into the den of lions in the first place? No. I was playing a hunch, I suppose. I had come to believe the tigers kept their word. That meant the second skin wouldn't make any difference, so why bother with it?

The truly monstrous size of the dreadnought became more apparent as we approached. It began blotting out more and more stars, becoming like a portable world to us. How many decades of construction had gone into making the thing? How many Lokhars lived aboard it? Hundreds of thousands of mechs and techs must be employed keeping it running. No wonder a *High Lord Admiral* commanded the dreadnought.

"This doesn't make sense," I told N7. "Why build something so big? I don't think it's a military reason. Instead of putting all of one's eggs in a single basket, a thousand battlejumpers would be wiser."

"Agreed," N7 said. "Perhaps it relates to its primary function: that of an exploratory vessel."

"I don't buy that either. The whole thing is weird, if you ask me." I shrugged. "Maybe the Lokhars are into impressive stuff and somewhere down the line they got carried away. You saw the High Lord Admiral's uniform. Hah, listen to the title. Maybe they think bigger is always better. So after giving themselves long titles they went and built the granddaddy of all starships."

N7 concentrated on piloting—not that he needed to. There was so much *space*. We passed through a monstrous portal with blinking green lights shooting along the sides of the oval opening. It reminded me of Christmas Tree Lane back in my old hometown. The vast entrance made our assault boat seem like a fly buzzing into a house. Soon, we flew over a hanger deck kilometers upon kilometers in circumference. If that weren't enough of a kick, on the deck below parked wingtip to wingtip were thousands upon tens of thousands of alien fighters. They were bulky with stubby triangular wings. I wouldn't have been surprised if someone informed me that I looked at more aircraft than the combined total of the U.S., China, Russia, Israel, heck, the entire Earth's air forces in any given year—or what Earth used to have.

A Lokhar spoke to N7 over the comm, guiding us over the hordes of assault craft. Finally, I saw a neon-red outline down there, a place for us to park beside all the fighters.

We went down and landed with a clang, N7 jostling us in our seats. I was too wound up to ask him why he'd made such a poor landing. Could androids be nervous?

N7 twisted in his seat, looking up. I did to, noticing he watched a video feed of what went on behind us. Oh. He watched the outer portal slowly slid shut. Is that how flies felt when I'd closed the door to my house as a kid?

"What do we do now?" I asked.

The answer came in the form of military hovercraft, twenty of them. They raced across the hanger deck, with turret cannons aimed at our assault boat.

"Trusting tigers, aren't they?" I said.

We suited up in regular vacuum gear and exited the boat. Good-bye Jelk tech and hello Lokhar. I hoped the tigers were honorable. I admit it was difficult walking toward what could be my last hours before horrendous alien torture.

At least one hundred battle-armored Lokhars filed off the hovers. The vehicles were bigger than any Earth tank, more like a Coast Guard patrol boat in size. The soldiers or legionaries marched in unison and carried laser rifles. They created a lane for us to walk down, with legionaries on either side of us. I felt like Moses walking through the parted waters of the Red Sea. The tigers towered over me as if each one was an NBA superstar. I noticed a range of Lokhar sizes, starting with seven feet and going up to eight.

Finally, N7 and I reached a ramp leading into a hover. With more than a little trepidation, I climbed the ramp. Would I regret this for the rest of my short life? Why did they want *me* anyway? I wasn't anything special, just one angry Earther willing to take a wild chance now and again.

I refrained from muttering a radio remark to N7. He likely wouldn't understand it anyway. He had Ella's disease: simian curiosity about just about everything. I imagine our android loved every minute of this, drinking in the details. That was one of the reasons I'd brought N7 with me. He had a photographic memory, storing the images.

We entered a narrow chamber with seats. Five armored tigers followed us, squeezing through the hatch in their armor. We all sat down and strapped in. I squirmed as the hover engine revved, and then we were moving.

It took an hour, if you can believe that. No tiger talked to us during the entire time. We drove, walked down kilometers of corridors and rode several different lifts. Forget about the feeling of moving through a city. This felt as if we moved through countryside and passed through several cities.

Finally, the Lokhar escorts brought us to our destination, stopping before an elephant-sized hatch. Within the massive door was a smaller man-sized portal. It slid up and N7 and I walked toward a lone tiger, a thin and recognizable one. Instead of armor, he wore a black uniform with silver trim. I was grateful to see we approached the Alien Contact Officer that had talked to the High Lord Admiral on the screen before.

The portal slid shut behind us, leaving us alone with the Lokhar. I take that back. The room was big, the size and volume of a football stadium at least. Along the walls in layered tiers one row above the other, sat hundreds of tiger technicians at their stations. Each of them monitored something, constantly adjusting and twisting dials.

You heard right: dials. Just like an old 1950s science fiction movie.

I looked around. So did N7. I spied various antennas on the ceiling. One dish twisted up there until it aimed at me. The massive room lacked any other furniture, just lots of open space and deck plates.

"Okay," I said. "What's going on? Are we zoo specimens or guests of the Lokhars?"

"You are Commander Creed?" the Alien Contact Officer asked.

I noticed he didn't use a translator, but spoke tiger-accented English. That was interesting. There wasn't any time lag between his moving lips and the sound.

"Yes, I'm Commander Creed," I said. I admit that the approach to the giant vessel, the interior journey and my predicament had cowed me. I wasn't feeling as aggressive as normal, and decided on a more cautious approach. First clearing my throat, I asked, "Is it against Lokhar protocol if I ask you what your name is?"

More of the antenna dishes on the ceiling swiveled toward me. And although we were too far away from them to know for certain, it seemed as if some of the monitoring tigers in the tiers moved their hands and arms more rapidly.

"I am Doctor Sant," the tiger told me. "Among my various duties, I am the chief xeno-psychologist aboard *Indomitable*."

Doctor Sant was the first Lokhar I'd seen who stooped a bit at the shoulders. He looked thinner than the legionaries I'd slain in battle. He had white in his facial fur and the eyes were a faded yellow. His uniform was a silver and black as I've said, with orange chevrons on the sleeves. He lacked a blaster on his belt, although he had what looked like an old telephone receiver hooked there. He also wore a ring, a gaudy, plastic-looking thing a little girl might have bought in a big bubblegum dispenser.

"The High Lord Admiral said you were the Alien Contact Officer," I said.

"I hold several titles," Sant said, and to my ear, he spoke with pride. "I am the most learned Lokhar aboard ship and hold several...hmm... I believe you would call them diplomas."

I found his vanity odd, and it struck a funny bone with me. Imagine the old time alien aliens in their silver saucers who picked up people and ran tests on them. Imagine if the first words they said were, "I am a pointy-headed university professor who lives in an ivory tower," and if he said that proudly.

I realize I didn't know enough to make judgments about the Lokhars. Still, Sant's words helped shake me out of my depression. They hadn't beaten me yet even if I stood inside the belly of the whale.

"You've been to school a long time, have you?" I asked.

Sant leaned a little closer as I spoke, as if he needed to in order to hear my words. He was over seven feet tall, making the movement ominous. Then he smiled, showing fanglike teeth, the kind vampires have in the movies. "Yes," he said. "I have studied longer than any aboard *Indomitable*. Despite my many duties, I am also taking a correspondence course from Regal Theology Cathedral."

"You're a religious man?" I asked.

He unhooked the old telephone receiver from his belt, clicked a button in the center and put the phone against his right ear. He spoke quietly and then listened.

"I see," Sant told me, as he hooked the receiver back onto his belt. "You're asking if I believe in supernatural phenomenon."

"Not exactly," I said. "What do they teach at Regal Theology Cathedral?"

"Higher criticism concerning the Creator and various alien holy books," he said, promptly.

"That's all very interesting."

"Yes, I think so, too," Sant said. "It is good we have a similar reference point. That will help us considerably."

The odd, funny feeling departed. I was a fool if I thought Sant was amusing. These creatures had practically annihilated us. I needed to get my head in the game. Doctor Sant was an alien in form, feeling and thought. An entire football stadium of Lokhars was absorbed with the task of monitoring me. Why go to such lengths if they were simply going to kill me?

"Are you studying us?" I asked. "Are they studying us?"

"Yes," Sant said. "That is correct."

"I take it you've never met a human in person before?" I asked.

"No, no, I've met several."

"Are they aboard your ship?"

"I'm afraid the High Lord Admiral did not permit that."

"The admiral had them killed?" I asked, with an edge returning to my voice.

"Yes. That's right. You are quite perceptive, which you might be interested to know I predicted would be the case."

I refrained from grabbing my Bowie and attacking the smug tiger. Other than the knife, I had no other weapons with me besides my fists and wits. I'd expected them to notice a gun, which is why I'd left mine behind.

The receiver at his belt made a loud hum. Sant picked it up and listened. His eyes latched onto me as he did. Warily, he hooked the receiver onto his belt and took several steps back.

"I would like to warn you, Commander Creed, that several sharpshooters even now aim at your chest. If you make any sudden moves at me, you shall die. That would be most unfortunate. So I suggest you contain your anger."

"I get it," I said. "Your monitors just saw an emotional spike and called to warn you. Yeah, you should know that I get unhappy hearing about Lokhars murdering more people. It makes my blood pressure rise."

The receiver gave off its tones once more, but Doctor Sant ignored it. Finally, he turned toward one section of wall and waved his right arm. The tones stopped.

"I perceive your outrage," Sant said, turning back to me. "From your perspective, I understand that you believe you are being reasonable."

"No! I know I'm being reasonable in hating the fact that Lokhars murdered humanity."

"Commander Creed."

"Just Creed will do," I said.

That brought the doctor up short. He appeared puzzled. "Are you not the commander?"

"I am."

"Then why would you prefer me to call you bare."

"What?" I asked.

"Bare," N7 said. "The Lokhars are a formal race. They enjoy their titles and prerogatives. He cannot understand why you want him to call you your bare name. It would be like you stripping and walking around naked."

Doctor Sant nodded. "Clever, clever, you are a clever beast. Excuse me," he said, as I began to bristle. "I realize you are not beasts. You are people, albeit hopelessly mired in a primitive stage."

So I had to go through this again. Okay. I'd use their arrogance against them just as I once had against Claath.

"Why do you think I'm so clever?" I asked.

"I've had you brought here for study," Sant said. "I mean this chamber, of course. Yet even as I study you, you study us, having brought a portable analyzer with you."

"Wait a minute," I said. "Do you mean N7?"

"Yes, of course."

"N7 is my friend. He's not just an analyzer."

Doctor Sant glanced sharply at N7. "It is a machine."

"With a bio brain," I added, "and with enough upgrades to have changed him."

"He is still a manufactured product," Sant said. "He was never born."

I didn't want them taking N7 away and dismantling him. If they called him a machine, they might not feel honor bound toward him.

"Let me say it again," I told Sant. "N7 is my friend, a friend to the human race."

Doctor Sant squirmed uncomfortably. "Commander Creed, let us reason this through."

I held up my hand. "Why do you care what I believe about him? What difference does that make to you?"

Sant twitched his whiskers and took a step closer to us. He lowered his voice, as he said, "You mustn't say such things in the High Lord Admiral's presence. To grant a machine sentient being is a primitive's response or the response of someone hopelessly superstitious. Neither of those will persuade the High Lord Admiral to commit to the experiment."

"What experiment?" I asked.

"Allow us to take one step at a time, Commander."

"Look," I said. "If you guys dismantle N7, I'll take it as if you've murdered my brother."

"Please, Commander, contain your emotionalism and primitivism. Neither will help me nor help you or your race in this grave situation."

"Doc, you're confusing the crap out of me."

"Yes, that would appear to be a natural problem with our situation. Still, the oracle has spoken. The High Lord Admiral wants to believe, but it isn't in his nature to submit to such indignities. I have had an extremely difficult time convincing him of the seriousness of the situation. You must aid me, not fight me."

"I don't know what you're talking about," I said.

"Please, do not call the machine your friend. It will hinder, not help, and it is extremely disconcerting to me personally."

I glanced at N7. The android pretended not to notice the scrutiny as he stared straight ahead. It made his features immobile as only a construct could do. For that moment, his face seemed to have the texture of a plastic Halloween mask, an eerie thing.

"He has no soul," Sant explained. "You realize that, do you not?"

"Why don't we forget about it?" I asked. "You leave him alone and I won't upset you with my beliefs."

Doctor Sant began to pace back and forth. "I had no idea this was going to prove so difficult. The High Lord Admiral was right in many regards about your race, about you. Yet we cannot ignore the oracle. If we're to learn the secret of the Jelk—"

"What did you say?" I asked. "This is about the Jelk?"

Doctor Sant regarded me. "It's too early to go down that route. We must know more about you first."

I massaged my forehead. "What does the High Lord Admiral plan to do with the freighters?" I asked.

Sant stared at me, and it appeared as if he was on the knife-edge of a difficult decision. "Do you realize our quadrant of the spiral arm is in a fight to the death against the Jelk?"

"I don't know much about that, doc."

He stiffened. "I am Doctor Sant. Do not demean my rank with your primitive informality. I cannot abide it and the High Lord Admiral..." Sant shook his head.

"Sure, Doctor. I can see you're...trying to understand us. We're on the same side, you and me." I didn't believe that, but he seemed more disposed toward humans than any other tiger. "I don't know much about quadrant politics. Your admiral bombed us into oblivion and the Jelk offered the last humans survival if we fought for them as assault troopers. What else could I have done?"

"The honorable thing," Sant said. "You could have proudly denied his insufferable offer and gone into oblivion with your human dignity intact. We tried to save you the ignobility of Jelk slavery."

They did that by killing nearly everyone on Earth? "Thanks a lot," I said, sarcastically.

Sant bowed at the waist. "You are welcome, of course. I hadn't realized some of you humans understood the situation. I should have realized you of all people would know."

"No, you don't get it," I said. "That was sarcasm just now. You—"

N7 laid a hand on my arm and shook his head. "He doesn't understand about sarcasm. Lokhars are all but devoid of humor."

Doctor Sant hissed, and he stared at me expectantly.

N7 let go of my arm.

"What do you have to say now?" Sant asked, triumphantly.

"About what?" I asked.

"The machine touched you and dared to admonish you in front of others. Do you wish it destroyed? I will grant you this boon as a matter of personal honor."

It took me several seconds. I finally looked up at the ceiling full of antennas. The tigers were even more alien than I'd first realized. They thought much differently about many things. Maybe it was time to change tactics, to begin playing the game their way. I was in a fight, a battle of wits. Doctor Sant and his High Lord Admiral wanted to use me somehow. I wonder what the oracle had told them. I had to use the Lokhars if humanity was going to get out of this mess. I didn't know the tigers well, but after these brief words, I had a clue as to the right way to act.

Straightening my uniform, I spoke sternly, "Listen to me well, Doctor Sant. I am Commander Creed, the leader of the last humans. I don't need Lokhars taking care of my honor. I will address the android my own way and in my own time."

"Of course, of course," Sant said. "I apologize. I did not mean any disrespect."

I nodded stiffly. "I take you at your word, Doctor Sant. The matter is forgotten."

The tiger brought his left paw-hand near his face, and let needle-sharp claws appear from the tips—just as a real lion or tiger could do. Delicately, Sant scratched under his chin. It struck me as something a man might do in rubbing his jaw or scratching the back of his head.

"You give me hope, Commander Creed. I hadn't realized— well, never mind. It probably wouldn't make sense to you. Perhaps some of you, warriors such as yourself, at least, can work with us. The others we tested…"

I could feel N7 watching me.

The android did so for good reason. I hated the idea of Lokhars testing humans. Sometimes, though, one had to swallow his pride. Sometimes, one had to go Starkien and get sneaky. I decided that as long as I was in *Indomitable*, I would act with tiger formality. I had to remember they were inordinately religious, too. Did the two go hand in hand? I didn't know.

"Here is how we will proceed," Sant said. "I suggest we familiarize ourselves with each other. I will...hmm...coach you on the correct way to address the High Lord Admiral. He is ultra-conservative in bearing and dignity. He is a Lokhar of immense gravity. It would be unwise to use any of your informality and primitivism with him. Can we agree to that?"

"I'd like to know your objective, Doctor Sant. Why has the Lokhar Pride attacked Earth one minute and now believe we'll help you the next?"

"The reasons are excellent as I'm sure you'll agree once I tell you."

"So tell me."

Doctor Sant might have. Before he had the opportunity, the door slid up. N7 and I turned around.

Tigers in elaborate dress uniforms and bearing baroque rifles marched into the chamber. Like WWI-style German soldiers, they had single spikes on their helmets. It made them seem nine feet tall. Then I realized these tigers were bigger than the ordinary ones.

"*Indomitable's* Imperial Guard," Sant whispered. "You must be on your best behavior, I implore you."

I wondered why that should be. The guards marched into the room, about thirty of them. They marched in perfect unison, parting around us until they encircled N7, Doctor Sant and me. Only then did the High Lord Admiral make his appearance. The tiger swaggered into the football-sized chamber. He wore his fancy braid and carried an ornate baton like a Sixteenth century marshal used to hold when artists painted his portrait.

The admiral halted, studying me as one might a trained pit bull.

Doctor Sant spoke in a ringing voice, "Bow low, Commander Creed, for you are in the presence of Prince Venturi of Orange Tamika, the High Lord Admiral of Dreadnought *Indomitable*, an Explorer First Class and a soldier of the combat school of Sha-karn."

11

I didn't bow. I didn't even incline my head. This bastard had ordered the death of my father and the Earth. I'd sooner stick my Bowie in his chest than grant him the slightest honor.

"My apologies, Prince," Sant said. "I haven't yet had time to teach him the correct protocol."

"Time isn't the issue," Venturi said in a gruff voice. "Besides, he is a killer and a savage. Protocol means nothing to such as him."

"Perhaps—"

Venturi raised a heavy paw. Lokhar fingers were blunter than ours were and shorter. Well, not in actual size, but in proportion to their larger bodies. He had three different fleshy pads on each finger, without hair. Like a human finger, there were three parts or joints.

The doctor fell silent.

"I am well able to defend my honor," Admiral Venturi said. "If I desire, my guards shall beat the offender to death. Nothing in fact would please me more…except obeying the suggestions of the oracle." He regarded me. "It is the only thing keeping you alive."

I waited, wondering what this oracle had said that would keep the tiger from killing me.

"It appears to understand patience," Venturi said. "That is a useful trait in a killer."

"Why don't you make your pitch," I said.

"Now see here, Commander Creed," Sant said. "You cannot speak to a prince of the Orange Tamika—"

"We will make allowances today," Venturi told the doctor. "The sands of fate run against us. We have no more time for useless arguing." He made growling noises before regarding me. "I find you offensive, human. Your stench, your arrogance and your buffoonery all conspire to enrage me against you. For your disobedience of my order concerning the Starkiens, I should rend you limb from limb."

I eased forward onto my toes, ready to draw my Bowie and attacked. If it hadn't been for the defenseless freighters racing to the Sun in an attempt to escape... I eased back onto my heels, waiting.

"Instead of gratifying my desires," Venturi said, "I will show you a marvel that confounds League scientists, holy adepts and emperors alike. It is a terror from beyond time, and I'm gambling your primitive mind has the wit to understand its significance."

The prince or admiral aimed his baton at the ceiling and pressed several buttons on the end. Half of the chamber darkened. Within the gloom, a holoimage of the Altair Object appeared against the background of stars. The Forerunner artifact was torus or donut-shaped as I've said before, with a black hole in the center. I'd been told the First Ones had constructed it ages ago. An asteroid maze orbited the object. On the circling rocks, the Lokhar Fifth Legion waited. To them this was holy space, the artifact venerated in the name of the Creator.

I don't know where Venturi got the footage, but he replayed the combined Starkien-Android-Assault Trooper attack against it. He used speeded images, slowing a few times to show a particularly savage conflict. Starkien ships expelled masses of assault boats, which closed against the maze and disgorged sled-riding troopers. All the while, Lokhar lasers beamed from asteroid domes, destroying attackers. The footage brought back bitter memories. Thousands of assault troopers perished that day, although Lokhar legionaries died, too. Finally, legionaries retreated toward the center Forerunner artifact. Then it happened again. The object brightened like something from Heaven before growing fainter and fainter.

Finally, it disappeared, taking a number of Fifth Legion soldiers with it.

"You witnessed a miracle," Venturi said in a rough voice. "The Jelk Corporation desired the artifact and went to great lengths to acquire it. Instead of allowing that to happen, it would appear that the Creator summoned the artifact home. Those who know about the sacrilegious assault believed such an event occurred, or the majority did anyway. What else could have caused a miracle?"

The Forerunner artifact had been troubling me for some time. What did it do? Why did the Jade League venerate it as something from the Creator if the First Ones had built it? And finally—

"Why did the Jelk want it?" I blurted.

"Eh?" Venturi asked, tearing his gaze from the holoimage to scowl at me.

"He does not understand his breach of protocol, Lord," Sant said. "He deserves a beating—"

"Cease," Venturi said. "Having him in my presence is belittling enough. Yet if I can stomach his nearness, I can endure his apish chatter, too, I suppose. He thirsts for knowledge, which is a sign of intelligence after all. We can be grateful for that."

"Yes, Lord," Sant said.

"Here I am an admiral, Doctor. I am not on homeworld at court. It is against the diktat of Purple Tamika for you to address me as nobility in this place."

"Yes…Admiral," Sant said. "I am abashed at my conduct—"

"Cease," Venturi said. "We have no time for strict formality."

Doctor Sant bowed his head.

Venturi regarded me. "As to your question, I believe the artifact has spawning implications."

"What does that mean?" I asked.

"Indeed," Venturi said. "Hmm… I spoke with Naga Gobo before he perished. I found the encounter demeaning but useful. You might be interested to learn that the Starkien knew you had turned a Jelk incorporeal."

"You know a lot," I said.

"The Lokhars and then the Jade League have warred against the corporation for generations. Yes, we know the basic nature of the Jelk. In essence, they are energy beings able to house themselves in bodies of flesh and blood. The holy adepts believe Jelk crave sensations." Venturi studied me. "I do not know if you have the capacity to understand this, but: the Jelk did not originate in our universe, but came from outside it."

"What?" I asked.

"Do you mean they originated in a parallel universe?" N7 asked.

Venturi's head whipped about as he stared at N7. The tiger growled low in his throat and hunched his shoulders as claws appeared at the end of his fingertips. "Keep your machine silent or I will destroy it."

"N7," I said.

The android nodded his understanding.

It took Venturi a few moments to settle himself. He tugged at the cuffs of his sleeves, brushing the orange chevrons sewn there. Finally, he resumed talking. "If you can understand the concept of parallel universes, yes, that will be sufficient. Jelk are *others* in the worst sense of the word. How they crossed from one space-time continuum to another, we do not know. It happened eons ago. Certain theorists claim the Jelk visited the early worlds, astounded at the life forms there, bewildered at flesh, blood and bones. Through a process of trial and error, the energy creatures built bodies for themselves a particle at a time. Some holy adepts think the Jelk first possessed or inhabited our ancestors' bodies and only afterward desired their own forms. In any case, in order to reproduce, a Jelk splits his energy in a similar manner as a single-celled organism or an amoeba. However, they cannot do so under normal conditions in our universe. They must stimulate whatever their space-time continuum did that allowed them to procreate. Our most learned scientists believe Jelk need powerful constructs like the artifact in order to render itself into two. As far as we know, these two *spawns* are granted the newness of vigor and desire of youth, but they maintain the knowledge of the older, single being."

"How does the Forerunner artifact help them split?" I asked.

"Firstly, our scientists do not *know* the Jelk must have the artifact for this. It is a theory, albeit the best we have to date. That is one of the primary reasons the Jade League guards each artifact with military power. We must unite in order to keep the Jelk from growing more numerous."

"I can see that," I said. "After watching Claath change and burn his way free of the battlejumper I'd agree they're as alien as can be. If the artifact can help him spawn, and Claath went for it, that would imply he needs to split or has a growing desire for it."

"Yes, of course," Venturi said. "It is an obvious deduction."

"So do you know where the artifact went after it disappeared?" I asked.

Venturi stared up at the ceiling.

Doctor Sant cleared his throat before addressing me. "It would be more seemly if you waited for the prince to give you this information. To grill him as if he were a recruit..." Sant shook his head.

Raising the baton, Venturi clicked more buttons. The asteroid-ship wreckage of the Forerunner battle, Starkien vessels and the entire Altair system faded into darkness. Slowly, a fuzzy world holoimage appeared in its place. The planet had a metallic sheen and jigsaw puzzle lines as if someone had bolted it together. Several, glowing, meteor-sized shimmers circled the spheroid.

"We do not know if the Jelk preplanned the event," Venturi said in a softer voice than before. "Imperial scientists and holy adepts have multiple opinions on the subject. The truth is we do not know how this happened."

I wanted to ask, "Know what?" The information pouring out of the tiger was too interesting, though, for me to want to jeopardize it. I wish Ella could have been here to see this and give me her opinion.

Venturi lowered the baton and stared at the fuzzy, metallic-looking spheroid. Its fuzziness was in the sense of bad TV reception, as in the days of rabbit-ears antenna.

"As I've said before," Venturi told me, "I am going to gamble on your intelligence. Why otherwise would the oracle have spoken about you? It is a mystery, one among many, I might add." He cleared his throat. "The Jade League has been on the defensive against the Jelk Corporation for many generations. We have fought them to a standstill in places. In others, in the past few years, we have gone onto the offensive."

"Admiral Venturi," I said. "During my time in corporation service, I heard otherwise. Claath told us the Jelk hadn't taken the offensive for generations."

"I'm not surprised he lied to you," Venturi said. "You were Jelk slaves, and they are masters of disinformation and misdirection. Now do not interrupt me again. It's too irritating and disrupts my concentration."

He breathed heavily, and I noticed the honor guards watching me more closely.

Finally, as he breathed normally again, Venturi began speaking in a low voice. "There are those of us who believe we should attack the corporation vigorously. Among those, Orange Tamika has argued the hardest for hammering assaults and we have filled the most command slots in the exploratory arm of Lokhar space service. We captain the dreadnoughts, the few we have. They are the largest vessels in known space, and there is a reason for their size. We have the engines, the power-plants and space-tearing components that let us enter hyperspace."

Venturi eyed me. "Do you know what hyperspace is?"

"I do not," I said.

"No doubt your machine could tell you," Venturi said, "but I will do so. Hyperspace lies between the parallel universes. Some suggest that hyperspace is a parallel universe all its own. I do not accept that. Rather, in hyperspace, the separation between the universes weakens. The most knowledgeable concerning the Jelk believe they used hyperspace to reach our space-time continuum. Based on the theory, our dreadnoughts search for the rent in hyperspace so we can find the original Jelk homeworld. Once found and the homeworld studied, many adepts believe we will have the knowledge to destroy the Jelk forever."

"Are the Jelk devils?" I asked. "Is their parallel universe Hell? They sure seem like demons."

"That is a quaint proposal," Doctor Sant said.

"And at this point in the discussion, also meaningless," Venturi said. "The point I'm trying to make is that we have a working knowledge of hyperspace. The First Ones were said to possess that understanding. After studying ancient holy texts of the First Ones, pious adepts first proposed hyperspace. The scientists told us that tampering with hyperspace would be dangerous, given it existed. If there were enough universes, whatever could exist would exist, and thus, we shouldn't attempt to reach them at peril to ourselves."

Okay, I thought. *What does that mean in reality?*

"I am of the opinion that your attack against the Forerunner artifact triggered a defense mechanism in it," Venturi said. "It must have known you were Jelk slaves, although that is a supposition."

I wanted to ask how a construct could know that, but refrained. Maybe I'd learn the answer by listening.

"Where did the artifact go?" Venturi said. "I believe you asked that. We might have never found out until too late, but fortunately, *Indomitable* was in hyperspace at the time. Hyperspace…it is a strange and terrifying place. The laws of motion work differently there. It is nearly impossible to navigate in any meaningful manner. Can you imagine my amazement when my signal's officer told me she was receiving Lokhar distress calls? I ran to her side, hovering over her instruments as she replayed the signal. It seemed impossible. This was hyperspace, but the call grew in strength as we homed in on it. Finally, we realized the distress signal came from the Lokhar Fifth Legion, the one guarding the Altair Object."

Venturi shook his head, and his eyes had a far-off look as if he stared at a distant point in the past that only he could see. "We increased velocity and the signal became clearer. A centurion of Orange Tamika spoke to us. He told us about the sacrilegious assault in the Altair system and the artifact's vanishing. Several hundred legionaries survived the artifact's transfer and reappearance at its new location." The admiral growled, and glanced at me. "The centurion asked what you

110

might have in his place, wondering if he'd been transported to Hell for the sin of losing the battle.

"I told the centurion he'd come into hyperspace. He told me he saw no space at all, but gleaming metal and incomprehensible machines." A raspy tongue appeared in the admiral's mouth. "It took us days of ship-time to reach them. During the interval, the legion's last adept used his holy book to decipher some of the planet's commands. The symbols were in ancient script that only the most studious adepts learn."

I wanted to ask the prince, "What planet?" but held my tongue.

"The implications of his words were clear," Venturi said. "The surviving legionaries were in yet another construct of the First Ones. This one, however…"

The admiral raised the baton and pointed at the fuzzy object. "The aliens attacked before we could reach the portal planet. They used jamming equipment, and almost cut our contact with the centurion completely. We would never have found the hyperspace planet if contact had been cut too soon. The planet was and is the only one of its kind that I or anyone else I know has seen or heard of. As far as our garbled transmissions could make out, the Forerunner artifact from the Altair star system had appeared in the center of the planet you see up there."

The admiral paused. "I heard the centurion say the Altair Object had fit into the construct as a hand fits into a gauntlet. It would seem by his words that the First Ones had constructed the Altair Object as a key for the portal planet. The implications are terrifying. It means the First Ones must have built the planet, if that really is an entire world. We never got near enough to know precisely. To my eye, the planet looks metallic, like a construct through and through. And the centurion said they were in the center of things as one would be in the center of a world-spanning engine."

"You spoke about aliens," I said. "They kept you from the planet?"

"You swung around *Indomitable* before docking your assault boat," Venturi said. "You must have seen the damage."

"We did. It was heavy."

111

"Almost crippling damage," Venturi corrected. "We voyaged close enough to take the video you see up there. Then the aliens attacked in unbelievable swarms. The craft darted with amazing speed, taking G-annihilating turns no Lokhar could sustain. Ships three times the size of one our fighters beamed a graviton ray, slicing through our shields and ripping hull armor. *Indomitable* barely fought free of the first wave. Then explosions occurred unexpectedly within our ship, the aftereffects of graviton beams. The outer engines took hard hits and the power cells drained one after another. Luckily, we had sufficient energy reserves to open a rip, escaping from hyperspace back into our own universe. The attempt to reach the planet cost me more than half my crew. That meant millions were dead…millions."

If the admiral wanted me to feel sorry for him, I didn't. I was glad these aliens had torn the Lokhars a new one. Strike one against the Earth killers.

"Look how his eyes shine with hatred against us," Venturi told the doctor. "These humans are thorough savages, made for war. I wonder at the oracle's wisdom. We should destroy them and be done with it."

My right hand strayed to my Bowie. If he was going to order us dead, I'd take him with me.

"I would love to hear the end of the tale, Lord Prince," Sant said.

Venturi didn't correct the doctor this time. The tiger prince looked wearily at the holoimage spheroid. "If you would have known what your folly would unleash, I wonder if you would have been so quick to follow Jelk orders."

Was he talking to me? I didn't have much choice at the time. Besides, I still didn't see what the hubbub was about, bub. So a few aliens had graviton rays—big deal, why should I care?

"Did Shah Claath know what would happen to the artifact?" Venturi asked no one in particular. "I cannot believe he did. No, he must have believed he could capture the Altair Object. Then again, maybe his sexual drive to split into two overrode all precautions in him. Maybe he couldn't have stopped himself if he'd wanted. I do not know."

The prince-admiral clicked the baton once again. One of the glowing areas near the planet opened like a flower. Within it swirled a black void. Out of the void drifted vessels shaped like giant snowflakes. From the snowflakes rained particles, drifting down onto the portal planet.

"You are witnessing the aliens, Kargs," Venturi said in a soft voice. "Before you belabor me with your chatter, I will explain the Kargs to you. My knowledge comes from the last transmission with the centurion. Their adept had found amazing databanks over ten thousand years old. The rest of our knowledge comes from the oracle. Have you heard of it before this?"

"No," I said.

"The oracle is the supreme Lokhar marvel of all," Venturi said, proudly. "It is a product of the greatest adepts of the ages."

"A gift from the Creator," Doctor Sant said.

"Perhaps that is so," Venturi said. "Its centerpiece also belonged to the First Ones. That is clear."

"A marvel of marvels," Sant whispered.

Several of the honor guards made what I took to be religious gestures, much as a Catholic would have done making the sign of the cross.

"The Kargs are a devouring species even more rapacious than the Jelk," Venturi told me. "They inhabit a much smaller universe than ours, with fewer planets per star. Those planets they have inhabited. When that became too little space, they demolished the planets and used the matter to create Dyson spheres around the various suns. They annihilated all other life forms but their own. They are xenophobic to an intense degree. It seems the First Ones visited the small universe eons ago, barely escaping with their lives. The Kargs know about multiple universes and it has driven them into a frothing rage to cross over and devour us. Given enough time—if the portal planet remains operative—they will come with billions upon billions of starships to conqueror our galaxy and then our universe. Clearly, the Jade League would never survive such mass and firepower. Maybe the Jelk would perish as well. Maybe the Jelk will escape and journey to a safer universe. I do not know. What I do know is that we must destroy the portal to the Karg universe and that means returning to the planet in hyperspace."

I stared at the fuzzy holoimage. "So…"

"Speak," Venturi said. "This time, I will allow you to ask me your questions. The time has finally come."

"Just to be clear," I said, "I'm thinking that you're suggesting the Forerunner artifact powers the portal planet."

"Ah…" Venturi said in a mocking manner. "That was logically deduced, savage. It also happens to be correct—such the centurion informed me. The Forerunner artifact is the key to opening the portals to other universes. The rest of the spheroid is the engine. The oracle has decreed that we must remove the Forerunner artifact from the center of the constructed world. It is the one piece of irreplaceable equipment, the one thing the Kargs cannot duplicate."

"So…how big is the world exactly?" I asked.

"Slighter larger than your Earth," Venturi said, "and with a bit more mass."

"And the Forerunner artifact is somewhere in the center of that?"

"Not somewhere in the center," Venturi said, "but in the exact center."

"Journey to the center of the metallic planet," I muttered. "Okay. I'm not sure what you're expecting from me, but the answer seems easy enough. Take all your dreadnoughts, whatever other war-craft you can into hyperspace, and return there. Defeat the Karg fleet and annihilate the planet. That should close the portal and end of story."

"How much firepower would it take to destroy your Earth?" Venturi asked.

"You've already destroyed it," I said.

"The nuclear warheads were less than pinpricks to the planet," Venturi said. "The bio-terminator was meaningless."

"Not to billions of humans!" I shouted.

The guards aimed their rifles at me and seemed eager to fire.

"Put those down," Venturi snapped.

The rifles smoothly returned to their sides, and the tiger guards stared straight ahead.

"You are failing to understand me," Venturi said. "You humans lived on the surface of the Earth. How many nuclear devices would it take to split the planet open and destroy the core?"

"Oh," I said. "I don't know."

"Notice the holoimage," Venturi said. "Those craft coming through the rip in time and space are giant Karg warships. The particles falling from them are titanic landers. It is likely that millions of Karg soldiers are already garrisoning the spheroid."

"Wait a minute," I said. "I think I'm finally getting this. You lost millions of legionaries when the Kargs blasted your dreadnought. Now you need replacements. You mean for us to do your dirty work, don't you?"

Admiral Venturi growled, with his facial fur bristling. "You have a high opinion of your soldiery worth. We are the Lokhars. We are the guardians of the holy objects. We will right this wrong you have started with the Altair system attack."

"Why did your oracle tell you to come to me?" I asked. "If you can take care of this, why are you here talking to me instead of getting ready to return to hyperspace."

"Have a care, human," Venturi warned.

"I don't think so," I said. "Your oracle says you need us. Can you image the gall? You obliterated ninety-nine percent of humanity. Now you want the last one percent to save your ass. That's rich."

"Vain primitive," Venturi said. "Your attack into the Altair system started this. Don't you have any appreciation for what you've done?"

"Not a whit," I said. "We were doing well enough on Earth on our own. Then you Lokhars showed up and nuked us."

"We did it in order to save you from the ignobility of Jelk slavery," Venturi said.

"Is that the party line?" I asked. "It doesn't impress me. Why didn't you bring some starships and dreadnoughts and help us defend our planet from the Jelk?"

"You were not part of the Jade League."

115

"That's it?" I asked. "That's your excuse? So instead you murdered my father and—"

"Please," Sant said. "Accusations won't get us anywhere now. The Kargs are as dangerous to you, Commander Creed, as they are to us."

I raised my eyebrows. "Is that what you think? My planet smolders below as a radioactive wasteland you created. The last humans are hightailing it in crappy junk freighters. We're almost kaput as it is. Now you're crying because you might be in the same boat as us. Phht! I don't care what happens to you."

"If we die," Venturi said, "you die."

"You don't listen very well, Prince. We're already dead."

"The freighters still carry humans," Venturi said, softly. "They carry millions of your kind. You are not yet extinct, although you could be in short order."

I stared at him. I got his point: no help from us, no more freighters for humanity. "Let's get down to it then," I said. "What are you willing to offer me in order for us to do what exactly for you?"

"I am offering you the opportunity to save your universe," Venturi said.

I shook my head. "You're going to have to give me something tangible."

"I am a prince of Orange Tamika. Our color is not ascendant."

"Maybe you'd better explain that," I said.

"Purple Tamika rules," Venturi said, curtly. "We are presently outcasts, awaiting our chance for glory."

"The colors are factions?" I asked.

"He speaks so crudely," Venturi told Sant.

"He is a primitive," Sant replied.

"Yes, true enough."

"Are you finished slapping yourselves on the back?" I asked. "If you can't offer us anything concrete because you lack the power, maybe you should take me to Purple Tamika and I'll talk to them."

Venturi stiffened and his slit pupils widened in what I assumed was outrage.

"My prince..." Sant said.

"No," Venturi whispered, "no. I have taken my last insult from this primitive."

"Remember the oracle, my prince," Sant said. "We must bargain with them despite their vulgarisms."

Prince Venturi remained motionless for several seconds. Finally, he said, "His words are incredibly demeaning. I desire to rip him apart and put his head on a spike."

"Yeah, and *I'm* the savage," I said.

Venturi roared louder than I'd ever be able to yell. It hurt my eardrums and I felt my body tighten. Was that an ancient atavistic dread on my part? He exposed his fangs and I could look down into the blackness of his throat. His bearing transformed with startling swiftness into something feral. With catlike speed, he rushed me and swung his baton at my head.

I'd already shaken off my dread, and I reacted like a trooper. Using the neuro-fibers in my muscles, I dodged the blow and grabbed the offending arm. He was big and heavy, and I felt the coordination in him. Just the same, using a combat move, I took the admiral down onto the deck plates. He grunted painfully. I drew my Bowie knife, deciding to slash his throat. He might keep his heart in a different place than a human would.

"Creed," N7 shouted, "don't do it!"

The battle madness departed me as swiftly as it had come. I dropped the knife. It clattered on the deck. I released the admiral. Looking up, I saw the guards aiming their rifles at me.

"High Lord," Sant said, rushing to the fallen admiral.

"No," Venturi said, brushing aside the doctor's hands and standing on his own. He looked down at me. "Impressive," he said. "I'd heard about your battle speed. It is not regular human reflexes, is it?"

I shook my head.

"Stand," Venturi said.

I did so, wondering how he could become so calm so fast.

He bent his head, growling to himself. Finally, he regarded me, and the shine no longer radiated quite so powerfully from his eyes. "You are a warrior race, an ancient project, I believe."

What did *that* mean?

"I know about the neuro-fibers," Venturi said. "No Lokhar would have allowed such sacrilege to his body. Nor would we don your filthy bio-suits, living tissues wrapping over our body like a cocoon. Our honor is too great."

I bent down and retrieved my Bowie. No one objected, so I sheathed it. Maybe I should have cut his throat after all. I was sick of his boasting.

"You are right in a few particulars," Venturi told me. "We lost many shipboard legionaries in our brief contact with the Kargs. Those legionaries were elite soldiers, among our best. But the problem goes deeper than that. Lokhars find it difficult enough to operate in hyperspace. It would be even worse for our individual legionaries."

"Why don't you just say it?" I asked. "You want us to fight for you. See, it's not so hard."

Venturi raised a heavy paw. "Let me finish, I implore you. We do not have time to quarrel. You hate me and I loathe you. That is clear enough. Sometimes, however, enemies join forces to defeat a worse evil."

"You can talk," I said, "and I can listen. Agreeing is another matter."

"Of course," Venturi said. He turned away, and he studied his baton. Soon, he pointed it at the ceiling. The fuzzy holoimage faded. In its place appeared a sharp metallic cutaway of a different spheroid. He hefted the baton before regarding me.

"This is a diagram," he said. "We do not know what the portal planet contains. The centurion suggested it had many failsafes and guardians. Likely, it also now possesses millions of Karg soldiers. I will take *Indomitable* to our great space dock for speeded repairs. Meanwhile, our leadership will summon the other two dreadnoughts. Once ready, the flotilla will return to hyperspace, with *Indomitable* leading the way. The plan is simple but desperate. We don't know how many Karg vessels will have reached the rip into our hyperspace. Whatever the number, the three dreadnoughts will fight their way to the planet. Then we will launch legionaries in a vast space assault."

Venturi clicked a button. A shimmering shield appeared, protecting, it would seem, the cutaway planet.

"The assault ships will have to travel slowly enough to slide through the defensive screen. If they have too high a velocity, the shield will stop them. Our ships will deposit ten million Lokhar legionaries onto the surface. Their task will be to fight downward toward the center of the construct."

"Ten million?" I asked. "Is that what you said?"

"That is the extent of our three dreadnoughts' carrying capacity, along with the assault ships and fighter protection they will need. The Kargs will no doubt attempt to stop us. It may already be too late, but surely the oracle would have said as much if that was so."

"Ten *million*," I said.

"I doubt ten million legionaries will be enough," Venturi said. "In fact, by its words, the oracle indicates it won't be. This will not be a classic assault, as perhaps you're envisioning. We already know that ten million is far too few for such an attack. We would need one hundred million to launch a full scale attack and win our way down into the portal planet's center."

"So what kind of attack are we talking about then?" I asked.

"This will be a commando raid."

I laughed. "You're joking, right?"

Venturi's eyes glowed. "I have told you once already, I do not kid or joke."

"Okay, okay, a commando raid with ten million legionaries. I doubt you've ever made a regular attack with so many soldiers."

"You are correct. We have not."

"But you want to call it a commando raid, huh?"

"The ten million legionaries will not be making the raid," Venturi said. "The oracle intimates that they would not be skilled or hardy enough to reach the Forerunner artifact."

"For that," I said, "you need us, right?"

"Yes," Venturi said, softly. Unconsciously, it seemed to me, he stroked the teal-colored medal pinned on his uniform. It glittered darkly after his touch. "For that, we need one hundred thousand assault troopers with neuro-fibers and symbiotic suits."

I stared at the bastard, and things began to click into place.

"That's why you want our captured Jelk battlejumper," I said. "It has the neuro-fibers and surgery centers. And it has the genetically engineered bio-suits."

"Yes," Venturi said.

"Do the symbiotic suits work better in hyperspace than powered combat armor?"

"That is an intelligent question," Venturi said. "And the answer is yes."

"How about that," I muttered. "There's something I don't understand then. Why did you unleash the androids against my ship? Why start out trying to kill us if you need us?"

"Naga Gobo did that on his own volition," Venturi said. "He did not do so at my orders. He did it as a Starkien, a double-dealing pirate."

I wondered if I could believe that. Maybe it didn't matter anymore—if what the prince told me was true.

"One hundred thousand Earthers," I said. "Supposing I agreed to this madness, it would take time to get that many people ready. At present, only one hundred and fifty of us are trained as troopers."

"I will aid you, of course, "Venturi said. "Even so, you would have two, perhaps three weeks."

I laughed. "That's insane."

"No, that is desperation. If we wait any longer, it will be too late. The Kargs have unimaginable numbers. We must destroy the portal planet before they move those numbers into position. I would think the opening has also caught them by surprise."

"Once we do all that, how do we escape from the portal planet?"

Venturi shook his head. "This is a one-way mission. There will not be any escape for any of us. The Kargs will surely realize what we're attempting to do. They will pour everything they have into stopping us. It will be a nightmare. But with the Great Maker's blessing, we just might be able to succeed."

"You're asking me to join you as a suicide trooper?" I asked.

"For the sake of our universe," Venturi said, "yes."

"No," I said. "I don't give a shit about the universe. I care about the human race. If they die, let the whole universe die with it. You murdered us. I don't mind seeing you murdered in turn. Let the Kargs pile onto every sentient being that didn't come to our aid."

"You would let the universe die?" Venturi whispered.

"That seems to bother you, huh?"

He just stared at me.

"Well," I said, "if you're so unbelieving, change my mind."

"You want us to torture you?" Venturi asked.

"How about instead of that, you offer me something worth my while," I said.

"What do you desire?"

"Okay," I said. "Now you're starting to sound reasonable. You want me to sacrifice myself for you. I want you to sacrifice Lokhar hardware and money to save the human race."

"Meaning what?" Venturi asked in a guarded manner.

"Meaning a fleet of warships that you hand over to us," I said. "And you give us the antidote to cleanse the bio-terminator from our world. Then—"

"You want more?" Venturi asked.

"Hey, you're asking me to die to save the universe. Why shouldn't you have to pay for that?"

He mumbled quietly.

"I want automated factories set down onto Earth and other technologies that will give us equality with the rest of the Jade League. Oh, and that's something else, too. I want membership on the League, voting membership."

"I am the prince of Orange Tamika. I am not a magician."

"Better pull in some markers then," I said.

"What does he mean?" Venturi asked Sant.

Sant shrugged.

"It means you'd better call in all your favors," I said. "Talk to Jade League members. Tell them the score. If you can guarantee these things and show me that it's going to happen— by starting with the fleet of warships—" I took a deep breath.

"Do these things, O prince, and I'll join your crusade against the Kargs. I'll sell my life as dearly as possible, because I'll have something to fight for then."

Admiral or Prince Venturi of Orange Tamika stared at me. He kept blinking those tiger-eyes of his. He finally turned away and began to pace. If he'd had a tail, I'm sure it would have been lashing.

"Yes," he whispered. "I can see your point. The oracle believes in you and in humans, it appears. That will have to be how I convince the others." He laughed sourly. "This will stick in the craw of Purple Tamika. Yes, maybe that will make my death worth it." He faced me. "I agreed to your terms, although I may not be able to convince the Emperor."

"Well you'd better," I said. "Otherwise, we're going to sit this one out. Tell your Purple Emperor that."

Venturi faced Doctor Sant. The lean doctor bowed low. Without another word, Venturi headed for the exit, taking his honor guards with him.

12

Several hours later, I was back on the battlejumper with a mass of Lokhars headed by Doctor Sant. He would be my liaison with the tigers.

I'd already contacted Ella and told her to forget about destroying our warship. Seven Lokhar pinnaces guarded the battlejumper. They were lozenge-shaped craft, each of them one-sixth the size of our Jelk vessel. The pinnaces used heavy particle beam cannons as their main armament, making them short-range warships. The Lokhars also left two hundred of their stubby fighters and several supply vessels. It amazed me how much hardware sat in the dreadnought. If the Jelk showed up, the Lokhars would help us give them a fight.

Indomitable already accelerated for the Pluto jump point. When it returned, I was supposed to board with one hundred thousand Earth assault troops.

I had several weeks to forge an army of commandos to save the universe. Talk about your melodrama. It sounded crazy, but so did aliens nuking the Earth into oblivion. So did a Rumpelstiltskin-sized extraterrestrial changing before my eyes into an energy creature. Why then couldn't there be hyperspace and rips into a Hell dimension?

At my order, Ella, Rollo and Dmitri lifted from Earth in the assault boats, returning with the troopers.

I sat in my room, thinking. Somehow I was in charge of humanity—me. I'd been a callow youth, spending a good part of my teenage years in prison with cons. Most of that time, I'd read books, history in particular and military stories and biographies the most. The rest of the time, I'd defended my honor with my fists and my wits. Unfortunately, in prison, a shiv or five-to-one odds quickly rendered fists unimportant. That's where wits came in. I'd read history in the prison library and in my cell, and learned about hard reality the rest of the time.

Let's be real. Humans could be nice, but sometimes people were more ruthless than starving wolverines. The last of us remained—the mean humans, the tough, desperate and ornery. Many of the survivors had former military training. That was a plus. The minus was that given the chance, most of the survivors would put a gun to my head, if they could, and demand I listen to whatever they ordered.

So, how did little old me stay in charge long enough to see this through? Once the Lokhars began the surgeries, implanting neuro-fibers, and once troopers received their symbiotic suits, how could I ensure that I remained the commanding officer?

I mean, why would anyone agree to become suicide troopers in the first place? Why would anyone obey my orders? At the moment, I had the sole warship. That was my only ace card trumping the captains or leaders of the freighters. Each of them, presumably, had their core of followers. Most commanded through terror along mafia or feudalistic lines. Mafia had gunmen, feudal lords had knights: same concept but in different environments. Some of the freighter leaders used religion to enforce their rule, and a few had voted on things. Those were in a minority. My point was that I was dealing with tough guys and gals, who thought and acted upon similar lines as prison cons. The real difference was the freighter leaders were smarter and likely tougher than those losers I'd known in the pen. So, once the Lokhars began giving us warships and setting down automated factories and cleansing the Earth, my ace card would vanish. Heck, I wasn't sure my ace card would survive a few days of training.

How could I maintain my advantages? One way, clearly, was by becoming the Lokhars' butt-boy. I could use their soldiers and ships to make the others obey me. That reminded me of the Spartans back in the day when they had squared off against the Athenians in the Peloponnesian War. In had been a

Greek World War fought with hoplites and triremes: spearmen and galleys. In the old days, the Spartans and Athenians had hung together and defeated the Persian invaders. After bitter years of fighting each other in the twenty-seven-year-long Peloponnesian War, the Spartans finally went to the Persian Great King and sought his financial and naval aid. That helped them finally defeat the Athenians. But in a sense then, the Spartans became the Great King's servants.

I wasn't going to do that here. If I couldn't stay in charge by my own wits, I wasn't going to call in the Lokhars to bail me out. I wondered if that made me too idealistic for this. I should use whatever I needed to make this work. But everyone has lines they can't cross. This was mine: end of the debate.

I'd give humanity a second chance if I could by killing enough Kargs and turning off this Forerunner artifact. Maybe some of you reading this wonder why I accepted such a crappy job.

I'm not sure why. I think it had something to do with the end of the world, the first time. Seeing those nukes raining down on our cities and the penguins keeling over spitting up black gunk—it did something to me. For one thing, it made me hate aliens with a desperate passion. I'd read a story once where the hero's heart had turned into a hellish icy hated. Nothing could reach the man anymore, not love, not cold, not disease, not pain, not compassion, nothing. The hatred seethed so deeply that he'd spent twenty long years as an oar slave. It had a been a Crusader vs. Muslim story, with a Turk breaking his word and killing in a nasty way, and later selling the crusader to a bitter life of torment. Well, that oar slave lived, and he found the Turk twenty years later and killed the man at the moment of the warrior's glory, but that's another tale. My point was that some of that infernal rage pulsed in me. My heart had frozen with hatred the day the Lokhars killed the Earth.

Aliens had poked their tentacles into our business and we'd almost died. Now we had a shot again, but another annihilating group of aliens planned extinction of everything this time.

Did I hate the Kargs? No. They were giving us this chance. But I had to seal that breach before I could deal with the

Lokhars and the Jelk how I wanted to. Does that sound egocentric: that *I* could do those things? Hadn't Prince Venturi said this was a one-way mission? Well, I didn't believe in one-way missions. I'd escaped the Jelk, and they had put a mini-bomb in my head. I'd find a way to beat the Kargs, plug the portal between dimensions and return to normal space. Then I'd give the Lokhars and Jelk grief enough so they'd stay away from my planet. I'd give Earth the chance my dad had tried to give me. From all my reading of history, I realized this was my time in the saddle. I had to draw the sword and hold back the raving hordes. I wanted to be like King David of Israel, the giant-killer. I wanted to be like Robin Hood of Sherwood Forest and William Tell, George Washington and the defenders of the Alamo. This was my time, and if I failed, I failed all those heroes of the past.

Therefore, as I sat at my desk in my room, scratching my fingernails across my scalp, I did some deep thinking. I engaged my wits, so when the time came to swing my fists, I could win.

Shortly thereafter, I spoke with Ella, Rollo, Dmitri and N7. I explained my ideas, my plan. Then I got on the horn and told the freighter leaders that it was time for a face-to-face, with all of us aboard the battlejumper.

***

Twenty-four hours after my talk with Prince Venturi, I presided over the first grand meeting with humanity's leaders.

We were in our old cafeteria: the one Claath had given us when we'd been aboard the battlejumper as his assault troopers. During that bad time, this had been the "beast" area of the ship.

We used only a small part of it, with the toughest, most cunning people to outlast the disaster.

Diana the Amazon Queen sat with her chief enforcer, a big black man—six-seven and easily over three hundred pounds—by the name of Demetrius. She was tall with wide hips, large breasts and handsome features. Her thick dark hair hung in a ponytail and she wore combat fatigues. Everyone from the freighters was unarmed, so she didn't sport a knife as she had the last time we'd met. Diana oozed cunning and sexual power.

Demetrius was huge, bald and athletic, with the eyes of a Rottweiler. He may have been SAS at one time. Rex Hodges sat beside Demetrius. As I said earlier, Hodges was a former football tackle for the Dallas Cowboys. Rex used to control the other half of their freighter. He had his own freighter now, but they sat together. It likely meant they had learned to cooperate with each other. Good. Maybe they had taken my words several months ago to heart.

Several of my troopers stood around the room. Each wore his symbiotic suit, complete with helmet. Many of the people in here dwarfed us in actual size. None was stronger or quicker, though. Jelk science had seen to that.

The freighter leaders and their bodyguards had been talking among themselves, a buzz of noise. That died down as I entered with Rollo.

I was the only assault trooper not wearing a battle suit. I did that for a reason. I didn't think anyone would try to take a shot at me now. Not that any of them were supposed to have a weapon. But let's face it, throughout history, people have been pretty inventive about sneaking weapons where they weren't supposed to be.

I raised my arms. The talking died away until everyone watched me.

I gave them a quick rundown of the battlejumper-Starkien fight, the dreadnought's appearance, its admiral's request and that I'd gone aboard later. Many of them knew all this, but I wanted to begin with a recap.

Afterward, I gave them the nitty-gritty, the whole story about hyperspace, Forerunner artifacts, the portal planet and Kargs. Naturally, some of the leaders questioned everything or wanted more details. I told them about my deal with Prince Venturi, how we would get hardware, cleansing agents and warships—

"In exchange for Earth soldiers," Diana said, interrupting me. "You sold people to the aliens as if they're a commodity?"

"Wrong," I said. "I agreed to an alliance. We'll supply one hundred thousand commandos, but first we gave them a list of items we want."

"You're turning one hundred thousand people into Hessians," she said.

The Hessians had been German troops back in the day that fought for the British. In essence, the Hessians had been mercenaries. They did a lot of dying during America's Revolutionary War, and they did some killing, too. The Hessian king received money for his soldiers' service. So in a sense, Diana had a point.

"Who will you send on this suicide mission?" Murad Bey asked. He was a square-shouldered giant of a man. He was Turkish, with the blackest hair I'd ever seen. He combed it straight back and had a burn scar on his neck. He called himself the sultan of the Freighter *Istanbul*, by the grace of Allah.

He'd also cut to an important point rather quickly.

"One hundred thousand is a large number considering how many people we have left," I said. "My thought is that some will come from each of your freighters, about twenty-eight thousand people from each. To make this work, the volunteers will all have to be former military."

That started a babble of shouting and questions. I let them get it out of their system. Finally, I whistled loudly, cutting through the hubbub.

"Listen," I said, "call it what you want. Maybe we are selling the Lokhars one hundred thousand soldiers. I don't see it that way, but maybe you do. I can't help that, so I'm not going to sweat it."

"No, no," Murad Bey said. "It matters. No one will willingly go if they believe they're alien slaves."

"Look, I'm no one's slave," I said. "You can believe that."

"You're going?" Diana asked.

Her question surprised me. "Yeah, of course I'm going," I said. "I'm the leader of the assault troopers. That's what they're going to need: someone who has done this before."

"You're willing to submit to slavery?" Diana said.

"Okay," I said. "It looks like I failed to make myself clear. We're going as Earth's soldiers. Think of it like this. During World War II, the Germans invaded and conquered Poland. Later, many Polish soldiers fought with the British Army, but as Poles, not as Brits. They fought in order to reclaim their national homeland eventually. Well, we're doing that. We're getting our homeland now, with hardware to protect it. Then we're sending off soldiers to fight to keep it free from these Kargs."

"If you're going," Murad Bey asked in a silky voice, "who will be in charge of Earth during your absence?"

The attendees glanced at each other as if they were junkyard dogs searching for the pack leader. That hadn't taken him long, had it? Soon, the talking among them started up again. Like before, I waited. Let them get it out of their system. Finally, the speechmaking died down and one by one, they looked up at me again.

"That's the billion dollar question, isn't it?" I said. "Before I answer it, I first want to make something clear. I'm coming back. Earth's soldiers are returning."

"You said the Lokhar told you it's a suicide mission," Diana said.

"That's right. He did."

She stared into my eyes. Hers were a startling green. "Then you're not coming back," she said.

I broke contact first. A man could drown in eyes like those. "I don't see why that's true. If the Forerunner artifact did its trick once, why can't it do it again in reverse?"

"If you can think of that," Diana said, "why didn't the Lokhar?"

I shrugged.

"He must have a good reason for not believing it will work," she said.

"People miss the obvious all the time," I said. "Aliens aren't any different. The Lokhar prince probably didn't even think about it."

Diana became thoughtful, finally asking, "Do you know how to make the artifact disappear and reappear?"

"I don't have a clue. All I know is that I'm not going as a kamikaze. Sure, this is going to be incredibly dangerous. Every space battle I've been in so far is. But I made it back before. Why not again?"

Murad Bey's face tightened. "Do you intend to rule Earth on your return?"

"I'm a soldier, a killer. I'm going to do what I do best. I've never been a politician. I imagine some of you where though. And if you weren't politicians before, I'm betting you're thinking about it now. As I see it, we have two questions, maybe three. The first question is: how do I recruit one hundred thousand soldiers, run them through the surgeries and train them well enough in time to board the dreadnought? Luckily for all of us, I've already got the answer."

"What is that?" Murad Bey asked.

I wanted their cooperation. We all had to pull together to make this work. But if we couldn't make this work, would the Lokhars step in? Yeah, of course they would. Why had Venturi left all those fighters and pinnaces? He wasn't leaving anything to chance if he didn't have to.

"Before I answer that," I said, "I want to tell you that I'm going to give up some of my power now. I know that's something each of you treasures. Let's face it. You're the meanest, toughest and most ruthless sons and daughters of bitches left to humanity. You're the cream who has risen to the top in each freighter. I know that, and I respect that. I could try to run things like a king, but I'm not interested. I want to beat the aliens too badly for that. I want to make sure humanity survives. That means I'm going to be too busy training to kill aliens for me to run everything. You're going to do that for me, or for humanity."

Murad Bey's eyes seemed to darken into jet-black gems. They shined as if wet, moist with ambition, I suppose. "Tell us more," he purred.

I gave him a lopsided grin. "Before you start, though, the Lokhars and I are coming to each of your freighters. We're going to come in force and recruit the candidates. You're all going to stay here as my guests for the moment. Now I'd rather do this in a friendly fashion with your cooperation, but I didn't know if I can convince you in time, and that's something we no longer have enough of."

"You're threatening us?" Diana asked.

I shook my head. "If it sounds like that, I'm sorry. I don't mean it that way. I'm trying to give it to you straight. I need soldiers now and I can't afford anyone trying to stop me."

"How does that share power?" she asked.

"I want you to vote and chose a council of three members," I said. "Each freighter gets a vote. In the divided freighters, you'll have to figure out how to agree. If you can't agree, if one of the divided freighter leaders vetoes things, that freighter gets no vote. The three-member council will work with me at first. After I'm gone, well, you're on your own then. But you should have warships by then and the first automated factories."

"Do you have a constitution written up?" Diana asked.

I almost laughed, but by pressing my lips together, I strangled the impulse. "It's not going to be like that yet with written constitutions and all. We're going to...to figure things out as we go along. Hey, we're flying by the seat of our pants. The three-person council gives us something to work with. It's a start."

"In other words, you still plan on making all the choices until you leave," Diana said. "This is simply a way to cover the mailed fist."

"Maybe it seems like that to you now. I don't mean it to be. We're at war. In the Sigma Draconis system, I fought my way back to the battlejumper. I came back to the solar system and freed you. That means I'm going to make a few critical choices right now. But it's not going to stay that way. That's what I'm trying to tell you. That's why we're setting up a council. Besides, I'll be going away soon. The council will have the power to run Earth and its new space fleet."

"Do you believe the Lokhars will keep their word?" Murad Bey asked.

"If they want our help, they'd better," I said.

"Tell us more about this oracle," Diana said.

She was sharp. "I wish I knew more," I said. "Look, there are a million things we could go over. But we simply don't have the time. If you're against this, tell me now."

Hard faces stared at me. No one spoke up. I don't know if they knew a story about Saddam Hussein, but they must have instinctively understood such a thing.

There had been a time when Saddam Hussein fought a savage war against the Iranians under Ayatollah Khomeini. It had been called the Iran-Iraqi War, and it had been a bloodbath with wave assaults and chemical bombardments. Ayatollah Khomeini said that Iraq had to rid itself of Saddam Hussein for there to be peace. That didn't have much influence until the Iranians started winning. So Saddam asked his council of ministers if he should pretend to step down from power. One man had the courage to speak up. Saddam smiled and encouraged the man. The minister said, "Let us fool the Iranians, sir. We will put someone else in your place for a time, but it is simply a pretense."

"Yes, yes, this is very interesting," Saddam said. "Come with me and tell me more."

The two men walked out of the room. Those in the chamber waited. A single shot rang out shortly, and Saddam returned to the council chamber with a smoking gun. No one else ever agreed that it would be a fine thing to trick the Iranians by pretending Saddam had stepped down from power.

The freighter leaders must have realized I would kill anyone who outright fought against me. They were right. I would if I believed I had to.

"Very well," I said. "You had your chance to disagree with me. Now, in order to let you vote for exactly whom you want to, and for each of you to politic without my interference, my troopers and I are leaving. I'm providing food and there is a restroom past that door over there in back. Yes, there. You will remain here until you've made your choices."

"Where are you going?" Diana asked.

"I have tasks to attend to," I said. "Good luck, by the way. The human race is counting on you."

With that, I left, and my troopers left with me. We locked the hatch behind us, leaving the leaders in the cafeteria. I would not let them out until they had chosen three to lead. I suspected that would take some time. During that time, I had to solidify my position in the commando army-to-be.

-13-

I'd talked to the leaders. During that time Rollo, Dmitri, Ella and others went down to Diana's freighter in Baja, California.

They took thirty troopers with them and the three assault boats. Their task was to return with two thousand recruits.

I learned there was some commotion with Diana's people in the freighter, but not much. She'd trained them to think well of me. I'd chosen her freighter for several reasons. One, it was separate from the others. Two, it was grounded and people likely wanted off bad. Three, Diana trusted me after a fashion and I believed she'd taken my idea many months ago to heart. I'd told her to create a secret society whose goal was to defeat the aliens. Four, the majority of the passengers were Americans. Did I think Americans were better than everyone else? No, but Americans thought like me, and I needed a core group I could trust.

The truth: people most easily trusted those like them. Many rail against the idea, but facts are facts. I didn't have time for wish fulfillment.

My troopers took over the freighter and set up an interviewing schedule. They searched for several qualities. One, I wanted independent operators. In other words, I wanted my people to weed out Diana's plants. The troopers were my political strength in the situation, if you want to put it that way. Two, I wanted those who hated the aliens and desired payback. Three, I wanted soldiers who could take orders and finally, I desired those who could dream with me and thus would become loyal.

It took a working day for the troopers to pick the two thousand and head up to the battlejumper. After Ella and Dmitri showed the recruits their quarters, I had a meeting with the remaining assault troopers.

We met in a different cafeteria from the freighter leaders. This one stank of onions and a hint of rotten meat. No one had ever liked eating in this place. As I'd expected, the freighter chiefs still hadn't chosen the three-person council. I got up before my one hundred and fifty-three troopers. I already missed those the sleepers had slain, and could have used them.

"Okay," I began. "Here's the situation in a nutshell. We used to be Jelk slaves but we fought our way free. Now we're starting over and already have an alliance with the Lokhars and hopefully soon with the Jade League. I think it's time to use a different frame of reference than our so-called beast master gave us."

More than a few troopers nodded.

"It's up to us to save humanity from the Kargs," I said. "If we fail, it is game over. Now, Claath called us legionaries and I suppose the Lokhars think it's a fine name. But you know what, I spit on his slave name." And I did spit right there in front of everyone.

"I know legionaries were a Roman name," I said. "They came from a proud people and they fought to defend a certain plot of ground. At this point, we don't have a plot of ground anymore. Sure, I want to clean up the Earth and repopulate it. That's a long-term goal. But right now, we have to take a leaf from the past.

"What I'm saying is this. The greatest conqueror in Earth history was Genghis Khan. His Mongols swept over an incredible area, riding across degrees of longitude and latitude instead of just hundreds of miles. Some of you may not know this, but early in his career, fellow nomads made a slave of Genghis. In that way, he was like us. But he wouldn't accept his slave yoke. Just like us, he tore it off, and to make sure he and his were never slaves again, he became the greatest warrior the world has ever witnessed.

"I'm telling you right now before all of you, we're going to outdo Genghis Khan. We have to defeat the Kargs first, and we have to create a commando army. Well, we're going to copy the greatest Earth warrior. Genghis Khan was a nomad and the Mongols were nomads. For a time, at least, we're going to be nomads, too, traveling with the Lokhars.

"I plan to steal several ideas from Genghis Khan's bag of tricks. One thing he did was make an iron law called the Yassa. We're going to have our own Yassa. One of its keys was never to leave one of your own men behind on the field of battle.

"Look around you," I said. "How many troopers do you see?"

They looked around.

"There's not a whole heck of a lot of us left, are there?" I asked.

"No," Ella said.

"That's why some of you went and got us some recruits," I said. "There are one hundred and fifty of us, and we're going to be the kernel of one hundred thousand troopers. That means we need a few more. I want a guard, a core that I can trust with my life. Napoleon had his Old Guard. I have you.

"We don't have much time. The two thousand waiting recruits will get the first neuro-fibers and symbiotic suits. They'll get immediate training by you.

"Listen, each of you is going to get ten to twelve people. You're going to be the sergeant of your ten. You're going to train them to a fine pitch, and when they're ready, Jen and the other nurses are going to operate and implant the fibers. We'll feed them the same growth hormones and steroid-68, too. But here's the critical thing. These recruits are going to be your brothers and sisters. You, and us, are going to live and die by how well we integrate."

They looked at me, and I don't think that too many got it yet.

"I spoke about changing our ranks," I said. "We're not legionaries anymore. We're tossing out all the rankings. I don't want to be like Jelk or Lokhars. Instead, we're going to use Mongol rankings because I think that suits a raider and commando mentality better. The smallest group is the *arban*, the ten brothers and sisters. You will live and fight together, and look out for each other. You will be the eldest in your arban, leading them to victory.

"Ten arbans will form a company called a *zagun* of one hundred troopers. Ten zaguns will form a *mingan* of one thousand. Dmitri will lead one mingan and Rollo will lead the other. Are there any questions so far?"

Naturally, there were plenty, and I answered them the best I could.

Afterward, Rollo, Ella, Dmitri and I went to see the new recruits. We'd try to put similar people together. We needed all the bonding we could get right now.

Time passed in a blur. A thousand things needed doing, and it seemed as if everyone wanted me to either do or decide the things. After speaking to the two thousand recruits, I spoke to Doctor Sant. He wanted to know the extent of my progress. I wanted to know how the prince was doing with his negotiations with the Emperor. Neither of us left happy.

I slept like Edison, a catnap here, a short siesta there. Jen gave me stims, but only if I promised that I wouldn't take anymore without her knowledge. I agreed, and I kept my word. The more I worked, the more I realized delegation was critical. I needed Jen for a host of reasons. To be my personal doctor was high on the list.

A hand shook me awake what must have been a day later and I found myself in the gym. I lay against a treadmill, with a towel around my neck.

Ella squatted beside me. "You're pushing yourself hard, Commander," she said.

I groaned, accepting a hot cup of concentrate from her. It tasted like chicken soup. In my younger days, I'd always kept a can or two around as my emergency medicine. When the chills of a cold or the aches of a flu hit, there was nothing quite like chicken soup.

"The council is ready to see you," she said.

"Already?" I asked. "That was quick."

"Two days?" she asked.

"It's been that long?"

Ella sighed, plopping onto her butt and sliding against the treadmill beside me. "I know you have a lot on your mind…"

"What's your question?" I asked, as I slurped chicken noodles.

She raised an eyebrow. Ella had gotten leaner. Her cheeks proved it, with a slightly sucked-in look. I'd seen a video once with a woman with cheeks like that. I'd seen the flick at a bachelor party, and I'd never forgotten the porn star's look.

"Am I that transparent?" Ella asked.

It took me a second to concentrate. "I know you, remember?"

She smiled wistfully, and I had to look away. "I don't think you do know me. I don't think anyone really does."

"Not even Dmitri?" I asked.

"No, he doesn't really know me either…" Ella became reflective. I drank concentrate as she mulled something over. Finally, she began to speak again. "I grew up in Siberia, in the wilderness, really. My father was a miner, but he loved hunting more than anything else. He taught me to shoot. I was his only child, and I think he'd wanted a son."

"Oh," I said.

"Do I bore you, Commander?"

"Not at all," I said. *Not as long as I have some chicken soup to sip.*

"The loneliness of Siberia drove me to books. I read all the time. People called me a bookworm, but I devoured them, and thought of myself as a book-lion."

"I like that," I said.

"I thought you might. My father, he drank far too much. It is a Russian stereotype, but it has a great basis in fact. When he drank, he would preach to me and tell me about Mary, Jesus and Holy God. He would get angry then, and he struck me more than once. I knew then that God could not exist, not how my father told the stories. I read books about evolution and we would have terrible arguments. Finally, I left him and I left Siberia. Because I read so much, I had excellent grades. I went to school in Moscow. There, I excelled."

Ella Timoshenko laughed sourly. "Wouldn't you know it that I was picked to go to Antarctica. That was an even lonelier

137

place than Siberia. My superior told me he had picked me because I must know how to handle the cold and isolation. I should have refused the assignment."

"What's troubling you, Ella?"

"This oracle the Lokhars possess, the Forerunner artifact and the ideas about the Creator...I cannot accept any of them. There must be hard scientific evidence for each, instead of these alien myths."

"Maybe you're right."

She glanced at me sidelong. "Do you believe in the Creator?"

"I don't think about it much, but yeah, I guess so."

"I do not," she said, as she made a face. I wondered if she'd looked that way in front of her father. "It is a preposterous notion," she added.

"What do you think about the Kargs?"

She drew up her knees and wrapped her arms around them. "I do not know enough yet to form an opinion."

"I know what you mean," I said.

She rested her chin on her knees, staring ahead. Finally, she asked, "Do you think we will survive the battle?"

"The Lokhars don't think so. But the Forerunner artifact vanished once. Why can't it do it again, taking us with it?"

"What caused the artifact to disappear from the Altair system?" Ella asked.

I grinned at her. "That's one of your assignments."

"Commander?"

"You're the nitpicker, Ella. You don't accept something just because others tell you it's so. I'm all for that. Observe, test and figure out. I want you alive once we reach the center of the portal planet. You're going to have to make the artifact vanish for us, taking us along."

She bit her lower lip. It made her beautiful. "This is a daunting mission."

"What combat mission isn't daunting?" I asked. "I was in Afghanistan. I used to crap my drawers during a firefight."

"Truly?" she asked, wrinkling her nose.

"Well...no," I said, and I laughed.

She laughed, too. I liked the sound.

With a groan, I worked up to my feet. "Was there anything else?"

"Yes. If you remember, I told you the council is ready to see you."

"Okay," I said. "Here we go. Wish me luck."

"Luck," she said. "But don't you think you should shower first? I'm sorry to say this, Commander, but you have become ripe."

I plucked at my sweatshirt, still a little damp from the workout. "I want you to keep doing that," I said.

"What do you mean?"

"Telling me the truth," I said. Then I yanked the towel from my neck and wadded it up, putting it under my left arm as I headed for the hatch.

***

Twenty minutes, a shower and fresh clean clothes later, in the cafeteria, I sat down across from Murad Bey, Diana and a man named Loki. He was tall, chisel-chinned and had hard eyes like coal. Only when he smiled did that change, giving him an electric sense of charisma with his ultra-white teeth.

The three of them looked better rested than I felt. I wonder how they'd managed that.

"Where's everyone else?" I asked.

"They have returned to their freighters," Murad Bey said. "Do you not remember giving the order?"

I waved that aside. "You three finally garnered the most votes, did you?"

"Diana had the most," Loki said smoothly. He had a rich voice, very suave. I learned later that he'd been a Swedish businessman worth a cool billion before the end of the world. "Murad Bey had half her number and I squeaked by."

"Diana is the president then," I said.

Murad Bey scowled. The big Turk was good at it. Loki examined his manicured fingernails and Diana kept her face impassive.

"What powers does the president possess?" Murad Bey asked.

"She's the spokeswoman," I said. "She has two votes on issues. Each of you has one."

139

"If she disagrees with us…?" Murad Bey said.

"Then the thing doesn't happen," I said. "But for something to pass, she needs at least one of you to agree with her."

"You accord her great power," Murad Bey said.

"He trusts her," Loki said. "He does not yet trust us."

"You Americans stick together," Murad Bey muttered.

"It has nothing to do with that," I said. "She had way more votes than either of you. It sounds to me as if the others trust her more, too."

"He has a point," Loki said.

"Bah," Murad Bey said. "He makes up the rules as he goes along."

He was right. Still, I trusted Murad Bey much more than I did Loki. The Turk spoke his mind. Who knew what the charmer thought? Loki struck me as more dangerous, especially as a politician.

"What now?" Diana asked.

"We have to accelerate the recruiting process," I said. "I want to keep the tigers out of that as much as possible. You can leave the training to me. What you need to focus on is gathering personnel for a space navy and deciding how to recolonize the planet once the Lokhars clear away the bio-terminator."

"Do you trust the Lokhars on a long-term basis?" Diana asked.

"No."

"What do you suggest we do once you leave?" she asked.

"I'm going to try to make sure you get as many weapons as possible. You're going to need soldiers, too. It's hard for me to tell you what to do. I'm leaving, probably not coming back. What I don't want is for one of you to become the dictator and creating a hell-world for the rest." I shook my head, thought about threatening them, and decided against it. I suspected there wasn't much I could teach these three about power.

Besides, my real trouble came with recruiting and training. Essentially, Prince Venturi had given me a hopeless task. How was I supposed to create a commando army in a few weeks, one that could defeat an unbeatable menace? The task seemed impossible, but for the sake of everyone, I had to give it a shot.

14

Our tight timeframe forced me to change my mind about the Lokhars and their help. Suppose I had three weeks to forge an army. That meant I had to skip parts or speed up others if I hoped to finish in time.

Diana suggested something novel. She told me about it several hours after the first council meeting.

I escorted her to a docking bay. Murad Bey and Loki had already left the battlejumper. N7 walked behind us, while a few Lokhars marched ahead. I could hear their servos whine in their powered armor.

Diana stopped, and she touched my arm. It shouldn't have, but the arm tingled.

I wasn't a high school kid in love with her. I loved Jennifer. Diana had sexual power, though. The lady oozed it. Maybe she wielded it with unconscious effort. No…I take that back. I think Diana always knew what she was doing. She wielded it with conscious ease.

"Can I give you a suggestion about recruitment?" she asked.

I shrugged.

She squeezed my arm. I brushed the hand aside and stepped back. She laughed, a throaty sound. "There's your problem right there."

"Yeah?" I asked. "What's that?"

She didn't answer directly, but said, "If you want the ex-soldiers in the freighters to step forward for you, you're going to have to tell them the truth. Talk to everyone over ship-wide intercoms. Right now, too few people trust you enough to step forward and volunteer."

I snorted. "Tell them the truth, huh? Who's going to join a one-way mission?"

"Why did you just step back from me?" she asked.

This lady didn't like to answer direct questions. I filed that away. "You know why I stepped back," I said.

"Of course I *know*," she said. "I'm wondering if you do."

"I already have a girl."

Diana smiled sadly. "I wonder if you can't admit the real reason to yourself."

"Admit what?"

"You don't trust people's motives, Creed. You're too suspicious."

"And that's bad?" I asked.

"Most of the time, no," she said. "In a case like this, yes."

"I'm not getting you."

"What kind of man picks up a gun in defense of his home and community?" she asked. "It isn't the coward, the self-server and the liar. It's the man of honor."

"You haven't been in too many armies, have you? There are lots of cowards, liars—"

"Don't lie to me," she said.

"I'm not," I said, indignant.

"We're talking about a certain kind of army," she said. "We're not talking about conscripts or those hungry all the time that they join up for a square meal every day. We're talking about a volunteer force, a militia, really, jumping up to save their homes."

"No. We're going to have to be professional if we're going to beat the Kargs."

"You don't have time to train that kind of force," Diana said. "I know what you're hoping. Many of those left are former military. That's a plus, maybe the key factor to your success. But that still doesn't answer the question. What kind of person will step forward now? I'll tell you what kind: the man of honor, the noble-spirited, those who understand duty. Humanity is down and almost out. Their service is going to buy us life. That idea will stir thousands of them, Creed. That will give you motivated people who will follow you to Hell—this time a literal Hell-world."

Maybe she had a point.

"So why did I step back from you again?" I asked.

"That's easy. You don't trust my motives."

She was right. I didn't. "You're going to give Murad Bey and Loki a real run for their money," I said.

"There's one more thing," she said.

"Yeah?"

"I know it goes against every grain in you. But you need to listen to me. Against Claath and the Jelk Corporation, you had exactly the right idea. They were screw masters. The Lokhars, however—"

"I hope you're not going to tell me to trust them, too?"

She stared at me. Those green eyes seemed to see right down into my soul, and she stirred something there. The corners of her mouth quirked upward the way a cat might smile upon seeing a fat limping mouse.

I hardened my heart, and then I mentally hammered steel sheets over that, driving the studs with internal arguments. I already had a girl, one I could trust. Why did I want a succubus?

"Creed…" she purred.

I shook my head. "Stick to the issue, Diana."

"Really?" she asked, and she touched the top button of her uniform, as if she planned to undress right there.

I would have liked to see that, but I turned to go.

"In answer to your question," she said, "yes, you should trust the Lokhars."

I faced her with a sneer. "Phht," I said. "No way. That's crazy."

She turned down the sexual wattage of her eyes and became all business. It transformed her, and I admit I already missed her trying to seduce me.

"It's logical, if you think about it," Diana said. "The Lokhars desperately want our help. In this instance, you should use them as much as you can, at least to help train your army.

143

If you think about it, you'll realize that you don't really have a choice."

"Is that it?" I asked.

"It is."

"Good-bye," I said.

"Think about what I said."

"Sure," I said. "N7, why don't you escort her the rest of the way."

He did. She didn't protest, and I walked the corridors alone until I reached a viewing port. I told myself to forget about her undressing in front of me. Diana was a viper waiting to sting. A fling with her would cost me bitterly later. Still, those eyes…

I swore to myself and glared out of the viewing port. Daytime Greenland reflected sunlight. The ocean water to the south of it looked so blue and clean. It wasn't. A Lokhar bio-terminator poisoned the world's seas and ice. Now Diana figured I should trust the murdering tigers.

I stood there for forty-five minutes. My mind whirled and my thoughts fought each other. In the end, I decided Diana knew a few things. In these instances, her logic proved diamond-hard.

I gave the ship-wide message, and I told everyone the straight scoop. You'd think I'd told them to sign up for free blondes, all the booze you could drink and a million bucks in the world's glitziest casino. The mass reaction surprised me, and it put a lump in my throat. The cons in the pen wouldn't have reacted like that. These people, though…

I figured if Diana was right about that, maybe she had a point concerning the Lokhars. They wanted our help, our one hundred thousand commandos. It wasn't because they loved us. No. They were desperate. It was time to use their desperation to get the job done.

For three glorious weeks that's exactly what happened. I felt like a rock star strumming his worldwide hits before a vast audience of screaming, cheering throngs. When I walked through the freighters, men and women clapped and cheered. Men shook my hand, squeezing with all their strength. Women hugged, pressing their breasts against my chest.

Demetrius the enforcer joined up, and he confirmed my suspicion about him. "I used to be SAS," he said.

"The world's best commandos," I said.

"Some people say that."

I put him in charge of training, along with Rollo and N7. Demetrius knew tricks of the trade—the man was scary.

The days blurred together, and they were among the happiest of my life. My personal belief was that man was made to work. Unemployment was one of the worst evils, as it stole a man's pride.

I worked. We all did. Maybe I worked harder than most. With Rollo's help and an occasional word of advice from Demetrius, I chose the tumen colonels.

The *tumen* was the Mongol division, composed of ten mingans of one thousand soldiers each. The commando army would have ten colonels. I was the only Earth general.

Maybe I should have picked my ten colonels from among the original assault troopers, but I didn't believe that was a smart idea. Command was an art, a hard one taking years to master. One wouldn't expect a first year car mechanic or welder to know the trade better than a ten or twenty-year veteran would. In the same way, none of the original troopers had trained for higher command. We were low-level ground pounders.

I know what a few of you are thinking. If I wouldn't chose colonels from among my veterans, why did I think I would make a good general? Like everyone else, I had double standards and made an exception for myself. Besides, I may not be the best leader, but I was the survivor, the symbol. Sometimes people needed a symbol more than they needed a strategist.

In any case, I sought long-term professionals, former officers who had combat experience. I wanted them young, too, in their early forties at the latest. They were going to learn many new things in a hurry. If they couldn't accept the new ways of combat, they would get good people killed. A good combat officer was seldom a nice person. He was a doer, a leader, a go-getter. What was the right way to pick them?

In the end, I had N7, Ella and Demetrius read the resumes. Those they chose, I interviewed personally. After four days, I made my decisions. The Lokhars provided instructors, training vehicles and masses of weaponry. That meant working closer with the tigers than I wanted.

Ella suggested that maybe that was a good thing. "You're going to be swimming in tigers soon. Ten million of them, in fact."

From the bridge of a Lokhar vessel we watched an orbital planetary deployment, with troopers swarming down onto Mars. The Lokhar landers screamed through the thin atmosphere at combat speeds, braking at the last moment. Troopers jumped out, using jetpacks to soften the final landing. Fifty-nine trainees crashed so hard they died on impact, sending up the superfine Martian dust. Eighteen lingered in the hospital bays several days before dying. Three hundred and twenty-seven broke at least one bone. That was out of seven mingans or seven thousand troopers.

"Not good," I said, examining an e-reader as I stood in the Lokhar pinnace. Two of them were in Mars orbit.

The next space drop seven hours later with another eight thousand troopers proved even worse. A Martian sandstorm rose up in the middle of the drop. The particles were superfine, as I've said, and the driving speeds caused them to scratch visors. We lost one hundred and ten recruits. There would likely be fewer injuries once they wore bio-suits and had thicker muscles, but...

I set down the e-reader and glanced at Demetrius.

"Harsh training saves lives later," he said.

"I know. I hate seeing anyone killed, though."

Demetrius's hard face went stone cold. He said in a low voice, "There might come a time on the portal planet when you have to order twenty thousand soldiers to their deaths in order to win. Can you do that?"

So this Rottweiler of a SAS man was tough as nails, huh? "You don't think I'm hardhearted enough?" I asked.

"Sometimes I think so," Demetrius said. "Watching you fret over this...I don't know."

"Thanks for the vote of confidence."

"I'm just telling it to you straight, sir."

"Yeah," I said. I kept wondering about him. Why had the man joined up? Was he honorable? Or had Diana told him to do it? Did the new president want someone like Demetrius on the inside of the commando army?

Maybe the answer was a little of both.

The first week passed too quickly. The second shot past even faster and the neuro-fiber surgeries killed three hundred and seven recruits.

"What's going wrong?" I shouted at Jennifer.

She wept as she stood in a surgery center aboard the battlejumper. There were cots, with torture-looking devices overhead of each. Lokhar doctors had done most of the killing, although many of their subjects had survived the surgeries.

My shouts only increased Jennifer's tears. I couldn't take it, and I consoled her. She hugged me tightly and wept even harder, with her face pressed against my chest. She wasn't getting much sleep either, and she had been here for many of the deaths.

"The Lokhars are too rough," she finally said, hiccupping as she did.

"They're off neuro-fiber duty as of now," I said. We didn't have an endless supply of humans, never mind the ethics of death during training.

"Then we'll never met the quota in time," she whispered.

I closed my eyes. There had been far too many training deaths, and it weighed on me. We did things too quickly. It was one thing being a trooper in action making hard decisions. I had done that against Claath without much trouble in soul. Making coldhearted decisions as the general—sending trainees to their death because we had no other choice—that was proving more difficult than I thought it would be. Was I the right man to be general?

"Okay," I whispered. "We'll keep the Lokhars here, and chalk this up for more payback against them."

"You're so bloodthirsty," Jen said.

"It's a character flaw," I said. "I guess I hate seeing humans die."

She didn't say much more, and soon we parted company, each of us hurrying to our next assignment.

***

The Lokhar Pride must have convulsed with effort; the same with the Jade League. The Karg menace meant the end of everything. It reminded me of America at the start of WWII, well, the start of the conflict for the U.S.

After the sneak attack of Pearl Harbor, Americans hated the Japanese and feared their navy. The Japanese flattops sailed supreme from the Indian Ocean to the Pacific. One of the only Japanese failings at Pearl Harbor came as a matter of luck. The three American carriers had been out a sea, and had thus escaped destruction.

Washington wanted those carriers to harass the Japanese in 1942 as the American Pacific Fleet rebuilt its numbers. The carriers did just that. Finally, the dreaded Japanese navy and the three American carriers fought a confused and error-prone battle in May in the central Coral Sea, the first true carrier-to-carrier action. The conflict was fought solely with airplanes, no enemy ships seeing one another. The Japanese sank *Lexington* and thought they'd done the same to *Yorktown*.

The Battle of Midway was fast approaching. America was down to two carriers to face the grand Japanese armada. After Coral Sea, the techs estimated it would take three months to make *Yorktown* battle-worthy again. American workers produced a miracle, repairing it in 48 hours of around the clock labor, like ants. *Yorktown* entered the lists for the Battle of Midway, which proved to be the greatest David and Goliath match of the war and one of the most decisive battles.

What's my point?

At the end of the third week, *Indomitable* returned to the solar system with its alarming damage repaired in record time, a Lokhar miracle.

With the dreadnaught came old Lokhar cruisers and missile-ships, seven of them. There were also thirteen supply ships filled with automated factories, a bio-terminator cleansing vessel and three hundred fighter-bomber orbitals. They were all payment to Earth for the commando army.

The time had come to test our new government. Who would get the Lokhar warships? How would that change the power structure? Could the last humans work together, or would they let the old diseases of envy, greed and vaunting ambition destroy the restart?

I wish I knew. I didn't have time to find out the plans or even the beginning implementations of the freighter leaders and their henchmen. I was too busy coordinating my commando troopers onto *Indomitable*. My last act was to divide the warships among them.

Diana got two, Murad Bey got one and Loki one. Then I let Diana, Murad Bey and Loki each choose an ally to receive a warship. For the last vessel, I put names in a bowl and drew one out, giving that captain the prized starship. I then divided the fighter-bombers evenly among the rest of the leaders.

As Mao once said, "Political power grows out of the barrel of a gun."

I'd given Earth a government and those people the biggest "guns." They'd have to decide what they could do with them.

Time had run out for my commandos and me. Prince Venturi was in a terrible hurry to begin the Karg campaign in hyperspace. I wondered if I'd ever make it back to Earth to find out what happened. And if I did make it back, would I have to fix the problems the council had made?

15

The first argument with Prince Venturi didn't take long. We'd landed one fourth of the troopers when Doctor Sant visited me in *Indomitable's* hanger bay. Well, in one of the countless hanger bays.

Just like the Jelk, the Lokhars had a nearly invisible membrane before a vast opening. Each entering shuttle stretched the membrane like a soap bubble and then—plop— the craft made it through and the barrier snapped back into place. I found it weird to see, but I watched anyway. Lokhar landers came through every minute, bringing more of my commandos.

I watched, with N7 and a zagun of troopers beside me, one hundred bad boys ready to wreak mayhem at my orders.

Doctor Sant arrived in a Coast Guard-sized Lokhar hover, joining me on the floor.

"Everything is working like clockwork," I told him. "You must have brought through twenty thousand troopers so far."

The doctor nodded stiffly. He seemed tense, and he glanced back at the Lokhar officers who had followed him off the hover.

What was their problem?

"Prince Venturi sent me to tell you the rest of the commandos are heading for *Defiance* and *Glory*," Sant said. Those were the names of the other two dreadnoughts.

My smile disappeared as I regarded Sant. He had lost weight during these past three weeks. I'd learned that tigers reacted to stress worse than humans did. But I didn't think that was it. Sant and I had been getting along. He wasn't too bad for an alien. The Lokhars behind him struck me as high brass. They seemed smug, and they watched the doctor a little too closely.

"Come again?" I asked.

Sant couldn't help but sneak a peek at the tiger officers. He straightened his spine afterward and spoke sharply, "I believe you heard me, Commander."

"We're Earth Army," I said. "That means we will all stick together."

"I...I am simply relaying orders."

Okay. I got it. The brass hats had come along no doubt to make sure Sant did as he was told. Maybe someone along the line of command thought he'd gotten soft. Well, I didn't care about that much. But there was no way tigers were going to split my command.

I told Sant but spoke for the benefit of the brass hats, "Then you will simply take me to Prince Venturi."

"I'm afraid that is out of the question," Sant said. "Perhaps in a few days—"

"Do you believe you've come to know me, Doctor?"

"To a degree," he said. He glanced at the officers and fidgeted with his paws. "I'm unsure if a Lokhar can ever fully truly *understand* a human, though."

Did they figure humans tainted tigers? I didn't care. Forget Sant. "Doctor, if you understand me even a little, you must realize that I'm a sovereign nation."

"I'm afraid the prince was unable to gain you Jade League admittance—"

"Okay. Two things," I said. "Why do you refer to him as prince instead of admiral? Has the Emperor changed his policy on that?"

"No..."

"They why call Venturi a prince?" I asked.

Sant scratched under his chin. I knew that meant he was thinking hard, hesitating to speak. "Admiral Venturi, if you please," he said.

I glanced at N7 before regarding the tiger again. "I think I understand," I told Sant. "You're on a death mission and you must belong to Orange Tamika. The goons standing behind you are also the same. Therefore, Venturi is your prince and you're going to damn well call him that from now on in defiance of Purple Tamika."

"That is crudely stated," Sant said.

"I know. I'm a crude person; vulgar, I believe the proper word is. Here's the second question. Don't you realize I'm not going to let you Lokhars push me around?"

"No one is *pushing* you—"

I snapped my fingers. "Venturi figures he's going to split up my army, divide my command against me? No way, doc."

One of the tiger officers lurched forward, speaking with a hiss to his words. "It is *Admiral* Venturi. You will accord the prince the highest respect."

"Who are you?" I asked.

The tiger glowered at me, looked as if he wanted to say more and finally backed away. He must have been under orders to let Sant do the talking. Yeah, the other tiger officer whispered harshly as if admonishing the first one.

"It is doctor, not doc," Sant said quietly.

"I know what it is," I said. "But if you can't respect me, I'm not going to respect you, any of you," I said, raising my voice.

Sant stiffened. "You must take care, Commander. You are aboard *Indomitable*—"

Stepping closer to Sant, I said, "Take me to him now or I'm going to gather my troops and storm the nearest transports. Then we're reloading and heading back for Earth, or our Moon, I suppose."

The tiger officers stopped whispering between themselves. They stared at me askance. Sant blinked repeatedly. It seemed as if none of them had thought I might react to their ploy.

"Your people will not follow such orders," Sant said. "They—"

"N7," I said, whirling toward him.

"Wait!" Sant said. "I implore you."

I let myself turn back to the Lokhar, but hesitated several pregnant seconds before saying, "I'm a sovereign nation, Doctor."

"I don't know what you mean by that."

"Ven—Admiral Venturi will understand," I said. "Take me to him."

Doctor Sant glanced at the tiger officers. The second one gave the slightest nod.

"Oh very well," Sant told me. "But he will not be pleased."

"That makes two of us," I said.

***

N7 tried to explain the situation to me. I waved him silent as we rode a lift through the dreadnought's main thoroughfare, on a rail system, complete with tracks. Our car zipped along at bullet train speeds. There was a constant *hiss*, though, and the slightest vibration against my back. My zagun guard remained with me.

It took forty minutes before we marched through fancy corridors. Silk hangings draped along the walls and from the ceiling. It gave the place a royal feeling. Finally, we reached a wider area where Lokhar Imperial guards wearing golden helmets stood around looking important.

"Beyond is the planning chamber," Sant told me. "The prince—the admiral is busy in a strategy session."

"Without me?" I asked.

"I believe they are deciding on the best fleet approach to the portal planet."

"Yeah, whatever," I said. "Announce me."

Sant scowled, went to the senior guard, spoke quietly and retuned to me. "This really isn't a good time, Commander."

"It never is," I said. "Think of it this way. The sooner we talk, the sooner we leave the solar system and save the universe."

"You are too frivolous, Commander."

"I'm a lot of bad things. You tell me that all the time. Now hurry along, there's a good fellow."

Growling softly to himself, Doctor Sant followed the senior guard through a door. The remaining Lokhars, including the two-watchdog officers, observed us uneasily.

"Why do you push him?" N7 asked softly.

"Because he's pushing us," I said.

"The Lokhars have the superior position."

"That's right,' I said. "It's even more reason why I can't back down. Look, all we have left is our pride and fighting skills. If we don't parley that into more, we're finished. That means I have to bluff and bluster."

"Your logic fails me," N7 said.

"I know."

Bigger doors swished open, and Admiral Venturi stalked toward us. More guards followed him, about thirty more. My zagun still outnumbered his boys, which was good.

"I'm very busy, Commander," Venturi said. He wore more braid than before, and his uniform was scarlet and impressive. I imagine the Emperor had bumped him up in rank. The sidearm was ornate and fancier than ever, and his baton had shimmering gilt wound around it.

"It is good to see you again, High Lord Admiral," I said.

There was a pause as the tigers stared at me in silence as if I'd made a gross blunder.

Finally, Venturi spoke gruffly. "My title has changed, Commander."

"Oh?" I asked.

Belatedly, Sant spoke in a ringing voice. "May I present to you, Supreme Lord Admiral Venturi of the Avenging Arm of Lokhar."

"It is an honor, sir," I said, deciding to get into the spirit of this. "On Earth's behalf, I would like to formally thank you for the seven warships, the supply vessels and the—"

"Commander Creed," Venturi said. "Your decorum is welcome and noticed. However, we lack time. Extreme urgency compels me to cut this meeting short."

"I see," I said. "Then I would like to inform you of a problem. It appears—"

"Doctor Sant has informed me of your irritation."

I'd gotten a handle, or the beginning of an appreciation, on Lokhar etiquette. They were formal. How they treated one showed exactly what they thought of the person. In that way they were much simpler than humans and many times more transparent. It meant I couldn't let his interruptions go unnoticed. "Clothes make the man," was an old saying. "Force

154

a Lokhar to treat you well, and he would automatically think more highly of you," could have been another.

"Supreme Lord Admiral Venturi," I said. "Despite your vaulted rank, I will not allow you to continue to interrupt me as I speak. I am a sovereign individual and—"

The tiger actually put the tip of his baton on my chest. I brushed it aside and stepped closer. His guards bristled. So did mine.

"Wait," Doctor Sant implored.

I put my hand on Venturi's chest and pushed the admiral backward so he stumbled several steps.

Claws appeared at the tips of his fingers. He hunched his shoulders and snarled. His guards aimed their weapons at me. Mine rushed forward, some kneeling and aiming at Venturi.

"How dare you touch me," Venturi said. "I am the Supreme Lord Admiral of this fleet. I am—"

"An underling of the Purple Tamika Emperor," I said loudly.

That stilled Venturi's rant, and it seemed to steal his thunder.

"I am no one's underling, purple, orange or otherwise," I said. "I am the ruler of Earth." That wasn't exactly true anymore, but I'm sure Venturi didn't know the difference. "That means no mere admiral outranks me. That means you will treat me with respect or I will take my soldiers elsewhere."

"Are you insane?" he asked. "We must defeat the Kargs."

"No and yes," I said.

"What?" he said.

"I am not insane and I agree: we must defeat the Kargs. No and yes."

Venturi turned to Doctor Sant. "Do you understand him?"

"He accords himself high honors," Sant said slowly. "If you desire his cooperation, I believe you will have to meet several of his demands."

Three painful seconds ticked by. I wondered what went on behind the prince's forehead. The tigers were proud, legalistic but desperate. Did Venturi have the wit to recognize he couldn't afford a rupture? His reaction would tell me what kind of leader he was: one who worried more about his honor or about winning.

Finally, ruefully, Venturi shook his head, and tension seemed to flow out of him. "I had forgotten human ways. I have been so busy these past three weeks and worked down to the claw..." The admiral squinted at me. He didn't like this: but he wanted to defeat the Kargs more. He turned and ordered his guards to back up.

I did the same with my men.

Soon, N7 and I faced Venturi and Sant. The extra tiger officers had moved back with the Imperial Guards.

"Why have you demanded to see me now?" Venturi asked. "We still have much to do and no more time to do it in."

"I want my entire army in your dreadnought," I said.

"Is that what this is about, truly?" Venturi asked.

"Yes," I said.

He frowned at me, glanced at N7, scowled and said, "Did you bring the machine along in order to goad me?"

"No."

"You know I dislike it."

"Look, Prince, this isn't about what you like or don't like. I take whomever I want with me when I come to see you. We're allies."

"Now see here—"

"No!" I said. "You see here. You came to me, asking for my aid. I didn't come to you. As you requested, I have brought with me one hundred thousand universe-saving troopers."

"I have ten million legionaries," Venturi said.

"Right," I said. "We're allies. We've joined forces. Your transports have brought part of my army here and informed me the other two thirds would go elsewhere. You didn't ask me if that was okay. You told me. Well, I'm here to tell you it isn't going to work like that. You have to either understand we're allies, or I'm leaving."

His tiger-like eyes smoldered, and I almost expected steam to hiss from his collar. He didn't like it. I was inferior, he believed, a savage. No doubt, he was the hero in his mind, the great tiger prince-admiral saving the universe. My words must have stuck in his craw.

"Logic dictates putting your forces in several dreadnoughts," Venturi said as if speaking to a simpleton. "If one vessel is destroyed, the rest can continue."

"Sure, that's one way to do it. But it isn't what I'd recommend."

"What *you* would recommend?" he asked.

I nodded.

"You are not—"

"Hold it," I said. "Let's think this through, shall we?"

His eyes widened, and he sputtered in building rage. I was doing two things now: making a point and finding his limit.

"The oracle said you needed human troopers. I told you what it would cost the empire. You failed to come through with everything, but I let that slide. Now, I'm beginning to think you think you can bluff me whenever you feel like it. Well, you can't. That's another thing I'm here to tell you."

"Silence," he hissed, and it looked as if he was going to take another whack at me with his baton.

My zagun of troopers was faster on the draw than his Imperial Guard. The tigers were surrounded by Lokhar hardware. They must have felt safe. My zagun was in enemy territory, and they were nervous like good guards should be.

Without a word from me, they jogged forward.

"Are you mad, Earthling?" Venturi said. "I can have every one of your—"

I stepped in close, and I used his body to shield my actions from his tigers. He must have seen the oil-wet sheen of my Bowie knife. I held the blade in my right hand, close to his lean belly.

"Admiral Venturi," I said softly. "I'm a savage, and I'm insulted much easier than you would believe. Lokhars killed my dad and killed my planet. You're Kargs to us, if that makes sense. If you want to threaten and bluster, then I'm going to suspect you can't accept our equality. That means you plan to double-cross us. So I might as well stick you in the belly and watch you bled to death. Then I'll kill your command staff and start a war to take over this fancy dreadnought of yours. I could use it."

His overactive eyelids told me I'd hit a nerve. Maybe for the first time, this Lokhar could actually hear what I was saying.

"You're going to put *all* my soldiers in here with me," I said. "Then you're going to protect *Indomitable* so it's the last dreadnought to go down. That gives us the greatest potential to storming into the center of the portal planet. The oracle said you needed all of us, not two thirds or one third."

"I am the commander of this mission," he said at last.

"Do you want me for an ally or not?" I asked. "Let's decide this here and now."

Venturi stood frozen, and I give him credit, he didn't seem to care a whit that I held a knife to his belly. His yellow eyes glowed with rage. But there was something else too—intelligence.

"I will lose face before my officers and guards if I back down now," he said slowly.

"Listen to me carefully," I said. "I don't care about your face. That's not my problem. You tried to outsmart me. I know it and now you know that I know. Eat crow, sir, and remember that I'm Commander Creed, your ally, not your underling."

"You are making things difficult."

"How about that?" I asked. "Do you think maybe that's why the oracle told you that you needed me?"

"It is possible," he said.

"Now we're getting somewhere."

He frowned, and he finally glanced at the knife. "You can put that away. I will not threaten you anymore."

I slid the Bowie into its scabbard.

"You have convinced me, Commander Creed," the admiral said in a loud voice. "I had not foreseen the Karg maneuver you just whispered to me. The oracle must have foreseen your strategic insight. I will not forget that again."

Venturi turned back to Sant and the brass hats. The admiral raised his baton. "There will be a change in policy. We cannot let the Kargs into our universe. To that end, we will need *all* the Earth troopers. They will remain in *Indomitable* with me. Our dreadnought must win through and survive contact with the portal planet. Everything depends on it."

If it had just been me, I might have laughed in a rude way. I might have told him he was a good actor. Instead, I told myself to remember he was just like Diana, Murad Bey and Loki. Everyone maneuvered to make himself look good. Humans did it and so did tigers. Was I expecting angels? No. He was intelligent and had his share of good points and bad. For the good of the mission, this overweening tiger-prince had backed down before me. For the sake of Earth, for the sake of my army, I could at least act a little graciously.

"I thank you for your wisdom, Prince Venturi," I said. "It is apparent to me why your pride chose you to lead this sacred mission. The fate of the universe rests on your military skill. The Commando Army of Earth proudly serves with the Lokhars, in this, the deadliest peril to life anyone has ever witnessed."

I stood ramrod stiff, and I gave him a precise salute.

Venturi studied me, and I couldn't tell what went on in his tiger brain.

The first self-inflicted crisis of the mission had passed. I doubted it would be long until we faced the next.

-16-

The Lokhar shuttles hauled every Earth trooper into *Indomitable*. I spent the next several hours making sure my people found their berths, had their symbiotic suits and weapons.

The tumen colonels had small staffs. I had a tiny one. We were doing this mean and lean. My eyes hurt after reading so many manifests and I wondered if I'd been better off as a Jelk trooper.

Freedom always took more work. Being a slave was easy, like a child. Let someone else do the thinking. I'd had enough of that in prison. Even so, I was tired, and I wouldn't be letting my eyes shut for quite some time still.

The Lokhars had sophisticated gravity-plates, better than what I'd seen on the battlejumper. I remember feeling a slight bump. I swayed, and grabbed hold of a rail.

I had been marching down a corridor with my security zagun, N7 and Doctor Sant. The two tiger watchdogs had stayed with Venturi.

Sant and I hadn't said anything about the last incident. It made me wonder if the Lokhars used bugs and hidden video cameras. I made myself a mental note to have that checked out later.

I grabbed the bar as the jolt made the security troopers sway just like me.

"Is there trouble with the ship?" I asked Sant.

"In what manner?" he asked.

"Didn't you just feel that?"

160

"Yes, of course I did. Lokhars have keen sensibilities."

"I'm sure that's true. What was that then? What caused us to sway?"

"We're accelerating," Sant said. "I believe…at three or four gravities."

"You're kidding."

Doctor Sant jerked at his uniform as if straightening it, which I'd come to learn was a sign that a Lokhar figured I'd insulted him. They were as touchy about their honor as Medieval Samurais.

What now? Then I understand what I'd done. "Doctor Sant, sometimes a humans says, 'You're kidding,' as a way of speech. It does not mean to imply the other is joking or being frivolous."

"Yes, yes, I know that, of course. I have been studying you for over three weeks now. I am the ship's xeno-psychologist."

I stared at him, and it clicked. "You know, Doctor Sant, I'm going to have to insist that every listening device and camera be removed from human…living quarters."

"But that's preposterous!" he cried.

"That you have them trained on us, or that you're unwilling to have them removed?"

He stood there frozen, and finally whispered, "How did you know? I cannot understand your insights, what I've come to believe are your intuitive leaps of thought, Commander Creed. You are an enigma to us, and that is making certain important people…"

"Nervous?" I asked.

He straightened his uniform. "I will see what I can do…concerning your request," he said.

"Thank you, Doctor Sant. Having you as the liaison officer has made things much easier for us than it otherwise would have been. I've learned to trust you and your insights."

"I don't see why you're saying—"

I held up my hand so he quit talking. Then I gave him a salute, one less precise than I'd given Venturi. But I believed it would help Sant in whatever internal debate he'd have to go through with the watching Lokhars. Clearly, he spoke for their benefit, and now so did I.

A glimmer of understanding sparkled in the doctor's eyes. His manner lightened. He gave me a similar salute, no doubt as a sign of respect. Then he took his leave with loping Lokhar strides. He seemed like the most athletic NBA stars, the natural athletes. The tigers weren't the most cunning aliens. The Jelk easily outdid them in that regard, but they did have size, strength and agility. Against an average human, I'd bet on the Lokhar. Against us modified and trained troopers...

I yawned, and I debated getting another stim from Jen. I shook my head. She was setting up an infirmary. It might have been a useless gesture, given we were headed to the last battle. But I wanted to do everything I could to make the troopers believe this was a two-way mission. A soldier who believes he can survive will take greater precautions during combat to insure that happens. Japanese *banzai* charges in WWII proved the idea. Suicidal soldiers become too reckless with their lives. I'm sure a suicidal soldier figured: *Since I'm going to die away, why not do it with abandon?*

Courage was critical to good soldiering, but so was survival. I believed George S. Patton's saying. "No bastard ever won a war by dying for his country. He won it by making the other poor dumb bastard die for his country."

The infirmary should have shown our boys that I believed what I said. I did believe it, at least until I went to the Lokhar strategy session.

That was wild, and it went bad in a way I would have never foreseen. If I hadn't gone to it, though—I don't like to think about that, either. Was it fate I happened to be there or just dumb luck?

What happened?

Supreme Lord Admiral Venturi belonged to Orange Tamika. The Emperor had bumped him in rank, and Venturi ran the three-dreadnought flotilla. Politics back home must have shifted, though. The Emperor must have had second thoughts, and he used the fastest Lokhar ship in the fleet to tell everyone his new decision.

***

Before I relate the strange strategy session, I should let you know something about the dreadnought as a class of

162

hyperspace vessel. I saw it later, but this seems like a good point to describe it.

Hyperspace, as I would discover, had many weird properties. I suppose that made sense given its aspect. Consider a universe, a space-time continuum, as a balloon. It could be a water-filled balloon, one crammed with helium or one that a kid just blew up with his mouth. Actually, that's a good way to think about it. Each universe had its own properties, its own realities: water, helium or mixed lung air. A fish couldn't swim in helium, just as a human couldn't exist in some of the theoretically different universes.

Suppose now that all those balloons were stacked or dumped into an auditorium. The balloons would lay against each other in a mass, piled one on top of another. The small areas between the balloons would be like hyperspace. It was non-space-time continuum, outside universes. Hence, it was different.

What kind of engine and equipment would it take to leave a universe, travel through hyperspace and enter another space-time continuum?

I'm not a scientist or much of a mathematician. Ella and N7 tried to explain the precise concepts to me more than once. Mostly, I blanked out those times with glazed-over eyes. Yet I suspect that the majority of you are how I used to be in grade school. If the math teacher explained a problem to me in her adult jargon, I got confused. If another kid explained it to me plainly, a light bulb went on in my head.

The balloon analogy falls apart here, because we couldn't jut tap out of a universe anywhere. There were weak spots in a space-time continuum, and we needed the right equipment to tell us where reality was frail. That meant we had to travel to a soft spot to enter hyperspace there. Then we had to travel through non-reality to reach the portal planet.

Are you with me so far? Good.

The energy needed to bust out of our space-time continuum was vast. From a human perspective, the engine doing the breakout proved to be colossal.

That meant the dreadnought had outrageous size. In the middle of the ship, with the volume of a small lake, was a globular area holding an artificial black hole in its exact center.

I know what you're thinking, because I thought it as soon as I learned about it. The Forerunner artifact, the torus object, had a black hole in its donut center.

The point is obvious. Black holes helped one escape a universe. Now I'm not saying *Indomitable* had a black hole in the middle of the ship. It had an *artificial* black hole. Both N7 and Ella assured me that made a huge difference.

Whatever, huh? When they talked like that, it made me want to pull him or her behind a gym and beat the crap out of them. Not that I'd ever done that before as a kid, mind you. I'm just saying.

Around the artificial black hole, around the lake-sized liquid volume, were billions of tons of special engines, computers and equipment. That gave the dreadnought its size. No one entering or leaving *Indomitable* ever went into that inner sanctum part of the ship. Sealed in there was a special class of Lokhars, a concentrated order half adept and half scientist. I'd been told they read ancient writ, chanted prayers and used semi-divine instrumentation and machines to take us out of our reality and into hyperspace.

What struck me was the size of everything more than the technology. It reminded me of old footage of the Apollo space missions. I'm sure you've seen all those Houston geeks in their white shirts and narrow ties, with their 60s buzzcuts and black-rimmed glasses. In the background would be the computers, banks and banks of them with less computing power than any laptop a kid would have used at school before the tigers dropped nukes on us.

The Lokhars were like the 60s Americans with computers able to get a man on the Moon. It struck me there should have been miniaturized versions of the hyperspace-ripping equipment. Instead, we had first generation stuff that could get the job done, but man oh man, it was honking bigger than what future Lokhars would use—if we could get to the Forerunner artifact and stop the Kargs from killing the future.

***

164

I lay down on my cot and shut my eyes. It took time for several of my back muscles to stop twitching. Finally, I fell asleep, getting a solid six hours. Before Sant returned to us, N7 woke me.

I sat up, groggy. You'd think with such a monstrous vessel that everyone would have plenty of room. No. I felt like a Japanese apartment dweller living in a coffin. There was a cot, a stand with my Bowie knife and an old .44 Magnum on it and a stool. Diana had given me the nickel-plated pistol as a gift, complete with a holster. How she'd learned I'd used one in Afghanistan, I didn't know. I'd been wearing the gun on the ship as a reminder I fought for those back home.

Anyway, N7 sat erect on the stool. If he leaned back, he'd be touching the hatch. If he leaned forward, he'd been hovering over me in my cot. My room was like a coffin.

I wiped accumulated gunk out of my eyes and groaned. My head hurt, making me wonder if I was coming down with a cold.

"Admiral Venturi has summoned you to a strategy session," N7 informed me.

"When?"

"It begins in an hour. If you leave now, you'll get there with ten minutes to spare."

"Sheesh. You'd think they would have a faster way to move around their own starship."

"I suggest you shower and eat immediately. You're running out of time."

"Yeah," I said, sliding down to the end of the cot.

N7 stood, the hatch opened and he stepped into the corridor. An officer walked past, glanced into the room and hurriedly turned away. We were learning to live together in these cramped quarters and give each other privacy by not noticing things.

"Where are you going?" I asked.

"To summon Ella," he said.

"To do what?"

"To join you," N7 said.

"I'm taking you to the strategy session."

"I do not suggest that, Commander."

This was interesting. "Does it bother you when the Lokhars call you a machine?"

"Do not be absurd," N7 said. "I am too logical to let bigoted comments affect my equilibrium."

"Then why don't you want to come? Aren't you curious what they're going to say?"

"I am curious, yes. But you have…hmm…ruffled them enough for now. I am also to inform you that Lokhar technicians have arrived and have begun removing spy equipment from our living quarters."

"So Sant succeeded," I said. "Good for him." I frowned thoughtfully at N7. "It seems to me they're doing what we want. Let's keep pushing so they continue to do so."

"There is a time to push and a time to relent. I suggest that now would be a good opportunity to show the admiral that you are able to cooperate as well as you are able to push."

N7 had a point. "I wonder why they don't like androids."

"Agreed," N7 said. "It is an interesting question."

"You don't have any ideas?"

"I suspect it has a philosophical reason."

"Which for the Lokhars means a religious reason," I said.

"I believe that is what I just said."

I ran my fingers through my hair. I must have been more tired earlier than I realized for me to feel this groggy.

"Time is running short, Commander. You should have already showered."

"Okay," I said. "Grab Ella. Tell her she's coming with me to the session. And alert my security team."

"I suggest you leave them behind today," N7 said.

"Nope. The zagun stays with me all the time. I don't have a great big ship and ten million tigers to call on. I don't have an empire. I have our small army. One thing I'm going to do is be strong at the point of contact as much as it's in my power to do so." I yanked on a pair of pants and began buckling on my knife and gun.

"By continuing to bring your zagun everywhere," N7 said, "you antagonize the Lokhars."

"I think that's what I just said."

N7 surprised me, and he let the corners of his lips upturn in the slightest smile.

"Let's hurry," I said. "Go get Ella."

N7 left, the hatch shut and I stretched good and hard before getting started. A strategy session; I wondered what that would be like.

-17-

In a way, this reminded me of the Starkien strategy session aboard their ship when I'd been a Jelk trooper. I don't mean the Lokhars sat on the floor or hooted like baboons. They were more formal and dignified than that.

We sat at a great rectangular structure. Each commander faced inward, surrounded on three sides by table, with staff standing behind him or her. I had Ella, and realized too late that I should have brought more people. It would have made me look more important. My security zagun was outside with the admiral's guards, but it was too late to grab one or two of them to stand behind me.

While the Lokhars didn't strike me as bureaucrats, they definitely had certain bureaucratic mentalities. The bigger the entourage one had, the more important he was. It went ditto for the more nifty uniform, medals, etc. I had compensated on the spot as Venturi's guards scanned my nickel-plated magnum. No lasers or needlers were allowed within the main chamber. The gun looked impressive, so I told them it was part of my uniform, an ancient Earth sidearm of harmless design. Lokhars didn't use gunpowder weapons and their scanners proved it wasn't electric in any way. The guards still balked, so I'd said, "It's like a medal of honor. I received it for courage in the line of duty." That they had understood, finally letting me pass with it.

Each dreadnought admiral sat at the gigantic table. There were also ten Lokhar marshals, one for each million legionaries. Fighter-wing generals sat at the table, the captains of suicidal attack-craft and the chief officer of the Lokhar teleportation missiles. Finally, a number of the oldest-looking tigers I'd seen so far, wearing shimmering orange robes with acolytes behind them, sat with us. They were holy adepts, akin to Catholic bishops, but in the Lokhar religious hierarchy.

I sat down at the end, directly across a great breadth of burnished metal from Supreme Lord Admiral Venturi. I might have pointed out that as the Lokhars' only ally, I should be sitting beside the prince. But I let this one pass. He had one end of the table. I had the other. Who was to say which person sat at the head of the table?

I cracked my knuckles and gained a few sour looks from the nearest legion marshals. I found it interesting the infantry soldiers sat down here at the low end. As far as I saw it, we were the key to everything. The flyboys and priests saw things differently. I guess such thinking held true for both human and tiger versions. Maybe we footsloggers had more in common than we realized.

The door opened and the senior guard announced Doctor Sant. He hurried to me.

"I'm to help liaison with you, Commander," Sant said quietly. "Does that meet with your approval?"

"Certainly," I said. "Thanks for coming." I lowered my voice. "And thanks for talking to whoever was in charge of spying on us."

He nodded curtly, and I wondered if he wore a bug. I didn't ask, and the meeting started soon thereafter.

The oldest tiger of all rose, with his robes shimmering. He gripped a metallic sphere in his trembling paws. The thing had the size of a bowling ball. Lifting his face toward the ceiling, the old Lokhar began to chant in what Sant informed me later was the speech of the First Ones. It sounded alien, and it made my spine tingle. He went on a long time, and finally, the globe in his hands began to pulse with an eerie light.

Tigers gasped. Many made holy signs. A few even cried out in what sounded like anguish.

The ancient one became more animated, speaking louder than ever. He raised the object in his paws and released it. The thing hovered in place.

169

At that, Lokhars began to roar and cry out. Some slumped forward, crashing their torsos onto the table, as if all their strength had left them. Many closed their eyes.

The radiance in the floating sphere reminded me too much of the Forerunner artifact in the Altair system. I didn't like it, and I expected to hear heavenly singing at any moment.

Instead, Ella bent near and whispered, "Interesting, is it not? I suspect that is a piece of Forerunner technology."

I half turned, staring at her in amazement.

"Please," Sant whispered, with a tremor in his voice. "You mustn't speak at a time like this. It is sacrilegious. That the globe shines shows us the Great Maker hears our prayers."

"You can't believe such nonsense," Ella whispered to him.

I grabbed her sleeve, gave her a significant glance and shook my head.

She made a face, looking as if she was going to say more.

"This is important to them," I whispered.

"The sphere isn't holy," she told me. "It's old, maybe ancient technology. I'd like to study it, Commander. Maybe it could be helpful to us with the object in the portal planet."

"No, no," Sant whispered, sounding scandalized. "Only the purest Lokhar can handle such a relic. For a human to touch it—we would have to kill every one of you and burn your planet. Now I implore you, compose yourself and feel the awe of this singular moment."

Ella looked pissed. She wasn't letting go of this.

I gave her a stern glance and tugged at her sleeve one more time.

Finally, reluctantly, she drew back. The tigers nearest us were too fixated on the moment to have noticed our whispered conversation, with their a glazed manner. I actually saw drool spill from one marshal's open mouth.

I wanted to view this through Ella's eyes. The radiance of the globe was making me edgy in a way I didn't like. If this went on much longer—

But no, the old adept raised his paws, mumbling liturgy, no doubt. With a deft and reverent move, he put his paws on the radiant globe. He pulled the object toward him, and the light dimmed. Finally, he tucked it away within his robe, although I noticed a bump there like a man with a big concealed carry weapon.

Tears glistened in the adept's eyes. He cleared this throat.

Tigers stirred, pulling themselves off the table, sitting upright. Many adjusted their caps and smoothed their uniforms. Others blew their nose and dabbed their wet eyes. It was an emotional occasion, and it took time for the Lokhars to settle down.

"The Great Maker grants us His blessing," the ancient adept said in a quavering voice. "We are His Chosen Ones to do His holy bidding. We have been given a sign that our task will succeed. If in it we die, we die."

"If we die, we die," the Lokhars chanted, every one of them, including Sant.

The old one looked as if he would continue to sermonize. Admiral Venturi must have given him a signal, though. The adept swiveled his trembling head until he faced the admiral.

"This is glorious news indeed," Venturi said.

"We are the Lokhars," the adept said.

"We are the Lokhars," everyone else chanted.

"We are the Lokhars," the admiral said in a soft voice.

Finally, the adept lowered himself until he seemed to sink against his chair. An equally ancient acolyte shuffled forward and patted the old one's head. That would have been demeaning to a man, but not apparently to a tiger. The pat must have signaled the end of the religious ceremony.

Venturi rose, and he held his own object. His was blue and small like a TV remote. In the end, that's exactly what it was. With a click, he switched on the table. I don't know what kind of technology you'd call it, but I could look down into the table and see what I took to be an estimation of hyperspace. It seemed as if the table sank twenty feet. I could see the objects on the screen with perfect clarity, even though I sat so close to it and peered at a sharp angle.

Ella told me later that she couldn't see the images as well until she moved in close to the table.

The admiral spoke about the coming mission, its importance, the objective and the heinous nature of the Kargs.

I learned then why the attack-craft were suicidal. The Lokhars couldn't exist for long in hyperspace except while aboard the dreadnoughts. The massive starships were special in many ways, with thick ultra-effective shielding holding back the baleful influences of hyperspace. Those in the fighters and other space vessels would have short lifespans. The same would be true for legionaries on the portal planet. Venturi speculated that the deeper the legionaries traveled *into* the planet, the more shielding they would have from hyperspace and the longer they could survive. Those who would remain on the surface in giant fighting tanks would only have a limited amount of time to achieve their military objectives.

Listening to the monologue drove home to me the suicidal willingness of the Lokhars to go the last mile. I didn't hear anyone balk about doing this. Every tiger looked dedicated and each seemed to realize there was no return from the Karg-held portal planet.

I wondered about that. What made them willing to die to save the universe? What had made a suicide bomber back home willing to kill himself? Why had the kamikazes flown their planes into American ships during WWII? In the end, it seemed to me, it had been a mix of love of country and their religious beliefs. In Afghanistan, I'd hated the suicide bombers. I'd lost friends to them. But that didn't mean I couldn't try to figure out the other man's motives.

From what I'd seen of the two races: Lokhars and Jelk, it was clear Claath and his brethren were smarter and filled with greater cunning than the Lokhars. But a Jelk wouldn't die for anyone or anything. He served himself. Their corporation worked to feed them. Lokhars had loyalty, courage and a willingness to die for the betterment of the group.

Eventually, Venturi sat down, opening up the discussion. One by one, marshals, generals, officers and adepts rose. They spoke about courage, devotion to duty, hatred of the Kargs and a desire to shut forever the dimensional door between space-time continuums. There was little talk about how to fight better or offer some sly maneuver. I had the sense the Lokhars understood one thing: how to advance into the teeth of enemy fire.

I was beginning to get a better handle why the assault troopers had beaten the tigers each time. The Lokhars had hurt us, but in the end, our superior tactics had won out.

As an adept sat down and another marshal rose, I spoke up. "Excuse me, Supreme Lord Admiral Venturi, but could I please see a projection of the portal planet?"

Silence descended and all the tigers swiveled around to stare at me. I'd never felt more like a pariah.

"It speaks," a marshal said, the one standing, a burly female with a five-claw symbol on her cap. I believe her name was Marshal Danyal.

Venturi stood.

One of the marshal's aides saw this, stepped behind Marshal Danyal and whispered in her ear. Upon seeing Venturi on his feet, the marshal hurriedly resumed her seat.

"Many of you have wondered upon our human...ally," Venturi said. "Their leader requested the honor of attending a strategy session. This I granted, for the oracle has stated its desire that an army of human troopers join us in our crusade.

"I'm aware of this ancient breach of etiquette. Yet the humans are also sacrificing their lives for the betterment of our race. Could I stand on the old codes when blood willingly stepped forward for such a holy cause?"

"We must obey the ancient dictates if we desire the Great Maker's blessing," the old adept said, the one who had lifted the radiant globe earlier.

"I do not want to pick a quarrel with you, Esteemed One," Venturi said.

"I am not sure I agree with Purple Tamika's reading of the oracle," the old adept added in a quavering voice. "The humans' presence in our dreadnoughts sullies our crusade. The Creator has chosen the Lokhars to guard the Forerunner artifacts. He has not chosen these ill-befitted creatures, these hounds of the devil Jelk."

"They soldiered for the Jelk under false pretenses," Venturi said.

The trembling old ancient struggled to his feet. He faced the admiral. "Let me repeat the key phrase of your statement, Supreme Lord: 'They soldiered for the Jelk.' How can you impugn us with their presence? No. I say we must slaughter these vile sub-devils and rid ourselves of any taint of evil."

"But the oracle—" Venturi said.

"Purple Tamika misread the oracle!" the old adept shouted. He aimed a trembling finger at Venturi. "You jeopardize the mission, Supreme Lord Admiral. You have accepted the underhanded reading of the oracle by a self-serving—"

Venturi pressed a stud on the table. A klaxon blared into life.

I clapped my hands over my ears.

Finally, the admiral removed his finger, and the blaring sound stopped. It left a ringing in my ears.

"I am Prince Venturi of Orange Tamika. I have led many Tamika raids, and I signed the Accord of Ten. There is peace between Purple and Orange, and because of that, I saved our Tamika from certain destruction. We have made our peace with Purple. They view the Great Maker and the oracle from the same vantage as us. Let me ask you a question, Esteemed One. Do you refute the Accord of Ten?"

The old adept had lowered his arm. He looked down as his shoulders slumped.

"Do you refute the Accord of Ten?" Venturi asked again, in a louder voice. "As leader of this mission, I demand an answer."

The old adept's head snapped up. "You demand?" he asked.

"I am on my warship en route to battle," Venturi said. "I am the Creator's representative in his hour. You know that, Esteemed One."

"You spout the principles of Octagon Lars."

"Yes," Venturi said in a ringing voice.

"I have no more to say," the adept whispered.

Venturi rapped the table with his knuckles. "No! First, you must answer me. Do you refute the Accord of Ten?"

The ancient one reached into his robe. "I hold the stone of God," he said. "Do you refute *it*?"

"No," Venturi said. "I would like to point out however that it shone with radiance in the presence of the human commander."

The old adept swiveled around to stare at me. His eyes burned with fervor. Finally, he withdrew his hand from the robe. "The stone has shone," he said. "I cannot refute the Great Maker's blessing. Now I will lessen and you will grow greater," he told Venturi.

"We both go to battle the menace of the age," Venturi said in a softer tone. "We both go to die."

"Yes," the adept said, and he sank back into his seat.

Venturi scanned the throng. Then he addressed me. "Do you still wish to speak?"

"I do," I said.

"Then stand, and tell us your words." Admiral Venturi thereupon sat down, waiting for me.

I stood up, and I scanned the assembled throng. The tigers were on a crusade, and none of them believed we were coming back. I didn't like that. How should I word this? I wasn't sure. I didn't want to make anyone angry. I wanted them to see sense.

"I am grateful for this chance to see the Lokhars in their glory," I began. "I had not realized until this moment that the Lokhars were the chosen of the Creator."

Tigers gasped, and stares of amazement filled many eyes.

"It is true. We of Earth…"

I wanted to tell them we of Earth would hunt every Lokhar them down and blast them to death as they had done to us by nuking our world. Instead, I bent my head, looking at the table. I had to control these surges of rage against my newfound allies. I had to think of the greater good.

"He is overcome with zeal," a tiger whispered.

"He is reverent toward our crusade," I heard another say.

I almost smiled. The tigers misunderstood my silence. Well, I suppose it was for the best.

Looking up, I said, "We face a terrible foe in the Kargs. It is good that two races from our universe join together to fight for life. I admire your willingness to sacrifices your lives. All here know that the Lokhars are the bravest of the brave. Yet as I've listened to you discuss strategy…"

I couldn't help but pause. I'd heard almost no strategy discussion at all. Maybe it was coming. Thus, I paused to let someone correct me. No one did, though. Instead, many tigers hunched toward me. I already knew enough to realize they were interested in my words.

"As I've listened to you," I repeated, "an idea boiled into existence. Perhaps the radiance from the Creator's stone lit my mind with understanding. I have been thinking deeply on ways to defeat the Kargs—"

"By fighting!" Marshal Danyal roared as she bagged a fist against the table. "We will defeat them through our valor and with our laser rifles. We will march to victory, killing and being killed to reach the holy object in the center of the portal planet."

Murmurs and cries of assent filled the chamber.

"Thank you, Marshal," I said. "Your ringing endorsement for the coming fight gladdens my heart."

"I—"

"Hold," Venturi told Marshal Danyal. "You must let our...our...*ally* speak."

"Thank you, Supreme Lord Admiral," I said. "I have heard about the valor of Lokhar legionaries. I have even seen them in action."

Ella sucked in her breath, but it appeared that none of the tigers present understood my implication.

"So I know that each of you here is dedicated to the mission of saving our space-time continuum. Since I am not a Lokhar, I view these proceedings from a different vantage point. I bring my human insights to the mix. I admire the idea of driving in with ten million legionaries, inexorably drilling to the center of the planet. We will slaughter ten billion Kargs."

"Ten *billion*?" Marshal Danyal asked. "There are ten billion Kargs on the planet?"

"He cannot know the precise number," the old adept said. The ancient gasped as if overcome by a new thought. "Do you have precognitive insights?"

"Are you a prophet?" Marshal Danyal asked me.

"No," I said. "Remember, I'm human. I speak from human perspectives. I don't know the actual numbers; just that it's going to be more than we have, right? We have ten million legionaries. So when I say ten billion Kargs, I'm simply expressing the idea that they'll have a lot more soldiers on the ground than we do."

Expressionless tiger-eyes stared at me.

"Many Kargs will be there," I said. "We will likely have to kill them ten to one to reach the Forerunner artifact."

"Can we achieve such a kill ratio?" Marshal Danyal asked Venturi.

"It could prove to be an impossible task," another marshal said.

Venturi rose to his feet. "Why do you say such things?" he asked me.

"Uh...well, among humans, when we have a strategy session, we usually discuss strategy, tactics and odds," I said.

Lokhars glanced at each other in amazement.

"Anyway," I said, "I have a way to solve our dilemma."

Reluctantly, Venturi sat. The others regarded me anew.

"I fought against Lokhars at Sigma Draconis," I said.

Scowls appeared.

"I did not do so because I wanted to. Shah Claath, our Jelk, desired the reach the Shrine Planet there. During the battle, I observed Lokhar battle practices. Many of your weapons and tactics impressed me, by the way. Again, while in Earth orbit, I saw the Starkiens use your famous teleportation missiles."

Many of the tigers stared at the T-missile officer. He was shorter than the others, and his uniform a dull blue color. Something seemed wrong with his left eye, and I realized it must be glass. The pupil never moved.

"In fact," I said, "it was through using a teleportation missile that I gained my freedom from the Jelk and inflicted great harm against Claath."

By the shine in their eyes, that had their attention.

"Therefore, I speak with more than a little experience about the T-missiles," I said. "We've just seen that we face tremendous obstacles against the Kargs. It will be a bitter and difficult fight to reach the center of the portal planet. Yet we *must* reach it. We *must* turn off the Forerunner artifact and close the rip into the Karg space-time continuum. To that end, I suggest we make it easy on ourselves and insure our universe of victory."

"How?" Marshal Danyal asked.

I nodded. "That's the right question." I'm surprised they hadn't seen it yet. "We gauge the distance to the center of the portal planet and teleport the missiles there. Kaboom, we obliterate the Forerunner artifact and turn off the rip into the Karg universe. We save ten million Lokhar legionaries and escape back into our continuum with our lives."

"That's brilliant," I heard Ella whisper behind me.

I stood there beaming. I'd thought it was pretty brilliant, too.

The tigers sat in shock. A few slumped back against their seats.

The ancient adept turned to Admiral Venturi. "Did you hear his words?" the old one asked.

Venturi also stared at me. Slowly, he nodded.

"It is the rankest blasphemy I have ever heard," the old adept whispered. "We must skin him alive and set him adrift in space."

"Set him adrift!" Marshal Danyal roared. "He desires to destroy the Great Maker's handiwork. He is a blasphemer."

"Oh boy," Ella muttered behind me.

"Wait a minute," I said. "You're wrong about that. The Creator didn't make the Forerunner artifact. I've heard you say the First Ones did it."

"Aeeiii!" the ancient adept cried. "He subscribes to the Waylander Heresy. The crusade cannot abide heretics. Admiral Venturi, you must skin him alive with your own blade and offer him in sacrifice. This is blasphemy, blasphemy. We are all tainted by his presence. We must purify ourselves. We must—"

Venturi pressed the klaxon switch. I knew now why it had been installed. The wailing noise stilled the adept thirsting for my blood.

Finally, the ancient tiger slumped back into his chair, exhausted. Only then did the admiral remove his paw from the switch.

"You have heard the human's words," Marshal Danyal said into the silence.

"Listen," I said.

"No," the adept wheezed. "We mustn't listen to another word he says. He taints us. He taints us."

"I ask my ally to resume his seat," Admiral Venturi said in a low voice.

Reluctantly, I sat down.

Ella patted me on the shoulder, and she whispered in my ear, "We're caught up in a war by a bunch of religious zealots. This is worse than Claath."

I shook my head. I didn't believe that. But this did look bad.

"I am shocked by his words, just as you are," Venturi told the others. "Yet we must remember that the humans are new to space. They are ignorant savages."

"Then why are they with us?" Marshal Danyal asked.

"Because the oracle told us to gather them," Venturi said. "It is that simple. Believe me when I tell you that I would rather exterminate every one of them. But the Great Maker has used the oracle. We have gathered commandos who will rid our continuum of the Kargs."

"You still believe this?" Danyal asked.

"They have yet to learn the Creator's ways," Venturi said. "Once they do—"

"They are heretics," the old adept said. "They can learn nothing. I have spoken."

"Perhaps they are heretics," Venturi said. "Yet you must recall that the Lokhars too once followed lost ways. It wasn't until we found the spire of the First Ones and the original writ that we turned to the truth of the Great Maker."

"Meaning?" the adept whispered.

"That once we held onto false beliefs," Venturi said.

"But the human spoke so confidently," the adept said. "He was proud in his heresy."

"I wonder if he is still proud," Venturi said. "Commander Creed, do you continue to believe that we should use thermonuclear weapons against the Forerunner artifact?"

"No," I said, lying through my teeth. "I spoke in ignorance, without understanding. Hearing Lokhar outrage has helped to rid me of my false thoughts."

Murmurs of amazement went throughout the assembled chamber.

"Do you hear?" Venturi asked the old adept. "Your words helped to teach him the truth."

The ancient one studied me with wet, red-rimmed eyes. "He is sly like a Jelk and a Starkien. How do we know we can trust his words?"

"Because the oracle called upon us to gather him," Venturi said.

"Circular reasoning," Ella whispered to me.

"Do you retract your heretical idea?" Venturi asked me.

"I fully retract it and stand embarrassed that I spoke such a thing to you," I said.

"I believe him," Venturi said. "On such a subject, I do not think that even a savage could spin deceit."

"A Lokhar could not," the adept said. "Perhaps a test..."

"A test!" Marshal Danyal shouted.

Before anyone could add their voice to the idea of a test, the main doors opened. Heads whipped around. A group of heavyset tigers marched into the chamber. Three guards with silver helmets led the way. Each of them cradled a laser rifle. Behind them followed an impressive Lokhar in a purple uniform with many medals on her chest. She had an ornate blaster on her hip, and she marched with a decided swagger. Two adepts followed behind her. They had billowing purple robes and with long trailing gowns sweeping the floor.

One of the purple-clad adepts stepped forward. "All rise and bow before the Maximum Princess Nee of Purple Tamika, the Emperor's third daughter-wife."

Chairs scraped back as everyone rose, including the ancient Orange Tamika adept. The old Esteemed One needed the help of two acolytes to do so. Admiral Venturi, his aides, the marshals, the captains, everyone bowed except for Ella and me. Maybe for our sakes, no one seemed to notice, least of all the Maximum Princess Nee.

"In the name of the Emperor, rise," Princess Nee said in a voice obviously accustomed to command.

Admiral Venturi settled back into his chair, as did those previously sitting at the table. The others waited from on their knees.

Discreetly, Ella knelt as well. She would have made herself conspicuous otherwise.

"This is an honor," Venturi said. "Yet I cannot understand why or how you are here."

"We sped here directly from the Emperor's Court," the purple-clad adept said. "We used a racer-ship, the fastest in the fleet."

Murmurs of amazement rose from the throng.

"There is no honor intended toward you with my presence here," Princess Nee said coldly. She moved closer to Venturi as the purple adept discreetly backed away.

"I have come at the Emperor's direct orders," Princess Nee said. "Since you left homeworld, there has been much debate at court concerning this mission. Soon, the light of the Creator shined in our thoughts. Everyone realized that it was inconceivable a prince of Orange Tamika should lead the great assault into hyperspace. The more the Emperor pondered the decision, the more he came to regret sending you."

"Orange Tamika commands the dreadnoughts," Venturi said.

Princess Nee made a sharp gesture with her right hand, chopping through the air. "It is not a matter of those who man the stations. This is a case of authority, of grave peril and the decision to see the task through with maximum chances of success."

"If the Emperor doubts my courage—" Venturi said.

"It is not a matter of courage," Nee said. "You excel in the Lokhar trait. You have valor indeed, Orange Prince. Do you have battle cunning, though?"

"Do you?" Venturi asked.

Maximum Princess Nee hissed like a wet cat. "Have a care, Admiral. I am the Emperor's representative. Speak to me as if you were speaking to him."

"I am the Supreme Lord Admiral of the Avenging Arm of Lokhar," Venturi said. "The Emperor himself gave me the commission."

"And I am here to tell you that the Emperor has taken it away."

"You cannot do so while I am on my own vessel," Venturi said. "You know the laws and customs of—"

He fell silent as the princess produced a scroll tied with a purples ribbon and stamped with a purples seal. "Take this, sir," she said, stepping near and handing it to him.

With a trembling hand, Venturi reached for the scroll. Then he paused.

"Look closely," Nee said. "This is the Emperor's seal. I know you recognize it."

Venturi's raspy tongue appeared. He seemed stricken. "This cannot be. The Emperor gave Orange Tamika the commission to wander hyperspace, searching for the Jelk homeworld."

"That was then and this is now," Nee said.

"But—"

"Instead of banishing you to death," Nee said, "the Emperor sent you into the limbo of hyperspace. Who would know that your task served the Great Maker? It is amazing. Now everything rests on the operation of this combat mission. The Emperor realizes he cannot trust Orange Tamika to see it through."

"You are rash to speak so here on my vessel," Venturi said.

"I am to be the new Supreme Lord Admiral of the hyperspace flotilla," Nee said.

"With Orange Tamika crews?" Venturi asked.

"What difference does that make?"

Venturi stared at the scroll, still unable to take it from her paw. "What is your plan of combat?"

"You cannot ask me that," Nee said.

Venturi's head whipped up, and his eyes shined. "I do ask you," he said. "I was to lead us to victory and death. The Creator granted me a boon, with the humans as the tip of the spear."

"Yes, the humans..." Nee said, turning to me, sneering. "The Emperor would find it revealing indeed to see a human sitting at the table of a strategy session. You do not obey the old ways, Venturi. You taint everything with your blindness.

There are ways to die and there are ways to live. You know neither."

"I stand by my question," Venturi said. "And I swear by the—"

"No, no," Nee said, waving her paw. "I will not indulge you in dramatics. This is a simple change of command. But, in order to speed the process, I will tell you that I have a completely different battle plan in mind. First, we will rid ourselves of the human scum. They will do nothing but float in hyperspace as an object lesson to the Kargs."

"We need the humans to complete our holy task," Venturi said. "The oracle has spoken."

"The Emperor says what and when the oracle has spoken. You are not in primacy. Now, take the scroll."

"You still have not told me your plan," Venturi said.

"Bah!" Nee said. "To take these valuable dreadnoughts and throw them away in a suicide mission is folly of the worst sort. We will await the first Karg wave, destroying them as they exit hyperspace and attempt to adjust to our space-time continuum."

"Madness," Venturi said. "This is madness. The Kargs will bring billions of vessels—"

"That is mere superstition," Nee said. "Now, take the scroll. You have no more options left."

"Sure he does," I said. I'd heard enough, and I realized it was time to act. Maybe that's why their so-called oracle had told Venturi to come and get me personally.

Maximum Princess Nee turned slowly, and her garments rustled in an ominous manner. "The savage actually address me? This is blasphemy."

"That's right I address you," I said. "What grounds do you have to say the Kargs lack billions? Admiral Venturi has solid proof."

"Silence your creature," Nee shouted, "or I'll silence it for you."

"Commander Creed," Venturi said.

"Hold it," I said, standing now. "I'm a Lokhar ally. I am a sovereign individual. I joined this expedition to destroy the portal planet. I—"

"Guards!" Nee screened, with her hands clenched into shaking fists. "Kill it! Rid me of this Orange Tamika filth."

The three purple-clad guards with silver helmets, the three carrying laser rifles, hurried forward. I'd heard more than enough. If this she-devil gained command of the flotilla, the Lokhars would attack our Commando Army. While my troopers were good, I didn't think they could take on ten million tigers.

Like a gunslinger from the Wild West, I drew my silver-plated .44 Magnum. With a deafening boom, I blew a hole in the first purple Lokhar guard. He catapulted onto his back as smoke drifted from the barrel of my gun. I think the loud noise startled the other two guards. Besides, they were royal guards. Had they ever been in desperate action before? I doubted it. In quick succession, I blew away the other two so they also clattered onto the floor.

The Lokhars watched in stunned amazement.

Maximum Princess Nee snarled with rage. "How dare you murder my guards? They have been with me since my commencement. You will—"

She didn't get to finish. Realizing that this was the tiger Emperor's daughter-wife, I turned sideways and lifted my magnum deliberately. I had to make sure. As if at a firing range, I pumped three .44 caliber rounds into her body. She tumbled backward, spewing chunks of Lokhar meat and blood, landing on her back, quite dead. The scroll landed nearby, unopened, with specks of blood soaking into it.

Lowering my arm, I opened the cylinder and dumped shell casings onto the floor. Then I reloaded and snapped it shut.

Things were about to get interesting.

18

I'd learned a few things about Lokhars these past weeks. As physical specimens, few could match them. Maybe the energy keeping them running cost in other areas. I'm talking about mental agility.

Now tigers, like people, had large gradations in abilities. You had smart people and dumb ones. The Lokhars were the same. The Maximum Princess Nee had struck me as more quick-witted than the rest. Those standing in shock in the strategy session chamber I saw as having their minds in neutral. The engine could be revving like crazy, but it wouldn't move any wheels because the gears weren't connected. I think their minds were spinning, but they couldn't articulate whatever was going on inside their gray matter.

I'd just saved the mission from certain disaster. Now we could all jump into hyperspace and get ourselves killed at the portal planet. We might even stop the Kargs while we died. Would the Lokhars be grateful to the trigger-happy human? I didn't give that a high probability. In fact, the old adept would likely demand my skinning. I had a gun, but there were an awful lot of tigers in here and I only had so many bullets.

It was time to act. I had the initiative, and I planned to keep it.

"Stay behind me," I whispered to Ella. Then I began backing toward the door.

The tigers were all staring at the dead princess. Marshal Danyal must have had good peripheral vision. Her head swiveled around in a rusty manner. She gazed at me with blank eyes. Something stirred there, though. Seeing me moving must have kicked in a basic chase instinct.

With a roar, Marshal Danyal bounded at me. She literally leapt onto the table, jumped onto the floor and charged fast and hard. I hadn't expected that.

BOOM!

Her head disintegrated as it snapped back. Lokhars were big and heavy, though. A .44 Magnum load only had so much stopping power and no more. She died, but her body kept coming, sliding across the floor at me.

I sidestepped the body, and I wondered if her aides were about to charge en masse. I wouldn't be able to shoot fast enough to stop all of them. I had to think of something else to do.

"The Creator has spoken to me!" I shouted. I didn't know what else to say that might stop them in their tracks.

That did it, though. An aide that lurched toward me paused, blinking with incomprehension.

I heard a tiger ask, "Can the Creator speak to a human?"

The ancient adept took the question to heart. He bowed his head as if in prayer.

In those few seconds, I reached the main door. "Get ready," I whispered to Ella.

"Even with the zagun," she said, "we'll never reach our quarters."

"You don't think I don't know that?" I whispered. If the tigers went crazy, one hundred troopers without symbiotic armor, or even with it, would not make it back to the Commando Army.

I opened the door.

"He's escaping!" a different adept shouted.

"No!" I said. "I'm calling in the guard."

Tigers stared at one another. They must have wondered why a human would summon the admiral's guards. This human wouldn't. I was going to summon my own.

Poking my head through the door, I said into the antechamber. "Princess Nee has demanded to see my zagun. Troopers, hurry in here."

Both human and tiger guards stared at me. The walls were soundproof, so I doubt any of them had heard the gunfire.

"Hurry!" I shouted.

My troopers understood that. They started for the doors.

"What of us?" the Lokhar senior guard asked.

"You are to remain vigilant," I said. "Princess Nee spoke of your alertness. She is pleased with you."

I had no idea if that would work, but it did. The senior guard stood more proudly. So did the Lokhars nearest him. Meanwhile, my zagun, with the Zaporizhian Cossack Dmitri at their lead, marched into the strategy chamber.

"Do exactly what I tell you," I whispered to Dmitri.

He had a crew cut, a sweeping black mustache and wide Slavic features. He was muscular and was as tough as they came. We'd first met in Antarctica aboard a Saurian-run lander.

The tigers in here were losing their shocked expressions. Maybe seeing so many armed humans among them helped speed the process. Even with my hundred, there were more of them here. They were also bigger, but not stronger, faster nor armed.

"He slew the Emperor's daughter-wife," the ancient Esteemed One said. "We all witnessed the terrible deed. He must die."

"I just saved the mission," I said.

"You slew in cold blood," the Esteemed One declared.

I laughed sourly. "You didn't happen to hear Nee order her guards to kill me?"

"Supreme Lord Admiral," the ancient one said. "I beg you to order the human's death."

"Order his death!" the mass of acolytes shouted in perfect unison. It gave the old one's words power.

"You just killed the Maximum Princess Nee," Venturi told me.

"And thereby saved you a load of heartache," I said.

Once again, Venturi stared at the dead princess. What was he thinking? He seemed smarter than the average tiger. That was a plus. But would it be enough?

Ella sidled up to me. "I hope you have a plan, Commander. This is about to get ugly."

She was right, and I didn't want to go nuclear. I didn't want to poison things between our races by murdering the high command. But I couldn't see how I was going to make it back to our quarters without doing something drastic. I needed something that would hold the other Lokhars at bay. The answer popped into my head.

The shining globe would do it, right? It was a holy object. Yet if I held it in my grubby humans hands, that might make the tigers berserk with rage anyway.

I grabbed Dmitri by the arm and dragged him beside me. With my lips an inch from his ear, I said, "Do you see that old tiger in the orange shimmering robe? The one that's talking smack?"

"I see," Dmitri growled.

"We're grabbing him and taking him with us. He has a holy object on his person. Make sure it says with him."

"What if other tigers try to interfere with me?" Dmitri asked.

"First push them away. If they persist, kill them."

Admiral Venturi spoke up. "Commander Creed, you must order your guards away. Then you must summon mine. You will lay down your weapons and await Lokhar justice."

I didn't want to make my play. You have to believe that. The Kargs were real. The portal was real. To fight among ourselves was crazy. To let them kill me would even be stupider. Yet I had to give sweet reason a change.

"Listen to me, Admiral. The Kargs are still coming through the portal. They're going to invade our universe. Are you going to let your Emperor make a foolish decision that kills everything?"

"He besmirches the beloved Emperor," the Esteemed One said. "You must do your duty," he told Venturi.

"Wait a minute," I said. "Are you serious? The Purple Tamika fool sent his daughter-wife to unseat you. The head tiger is a fool. Screw him and his ideas."

The Lokhars began to murmur in outrage. A few started shouting for my death.

"You have no idea what makes Lokhars tick," Ella told me. "You're not going to talk them out of anything."

"You have to impound the princess's racer-vessel," I told Venturi. "Then you have to complete the mission and save our space-time continuum."

"I must read the scroll," Venturi said in a lifeless voice. "The Emperor has sent me a personal missive."

"Now!" I shouted at my zagun. "Let's do it."

I started across the chamber for the Esteemed One. Dmitri and Ella followed, and with them came my one hundred troopers. The tigers must have suspected my intentions. A few charged my men.

Instead of shooting the Lokhars, a shoving match ensued between them and my men. As the tigers weighed more, they had the advantage, and forced the zagun inward.

"Knock them down!" I shouted.

Neuro-fiber enhanced speed together with steroid-68 increased strength caused mayhem. There were meaty, hard-hitting smacks and Lokhars sprawled onto the floor. More tigers threw themselves into the fray, charging us. This wasn't going to work.

"Shoot to kill!" I roared.

Troopers unslung carbines, leveling them into firing position. Lasers sounded with a distinct combat noise. Tigers crumpled onto the floor with smoking holes in their foreheads and chests, and that started a panic. Lokhars surged away from my zagun, giving us the opening I needed.

I dashed to the head of the table and beyond, scooping up the scroll. As I did, Dmitri grabbed the old adept. My troopers surrounded the two, forcing the acolytes away.

"Listen to me!" I roared. "Listen!"

The Lokhars were too busy shouting and cursing us. I shoved Admiral Venturi hard so he stumbled against the nearest wall. Then I pressed the klaxon switch. It blared with noise. When I released it, the screaming and Lokhar shouting had ceased. Tigers panted, though, watching me with hate-filled eyes.

"Here's how it's going to be," I said.

189

No Lokhar gave me his attention. So I jumped onto the table, and I swept my .44 at the crowd lined against the walls. They looked at me then.

"Good," I said. "This is going to be short and sweet. Even though your Emperor's bitch ordered me dead, I still consider myself allied with Orange Tamika. Defeating the Kargs trumps everything. Unfortunately, Lokhar intelligence hasn't impressed me much, certainly not today. You're overemotional and relic-crazed. Nevertheless, we can still do business together. But I need to keep you from killing me until you regain your senses. I'm taking the Esteemed One with me, together with the stone of God."

Lokhars wailed in anguish, and I could feel a charge building up in them, like a giant plasma cannon building up a heated shot.

I fired a round into the ceiling. The magnum was deafening. Bits of construction dribbled and fell in chunks onto the table. One busted apart, sprinkling smaller driblets around it.

"I'm a savage, remember?" I shouted. "If you come at me, if you try to kill my troopers, I'm going to blow apart the stone of God with my gun. Then what, huh?"

That got their attention. The babble tied down, and the tigers stared at me with blank eyes. The evil I threatened to commit—at least in their eyes—was so terrible it probably hardly made sense to them.

Admiral Venturi stepped forward. He spoke with a hoarse voice. "You cannot mean such vile sacrilege. The stone is the oldest and most holy artifact in Orange Tamika possession."

I scoffed, "You doubt my willingness to do it? Dmitri," I said.

The stocky Cossack hustled the old adept near.

"I implore you," Venturi said. "Do not do this."

I pointed at the admiral with my magnum. "I want you to have the stone of God. I'm not going to touch it. You have my word on that. After we reach the portal planet, I'll return the relic and the adept to you."

"You will destroy it," Venturi said, sounding desperate.

190

"As long as you treat us as allies, I will do nothing to the artifact. I'm taking the Esteemed One with me so he can hold the stone. If you attack us, though, know that we will smash the Forerunner relic and kill as many Lokhars as we can. We will start by killing him," I said, pointing at the old adept.

"What are your final intentions?" Venturi asked.

"They haven't changed," I said. "We'll still march to the Forerunner artifact in the portal planet. We'll fight with the Lokhars with all our strength, battling the Kargs. The princess threatened to kill all the humans. Do you remember? She said the Emperor gave the order. Maybe you think that's seals the issue. You can bet I don't. I'm not under the Emperor's command. If he tries to kill us, I'll kill his as I've already done. I would do it again a thousand times over. Look at her body and think about that. Play fair with us, Supreme Lord Admiral, and we will play fair with you. Try to harm us, and we're going to unleash the biggest load of whup-ass you've ever seen."

"Leave the Esteemed One and the stone of God here," Venturi said. "I will give you my word of honor that none will harm you."

I considered his offer for all of a second. A glance at the glaring, hate-filled tigers told me I'd be a fool to trust anyone's word, especially as I had the one thing they held dear.

"I believe you, Admiral, but I don't believe *them*," I said. "Now get out of our way. Otherwise…"

"Do as he says," the admiral said hoarsely. "We cannot risk the Great Maker's wrath."

Reluctantly, the tigers knelt, even as they glared. Then me, the Esteemed One, the stone of God, Ella and my zagun begun our journey back to the Commando Army's quarters.

19

Doctor Sant insisted on joining us. He said to insure good treatment for the Esteemed One. I nodded, but told him, "Stay behind us then."

We hustled through the corridors, with the adept and his "stone" in the center of our formation. My zagun aimed their carbines everywhere. I wondered if I should have included gas masks in their kits. I told Dmitri in a loud voice to blow away the artifact if the Lokhars gassed us. If the tigers used listening devices, they now knew better than to try such a move. Even so, the trip was tense and nerve-racking. Finally, we reached the monorail and piled into a car. The thing zipped along at its usual high speed.

The Esteemed One never said a word. He sat erect, no doubt expecting indignities at any moment. I finally told him, "Look, you're going to be okay. Doctor Sant is along to see you're treated with respect."

The ancient adept glared at me, but he said nothing.

I wanted to ask how he liked being in the minority. Should I start talking about his extermination as the Lokhars had done in there about us? How would he like that? Probably, he wouldn't understand what I was getting at, so I didn't bother. Besides, I wouldn't want to seem petty.

Ella drew me down the aisle away from the adept and from Sant. She'd already suggested I stay away from any windows. Maybe the tiger had sharpshooters out there, waiting.

"This will never work," she said.

"Do you have a better suggestion?"

"Yes," she said. "We leave the expedition and go home."

"Right," I said. "How do you propose that? Even if they gave us a ship, they'd just blow us away the moment we moved far enough from the dreadnought."

She scowled. "This is a mess."

"I have it under control."

"Why do these things always happen to you, Creed?"

"The Maximum Princess Nee started this, not me."

"No. The Purple Emperor did, if you want to be specific. In a way, I can see his point. The dreadnoughts must represent a vast portion of Lokhar wealth. They're also the only things that can enter hyperspace. If we're going to lose them in battle—"

"That's not a given," I said.

"Do you really believe that?" she asked. "You gave the Lokhars excellent advice back there. Use the T-missiles on the Forerunner artifact. No. In their blindness, they reject the obvious. It is always the same. I do not predict success if they can't even make the correct decisions."

"The T-missiles did seem like a good idea," I said.

"Yes," she said. "That is our biggest problem. The Lokhars think differently from us."

"I think the bigger problem is that they want to kill us. I wonder why they're worried about that anyway. The Kargs are going to devour all of us in the end."

"This is a terrible situation," Ella said.

"Maybe," I said. "But it was worse in Antarctica aboard the Saurian lander, and we lived through that."

Ella peered at the ancient one. Then she looked at me. "I'd like to study his artifact."

I stepped up and put a hand over her mouth. Angrily, she brushed it away.

"Listen," I said as quietly as possible. "They could have the car bugged. I'm sure they do." I winked. Then I pushed her so she staggered backward. "I have given my word. No one touches the stone of God but for the Esteemed One. As long as I live, that is what I will do."

Several of my troopers looked up at me.

Ella muttered darkly and took a seat.

The rest of the journey proved uneventful. We made it back to our quarters. Once there, I had a meeting with the colonels, explaining the situation.

"Expel all tigers from our area," I said. "We will set up a patrolling roster and treat this... Well, we'll try to act like cops first. If the Lokhars continue breaking in even after we escort the first few out, we'll kill the others."

"Do you expect them to break in?" a colonel asked.

"I expect everything so I'm not surprised when it happens. This is a combat situation, with our lives at stake. I don't know if the Lokhars can see reason."

"Maybe we should attempt to take over the dreadnought," a different colonel said.

"We're better fighters than the Lokhars, no doubt about that," I said. "Unfortunately, they have over three million legionaries on this dreadnought alone. We have one hundred thousand troopers. Can each of you kill thirty tigers before they get you?"

"Why are they acting so crazy?" a colonel asked.

I shrugged. "I suppose every race has their own taboos. The tigers aren't any different. We're breaking them left and right. It's amazing we've gotten as far as we have. Now it's a matter of waiting and hoping logic gets through to them."

We did wait, for three days. We felt the bumps now and again. Each one indicated higher speeds or greater slowdowns.

During that time, Ella visited the Esteemed One in his holding cell. I had a camera and audio pickup preinstalled and recorded everything. Each night, I watched the recording. This is what Ella did:

While wearing a flowing nightgown, she came into his cell, kneeling and sitting on her heels, bowing her head and folding her hands in her lap.

This was Ella? I hardly recognized her. She knelt that way for five minutes, ten, twenty, for two hours in fact. She never said a word. She never looked up. She waited in reverence as the old adept studiously ignored her.

Finally, the old one stirred. He'd been lying on his cot. Turning his head, he asked, "Why do you mock me?"

"It is not mockery," she said in a soft voice.

194

He studied her and finally stared at the ceiling again. Another hour passed.

Weren't her knees sore? I couldn't have done that. Well, maybe I could have with someone holding a gun to my head. Then again, I'd already probably have tried for the gun. Clearly, Ella wanted something, and she wanted it badly.

With a sigh, the old Lokhar sat up. "You must leave. Your presence offends me."

Without a word, as demurely as possible, Ella rose and left the room.

I decided to leave it alone. If I asked, she'd want to know how I knew what she'd done. She must know we had bugged his cell, though.

The next day, she reentered his cell and did the same thing. She just knelt like a virgin priestess before a holy icon. The Lokhar ignored her just like before.

Time passed—three hours before he spoke with his paws resting on his frail chest. "Why do you persist in this?"

"I wish to learn," Ella said.

"Learn what?" he asked. "How to provoke a Lokhar high adept?"

"If my presence disgusts you, tell me please. I will leave."

"Yes, go, he said. "Your presence hinders my meditations."

She rose demurely and turned to go.

"That is all?" he asked.

With her back to him, she asked, "I do not understand, Esteemed One."

Air hissed through his nostrils. "I have watched you humans. Your commander is a rash barbarian, without any sense of decency."

"He is a fighting man," Ella said.

"Lokhar fighters have greater humility and reverence for holy things than your commander does."

"Yes. I have seen this to be true, Esteemed One."

"When have you?"

"Commander Creed forced me to attend the strategy session."

"You were there?" he asked.

"When you raised the stone of God…" Ella's head drooped until her chin touched her chest. "The radiance burned in my eyes and it made my heart thud."

"Interesting," the adept said. "I wonder if it was possible that it burned some of the human dross from your heart. Did a miracle take place?"

"Do you believe so?" she asked, and she turned, looking at him with hope.

Was Ella faking this? Why would she…it struck me then. I knew what she was trying to do. She'd wanted to study the Forerunner artifact. Ella was a clever woman indeed. I hadn't realized she was this deceptive.

"I had not thought this possible," the adept said. "Yet your actions these past days…you have acted with Lokhar humility."

"I have felt different ever since witnessing the radiance," Ella said.

"Why did you don robes?"

"It…it seemed like the right thing to do."

"Hmm," the Lokhar said, scratching his chin.

Ella took a step closer. "Esteemed One, could you teach me Lokhar ways? Could you teach me about the Creator and how He left these wonderful artifacts for your race?"

The old one stared at her. He shook his head. "I do not believe that would be wise."

"I understand. I am unworthy for such a task."

"What task is this?" he asked.

"To teach my fellow humans the truth," Ella said.

Ten long seconds passed. It seemed forever, as if he'd turned into a statue. Finally, the ancient adept stretched his arms and claws appeared at his fingertips. "I will do it," he said, in a lofty manner. "Perhaps this is the Great Maker's…well, never mind." He pointed at a spot near his cot. "You will kneel and listen, and I will begin to enlighten your heart."

Ella did as requested, a fierce light welling in her eyes. I wondered what she'd bring away from this. We needed more knowledge concerning Forerunner artifacts. It might help us later. In any regard, Ella kept the adept busy. She had more time alone with him because I kept sending Sant to Venturi.

I wanted another meeting. The Supreme Admiral balked at first by always being in conference, unable to reply. Finally, at the end of the third day, Sant returned with a request.

"The admiral is willing to speak with you," Sant said. We stood before a holoimage viewing port. It showed star formations I didn't recognize. One cluster near the upper left corner had different colored lights: blue, orange and red. I'd have liked to visit there.

"Naturally, I'm willing to speak to him, too," I said.

"The admiral asks that you come alone and unarmed," Sant said.

"Nope," I said.

Sant faced me, looking earnest. "The admiral is insistent on those requirements for personal communication."

"That's nice, and I understand. For I also am insistent, but I'm insistent *against* his requirements."

"You must understand his position, Commander."

"Stop right there," I said. "I don't have to understand anything of the sort. Tell him I'm getting nervous locked away in here. Tell him when humans get nervous, they break things. The holier the thing they can break, the better."

Sant stiffened. "You should not even…joke about such things."

"You insult me, Doctor. I'm not joking. I am getting ready to… Well, I don't want to break the artifact. But I am getting ready to study it."

"No!" Sant said. "That would be sacrilege. It is a Lokhar artifact, particularly venerated by those of Orange Tamika. For humans to sully the relic by their touch would lessen its sacred purity."

"I guess I don't see it that way."

Sant's shoulders slumped. "You disappoint me, Commander. I had hoped—but no, I will keep silent on that regard. The admiral anticipated your stubbornness. He gave me a predetermined response. I can see you are intransient. Therefore, the admiral is willing to come here. But he will come in state."

197

"You mean with an honor guard?"

Sant nodded.

"Wonderful," I said. "When does he want to meet?"

"Two hours from now?"

"Sure," I said.

Sant left to deliver the message.

I picked a nice spacious room. It had tables, benches, water and food. I lined the walls with two zaguns of troopers. They wore symbiotic armor, complete with helmets and grenades.

At the end of the two hours, the Supreme Lord Admiral with a retinue of three hundred honor guards, acolytes and adepts solemnly entered our corridors. Some of my soldiers had bagpipes. They wailed Scottish tunes on them, and the tigers looked impressed at the racket.

I also wore bio-armor. If they were going to assassinate me, they'd have to at least shoot well enough to hit me in the head, as I didn't wear a helmet.

Venturi's guards and acolytes had to stand in the center of the chamber. It turned out I'd barely picked a room big enough to hold everyone.

"Before I sit with you in conference," Venturi said. "I would like to see our Esteemed One."

I'd anticipated that, and swept my arm to the rear. Dmitri opened the door, and there stood the old and rather forlorn-looking adept. Ella stood behind him, wearing her flowing nightgown.

"Have they touched the stone of God?" Venturi asked.

The room grew deathly silent. Every Lokhar leaned forward to hear the answer.

"No," the ancient said. "They have awe regarding the relic. I…I am surprised. They esteem what should be esteemed."

Admiral Venturi turned to his honor guard and to the adepts and acolytes. "It is as I've said. The oracle does not lie. It told us we would gain honorable allies in the humans. They are different from us, but they are able to regard with awe what should be so regarded."

Dmitri closed the door and that was all we saw of the Esteemed One.

Venturi sat down across from me. His aides flanked him at the table. It reminded me of old pictures I'd seen in *Time* magazine as a kid. On one side of a SALT II negotiating team had been large dour Soviet delegates. On the other side of the table had sat leaner Americans.

"I am pleased you have treated the Esteemed One with regard," Venturi told me.

"He carries the Creator's…" I groped for the right word.

"Stone," Venturi said. "It is the Great Maker's stone."

"Thank you, Supreme Lord Admiral," I said.

We stared at each other. He spoke first once again.

"Perhaps you have tainted me, Commander Creed. I have done a terrible deed."

"Yes?"

"After much thought, I impounded the Emperor's personal race-vessel. I have kept the crew quarantined from my people. I did this as you suggested, so we could carry on our mission."

"You have done your duty to your people and to the universe," I said.

"You understand me, I see. Many of my highest officers do not."

"It is why you lead Orange Tamika and not them," I said.

"Yes. I believe this myself."

"How can I assist you?" I asked.

"Return the Esteemed One to us," Venturi said promptly.

"I will…once the Commando Army leaves *Indomitable* and heads down to the portal planet."

"You are making this difficult."

"Perhaps you're right," I said. "But could it be that the Emperor has made it difficult for both of us?"

"He has," Venturi said. He looked away, sighed deeply and regarded me. "It cannot be as it was. You realize this, yes?"

"How was it?"

"I took you into our confidence. I let you into the strategy session. That can never happen again."

"It doesn't matter," I said. "If we close the portal, I am glad and we will have done our duty."

"The Lokhars can never trust the humans again," Venturi said. "After this is over, we will have to go to war against your world."

I couldn't restrain myself at that. "You already went to war against us once."

"No. That was to save you—"

"Okay," I said. "I can't do this your way. It's too slow and it gives me a headache. We have your stone. Are you going to stay on task and attack the portal planet?"

Venturi glowered, but said, "I am."

"Do you want our help closing the portal?"

Venturi's chest swelled, and he leaned forward. "You are rash, Earthman. I, too, can throw aside ancient customs and speak as my heart compels me."

"It's about time," I said.

He snarled, a loud sound, and he slammed a fist onto the table. "If you touch the artifact, I will return to your world before engaging the Kargs. If you give it back now—"

"I won't," I said. "You get the stone once we leave your dreadnought."

He glared at me, and I felt his desire to slash my face into ribbons. He rose, I rose, and our people rose with us.

"There is nothing left to say," Venturi told me.

"How about we practice our maneuvers together against the Karg menace?" I asked.

"No," he said. "I will do this without you."

"Is that what your oracle said?" I asked.

He raised his head and roared like a lion from the African veldt. It put a chill in my spine, as my hand strayed to my weapon.

With a trembling arm, he pointed at me. "You are untrustworthy. I sense it in you, Commander Creed. But I am the Supreme Lord Admiral Venturi. I adhere to my word. On my last mission, I will not sully my honor because Earthmen cannot act with decorum. You will join in the assault once we of Orange Tamika have prepared the way on the portal planet."

"Don't get too puffed up," I said. "We're the ones who have to go through to the end. It's not how you start a mission that counts, but whether you finish it or not."

"This is the last time I will speak to you face to face," he said.

"Sure," I said. "But there's one more thing. I want you to install a viewing screen for me. We need to see the enemy in action so we can figure out what to do, and do better, when the time comes."

"That makes no sense."

"Not to a Lokhar," I said. "But you've already admitted that we're much different. Let us do things our way while you do it yours. We need to see the enemy. We need to get an idea about hyperspace. Install the screen and a communications system between our two commands. You know as well as I that we're going to have to coordinate this."

"Did you not just hear me?" Venturi asked. "I despise your face."

"I heard you. We won't be talking in person, so you'll be keeping your oath. Look. This isn't about us anyway. You sought me out because the oracle told you to. It must have done that for a reason, right?"

"You have battle wisdom," Venturi admitted slowly. "But you lack decorum."

"We all have to live with our faults," I said with a shrug.

Venturi hesitated before saying, "Let me see the Esteemed One again."

"Nope," I said. "Once you install the screen and communications between our command centers, then and only then can you or your representatives see him again."

"You guarantee to do this?"

"I do," I said.

Without another word, without a salute, Admiral Venturi headed for the door. His retinue hurried after him. As meetings went with Lokhars, this had been short indeed.

The next time I'd seen his face again, the Kargs would be attacking. The problem was, that happened far sooner than any of us anticipated.

-20-

In our area of *Indomitable*, the colonels ran their tumens through brutal exercises. As they did, Lokhar techs linked a screen to the dreadnought's main bridge.

Several days passed in tedium. Then the terrifying announcement came: we were about to enter hyperspace.

Ella had spent many long days with the Esteemed One. Through him, she learned some interesting things. As we'd suspected some time ago, the First Ones had made the jump routes. They had done so with their Forerunner technology. The former Altair Object had been one of those, at least according to the Esteemed One's lore.

Jump routes were like folds in space, and they allowed us newer races to zip from star system to star system without having to pay the time cost of Einsteinian physics. They also made some star systems more strategically important than others.

The three dreadnoughts had used jump routes. We'd hardly noticed, however. Usually, entering a jump point was physically hurtful. People threw up, got headaches and felt as if they had the flu. The fantastically thick outer hulls, together with extremely bulky tech, had kept us from feeling those normal jump effects. That was a military advantage, I thought. It came at great cost, though, a literal high construction price.

Through the Esteemed One, Ella confirmed our suspicion that dreadnoughts cost oodles of money. The reason for the price became obvious today.

Klaxons wailed, and onscreen, a Lokhar officer informed me that we would be entering hyperspace in another hour.

I'd set up a control center in the human area of the ship, similar to what I'd had on the Jelk battlejumper. Through N7, Ella and other bridge officers, I issued orders. All but a few corridor guards were to head to their sleeping quarters and strap down. We'd heard enough about hyperspace to figure out this was going to be bad.

I'd had cots installed on the bridge for us. Time passed, more klaxons wailed, and each of us lay down. Our main screen showed what the tigers saw on their main screen. We also had a link to some of their sensors.

"Commander," N7 said. He'd elected to remain at his station while the rest of us lay down. His uniform rustled as he made adjustments. "My board shows a weakening of the space-time continuum at grid 24-A-12."

"You should have let Sant onto our bridge," Ella told me.

"There's no time for that now," I said. "Besides, Sant assured us he could not take the initial hyperspace effect as well as we could."

"Observe, Commander," N7 said. "It's beautiful."

His words startled me enough that I unstrapped myself, stood and switched my station's screen to N7's panel. I don't know why he'd failed to put the image onto the main screen. A riot of colors erupted against my eyeballs. They twisted like rainbow-colored snakes in an obscenely pornographic way.

I glanced at N7. The android's mouth was slack. What was going on inside his bio-brain?

The colors swirled faster and faster. Then it seemed as if more rainbow snakes entered the passionate rioting. They merged and darkened to an inky blackness that blotted out stars.

"This must be the rip that will let us out of our universe," N7 said.

My mouth turned dry. Then the darkness became complete, and something sinister and vile appeared there. It seemed to be a nullity of existence, nothingness beyond even empty vacuum. It appeared to me that this was true nothing, if such a phrase even made sense.

A hole appeared with swirling rioting rainbow colors along the edges. Dreadnought *Glory* slid through the opening into hyperspace, with the second dreadnought following. Finally, it was our turn.

A fear I couldn't explain hit me, worse than any stomach-churning bogyman feeling I'd had as a kid. Once, as a teenager, after listening to Art Bell on the radio on a show about demons, I'd had the worst nightmare of my life. I'd lain in bed, and it had felt as if a nine-foot demon hovered over me with a wavy-bladed dagger in his scaly hand. That doesn't sound bad in the light of day. But it was as I'd lain in bed, too frozen with fear to move. I could feel that demon-knife inching closer and closer to my face. My throat had locked, my lips wouldn't work and I'd just about pissed in my bed.

At the last moment, my mom opened the door and flicked on the lights. I thought to see swirls of inky darkness where the demon had been. Then I moved my head and looked over at my mom.

"I thought you had the dog in here," she said. "I heard whimpering as if the dog wanted to go outside. That couldn't have been you, could it?"

I still couldn't have spoken, but I'd shaken my head.

"Good night, dear," she said. The door closed.

I hadn't gone to sleep for hours, and every few minutes I'd checked where the dream demon had stood. It had been the worst nightmare ever.

I'd almost forgotten the feeling. I remembered now, because a similar fear came upon me in waves. Was that the extent of real demons: non-space, non-reality?

I stood there, gripping the station's edges, trembling, trying to get my fear under wraps.

Then a puking sickness struck. I couldn't hold on to the post. I was too busy with my arms wrapped around my gut as I spewed onto the floor. We all did. I kept vomiting. I wanted to stop. We'd never get anywhere if this continued the entire trip.

Soon, there was nothing left to spew. With a sweaty face, I resumed my spot at my commander's station. I glanced at a few of the people on the cots. Tears streaked their cheeks and some had vomit stains on their chins.

"We're okay," I said, in a weak voice. I tried to clear my throat. The fear was still too stark.

"Hyperspace is haunted," Rollo groaned.

"Yeah," I said.

"Nonsense," Ella whispered.

"You can say that after having seen the holy relic?" I asked.

"Of course I can," she said, and she sounded angry. With the anger, strength entered her voice. Maybe that was the trick.

I tried it, drumming up rage against the Lokhars for nuking Earth. It helped, driving away some of the fear just as my mom flicking on the light switch that night had helped. I told the others about my find.

"Yes. It makes sense," Ella said. "The angriest person we have is our leader. Maybe that's why the oracle supposedly chose him. Hmm...I wonder why a similar process doesn't work for the Lokhars."

"Different races have different reactions," I said. "I want everyone to concentrate. Think about what pisses you off the most. Fixate on that."

Slowly, my command team resumed their posts. Everyone scowled.

I studied the screen afterward, which was black, just black, a viral nullity.

"Imagine spending years out here," Ella said.

"Why do you say that?" I asked. "We won't be here that long?"

"Because that's how long the dreadnoughts have been patrolling this region as they search for the Jelk universe."

We fell silent as Lokhars in the real command room began growling at each other.

"What are they seeing?" I asked. "Why do they sound worried?"

"I'm bringing up a far scan," N7 said, "and putting it on our main screen."

I glanced there, and in the blackness were three snowflake-shapes. I had no idea how far away those things were.

"Do you know what they are?" Ella asked.

It clicked. I knew, and I said in a quavering voice, "Those are Karg ships. Don't you remember seeing them in the video?"

Klaxons rang.

"Are we running away?" Ella asked.

"Negative," N7 said. "It appears as if our flotilla is changing course. We're heading toward the Kargs."

"If they are Kargs," Ella said.

"What else would you expect to find in hyperspace?" I asked.

"If they're Kargs," Ella said, "aren't they a long ways from the portal?"

"The Lokhars are firing," N7 said.

I kept looking at the main screen. A gigantic laser beam flashed across the distance. Then another joined in and one more. Each dreadnought sent a searing beam of concentrated light at the nearest Karg vessel.

"How big are those beams?" I whispered.

"Larger than the biggest Jelk laser," N7 answered.

The three lasers kept reaching out. They seemed to be moving slower than they should be, almost as if we watched the light move. Finally, I had a little bit of an idea on the size of the Karg vessels. The lasers burned into a tiny section of the snowflake. It would be like needle-pricks sticking a bull, flea attacks. Despite the miniscule size, that piece of snowflake apparently disintegrated and crumpled. As if falling, the piece went down, down, down. Then small sections of the piece turned and headed our way.

"What's going on?" Ella asked.

"What are those?" I said.

"I'm magnifying the images," N7 said.

A fuzzy Karg vessel leaped into view, long, with a dark energy tail spewing behind it. That the dark tail showed up against black hyperspace was interesting. Clinging to the pod were moth-like ships with glowing nuclear eyes. I don't know how else to describe them. What would have been wings on a moth—or a ship—twitched.

"Are those things alive?" Ella asked.

"What?" I asked. "Living creatures in space? That's preposterous."

"No," Ella said. "That would make it different from us, but it wouldn't be preposterous. Scientists have long ago foreseen space-living creatures."

"They must be robots," I said, "androids like N7."

"I cannot live in space without a suit," N7 pointed out.

"Well, you know what I mean," I said.

"Perhaps the moth-ships once fed off sunlight," Ella said. "The wings might be like giant solar panels."

"Whatever energizes them," I said, "they're detaching from the pod."

Twenty or more moth-ships detached. They spewed a brighter colored exhaust as the vessels accelerated toward us.

The dreadnought lasers switched targets, like a kid with his finger on a garden hose spraying his sister. You could actually see the last light bolt. When he switched targets, you could see the last stream of water but with nothing else behind it. That's what it was like today, with a last stream of light. Hyperspace had different physical laws all right. This was evidence of it.

Three dreadnought lasers concentrated on one moth-ship. They struck at the head with its twin eye glows. N7 magnified. The lasers chewed into the ship's hull. We saw heated sections bleed away. Then the lasers stabbed into the vessel. There might have been mini-explosions. Bright objects and glowing sections of ship broke apart and tumbled away as if someone had lit a firecracker in the thing and we watched the reaction in slow motion. There was a molten core. Maybe it was the alien engine. Maybe it was the guts of a space moth. At this point, we didn't know. From the images, though, we saw the rest of the moth-ships continue to bore toward the dreadnoughts.

As our lasers retargeted onto a new moth-ship, miniscule objects or dots appeared at the farthest edge of the screen from the Kargs. The dots came from the direction of the dreadnoughts, so I assumed they were ours. I leaned forward, trying to understand what I saw.

"Fighters," N7 announced. "Fifty fighters from Dreadnought *Glory* are attacking."

"That doesn't make sense," Ella said. "The fighters couldn't have gotten there that fast. Our lasers—"

"Whoa!" I said, interrupting her.

"Is there a problem, Commander?" N7 asked.

"Our lasers must have incredibly short range in hyperspace," I said, "and they fire much slower. Maybe in comparison, it's like shooting a bullet into water. The bullet won't travel nearly as far or as fast as if fired in the air."

"And the fighters?" Ella asked. "They would also be slowed, yes?"

I thought about that, and I might have figured it out. "A bullet shot in the water travels faster than a diver can, but the differences aren't as stark as an air-shot bullet compared to a sprinter on land. The faster something goes, the more it is slowed, bringing everything down to a similar level."

Ella nodded thoughtfully. "You are observant, Commander. Yes, I believe you're right. I congratulate you."

Before the fighters reached the moth-ships, the eyes on the nearest Karg vessels glowed more brilliantly. They seemed to bubble as if made of red-hot lava. Then a red ray beamed. To my eye, it traveled marginally faster than our lasers had. A single touch of the ray melted a fighter. The rest of the fighters began jinking, swerving out of the way.

"What kind of beam is that?" I asked. "What are you reading on your sensors?"

N7 worked his panel. He finally looked up. "It must be the graviton beam Venturi told us about."

The moth-ships destroyed many of the fighters, their rays like a laser light show at an old rock concert. Fortunately, at the same time, the dreadnought lasers worked over the Kargs, destroying them one by one. Ten fighters made it into particle beam range, and then we had a better estimation of the moth-ship's size.

"Commander," N7 said. "The moth-ships...according to my sensors, they're a tenth the size of our dreadnought."

That slammed home hard. It made the moth-ships massive, bigger than anything I'd seen so far except for the dreadnoughts themselves. Now I realized each Karg snowflake-vessel was many times larger than a dreadnought.

Of the three original snowflake-vessels, one had completely disintegrated. Yet that was a mistaken observation on my part. The snowflake-ship hadn't fallen apart, but launched its component warships. Those warships were colossal pods carrying moth-ships each a tenth of the size of a Lokhar dreadnought. It seemed a Karg snowflake turned into one hundred moth-ships, or ten times the mass of one of our vessels. The three Karg snowflakes represented ten times our flotilla's mass.

"I'm guessing we can't win this battle," I said.

"Our lasers outrange anything they've shown so far," N7 said.

"That's hurting but not stopping the Kargs," Ella said. "Look, another of their main warships had begun breaking up into its components."

Even as we saw that, the last of the initially launched moth-ships neared the dreadnoughts.

I opened communications with Admiral Venturi. At least, I attempted to do so. The tiger lord ignored me.

The battle turned disastrous then as the nearest moth-ships beamed *Glory*. Those graviton rays burned through the dreadnought's electromagnetic fields in an amazingly short time. Fortunately, the last of the near moth-ships died even as they began churning into *Glory's* hull.

"Admiral Venturi!" I shouted. "I demand your attention. If you want the stone of God to survive—"

Venturi appeared on my panel. He sat in a command chair, hunched forward, with his right elbow on his knee. He looked stricken and resolved.

"What do you desire of me?" he growled.

"Can we win this battle?" I asked.

He tightened a fist. "We must," he said in a hoarse voice. "Otherwise, the universe is doomed."

Too much struck me as odd about the battle. I was still trying to get a handle on hyperspace. "Visual range must be extremely short here. I think the same holds true for radar."

"Yes, yes," Venturi said in a heavy voice. "The Kargs surprised us. We had no idea they patrolled so far out."

"Okay," I said. "In hyperspace there are short detection ranges. Therefore, if we slipped away now, we might be able to escape from the Kargs."

Admiral Venturi blinked at me, as if the idea had never crossed his mind. "It is possible. Yet why are the Kargs out here? If we leave, they might slip into our space-time continuum."

"That's something that has been bothering me for a long time," I said. "They need the portal planet to break into hyperspace. That would imply they don't have their own technology to do such a thing. That would mean they can't possibly break into our universe from hyperspace."

A Lokhar marching behind Venturi halted, turned his head and stared at me. A muffled call caused the aide to step out of view.

Meanwhile, the admiral glared at me. "The portal planet will open the way into our universe. The Forerunner artifact is keyed to us."

"Which means I'm right about fleeing," I said. "On all accounts, we must reach and close the portal."

"By the Great Maker," Venturi whispered. The Lokhar straightened, and he began to issue terse orders. I kept the link open, to listen in, and the admiral did not close it from the other side, so I watched the progress of the battle.

Our three main lasers concentrated on the second wave of approaching moth-ships. Then a second swarm of tiger fighters appeared. The melee turned bloody as hell, with charred and tumbling fighters breaking apart from the slicing graviton beams. Then an enemy vessel exploded. I don't mean it burst apart in slow motion. This time, the moth-ship disappeared in a titanic flash that radiated its blast outward in a perfect sphere. Two hundred tiger fighters simply vaporized within it. Another two Karg warships also took direct hits. That left two more, which the lasers finished in short order.

From farther away wore moth-ships came, though, several hundred more in an unbeatable mass.

"Let's get out of here," I told Venturi. "It's time to scram."

I don't think the tiger heard me. He was too busy rattling off orders and listening to officers' reports.

I felt a bump, though. N7 and Ella swayed at their stations. We must have engaged the main engines. It seemed the Supreme Lord Admiral had some sense after all.

Thirty seconds later, Venturi roared in anguish. He shot to his feet, and he spoke in a low voice. I don't know what he said, but soon we felt another bump.

"What are you doing?" I shouted at Venturi. "What's the plan?" I looked at the enemy on the main screen. I think we'd slowed down.

The Lokhar slumped back into his command chair. Then he straightened, and there was fire his yellow eyes. "It is time to fight," he told me.

"There are too many Kargs for us to defeat."

"I must do my duty," Venturi rumbled.

Another look at the main screen showed me Dreadnought *Glory* by itself, badly wounded, with a ruptured hull along its spine. Vapors billowed out of it into hyperspace. It must not have accelerated with us. Maybe it couldn't.

"We cannot desert *Glory*," Venturi told me. "The Kargs damaged the outer engines. But given time, we can repair the ship."

I studied the main screen. Hundreds of Karg moths-ships accelerated toward the stricken dreadnought. Those hundreds represented a much greater mass than our flotilla. If less than twenty moths had done that to one dreadnought…

"Admiral Venturi, you must listen carefully. The Lokhars cannot win this head-to-head fight."

The tiger glared at me, and he expanded his mighty chest. "You do not know the Lokhars. We never abandon our own."

I knew that wasn't true. I'd seen Lokhars flee before. Heck, I'd seen it in the strategy session chamber. Maybe now wasn't the best time to remind him of that. I had to use reason—no. That likely wouldn't work either. There was only one way to appeal to Venturi.

"I would ask you a personal question, Admiral," I said.

"Is this another of your insults?"

"I am a savage and a barbarian. You've told me so more than once. But even I know where my ultimate duty lies."

"What are you implying?" Venturi asked.

"We have one goal: to close the portal. If we do, our universe survives and the Lokhars live. If we fail, we all perish. You can save life, Admiral Venturi, but only if you reach the portal planet."

"No!" he said. "I can do that only if I can reach the Forerunner artifact in the portal planet. For that, I need *Glory's* legionaries."

"Yes, you must reach the artifact, and that will take us humans. Do you suppose I foresaw this battle?" I shook my head. "That would be absurd to think so. Then what caused me to insist that all the humans remain aboard *Indomitable*? Why, the Creator must have moved my tongue."

Venturi glared at me with red-rimmed eyes.

"We have what we need to win, Admiral. If we all perish here, though, it's over. You must allow *Glory* the privilege of holding the Kargs at bay while we make our escape into hyperspace."

"I have two more dreadnoughts to hurl into the fray. Orange Tamika will survive."

"You could be right," I said. "Yet let us consider the odds. Forget that a fraction of their strength already did this to us. If you lose the coming battle, all is lost for our universe. If you lose *Defiant* in the fight, it makes our odds of battling down into the portal planet even less than before. If you lose *Indomitable* and *Defiant* survives, you have lost the humans the oracle said you needed for success. No, Prince Venturi, you have one duty. That is to reach the portal planet and land us on it. Make our deaths in hyperspace worth something by defeating the Kargs for good."

"Do you realize how many Kargs will be at the planet if there are already three such Karg snowflakes out here?"

I hadn't thought about that. But it didn't matter now. "Do you truly believe in the Creator?" I asked.

"How dare you ask me that?"

"I am asking. Do you?"

"Yes!" he roared, pounding the arm of his chair.

"Then know that He chose you for this mission for a reason. That reason wasn't to die uselessly. Maybe only you out of all the Lokhars have the sense of duty strong enough to leave *Glory* to her fate. We have our own to meet. And we can't win everything here, but we can if we win at the portal planet."

"I despise you, Commander Creed. I hate and loathe you to the depth of your being."

"That seems to be the way of things," I said. "I tell the truth too often, and no one really likes to hear it. Well, what's it going to be, Admiral?"

The big Lokhar bowed his head. I didn't envy him. It was one thing to know what to do. It was quite another to leave your friends behind to face certain death. This would weigh on his Lokhar soul for the rest of his life.

Admiral Venturi stood up, and he quietly issued what must have been the hardest commands of his life.

Shortly, I felt a bump again. We watched the main screen, as the moth-ships converged upon *Glory*. Beams began to rage as we fled from the fight. We had a greater destiny than to die today. Before the stricken dreadnought perished, it faded from sight and then from the range of our short-ranged radars.

There was no such thing as long-ranged radars in hyperspace. The flotilla now had two dreadnoughts instead of three. We had a little less than seven million tiger legionaries and one third fewer tanks, fighters and attack-craft. We also knew that the Kargs would have overwhelming numbers at the planet.

The success of our mission seemed even more hopeless than before.

I began watching battle video like a Big Ten football coach. Sometimes, N7 joined me. Sometimes, Ella and Rollo sat down. We took notes, compared them and talked late into the night.

It would have been good to capture a Karg. It would have been better to get hold of their weaponry. Maybe if we could have captured several moth-ships, and they turned out to be regular vessels with crews, we could have slain the Kargs. Then we could have used the moth-ships as scouts.

All we had were these videos of a losing space battle. So let's see, from that and from previous data we could figure they had more ships, more troopers, better weapons and already held onto the property. What did we have? We had stout hearts and determination, oh yeah.

The days passed. We avoided Karg vessels. Each of them headed for the weak spot into our space-time continuum. Did that mean they had a way to break into our universe without the portal planet? If that was true, even if we closed the portal, there were going to be a ton of Kargs in our space-time continuum. I didn't like to dwell on that, though. One problem at a time was my dogma.

After one lengthy session of note comparing, and after Rollo had left, Ella turned her chair around, draping her arms over the back. We were in my makeshift office and had watched the battle for the thirteenth time.

I'd called thirteen my lucky number since grade school. I guess I'd already been contrary then. I recall one of my teachers telling the class to pick a number between one and one hundred. I chose thirteen. The teacher stopped the contest right then. He told us he'd met his wife at table thirteen in college: his lucky number. Anyway, I'd won the right to pen a letter to the President about something the class had done a project on. I can't remember what the letter was about, since I never wrote it. I'd won the contest but disliked the idea of writing a letter. I'd been eleven at the time, interested in eleven-year-old things like hide and seek, riding my bike and playing sandlot football.

My luck has always been a mixed bag.

In any case, Ella let her arms hang down over the back of the chair. I noticed she wore a silver ring on her middle finger. It lacked a gem, being a simple band.

"I think we have learned all we can from the video," she said.

"Maybe," I said. "Maybe we're missing something obvious."

"Do the Lokhars know more about the Kargs they aren't telling us?" Ella asked.

"In case you haven't noticed," I said, "the Lokhars aren't talking to me much anymore."

"I will have to ask Ulmoc."

"Who?" I asked.

"Oh," Ella said. "I shouldn't have said that. Ulmoc is the birth name of the Esteemed One."

"Are birth names sacred or something?" I asked.

"Very much so," Ella said. "A foe can use it to cast evil magic against you if they know your birth name."

"Wait a minute," I said. "Some things aren't making sense here. First, the Esteemed One has learned to trust you enough to give you that kind of info?"

"He has."

"Secondly, Lokhars believe in magic?"

"Why should that surprise you?" Ella asked. "They believe in the Creator."

"You still don't?"

Ella cocked her head. "Why would you think I've changed my mind?"

"Ah...all the time you're spending with Ulmoc," I said.

"I am a scientist. I study where and when I must to achieve my goal. The Esteemed One holds an artifact."

"Have you seen it yet?"

Ella shook her head.

"Anyway," I said. "Magic is quite another thing than belief in the Creator."

"I profoundly disagree," Ella said. "Both are rank superstitions."

"I don't get it. How can you fool the Esteemed One with an attitude like that?"

"I am a scientist. I do what I must."

I grinned. "Tell me, Ella, where did you learn to playact like an acolyte? That's not something that just happens."

She drew her arms up to grab the top of the chair. While biting her lower lip, a far-off look drifted into her eyes. "I grew up in Siberia," she said.

"I remember you telling me."

"My father was Russian Orthodox."

I shook my head. I didn't know what that meant.

"I thought you were an amateur historian," she said.

"One, I don't know everything. Two, what does Russian Orthodox have to do with anything?"

"Russia became the home of the Eastern Orthodox Church," Ella said. "The Byzantine Greeks sent missionaries to the Slavic tribes long ago. The Orthodox Christians also warred against the Monophysite Christians in the Middle East. The Copts in Egypt belonged to what the others thought of as a heretical sect."

"So?" I asked.

"When the Muslims came into Egypt, the Coptic Christians liked them better than the Orthodox priests who tried to tell them how to worship. Coptic hatred toward the Orthodox helped the Muslims overrun the land." Ella shrugged. "In any case, when the Turks finally stormed Constantinople, the Russian tsar and his priests believed that Moscow had become the third Rome. The second one used to be Constantinople."

"I know about *that*," I said. "The Byzantine Empire was often called the East Roman Empire."

"To answer your original question," Ella said. "I grew up learning Orthodox rites. Once I went to school in Moscow, I learned about the Coptic Christians, the Catholics and Protestants. It was simply another point showing me the foolishness of belief in God."

"I don't see why," I said.

"If God is real, why would He allow all these differences?"

I shrugged. "Not being God, I don't have any idea. But I do know that people are different. Why not different churches for different folks? Some people like doing their services one way, others another."

"I do not accept your theory," Ella said. "People believe in magic, God and other superstitions. The same is true for the Lokhars. I fooled my father for many years, and he knew me much better than Ulmoc does. It is easy to playact again in the name of science. Soon, now, I will see the Forerunner artifact."

My thoughts had already drifted from her preoccupation. I wanted to figure out how to defeat the Kargs on the portal planet.

"It's really crazy we're not coordinating better with the Lokhars," I said. "We're probably only going to have one shot to do this. We need to get it down to a science."

"Agreed," she said.

I dimmed the lights, and I turned on the machine. Ella left, and I resumed watching the battle, trying to find an angle, trying to figure out the Kargs by how they'd fought the dreadnoughts.

I awoke to the sound of graviton rays. I'd fallen asleep on the cot I'd installed. I'd also looped the video some time ago so I didn't have to restart it. As I raised my head, I saw a moth-ship's eyes glow like a lava pit and then the beams burned outward. The Kargs—

Before I could finish my thought, N7 entered. "It is urgent, Commander. Admiral Venturi demands an immediate conference with you."

"Pipe it in right here," I said.

"No. He wants a face-to-face meeting."

That brought my head up. "You're kidding, right? Venturi swore an oath that he'd never—"

"In my estimation, the admiral is terrified. Something has happened to change everything."

I rubbed my eyes, trying to clear my head. I needed some coffee. "When and where does he want to meet?" I asked.

"He will come to our quarters with a three-man escort. He asks you do the same."

"Done," I said. "Do you have any idea what this is about?"

"I do not, Commander. He is waiting outside our corridors. He desires an immediate conference."

"Right. Now where's some coffee?"

"I will bring some," N7 said.

"Don't bring that scalding stuff you drink. I need regular coffee."

N7 nodded brusquely. "You must hurry, Commander. The admiral is urgent."

I didn't like this insistence. What did it portend? Nothing good, I bet. "Okay. Let's go, and get me the coffee."

Ten minutes later, I sat at the same long table as before. I had N7, Ella and Rollo with me. A haunted Admiral Venturi entered the room. Doctor Sant had joined him, together with two extremely tough-looking tiger guards. They wore orange chevrons on their collars and bronze biceps bands, showing that these had thicker arms than the others did.

I sipped from a cup, black coffee that put dirt on my tongue. I still felt foggy, but with an unnatural alertness.

"I'm glad we can talk, Admiral," I said, rising to my feet.

Venturi stopped short. His eyes were red, and if ever the tiger looked hangdog, this was the moment. The normally crisp uniform was rumpled, the military cap sat at an awkward angle and he seemed dazed and confused.

"Commander Creed..." he gestured helplessly. "I have broken my solemn oath to meet with you here. I am foreworn and useless now. But what I have just seen and heard..." He shook his head. "We are doomed. We are all doomed, everything. The end has come."

"You mean the Kargs?" I asked, with urgency in my voice. "Have they found us?"

"It is much worse than that," he said. The tiger lurched and almost stumbled to his chair, collapsing into it.

I sat. I'd never seen any of them like this. What had happened?

Venturi produced a glass chip. "The Kargs are the Great Enemy. It is unbelievable. The ancient writ spoke of this time, but I never realized until Abaddon spoke to us that it was so. How could any of us have known?"

I waited. He was obviously stricken to the core. He'd have to tell this at his own speed. All the same, I'd wish he'd hurry up for once.

The raspy tongue appeared, and Venturi aimed his red-rimmed eyes at me. "I must play the message. Perhaps you'll understand then. Perhaps you can..." The Supreme Lord Admiral shoved the glass chip into a slot. He pressed a button, and a holoimage appeared. "The Kargs sent us a message," Venturi whispered. "This is it."

"Did they beam it directly to you?" I asked.

"The message was broad-beamed," he said. "I do not think they yet know our precise location. It does not matter, though."

"Hello, Lokhars," a gravelly voice said.

The holoimage was fuzzy like bad analog TV reception. There was the outline of a possible head within the grainy fuzz. Those might have been shoulders and possibly red glowing eyes. For a second, I thought I could see. Then the image distorted again.

"We captured your dreadnought, the one you laughably call *Glory*," the Karg said. "Some fought, as useless as the pitiful gesture proved. Let us show you their fate."

The fuzzy distortion quit. I saw a Lokhar strapped down onto something. A knife appeared held in a metallic tentacle, and it committed unspeakable atrocities that made the tiger captive rave. Blood and gore, and torn organs tossed onto the floor—it was a wretched and ugly sight.

"Some died even harder, mewling like wounded kittens," the Karg said in his ear-hurting voice. "All provided us with limited sport, as you too will provide us when we find your pathetic ships.

"I now know you by name, Supreme Lord Admiral Venturi, of the Avenging Arm of Lokhar. You belong to Orange Tamika and are here to halt our invasion. That is ironic, don't you think? As your frail ship has given us the means we've sought for jumping the last lap into your space-time continuum."

"Is that true?" I asked.

No one seemed to have heard my question. They kept staring at the distorted holoimage, glued to the Karg's words.

"I know your mission, Lokhar. It is to reach what you call the portal planet. Do you think you can slip past hundreds of Karg invasion torcs? No. We know you, Admiral Venturi. We have the composition of your frail dreadnoughts imprinted on our sensors and we will obliterate your craft on sight if you dare approach near enough to the portal. The others here have your patterns. There is no chance you will successfully land one legionnaire onto the portal planet's surface. If we find you before that, we will storm your ships, capturing you for our amusement."

His words troubled me deeply. Maybe we should have stood and fought to protect *Glory*. I hadn't foreseen this.

"You have once chance for life, Admiral Venturi. Come to us begging on your stomachs and we will let you live as slaves. You will be the last to perish in your universe. Yes, you will tell us everything you know and earn your final days, or you will linger in extreme agony for untold years if you persist in your useless quest."

"That's important," I said. "We still have things he wants. That's why he sent this message. He wants us to surrender because he's afraid. I certainly don't believe all his boasts."

Venturi turned haunted eyes upon me. I had the feeling I hadn't heard the worst.

"Surrender to me, Lokhar, for I am Abaddon. I am the bane your worlds have feared for many millennia."

Venturi shuddered. So did Sant and the tiger guards.

"I have arrived at last," the Karg calling himself Abaddon said. I seemed to have heard the name before, but I couldn't place it. "I have brought my multitudes with me. I have returned from the locked pit and my wrath shall not be appeased. You cannot win. You cannot harm me. Nothing can. Surrender, *Supreme* Admiral, and I will teach you the meaning of power as I rend your space-time continuum into smaller and smaller pieces of death and destruction. Abaddon has spoken, and my word is a promise of destruction."

Abruptly, the holoimage went blank. A second later, Admiral Venturi clicked a switch and took his glass flake from it.

"Who is Abaddon?" N7 asked.

"This is a coincidence, nothing more," Ella whispered.

"What is?" I asked her.

"His name," she said.

"You've heard it before?" I asked.

"It is written in the Book of Revelation," she said. "Abaddon is the name of the chief demon let out of the pit."

"The Karg spoke about a pit," I said. "Does he mean their universe?"

"You have heard the name before?" Venturi asked in shock. "This is astonishing. We, too, know that in the last days as spoken in the ancient writ Abaddon will reappear to bring death and destruction. His name means 'destroyer.'"

I sat back, stunned. The Kargs had a leader named Abaddon, and both the Lokhars and we had that name written down from long ago? This seemed a little more than coincidence to me.

I recalled then walking across the old cathedral in Germany. I'd squatted beside a stone gargoyle. The statue's face had resembled Claath's far too precisely. Could the Jelk have more to do with the Kargs than any of us realized it did?

"Okay," I said. "We have to break this down one thing at a time. A couple of items strike me as important."

"No, no," Venturi said. "Don't you understand that our mission cannot succeed? We have failed. We are doomed, and our universe will perish with us."

"I don't accept that," I said. "We have two ships filled with soldiers. I breathe. You breathe. We're far from doomed, and the Karg's message proves it."

Venturi shook his head. "You are mad, Earthman. Here is the evidence before your eyes and you cannot see. We have failed the Great Maker and He has unleashed the great evil against us."

"That's one way to view it. I prefer to believe we're here to stop the evil by fighting harder than any of us ever has before."

"How?" Venturi asked. "I had one hope: to fly through Karg formations, to use boldness to reach the portal planet. Now Abaddon has blocked the route. The Kargs know us by sight and sensor, and will destroy our ships if we get too close."

I found it hard waiting for the tiger to finish talking. When he did, I said, "That's point one in my reason for thinking Abaddon is bluffing. Why bother sending the message if we can't do anything to him anyway?"

"Maybe because instead of destroying us, he wants our dreadnoughts," Ella said.

"Exactly," I said.

"Why would Abaddon want or need our paltry ships?" Venturi asked.

"The answer is obvious," Ella said. "He boasted, as Commander Creed suggests. He didn't get to *Glory's* core, but captured enough Lokhars to have learned about hyperspace rips separate from the portal planet. Now he needs our ships intact to get the drive."

Venturi sat like a statue until finally his eyes began blinking. "If you are correct," he said, "we must self-destruct at once."

"Come on!" I said, exasperated. "Will you listen to yourself? That makes no sense. If we fail, the portal planet will open a route into our universe anyway. He doesn't need our dreadnoughts. His fear must be that of our successfully closing the portal. That's the victory. That's the game winner here. The message has one reason and one reason only: to discourage us. Besides, did you ever stop to think that maybe there are others with him?"

"What are you suggesting?" Ella asked. "I do not understand what you're saying?"

"He broke his captured Lokhars," I said. "We saw the evidence. Did he do that for pleasure? I don't believe it. He must have done it in order to discover what they knew. Maybe these Kargs are swift-thinking bastards. In their questioning, they found the name Abaddon and his legend of the end of time. That sounds close enough to what they're doing, right? So the Karg figured: I will call myself Abaddon in order to paralyze their will—our will. Such a thing has happened before, you know."

"Are you mad?" Venturi asked. "This has never happened anywhere. We are discussing the end of everything."

"I mean the general principle of the thing. On our world, there was a man named Cortes. He sailed to the New World with higher technology than the Aztec Indians. Early in his march inland, he got hold of an Indian woman named Dona Marina. She told him all the Aztec legends and beliefs, and she helped him trick the Indians who had sold her into slavery. They thought Cortes was Quetzalcoatl, the legendary light-skinned god who was supposed to return out of the sea. Cortes played off the Aztec legends and thus weakened their desire to fight back against him until it was too late."

"Yes," Ella said. "Thank you, Commander. That makes perfect sense. I think that is exactly what has happened here. The Karg acts a part by calling himself Abaddon. That makes more sense than…than the other possibility."

Venturi glanced from Ella to me. "I do not understand you humans. The evidence is before you. To attempt talking yourself into believing otherwise…" He groped for words.

"No," I said. "We're right. The Karg isn't Abaddon. He's using your old legend about him to weaken your resolve to fight." *And if the Karg really* is *Abaddon, how does it help us fight him if we believe we're already doomed?*

"I wish to add a comment," N7 said.

"Go ahead," I told him.

"If the Karg is pretending to be Abaddon," N7 said, "then why is the name in both Lokhar and human holy books?"

"Yeah," I said quietly, not liking the coincidence. "That's an interesting point."

"No it isn't," Ella said. "Abaddon simply means Destroyer. It makes perfect sense for two different supposedly holy books to talk about a destroyer obliterating the world at the end of time."

"This is a useless conversation," Venturi said. "No matter if Abaddon is Abaddon or a pretending Karg, they have blocked

223

the way to the portal planet. Surely, hundreds of the biggest Karg vessels now ring it. They will know what to look for—us. The moment they see our dreadnoughts, they will unite and overpower our paltry force."

That did seem to be a problem, however... "Maybe we have a bit of time before that happens," I said.

"Explain," Venturi said.

"Radio transmissions can't go as far or fast in hyperspace as in our universe," I said. "Maybe the Kargs at the portal planet haven't yet heard the news."

"Surely they have relay ships passing the information from vessel to vessel," Venturi said.

I snapped my fingers. "I have an idea. We can still slip onto the portal planet even if this Karg has broadcast about us. Well, we can at least slip past the patrolling Kargs."

"No," Venturi said. "It is impossible. We are doomed."

"If you mean attacking the Kargs head-on, I agree with you," I said. "But we're not going to do that. Instead, we'll go around and come through the portal like other Kargs."

"What do you mean?" Venturi asked.

"We have hyperspace-ripping equipment," I said. "So we use it to break into the Karg universe. Then we join the other Karg vessels on their side going through the portal into hyperspace. We'll have to hope Abaddon's message hasn't gone through the portal back into their universe. As those other ships pass the planet, we unload and attack."

"The other Karg ships—the ones already in hyperspace—will see and destroy us anyway," N7 said.

"They wouldn't have any reason to do that," I said. "They're watching for us to come in to them, not waiting to see us come from their universe. Look, according to what Admiral Venturi originally learned, only Kargs live in their space-time continuum. If they think anything at all upon seeing us, it's that we're a new design, or an old one, for all I know."

"You are making blind leaps of speculation," Ella told me.

"Maybe," I said, "but that's better than giving up."

For several seconds, we all stared at each other.

Finally, Admiral Venturi made a low growling noise deep in his throat. It reminded me an old time muscle car on Earth, one that caused the car to shake with doglike anticipation. "You humans are mad with a hope that doesn't exist. Your wordplay means nothing. You cannot see the truth, so you foolishly persist in trying."

"And how is that worse than giving up and letting everything go to hell?" I asked.

"I do not know," the Lokhar admitted.

"Yeah," I said, "neither do I. So how about it, Prince? Let's give this bastard a run for his money. Let's fight until we're dead or lying on a cot with a Karg knife spilling our guts. What I'm not going to do is stop any iota sooner than that."

"I begin to perceive how you defeated your Jelk overlords," Venturi muttered.

"Let me ask you a completely different question," I said to Venturi.

"I am still," he said.

"What?" I asked.

"That means the prince is listening," Doctor Sant said.

"Oh," I said. "Do you believe there's a connection between the Jelk and the Kargs?"

Venturi considered that. "Both come from different space-time continuums. Apart from that, I do not think so. The Jelk do not possess such murderous technology as the Kargs."

"What are you implying?" Ella asked me.

"I saw something in Germany," I said. "Claath looks like a devil, a small one to be sure. Abaddon is a devil, as well."

"A demon," Ella corrected. "In the Bible, in any regard, the devil refers to Satan. He is one. The demons are his servants and they are many."

"Sure," I said. "Claath looked like a stone gargoyle I saw on a cathedral. I'm wondering if that's just a coincidence or if it happens to mean something."

"I highly doubt it means anything significant," Ella said.

"I know your worldview doesn't want to accept such things," I said. "But it doesn't even have to be supernaturally related. What if ancient men saw space travelers and wrote about them?"

"Are you referring to *Chariot of the Gods*?" Ella asked in a mocking tone. "The ridiculous book scorned intelligent scientific study."

"I guess," I said. "But suppose some of what it said actually is true. Then you could trust old eyewitness accounts written in the Old Testament or in Revelation about Abaddon or demons."

"You are reaching, Commander," Ella said.

"Enough of this," Venturi said. "We must decide now what we are going to do. Either we must destroy our ships to prevent our technology from falling into enemy hands or—"

"No one is destroying *Indomitable*," I said.

"That is not your choice," Venturi told me.

I silently counted to three, working to hold my temper. Threatening to try to storm his dreadnought wasn't going to help us. I had to convince the prince to go the last mile.

"If there is even one small particle of hope for victory," I said, "we should take it. The oracle told you to get us. Now you know why. We humans fight to the finish. We don't quit. Do you want it said that the Lokhars lacked the fire to keep fighting when the rude Earthmen still had the guts to try?"

"Who will say this in a destroyed universe?" Venturi asked.

"How about the Creator when your soul stands in front of Him?" I asked.

That made Venturi squirm.

"Do you guards want to quit?" I asked the two tigers in back.

Venturi turned around.

"Lord Prince," the smaller guard said. "These humans insult us. Let us kill them and die with honor."

Venturi's big shoulders slumped. With an old man's slowness, he regarded me. "I hate you," he said in a listless voice. "I do not understand you at all. But you will never march farther than a Lokhar. Where you go, we will go, too. We will prove ourselves greater than you in all things."

"That's good to hear," I said, and I began to outline the specifics of my idea.

-22-

Before we were ready to break into the Karg universe, Admiral Venturi made a few adjustments. He strengthened the link between our two command centers, making this an emergency bridge just in case the worst happened. He thus provided us a link to the interior portion of the dreadnought. I mean we heard Venturi talk to the priests in the sealed portion of the ship that held the artificial black hole. They spoke in the High Speech of the ancients then. It meant we would have to bring Ulmoc in here in order to communicate with the priests—if the time came where we needed to try.

Ella spent even more time with the Esteemed One. He began to show her the artifact. I figured I'd get a better look at it, too, by studying the video. That's when I discovered the equipment wouldn't record. It simply went blank whenever the adept took out the Forerunner object.

I was beginning to like certain aspects of this less and less. Angels, demons and old prophecy…what did any of that have to do with space battles? Nothing, I kept telling myself. This wasn't anything what I'd expected outer space to be like.

Our two-ship flotilla began to tiptoe through hyperspace, even though time was against us. We kept waiting for another broadcast from Abaddon. The devil, demon or Karg kept silent, though.

From my extended video battle watching, I decided the moth-ships were indeed structures with crews. Even with full magnification, it proved impossible to gain conclusive evidence. But some of the debris struck me to be floating crewmembers. What did the Kargs look like? What kind of soldiers would we face on the planet? Could they use graviton rays in rifles? That might cut through our bio-suits with pathetic ease.

Time passed as we trained, watched and waited. Finally, Admiral Venturi said over the link, "The technicians have found a weak spot in hyperspace. The problem is that they cannot assure me it will lead into the Karg universe."

"Can they give us odds?" I asked. Venturi was on his bridge and I was in mine.

"That is not the Lokhar way," Venturi said.

"How far are we from the portal planet?"

"At these speeds?" he asked.

"If we rushed there as fast as possible," I said.

"Three days journey from here," he said.

"Well, let's suppose that proximity to the portal means we're near the Karg universe."

"Hyperspace travel does not correlate so easily."

"Yeah," I said. "Let's do it anyway."

Venturi was silent for a time. Finally, he said, "Yes. In an hour, we will make the attempt."

Before the dread hour came—were we going to make a rip into Hell? I didn't know. In any case, before the attempt, Ella walked into the control room. She didn't walk with her usual confidence. She moved in a dazed manner. I knew she'd been with Ulmoc.

"Keep me posted concerning any new developments," I told N7. Then I intercepted Ella and took her by an elbow. I steered her to the hatch, walked down a corridor and brought her into my office.

Ella Timoshenko didn't say a word as she stood like a zombie. I poured her a cup of coffee, adding plenty of cream and sugar, as she liked it. There were even stale pastries, a close approximation to Earth norms. I chose one with a pink jelly center. She finally sat in a stuffed chair, with her butt on the edge as she kept staring at the floor. Well, not staring, her eyes were blank. I handed her the items, and she automatically took them and held them out from her body.

"Ella," I said gently.

"Hmm…?" she asked, while holding her stiff pose.

"Eat," I said. "Drink, and tell me what happened."

She glanced at the pastry, nibbled on the edge and slurped coffee. After gulping the liquid, she switched gazes from the floor to me.

"I cannot believe what I just saw and heard," she said.

"With Ulmoc?" I asked.

She nodded slowly.

"Well?" I asked.

She took a bite this time and practically gulped the pastry piece. That started her coughing, half-choking. Finally, she slurped more coffee, coughed a little more and set down both pastry and cup. The words began to gush out of her then as she spoke in a rush:

"I've been anticipating this moment for longer than you can believe. I have calluses on my knees and my lower back hurts every night. The ancient one—Ulmoc—is extremely condescending. He believes we're a lower order of species, possibly too stupid to understand the higher ways of Lokhar."

"You say that as if Lokhar was a person," I said.

Ella nodded. "Oh, yes, Lokhar was the first person as Christians, Muslims and Jews believe Adam was the first man. Ulmoc can quote pages and pages of their holy writ. It's very tedious. He waxes philosophical on everything. I can't tell you how many times I wanted to clap my hands over my ears and run out screaming. The tiger infuriates me. But I smile. I nod and listen to every word. I've been waiting for him to show me the artifact."

"He already has several times before this," I said.

Ella's head snapped up so one of her neck bones popped. Suspicion shined in her eyes. "You've been spying on the cell?" she asked.

"Of course I have. I'd be crazy not to."

"Then you've seen everything, I suppose."

"I've seen some," I admitted. "Every time he drew out the artifact, the sensors stopped recording."

A slow smile spread across Ella's face. It made her prettier when she did that.

"Interesting," she said. She laughed before pressing her lips together, as if her laughter might turn into insane shrieks. "What I've witnessed today…" She stared intently into my eyes. "Commander, the artifact is alive."

"What? How is that even possible? Isn't it supposed to be thousands of years old? Nothing can live that long."

"I still don't know enough yet," Ella said. "But I know what I heard. Maybe the Forerunner object is like N7, a construct. It spoke in High Speech to Ulmoc, and he spoke to it, trying to silence the thing, I believe. It shocked the high priest when it began speaking in my presence. I think that's making Ulmoc reassess some of his beliefs about us."

I pursed my lips. Okay. The artifact was a thinking machine. That made better sense than it being alive did. The Jelk produced androids. The First Ones simply made their models more durable and long lasting.

"This all sounds interesting," I said. "But why does any of this have you up in arms?"

"Surely you jest," Ella said.

I shook my head.

"Why, it speaks, it talks, it communicates. The object belonged to the Forerunners, the First Ones. That means I can ask it questions about then. I can riddle it concerning the Altair Object and the portal planet. It may be the key to our victory. It certainly could be the key to unlocking our understanding about the universe."

Oh. Yeah. Those were interesting points. "Do you *really* believe it's that old?" I asked.

"What are you suggesting?"

"Maybe someone else built it and called it Forerunner tech."

"Yes, yes, that is certainly a possibly," Ella said. "Yet the Lokhars believe it a treasure from the distant past. Surely, they must know something concerning it. This is incredible."

"I suppose so."

"No," Ella said. "If you are this calm then you do not understand its significance. This is as if the Sphinx started talking and told us about ancient times. This is scientifically exciting."

"I'm more interested in what it can tell us about the Altair Object and the portal planet."

"Exactly," Ella said, and her smile became predatory.

"What now?" I asked. "Am I missing something?"

"You of all people should understand the next step."

I frowned, and then it hit me. "You're talking about taking the artifact with us."

"I most certainly am," Ella said.

"Venturi isn't going to agree to this."

"He won't be alive long enough so it matters," Ella said.

"You don't think we can beat the Kargs?"

"I don't think any of the dreadnoughts are going to survive our initial landing, provided any of us can even make it down to the planet. If the creature calling itself Abaddon is right, and the Kargs swarm around the planet, we're going to be lucky to get anyone down. Remember, Commander, our battle plan calls for successive waves of troopers and legionaries to secure surface area and then bore for the center. Yet we don't have enough shuttles and dropships to land seven million soldiers all at once."

"Yeah," I muttered, "that's a problem."

Klaxons began to wail, and we both knew what that meant. The time had come to jump into the Karg universe.

"Let's hurry," I said, as I eased forward on my chair.

"We're going to have to use the T-missiles in some innovative manner," Ella said in a rush.

My mind had already drifted onto other subjects. I stood. She stood, and we raced for the hatch.

What do you want me to say? How specific should I go into what happened next? We reached the control room and lay on the cots as N7 kept his station.

Our android didn't declare the beauty of the shift out of hyperspace. Our guts did shrivel—at least mine sure did—but none of us puked that I could hear. I tell you the truth, this time we each sensed a greater feeling of dread than before.

It wasn't like a demon standing over me. Instead, I felt hopelessness as waves of despair attempted to drown me in the apathy that leads to suicide. How could a space-time continuum provoke such a feeling?

I heard weeping around me, and I felt dejection ten times worse, a hundred times worse, than when the judge had pronounced my sentence and said I was going to prison. I had the feeling of bars clanging shut times one thousand, or like a guy's first hot girlfriend telling him she was splitting up with him. It was that ache deep in the gut welling outward with waves and waves of anguish.

Yet humans are creatures of thought, not just feeling. Despite the weeping, the dread, the loneliness and the uselessness of everything, I unbuckled my straps.

N7 stood transfixed at his station. He stared at the screen in his panel. He said nothing and neither did he move.

I swallowed in a parched throat. Did I want to see this? No. But I was going to do it anyway. I'd once broken free of the Jelk bastard Claath. I was going to beat this, too.

I stood up, shuffled to my station and studied the screen. What I saw boggled my mind. First, I saw dust as the sensors registered vast fields of gas molecules. Then I saw worlds, planets, thousands of them, hundreds of thousands perhaps, drifting uselessly. Among them were cool black dwarf stars and neutron stars. In the far distance, I saw something much worse and more intimidating: a mighty glow of superheated matter and it seemed to stretch everywhere, from one end of the horizon—if one could say such a thing regarding space—to the other end.

Glancing at the sensors, I was startled at the radiation levels emanating from it.

"That thing…" I whispered.

"I assume you mean the accretion disk," N7 said in a hollow voice.

"What?" I asked.

"The incredible quantity of glowing matter is an accretion disk," N7 said. "It circles an enormous, supermassive black hole. My sensors say the black hole is trillions upon trillions of solar masses."

I tried to understand his words. A solar mass was the amount of matter that made up the Earth's Sun. Trillions upon trillions of solar masses meant an inconceivably huge amount.

That meant the accretion disk—the stuff circling the black hole—must be the remnants of billions of black dwarf stars, planets and other interstellar debris. The supermassive black hole was in the process of devouring *everything*. It must have been doing so for...an amazingly long time. I remember reading that black holes were messy eaters, and that not all the matter would descend into the singularity. The continual breaking down of atoms released gobs of radiation up and down the spectrum.

"The gravity from this universe's last supermassive black hole pulls at our dreadnought," N7 said. "You can hear our engines strain."

I did, and it worried me. "How far are we from...it?" I asked, gesturing helplessly at the horizon.

"Fortunately, many light-years," N7 said, "but the inconceivable mass makes the black hole irresistible."

I thought about that. Looking at the accretion disk, the way matter went down into the center...it reminded me of the times I drained water from a bathtub. I'd watched that happen a thousand times as a kid. The last water always swirled *around* the drain, but in the end, all the water was sucked down and disappeared.

My few words dried up. I concentrated, but I still couldn't talk. Getting angry had helped last time. I needed something different, because I couldn't even generate the resolve to get mad.

I sighed deeply once, twice, three times and felt overwhelming misery build in me. This was unnatural. Could a universe emotionally defeat someone like this?

It is doing it. Instead of theory, you need action. Yeah, but first I need to believe my action can help anything.

The thought put a seed of, of...*hope* in me. If we were lucky, heck, if the Creator really was with us, maybe we could survive. I clung to the idea, because I tell you the truth, I didn't have anything else.

"N7," I whispered.

The android moved with infinitesimal speed. It agonized me to watch his slowness. His haunted eyes finally looked up into mine.

"What exactly is all this?" I asked.

"You are observing the Karg universe," N7 said in a monotone.

"Why are all these planets, dead stars and supermassive black hole in such close proximity with each other?"

"Indeed," N7 said.

I studied the screen. We passed near a dead hulk of a planet, like Hell with all its fires gone out, with giant empty pits, cold mountains and steely ghost cities of empty buildings. And then I realized what must be the truth of this space-time continuum. If a universe expanded—think Big Bang—couldn't it contract? And if it contracted—they called it Big Crunch—couldn't there be a time when a universe became small indeed? If that small universe still had stars and planets—matter—wouldn't they all be squeezed together like this into the last super-supermassive singularity devouring it all?

I looked upon the black dwarf stars, neutron stars and the incredible black hole once more. The Kargs *had* to escape this place, for it was shrinking back into what—a single singularity? I wanted to shriek like a madman. I'd read stuff on the end of the universe before. Scientists and ivory tower eggheads had argued like crazy over these things. Once, people pushed Big Bang theory hard, until they realized that implied a start to the universe. And if there was a start, who started it and put the matter there to Big Bang in the first place? Had the matter always been there? That didn't make sense. But something couldn't come from nothing. That did seem to imply a big "C" Creator because a cause needed a reason, and for something to be there—as it is and was—there had to be a self-caused thing or being to start everything. Therefore, some scientists no longer liked the Big Bang theory so much. Others, particularly the Intelligent Design guys and gals, loved it. In any case, other theories began to abound, flat universe, open universe and closed universe. Only in the closed universe did you have the Big Crunch. I don't know about other space-time continuums, but the Karg universe was as closed as could be and getting closer every second. Could it be a pocket universe?

"Commander," N7 said in his monotone, interrupting my thoughts. "There are massive levels of X-rays, gamma rays and other radiation striking the outer hull. We are shielded for a while. But we can remain in this universe for only a limited time until we all die from radiation poisoning."

I nodded even as the desolation of this place pulled at me again. How had the Kargs managed to survive in this shrinking universe? Where could they live to outlast the radiation?

That didn't matter now. Hope. We needed hope, otherwise... I opened a wide channel with all my troopers. I spoke to them about hope. I spoke about the Creator and that we were the ones who were going to save our universe. I told them to fight doubt, fight the dejection in their hearts. We had a duty and a purpose. I didn't want them to despair.

What would have happened if I hadn't gone on the horn? Let me tell you what did happen. During our short time in the Karg space-time continuum, one third of the troopers gave into the misery pounding at their hearts and minds. They used grenades, rifles and knives and did what they needed to escape the insufferable gloom closing down around them. In three words: they committed suicide. I wish they hadn't. We needed everyone, but we no longer had a full one hundred thousand soldiers, but two-thirds of our former numbers.

Fortuitously for us, lucky for the universe maybe, the Lokhars didn't have that problem. Despair led Lokhars to extreme indifference and lassitude. It didn't cause them to take their own lives.

"Look," I heard Admiral Venturi over the comm. "I'm patching through to your main screen," he said.

I turned to the screen. I saw the hatching of an armada and an answer to my question about where the Kargs lived. I never wanted to see something like that again. A husk of an earth-sized world floated in oblivion. It had dried seas and cold mountains, with a flat silver area like a molten lake that had hardened. I wonder what that had been. In any case, the great breaking began on the flat silver. It split apart with lightning zigzags. That jagged line grew into a worldwide catastrophe. Mountains of debris fell away as the gigantic crack deepened, as if God used a titanic invisible chisel to break the world in two. The halves separated, and the core of the planet was cold and hollow. Out of it flew more than one hundred Karg snowflake-shaped vessels. To escape the radiation perhaps, they had burrowed into a world's cool center. Perhaps they had kept things going by feeding nuclear reactors with the core iron-nickel mass.

There was nothing majestic or awesome about the spectacle. Instead, there was something vile and evil in the action. It reminded me a black widow spider sac, one guarded by a poisonous mother. I'd watched once as a child, absorbed with the tiny hatchlings crawling out of a silk egg sac. I'd watched until my stepdad crushed the sac and the black widow with the sole of his shoe, twisting his foot back and forth. A hard smack to the back of my head and a stern lecture taught me why I shouldn't have been bent over like that, watching.

"You kill black widows whenever you can," my stepdad had told me. It had been one of his few useful lessons.

"The Karg vessels are accelerating," Venturi said. "I will follow them at a discreet distance."

"Right," I said. "They must be heading for the portal."

"I am of a similar opinion," Venturi said.

For the next several hours, we followed the Kargs. Another burnt-out planet burst apart, and more giant, snowflake-shaped vessels headed in the same direction like a horde of lemmings, only these were fantastically massive ships instead of rodents. And these lemmings didn't head for a cliff to dive into the ocean and oblivion. The fleets headed for a portal that would give them life and endless combat in a new, fresh universe. Their numbers were staggering. I was witnessing thousands of ships, masses that should never exist.

How many vessels would it take to conquer a galaxy, two galaxies or three, four or more? Well, I was witnessing the recruiting ground, or recruiting space-time continuum for such a campaign. Sure, it would take the Kargs a million years to get the job done, but they would be starting with our spiral arm of the Milky Way Galaxy.

"Admiral, you might need to jump to the head of the line," I said.

"I have reached a similar conclusion," Venturi said.

Seconds later, there came a bump, and then another and another as the dreadnought increased velocity.

The gas molecules and dust made our shield red with energy. That was bad. If the dreadnought's electromagnetic field overloaded…

"I suggest you get your troopers ready," Venturi said.

"Do you see the portal?" I asked.

"Not yet," he said. "But if this universe is shrunken to this tiny area, I doubt the portal will be far from here. Look at the masses of ships."

I observed the big screen, and there were tens of thousands of enemy starships in long lines, all heading inward toward the portal presumably. The inner misery threatened to return in my heart. I shook my head. I refused to give up. I never had yet. Why begin now here in this infernal pit of a universe?

Yeah, it was time to get ready. Time to don a symbiotic suit, check my rifle and make sure I had a ton of grenades ready. Time to talk to my colonels and number off. Seeing these Karg ships, I imagined that the portal planet swarmed with vessels the way ants swarm an open jar of honey. The only good I could see from this would be that the new Karg ships would push the others away to make room for more, more, more. It also showed me there was only going to be one attack wave for us, the first one. That meant loading each transport and dropship with three times the regular numbers. Every inch of each aisle would be crammed with troopers. Even that probably wasn't going to be enough.

During the next few hours, I found out that I was wrong. The colonels soon informed me of the many suicides. By tripling the numbers in the drop-boats, I could now take every human left alive on the dreadnought.

I worked hard, cajoling, pleading, shouting and slapping endless backs. Halfway through the proceeding, Venturi informed us he saw the portal.

A ragged cheer went up as I oversaw troopers.

"Let's load up the boats," I said. "Once we're back into hyperspace, I don't think we're going to have much time but to race into combat."

Work helped keep me from despairing. The bio-suit also helped. Had Claath known about this universe and its effect on humans? Had his scientists done things to the symbiotic suits

237

that allowed us this extra margin? Had his reason for coming to Earth been different from what he'd told us? Maybe the Lokhars had known more than they told us, too.

Bloody aliens; there was nothing good about them opening our eyes to the greater universe. Everything I'd seen had brought more heartache. None of this had solved our problems, as some believed extraterrestrials would do for mankind.

The uploading became a madhouse. There were massed body-jams in the corridors. The hanger bays were a giant mob of shouting, pushing troopers cramming themselves into the dropships. This place tore down our discipline.

I shoved my way aboard with my zagun with me. I was still linked to the admiral.

"Well, are we near?" I asked him.

"Commander Creed," Venturi said, "I wish to state for the lore masters that you are a unique individual. I find you loathsome, yet filled with courage and a Lokhar's heart. The oracle was right to summon you. Soon, we shall pass through the portal. I do not believe I will live once we begin the landings."

"Come with us," I said. "Join the surface attack."

"I cannot," Venturi said. "I am the admiral."

"I know you play by the rules. And normally, for you at least, that's good. Why not change the rules this time?"

"No," he said, in a stern voice. "I am the Supreme Lord Admiral. With the authority comes responsibly. A Lokhar knows this. I will fight from the bridge where I belong. I refuse to desert my post and give my duty to another."

"You're a tough Lokhar, sir," I said.

"I am sending Doctor Sant to you. In fact, I believe he has already boarded one of your assault boats."

"We welcome him," I said. "Admiral, there is something else. If you will permit me, I have a few battle suggestions."

"I am still," Venturi said.

I wasn't, as a mob almost shoved me off my feet. I felt elbows jab my back and the toes of boots kick my calves. I pushed back even as I spoke:

"Look, I know you hate the T-missiles. No, that isn't right. You hated my first suggestion. Now I think you should use them to pepper the inside of the portal planet. If there are Kargs inside, waiting for us, you need to pop those thermonuclear warheads amongst them. Try to create a lane for us to the Forerunner artifact."

"Yes, that is a wise suggestion," Venturi said.

"Another thing," I said, "but it's going to sound heartless."

"Speak."

"You've seen the Karg numbers. It's crazy. Overload your landers with legionaries. You're only going to get one wave down there. Use that to get as many legions down as you can. Once you've done that, I'm sure the Kargs are going to turn every graviton ray in range on your ship."

"I will attack them with ferocity," Venturi said.

"You could, but I wouldn't. You risk disablement and capture that way. We can't afford having the Kargs get your universe-ripping equipment. With all that said, you can also aid us in a better manner."

"How?" he asked.

"Once our first assault wave is in space," I said, "you need to build up as great a speed as possible with those dreadnoughts. Then you need to ram the planet as close to our landing zones as possible. Fire nukes as you go down, but use the giant ships to wipe out two vast areas. That might give us just a little more time to burrow into the world and start the journey down."

"You are heartless," Venturi said.

"I didn't think you'd like the idea."

"No," he said. "It is brilliant. But if I do this, Commander Creed, you must swear to me that you will make it to the Forerunner artifact and cause it to go elsewhere."

"I'm going to try my damndest," I said.

"No," he said. "I want you to swear you will succeed."

"I can't know that."

"Swear it, Commander Creed. Let me know that my sacrifice will be for a higher purpose."

"Swear it," Ella told me.

I hadn't realized she was here. She clutched an ammo bag against her suited chest. She must have filled it to capacity, because it kept moving, squirming. I frowned at her.

239

"Commander Creed," Venturi said over my helmet-comm.

"Okay," I said in a grim voice. "I'm going to swear to you, Prince-Admiral Venturi of Orange Tamika, of the Avenging Arm of Lokhar. I swear with all my heart to battle down to the Forerunner artifact and make it go where no man has gone before."

"By the Great Maker, swear it," Venturi said.

"Sorry," I said, "I can't do that."

"You do not believe in Him?"

"I do," I said, "but I believe it's wrong to swear by His Name."

"Ah…" Venturi said. "Thank you, Commander, thank you. We Lokhars also believe that. Now I know the oracle choose wisely. The portal approaches. I have never wanted to leave a place more than this forsaken universe. Too many Kargs have already made it through. But so many more are coming. It will be a pleasure besting these foul creatures."

"Yeah," I whispered. The fun was about to begin.

This was my Battle of Armageddon phase one. It was terrible and glorious. It was sick, mad, lovely, awe-inspiring and gut wrenching as only commandos and dirt-grubbing infantrymen riding landing craft can understand.

Each era of war has its bloody hazards. Who is to say which is the worst? Imagine marching in a line with your buddies during World War One across no man's land. Machine gun fire mows down hundreds on your side so they topple like trees. Artillery shells knock down even more. Then you have to crawl through enemy barbed wire, where you hang like a fool until you die, torn by shrapnel. Or imagine yourself with a sword in hand during the Third Punic War against Carthage as you charge the city wall. You reach a siege ladder and scramble up as the defenders pour boiling oil on your head and your skin melts from your face.

War! What is it good for? Well, it's good for businessmen making munitions. It's good for dirty politicians who need people to think about something else. It also helps getting rid of bastards and evil empires. Sometimes it can even save your space-time continuum.

Crammed to the gills, our assault boat lifted off the hanger floor. The engines thrummed so the deck plate vibrated against our boots, a good sound and feeling. We were done with our puking due to reentering hyperspace. The grim despair had departed, and that was a fantastic relief.

"Power up," I said, and the outer boat cameras showed us what went on around the vessel. I put that on the dropship's main screen in front, as if it was an airplane movie. Ella sat beside me on a crash-seat. Other troopers sat at our feet and few more were in front. The rest of the extras jammed into the aisles.

The boat was still in the belly of *Indomitable*. Well, the landing craft wasn't in the belly exactly, but in one of the huge hanger bays, as I've said.

A collective "*Ahhh...*" filled the assault boat. On the screen we saw hundreds of other dropships like ours. Each was a sleek armored tube with landing skids, a big exhaust port and sides ready to explode open. We used a rugged Lokhar boat, with an Orange Tamika sword emblem blazoned on the sides. Taken all together, our hanger bay held half the Earthmen ready to rock and roll against the Kargs.

"Switching to an outer scan," our pilot, N7, said.

He shouldn't have done that. The good cheer evaporated. I could feel morale drop like lead in a lake.

First, we saw *Defiant*. Then we saw giant Karg snowflake-ships. I'd say there were twenty of them between the great metallic planet below and us. Our two-vessel flotilla had pulled away from the stream of ships exiting the portal every few minutes. One thing that helped slow the flow was the size of the portal. A giant Karg ship couldn't fit through. It meant the snowflake-shaped craft split into component moth-ships, zipped through and reformed on the other side. We could barely make out the portal and a last glimpse of the hell-universe on the other side.

None of us looked there long. As our two dreadnoughts nudged out of line and moved toward the metallic planet, the Karg vessels in our way began to disintegrate. The moth-ships—the fighting vessels—were getting ready to engage us, was my feeling.

I'd come to appreciate what the Kargs did with their moth-ships. The snowflake-vessel had a skeleton and a vast engine. I imagine all the moth-ships, once docked on the skeleton, added their power to the thrusters. That gave the snowflake-vessel its greater motive energy. Once the moth-ships detached, I suspect they had slower rates of acceleration and burned up fuel faster. Why otherwise fly linked together like that?

More Karg super-ships between the planet and us began breaking down into the smaller moth-ships. A few already turned to face us.

"Oh boy," I muttered. "It looks like the welcoming committee is on the ball."

"Commander Creed," my headphones said. I wore a helmet. We all did in here. Admiral Venturi was on the line.

I chinned my comm-unit. "I'm right here."

"We will offload you now," Venturi said.

"There're some Karg vessels between us and the planet," I said.

"Yes," Venturi said. "Good luck, Commander Creed. Remember your oath to me."

"I haven't forgotten."

"I pray the Great Maker grants you victory."

"Roger that," I said.

As we spoke, the Lokhars began the attack. They'd learned one trick from me. When working for Claath in the Sigma Draconis attack, we assault troopers had stormed a Lokhar Planetary Defense Station. In it, we'd found a teleportation missile. After gutting the thermonuclear warhead, we'd teleported straight out of the PDS into Claath's flagship. We hadn't launched the missile first to fly in space.

Instead of launching the T-missiles outside of the dreadnoughts, the Lokhars launched them from within *Indomitable* and *Defiant*.

Even as the dropships began to disgorge from the giant hanger bay, the first T-missile left the dreadnought.

I watched on our main screen. I imagine we all did. There was nothing else to do except worry, and that wasn't any fun. T-missiles began materializing among the disintegrating snowflake-vessels. Seconds later, massive thermonuclear explosions made our presence fully known.

Cheers erupted in our boat, and I realized I shouted the loudest of all. We pumped our fists in the air.

"The Lokhars and Earthmen are among you!" I roared. "It's time for you to fear."

Our dropship passed through the huge hatch, leaving the hanger bay for good as we accelerated directly for the atomic

243

flowers blossoming into existence. A nifty byproduct of teleporting nukes was that if one timed it right one could send them in one right after another. The first warhead didn't destroy the next one because it wasn't there yet, and the EMP blast had already washed the area and moved on when the next warhead finally did materialize.

Admiral Venturi did the opposite of encroaching artillery fire. In ground combat, there's a dangerous way to help masses of troops attack the enemy. That's to have the artillery shells "walk" toward the enemy line. As those shells fall closer and closer, friendly troops follow. It had to be done perfectly, though. And that took lots of training or many battles to learn how to get it right. Because what often happened was friendly shells fell on friendly advancing troops, and that made infantry bloody angry.

Here, Venturi started close to us and had the T-missiles appear farther and farther out as the dropships headed for the portal planet.

This was called running the gauntlet in the worst possible way. The T-missiles killed many Karg moth-ships in our flight path, but didn't get all of them. The survivors started beaming our assault boats.

That was the right move for them.

Even as we drove in, stubby Lokhar fighters accelerated ahead of us. They engaged their particle beams from too far out, probably to get the enemy's attention. A few of the fighters carried missiles, launching them at the moth-ships.

I had a feeling what it must have been like during D-Day onto the Normandy coast of German-occupied France. Screaming shells, spouts of cold ocean water soaking you and the terrible rocking of the landing craft, making you spew because of seasickness. This was better and this was worse. We didn't rock. We watched the bigger battle, and we couldn't do a damn thing about it.

Troopers began shouting with rage. I let them. They had to let out steam somehow. Better to rave than to despair.

Lokhar fighters flew to their doom, taking the battle to the moth-ships. If the Kargs ignored them, the fighters pumped particle streams into the giant ships. If the red rays destroyed fighters with pathetic ease that at least meant for the moment, the enemy left the assault boats alone. Only one thing counted in this battle: us getting to the center of the planet.

Indomitable's heavy laser and their host of short-range particle beams now came into play. This was like a giant game of chicken, with two sides roaring at each other and with riders blazing shotgun blasts and rifle fire at the enemy. There wasn't much finesse, unless you figure drawing a knife and shoving your arm down a roaring lion's throat to get to his heart is crafty tactics.

We advanced. We died. Fighters died. Moth-ships died and the two mighty dreadnoughts accelerated.

As we did all this—hopefully, materializing T-missiles into the metal planet—Karg ships began converging on the two main interlopers.

Our trick of coming through the portal "behind" the planet had worked for the moment. We'd gained initial surprise and a chance to offload. Now, however, the alien Karg vessels focused beams onto the dreadnoughts. This fire didn't only come from the ships between the Lokhars and the planet, but from behind them, from those enemy ships coming through the portal.

Our dropship sped for the surface. We hadn't even reached the atmosphere yet. I gripped the armrests of my crash seat, and I saw an unholy thing. Red beams of tremendous size cut into *Defiant*. They gored the mighty vessel. They poured heat and destruction into the ship as more rays added their power. The electromagnetic field hadn't stood up long against the annihilating graviton beams. The armored hull lasted slightly longer, taking horrible punishment. Heated globs of metal floated everywhere.

"What if the dreadnought blows?" Ella asked me.

I thought about an exploding moth-ship the first battle. It had wiped out one hundred fighters like a man swatting a mosquito.

The *Defiant* didn't blow. The Rhode Island-sized vessel cracked apart as red-glowing sections fell away. The graviton rays acted like slicing knives. Here a slice, there a slice, everywhere a slice, slice.

As fury bubbled in my gut, I stood and shook my fists at the Kargs. It meant nothing to the battle, but it helped my raving heart.

A crackle of sound brought me around. "Commander Creed," I heard through static.

"This is Creed," I said, slouching back into my crash-seat, snapping the buckles back into place.

"We are about to rush for the planet," Venturi said.

"Give them hell, Prince," I said.

"No, I will give them a defeat," the Lokhar said. "They are too many of them, but you have faced too many enemies before and still won the battle."

"That's true," I said.

"Even if we close this portal, I wonder if our space-time continuum can defeat these far too numerous Kargs that have escaped their universe."

"That's not our problem, Admiral. Our purpose is to give our universe a fighting chance."

"Yes, I believe this, too."

"We are in agreement," I said.

"We are in agreement," Venturi said.

"I am still," I said.

"May the Great Maker bless you, Commander Creed."

"And you, sir,"

Those were the last words I heard from the Admiral-Prince Venturi. If you can believe it, I felt as if I'd miss the old tiger. He was all right. He was a man's man even if he was a Lokhar. He knew how to finish his life in a blaze of glory. I admired that.

The accelerating dreadnought, the last of its kind, soon sped past our swarm of assault boats. Karg moths beamed the giant vessel, and they brought down the protecting shield. They tore up hull armor. In return, Lokhar lasers killed two moth-ships; and the great vessel from our universe smashed against three Karg craft. Then the colossal ship glowed fiery red as it entered the portal planet's atmosphere. I wondered if they had managed to pump T-missiles into the thing.

I laughed wildly, realizing I witnessed one of the greatest charges in history.

Indomitable went down like a blazing meteor, accelerating the entire time. It left a fiery tail as it plunged down, down. Then the great starship struck the portal planet.

I would have liked to hear the clang, like a gong of doom from our universe to theirs. Did the planet wobble? I couldn't tell. A vast dent appeared but I didn't see that either. N7 told us about it. A giant mass of metal, plastics, water, bodies and other material flattened, exploded, burst into fire and did other contortions before billowing upward in a great mushroom.

"Strike one!" I shouted.

"Are we strike two?" Rollo asked from behind.

"If we can get down and burrow under the surface in time, yes," I said.

"What is strike three?" he asked.

I turned to Ella. "That isn't extra ammo you're holding, is it?"

She shook her helmeted head.

"You have the Forerunner artifact," I said.

"I do," she whispered.

"Did the Esteemed One willingly give it to you?"

She sat silently, hugging the bag tighter against her chest.

We all do bad things. We're all human, right? No one is perfect. Maybe there's a time to murder the innocent. I'm not saying that's what Ella did to Ulmoc. Ella wasn't talking about it, and there was a guilty feel to her. I'm glad she had the artifact however she'd gotten the thing, Ulmoc was dead now anyway. Would it have been better for Ella to leave the little relic behind? I didn't think so.

I jerked a thumb at Ella. "Our scientist has a tool that might come in handy for strike three," I said. "Of course, we're going to have to make it down onto the planet first."

"The Kargs are converging on us," N7 radioed.

"Give me a snapshot of it," I said.

On the dropship's main screen, I saw giant snowflakes to the side of us turning our way. Whatever we were going to do, we would have to do fast.

"How much longer until impact?" I asked N7.

"ETA, ten minutes," the android said.

247

"Will the debris from the dreadnought have settled enough?" Ella asked.

"We're not going to land there," N7 said, "but beside the radius of destruction."

Like a vast swarm of bees, the lead invasion craft entered the atmosphere with our assault boats in the center. The air was a blue-green methane mix, and it created hot yellow flares as the first dropships smashed into the upper levels. Then the rocking and shaking started for us. It threw those on the floor and in the aisles all over the place.

"I'm getting a message," N7 said over my headphones.

"From the Kargs?" I asked.

"Yes, Commander," N7 said.

"From the great Abaddon?"

"Yes, Commander."

I'd been waiting for that. "Patch him through to me," I said, "but just me. We don't need to give him an opportunity to demoralize us."

"Are you sure that is wise?" N7 asked.

"What are you thinking? Spill it."

"Maybe the Kargs have technology to know who hears the message. If so, they will discover who our leader is."

"Good point," I said. "Here's what you do. Reroute it to one of the Lokhars. Make sure it's the captain of the most damaged fighter left."

N7 followed my orders.

Meanwhile, the shaking, the screaming sound of metal with building heat, buffeted us and rattled our teeth.

"Anything?" I asked N7.

"Observe," he said.

"Put it on my HUD," I said.

"I have."

I watched as a seeking red ray switched from the human assault boats to an outer Lokhar fighter, one of the few left. The beam stabbed the fighter, destroying it in an instant. Once done, the graviton beam began torching Lokhar assault boats.

"Was that the ship that received Abaddon's message?" I asked.

"Yes, Commander."

"We haven't figured out all their tech yet, that's for sure," I said. "Do you know how he knew?"

"No," N7 said.

The shaking became too much then. I clung to the armrests and lay my head back. The entire dropship slung from one side to the next. We went up and down. I was hardened from entering hyperspace, though. It did nothing to upset my veteran stomach.

Who had made this portal planet? The Forerunners, right? Why had they bothered? Did it have anything to do with the Kargs? I would bet yes. Had the First Ones forced the Kargs into the strange space-time continuum? Why would they have done so? And had the eerie universe already been on the brink of destruction back then? Or did time flow much faster there than our cosmos?

I had questions and few answers. Yet now we had an artifact from that era. I wondered if Ella could speak to it. She said it spoke High Speech. None of us knew it, just Lokhar adepts. Most of them were dead, or would be very shortly.

"I urge everyone to hang on," N7 said. "We are taking evasive action."

"What?" I shouted. "Why? What's going on?"

"There are planetary cannons," N7 said. As he spoke, our assault boat flipped, and it hailed troopers down onto those strapped in their crash seats.

The next few minutes became a jumble of confusion. I couldn't focus on the screen anymore. I dodged unsecured troopers. I grunted at heavy impacts. Bringing the extra soldiers might have been a mistake. Some broke limbs. Worse, they did the same to those buckled in. Without the symbiotic suits, many of the crash victims would have died. Because of the bio-armor, those with broken limbs could still function, the suit supplying extra stability for the broken or cracked bone.

N7 leveled out, and I heard groans and saw troopers squirm in agony. The boat's shaking continued. We dropped through green clouds. A massive something sped past us, heading into space.

"That was an enemy shell," N7 informed us.

The shaking and rattling become worse. Small pink clouds now appeared for no good reason. I took those to be exploding anti-dropships shells, like flak. Metal rattled against us. Three pieces tore through, killing a trooper. The wind shrieked, and then we dropped almost straight down. It made my gut flip and I clawed at the armrests.

On the screen, I saw another dropship, and I saw something reach up from the planet. The thing exploded, and there was a white-and-pink fog of vapor and hot smoke. I watched for another second. The other assault boat was gone.

"Landing in ten seconds," N7 said in his cool android voice.

On the surface, I saw pleochroic domes. They shifted with a bewildering array of brilliant greens, blues, reds and purples. Through the brightness, I realized they were great metallic hemispheres with giant gun barrels sticking out of them. They boomed, sending hardware into the sky. Another dropship disappeared in a pink cloud. I felt like a rat on the Titanic. The domes dwarfed our boats. So did the planetary cannon tubes.

"Get ready for impact," N7 said.

I did, and like an out-of-control helicopter, our android smashed against the metallic ground. We skipped, hit down again, skipped again and spun like a careening bumper car. Then we slid with a shrieking sound of metal.

At last, the dropship came to a halt. I panted in my seat, trying to get my eyes to focus right. Then the sides of the craft blasted open. I watched a section of detached hull tumble end over end. It finally struck the ground and skipped across the metallic surface. The heavily methane mix rushed in. That killed three troopers who hadn't sealed their helmets properly. Stupidity was a bad way to die. I wanted to kick their butts, but it was too late for that.

Besides, I didn't have time to worry about the dead. We'd reached the portal planet, or its surface at least. Now we had to get to the center before the Kargs could kill us.

-24-

The atmosphere was alien, with milky threads drifting like rivers of smoke. Illumination came from atomic fires raging in the distance. Giant red beams stabbed down from space and areas of the metal planet composed of a pleochroic substance shimmered with eldritch lights.

Too many troopers never made it out of the dropship. It would have been good to set up a hospital area for the badly wounded. I stopped then, staring at a gun dome three times bigger than any football stadium I'd seen. The boom would have been deafening without a helmet to dampen some of the noise. The concussion of sound hit like a wall, staggering me backward.

I stopped because I had no idea where Jennifer was. She hadn't made it to my assault boat. I'd had far too little time for her lately. In fact, we'd grown apart. It was unconscionable that I didn't know where she was, but I didn't. Maybe that made me a heartless bastard. Maybe it meant I was on a mission to save our universe and nothing else mattered, not even my shattered love life or the life of the woman I loved.

More assault boats landed. Even more crashed and crumpled with a scream of metal. They leaked blood and gore, and the losses sickened me. I couldn't think straight with the continuous roar of the planetary cannons, the sounds like waves pushing against our bodies. The flashes of intense light—

"We have to get down before we can count off," I shouted.

"Down where exactly?" Ella asked me.

I pointed at a radiant planetary cannon dome. I labeled it a PCD. The giant tube sticking out of the opening belched orange fire and spewed a heavy projectile. The firing tube recoiled out of sight into the dome. Then it reappeared as blue smoke curled from the mighty orifice.

"We break into one of those structures and kill the Kargs," I said.

"And if the domes are automated?" Ella asked.

"Let's find out," I said, starting for the nearest one.

A trooper grabbed my arm, stopping me. I whipped around to see Rollo.

"We can't just charge in," he said. "We need a plan."

I laughed crazily.

"This isn't a solo mission!" he shouted. "You aren't just charging a Saurian lander this time. This is a planet, Creed."

"I've always been a follow-me type leader," I shouted back. I ripped my arm out of his grip. Transmitting on a wide channel, I said, "Listen up, you grunts. We're going to take that dome." I raised my arm, waved it and pointed at the huge metal thing. "We don't have much time. The Kargs upstairs are going to start beaming down with greater precision and killing more of us. At least, I would in their place. That means we have to act like gophers as fast as we can. Find your sergeants. Find your zaguns. Then follow me and kill everything that doesn't look like us."

I took a step forward before spinning around. "Ella!"

"Here," she said. Like everyone else, she was black with her symbiotic suit. She wore an air converter, a bulky ammo pack, had a Bahnkouv laser rifle, old-style Jelk grenades and the most important thing of all, the little Forerunner artifact clutched against her chest.

"You stick to me," I told her. "That thing you're carrying is probably the only way we're going to win."

"Roger," she said.

"I mean stick tight," I said.

"Yes, Commander," she said. "I understand."

Amid the landing boats, the hail and clang of others, we started for the nearest gun dome. The gravity struck me as slightly more than Earth norm. We could easily move in it, as we were stronger and many times faster than normal humans were. Our Lokhar allies landed and would continue to land for the next few minutes. They would come down in a circular circumference around us for at least one hundred kilometers in width. They were the outer shell. The humans were the inner. This arrangement was part of the plan. Would a Karg admiral noticing this decide the inner part was the bull's-eye? I'm guessing that was more than likely.

I wanted to make this hand-to-hand combat as quickly as I could. The Kargs had the heavy hardware with their spaceships acting like orbital platforms. They had infinitely more numbers, too. Were they any good at face-to-face fighting?

The landscape was eerie, stark with giant metal towers and the brilliantly lit PCDs, lonely as all get out. There weren't any stars up there. There sure wasn't any sun. There were Kargs, though. Fiends maybe; deadly aliens for sure.

I shook my head. Lokhar tanks wouldn't have a chance on the surface. All our plans went out the window as far as I could see. We had to be commandos indeed. I had the One Ring—the Orange Tamika Forerunner object—and the center of the planet was the Crack of Mount Doom.

Wasn't that funny? Venturi and I had made all these plans of moving big armies. We'd played sandbox general for weeks. Ten millions Lokhars advancing, holding, deepening the pit, and then bring in the drill that were the human assault troopers. Instead, our strategy was shot to hell with a portal planet swarming with ten thousand Karg space vessels or more. All they had to do was beam wherever we landed, and soon all of us would be cooked, crisped corpses, smoking like hot pork.

The giant dome came into better relief. Were there doors into that thing, hatches? If there wasn't a way in—bingo, I saw one.

"Look at that circular hatch!" I said over the open channel. "Dmitri, Rollo, do either of you see it?"

"I do," Dmitri said.

"Blow it down," I said.

I'm not sure how many troopers Dmitri had of his mingan, maybe two thirds, maybe half: meaning seven hundred fifty to five hundred troopers. Three squads set up portable plasma cannons on their tripods. Seconds later, the first heated orange blob splashed the big metal hatch. Here was the test, eh? Would our firepower prove good enough to crush Forerunner construction?

The answer proved to be a resounding yes. The first shot created a breach, the second opened it wider with glowing-hot edges and the third made room for us to jump through it.

I'd expected darkness inside. Instead, I saw yet more intense brightness, and my visor polarized deeper to compensate.

A few swift glances around showed me I had something like four mingans worth of troopers. That meant four thousand tough guys from Earth. Was that enough to clear out one of the giant domes? We were about to find out.

A regular mingan led by Demetrius charged through the opening first. In seconds, radio chatter told me the closest halls and corridors proved empty. Then the Kargs in there struck, and the first gun battle with their infantry began.

They fought savagely, as you'd expect fiends to. They should have slaughtered Demetrius's mingan, right? Wrong, my friend, wrong, wrong, wrong. We were on a mission from the oracle. It had told the Lokhars to get us for this assignment, and it must have done so for a reason.

I learned several things fast. One, the big dome had decks, levels, turning this into a three-dimensional battle. That made it like old time PDS fighting in the Sigma Draconis system. That brought back memories and ideas. I started acting like a general again.

Ella spread out a computer scroll for me. I already stood inside the gun dome, giving orders. Dmitri to the left, Rollo to the right, climb, go down, encircle and fire from all sides. Demetrius dug in. Well, he couldn't do that in metal. But he and his troopers held their locations while Rollo, Dmitri and Ms. Chan, the last mingan commander, followed my orders.

Once they engaged in a fight, the Kargs didn't know how to retreat, just charge harder than Lokhars would have done. That helped. I've spoken about suicidal troops before. They bled too hard compared to soldiers who wanted to live for another day. With high-tech weaponry, caution usually saved lives.

It might have helped that we had heavier personal weaponry. I saw a Karg infantry-creature soon enough. So maybe I ought to let you know what they were like. I don't know that I'd call them robots. I didn't know enough to make the call. These things seemed built and grown, though.

A Karg—or a Karg soldier—had a barrel body with a horny shell like a beetle. He had a triangular head with the same tough substance and complex eyes like a common Earth housefly. He had a wet orifice for a mouth with chitin teeth. Then, if you can believe it, he had two metallic tentacles with metal pincers on the end. We'd seen such a tentacle before holding a knife that had sliced a strapped-down Lokhar. A Karg had three shorter tentacles on the bottom for mobility, scuttling from place to place. He spoke in clicks. So I had no idea how the Abaddon character had spoken to us. That made me wonder if these were designed cannon-fodder types. I guess they could breathe in this atmosphere.

The Kargs didn't have graviton-ray infantry weaponry. That was encouraging for our side. They had rifles with odds shapes, sizes and big calibers like riot guns. In the beginning, I didn't see what made the weapons fire. I'm taking about hammers striking pins, as you'd find on Earth bullets. The Karg rifles launched big exploding rounds. They had knife blades for hand-to-pincer combat and they had sonic grenades that proved useless against us, although they made our ears ring as if we'd been standing beside speakers at a heavy metal concert.

Maybe these Kargs were the workers. Maybe these things were specialty bozos. There were enough of them, and they went *banzai* against us, selling themselves to get to Demetrius's mingan.

We completed the tactical maneuvering just in time. Demetrius's troopers switched to grenades because their Bahnkouvs began overheating and shutting down.

Surrounded, the last Kargs hesitated. What did they say to each other? After ten seconds of deliberation, the aliens attacked in all directions, and we finished the first battle in short order.

"Go, go, go," I said. "And keep looking for hatches leading down. Oh, and grab some Karg weaponry. Don't overload yourselves. But it's a good idea for us to save our lasers for the toughest fights."

"You do not believe this was it?" Dmitri radioed.

"Do you?" I asked.

"I would like to think so."

"No. It's going to get a million times worse," I said. "This is as easy as it's going to get. Now start moving."

Those were grim words, but one small victory in this dome hadn't won us much. We needed to descend at least several hundred meters. I expected more Karg moth-ships to reach orbital station any minute.

We hit the main chamber shortly thereafter. Squat creatures with rough, scaly skin and stunned heads without necks ran the computer systems. The tentacle-weaving Kargs had been half the size of a human. These things were built on a Lokhar scale. They didn't communicate with clicks and whistles, but spoke with mouths and lumpy tongues.

Were these the true Kargs? I had no idea of knowing. We kept no captives. We slaughtered every freak. We gutted the planetary cannon dome, silencing the thing, likely letting the Kargs upstairs know we'd made it in here.

That's when Demetrius found a great big hatch going down. He radioed me.

"Speed," I told my mingan leaders. "This is all about speed."

"We need to coordinate the entire landing," Demetrius said. "We have to use localized advantages to beat the Kargs in detail."

I could see the former SAS soldier had big ideas. I'd reached different conclusions, and I'd been the one who had fought aliens before. Everything struck me differently than we'd planned, due to having gone through the Karg universe. The sheer scale of enemy numbers, the super-supermassive black hole—I couldn't get that out of my mind.

"Demetrius," I radioed, "listen to me. Get down. Go as many levels toward the center as you can. Time is running out for us. Time's running out on our universe."

"You can't expect to walk all the way to the center," Demetrius radioed. "It would take weeks."

He was right, but now wasn't the moment to worry about it. Escaping the graviton rays about to come mattered more than plans and high ideals. I knew the beams were coming because it was obvious. It's what I would do.

Nor was I wrong. We fought another battle, this time with twice the number of tentacle-waving Kargs. Just like the first fight, we stood in place to pin them down and maneuvered to flank them from up, down and all around. The slaughter had barely finished when the first graviton ray burrowed into one of the flanking mingans, destroying three hundred troopers in puffs of vapor.

Panic might have finished us if there had been any Karg soldiers left. Fortunately, they lay smoking on the floors, leaking blood. I shouted at troopers. I raved at my commanders, and Demetrius found another hatch down.

We fled into it, causing jams at times. Demetrius used his big body, crashing into troopers, hurling them out of the way. Finally, I reached the spot. Did my voice help? Troopers were used to obeying me. I brought a semblance of order to the traffic jam, and we soon all plunged deeper into the portal planet.

We fled down circular corridors a giant snake might have used. We passed sewage, steam, computers, I think, lights, walked across thin arches with a bottomless pit below.

"If we could fly down..." N7 said.

"Do you have a flyer?" I asked.

We tiptoed across the narrow walkways, joining the others. In a word, several words, we outraced the depth of the graviton rays. That's what I'd been hoping for. The Kargs needed the portal planet. That meant they had to be careful how powerful of a beam they shot down at us.

Still, how many Earth troopers had survived the rays sweeping the surface? At this point, I had no idea. As far as I knew, we were the last ones left. My group had already been whittled down to a little more than three thousand men and women. Waiting Karg soldiers, planetary cannons and rays likely meant they had already slaughtered millions of us; well, millions of Lokhars, at least.

"This is hopeless," Rollo said a few minutes later, as he jogged down a pleochroic corridor of intense colors. Masses of troopers ran all around him.

"No," I told him. "We have hope."

He shook his head. "*You're* hopeless, Creed. You don't know when you're beaten. What chance do we have? Soon, the planet will be swarming with Kargs chasing us, and we have to get to the *center* of a *world*?"

"Yeah," I said. "That's why we need to find a spot to rest."

"Rest and do what?" Rollo asked.

I turned, starting at Ella. She still clutched the small Forerunner artifact in her ammo bag. It reminded me of a female chimpanzee and her baby. Is that what the relic had become to Ella?

"We need to figure out how to communicate with that thing," I whispered. "It might know stuff about this planet that no one else does."

"Do you think so?" Rollo asked, with hope tingeing his voice.

"I most certainly do," I said.

-25-

Our four bleeding mingans loped through subterranean corridors fit for giant snakes a block in diameter. Sometimes, brilliant lighting from embedded ceiling fixtures polarized our visors. Sometimes, darkness held sway and we switched on our helmet lamps.

I imagine that high above the planet the Karg Imperium shuddered with dread and horror. The impossible had happened. Alien life forms—us—had reached the surface and burrowed into it. The planet powered the portal. If we could reach the center, we could turn it off, and trillions of Kargs would forever remain stuck in their shrinking space-time continuum to die by supermassive black hole.

Abaddon had told us we couldn't even reach this far. By their numbers and the odds, we shouldn't have been able to do it. Now the Kargs would have to attack with fierce desperation to make good on their leader's failed boast.

Static blanketed all but the nearest communications. I had no idea if Lokhar legionaries still lived. Certainly, any land tanks would be smoldering wrecks by now. Could less than four thousand assault troopers be the extent of our numbers? I didn't want to dwell on that.

The fact was this was a death march without mercy or pity. You had to keep up or die. At times, a wounded trooper collapsed onto his butt to rest or an exhausted soldier slumped against a metal wall. Most of those we never saw again. At other times, distant, echoing battle sounds penetrated to us, and we'd hear snatches of radio chatter.

"There are others of us that are still alive," Rollo told me.

This was good to know.

By this time, we'd made it a half a kilometer underground. That was a long way already, but just a fraction of how far we needed to go. It should have gotten hotter, at least by Earth physics. The deeper one went in the Earth, the hotter it became. Did giant gravity plates change the equation in this place? I imagined so, or some similar technological reason.

"Commander," Demetrius radioed me. He was point man. "My people are badly fatigued. We need to rest before everyone collapses."

My throat burned and my sides ached. I wanted to stop as badly as the next person did. The idea of avenging Kargs following us had kept me going. But the SAS man knew his stuff.

"All right," I radioed my mingan leaders. "We're going to take five and try to recoup some strength."

In our curving, downward-slanting corridor, Rollo gave the order to his people. We practically all fell down as if knockout gas had hit us. Everyone wore symbiotic suits and air-converters and bulky ammo-packs. Black forms lay on metal floors. It felt glorious to rest, and I closed my eyes.

Maybe Ella should have used this time to try to communicate with the artifact. She was too fatigued just like the rest of us. It could have been she went to sleep as many of us did.

"Commander!" Dmitri shouted into my headphones.

I snapped up to a sitting position. There must have been three hundred troopers in sight of my helmet lamp. I was about to ask what the problem was—

A stabbing red light appeared on my HUD. It was a graviton ray as thick as a giant stanchion poking nail-like into metal and through layers upon layers of planetary decking. This was video-fed from a nearby trooper several levels above me. I immediately realized what I saw.

The graviton ray quit beaming as glowing hot globs of dripping metal cooled. Our scout must have maneuvered a drone eye above the slags of metal to look up the hole created by the giant drill. The drone showed space, and then space darkened as a tube or pod plunged into the hole. The pod slammed down like a shotgun shell into a chamber. It clanged against the end corridor where the scout had set up his post.

Seconds later, the pod's sides exploded, and out boiled a squad of Karg infantry with their metallic tentacles. The scout had time to lift his rifle into firing position before exploding bullets tore holes in his bio-suit. His flesh rained, and the scout died. Seconds later, so did his camera.

The battle had just entered phase two of our Armageddon. The nightmare was truly beginning for us.

In a thrice, the mingans rose, and we ran away from the attacking Kargs. While at full strength, we learned, a human could outrun a Karg fighting-creature. They had the stamina, though, and it was clear they would eventually run us down. Therefore, I planned as I sprinted. Soon, I coordinated our flight, and we set up a now classic Karg-killing ambush: one group stayed in place, fixing the enemy. The rest maneuvered to hit the flanks and hit the bottom and sometimes the top of the enemy formation.

The firefight fatigued us again, but afterward, we kept descending into the planet.

We passed through cube-shaped chambers bigger than a Macy's store. There, strange lights played along the walls and titanic equipment shined as if it was a vast jewelry display. The worst were eerie voices that turned into heavenly song. Once, as I scaled down pieces of brilliant equipment in order to get to the next floor, a ghostly apparition appeared—a hologram, I'd like to think. But the thing looked at me with yellow eyes that raged like a sun. It seemed to know what we were doing, yet it appeared indifferent to our actions. What was its shape? I seemed to know for a moment—snakelike with hundreds of centipede legs—but there was confusion in my brain and I couldn't be sure. The ghostly holoimage terrified me. I wanted to get away from it and its knowing eyes. So I did something stupid. I pushed off and plunged thirty meters to the bottom.

The floor rushed up. I saw a Karg rifle lying there in my way. I tried to shift. Then I landed with a crash, rolling, and heard other thudding troopers alighting beside me. Several people busted legs. That didn't happen to me, but the soles of my feet hurt worse than the time I'd kicked a tree. Yeah, I did that as a kid. A branch had broken and I'd fallen out of it. Getting up, I'd kicked the damned trunk as hard as I could. I think I'd been ten years old at the time. I learned right there it was stupid to try to hurt inanimate objects, and I'd limped for days.

I got up and limped away now. A few troopers helped those with broken legs as the symbiotic suits adjusted. We weren't going to willingly leave anyone behind.

We fought, we fled, and at strategic intervals, we turned at bay to kill our fastest pursuers. How long did that go on? I'd say for five hours, solid. As I've said before, we used Karg weaponry against our enemies. We saved our Bahnkouvs for later. I got used to firing the Karg rifles and hosing enemy down with Karg machine guns. We used their sonic grenades against them and watched flesh melt from metal frames.

What were these things? Were they robots, cyborgs or some new invention from a different universe? The answer was I didn't know.

Our numbers kept dwindling, though. We must have been down to two thousand by then. The enemy's attrition tactics would have finished us in another few hours, until two things changed the dynamics of the situation.

First, a mixed band of Lokhars and humans with Doctor Sant stumbled into us. That brought our numbers back up to four thousand troopers and maybe five hundred Lokhar legionaries.

We didn't have time or the strength to slap backs and congratulate each other. Another pod-drop of Kargs pushed against our rear ranks.

"This isn't working," Demetrius told me via radio. "We can't gain any separation from them."

He was right. We'd been at this for hours. I reeled from exhaustion. It had become hotter down here. We'd made it a kilometer and a half or so underground, maybe a little more. We'd never reach the center of the planet this way.

I knew the Kargs had an endless supply of the tentacle freaks to throw at us. It would just be a matter of wearing us down long enough. I was surprised they weren't ahead of us.

Maybe Abaddon hadn't trusted his soldier-creatures *in* the planet before this, just on its surface. Maybe this place was holy to them in ways we couldn't understand. The Kargs should have already been down here, but they weren't, and that's what gave us a chance.

"What do you suggest?" I asked the SAS man.

"I never did like running much," Demetrius said. "It always was the worst part of the training. Sometimes, I wanted to strangle the sergeants leading us up hill and down. You'd better believe this. I'm not going to end my life puking my guts out with sweat dripping down my eyes. I've had enough of this. I don't know how it happened, but my mingan is facing the Kargs right now."

We'd maneuvered, run and turned at bay so many times, that our point mingan had become our rear-guard mingan.

"We can set up another ambush," I said.

"I'm telling you to forget about that," Demetrius said angrily. "You know, Creed, I always wanted to kick your ass. Now that I have these fibers in me, I know I could knock you up one side and down another. But I'm never going to get the chance."

"Listen—" I said.

"No," Demetrius said. "You listen to me...sir. We're going to stay right here. We're loaded up on their weaponry, and we're going to kill Kargs until we die in place. You ever heard of the Spartans?"

I felt a constriction in my throat. I understood his idea, and it was the right one. We needed separation from the enemy, and we needed time for Ella to communicate with her relic. Still, to let Demetrius do this for us...

"I'm going to stay with—" I said.

"Belay that, Creed," Demetrius said, sounding angrier by the moment. Then his voice softened. "You tell Diana what happened to me. She'll want to know."

I wanted to tell him all kinds of things. *Greater love has no man than this: that he lays down his life for his friends.* What Demetrius was doing...

"Yeah," I whispered. "I'll tell her."

263

"You'd better," Demetrius said. "Now I have to go. The Kargs are coming. I can hear the echo of their metal legs clicking against the floors. I'm going to be busy for the rest of my life."

I squeezed my eyes together, shook my head, and I bellowed at my troopers to run. We needed to get separation, and then it was time to see if we still had a chance to do this.

We ran, we endured and cramps hit over half the troops. Finally, in one of the giant cube areas—this one made of a shimmering mirrored surface—my zagun and I, together with Ella, collapsed in exhaustion.

Others camped around us in various corridors and substructures. It daunted me to think of the entire metal planet honeycombed like this. There had to be engine areas, fuel depots and who knew what else. I sipped concentrated fluids, gulped vitamins and allowed the suit to stim me. Even then, I almost found it impossible to keep my eyes open. To lay on my side and rest would be glorious.

None of us could lie on our back because of the bulky ammo-packs and equipment we carried. A lot of that was life support, and most of that was breathing apparatus. In the end, I lay on my side like many others and closed my heavy eyes. After fifteen perfect minutes, I forced myself to a sitting position. I shook Ella awake.

"Leave me alone," she muttered.

"Nope," I said, in as cheery a voice as I could summon. "You picked yourself some time ago. Now we talk to the relic."

"Go away," she said in a raw voice.

"Ella, don't you want to know what this really is?"

"Futility," she said.

"I know you're curious. You need to know about the Kargs, the portal and Forerunners."

"I just want to sleep."

"Perchance to dream?" I asked.

"What?"

"Let's do this, Timoshenko. Let's awaken the ancient spirit of inquiry."

"Has anyone ever told you that you're a pain in the ass?"

264

"Pretty much everyone I've met says that to me sooner or later," I said. "Why do you think that is?"

Ella groaned as she dragged herself to a cross-legged position. She did it while clutching the bagged artifact. It didn't look like she could let it go of it even if she wanted to.

"I hate this place," she said. "I hate this chamber. Why did the Forerunners make this planet?"

"Ask your little relic," I suggested.

Hesitantly at first, she grasped the zipper and zipped open the ammo bag. Then she withdrew the precious item. Smaller than I remembered, it was about the size of a bowling ball, although it didn't seem to be as heavy. I recalled the adept releasing the artifact and watching it hover. Had the relic done that for him as a favor? I wished we'd brought the old Lokhar with us. I was more curious than ever how Ella had taken it from him. Belatedly, I glanced around. Fortunately, there weren't any powered-armor Lokhars in our midst. They might believe it was heresy for a human to hold Orange Tamika's greatest holy object.

Ella glanced at me.

All I saw was the polarized surface of her visor and me staring at her in reflection. She likely saw a similar image off my visor. That reminded me of the Apollo astronauts bouncing around on the Moon. I'd seen old video of that in my dad's living room.

"Talk to the thing," I suggested.

"I already tried that earlier," Ella admitted. "Nothing happened."

"Shake it."

"It's been shaken like mad for some time," she said.

"Give it to me then," I said.

Ella shook her head and clutched the round or oval, rather, artifact against her chest. "No," she said.

This was interesting. "Why not, Ella? Can't you let it go, or don't you want to let it go?"

"Of course I can let it go," she said mulishly.

"Then do it."

She hesitated before saying, "I don't want to."

I laughed hoarsely. I sounded like a sleepy smoker with pneumonia. I felt as powerful as one, too, which was to say as weak as a baby. Did the Kargs use radar, or what passed for radar, as they searched for us? Maybe. That meant we couldn't stay here for long. But the truth was that we needed something better than our legs. Walking to the center of the planet wasn't going to win us this war.

"We have to do something now," I told Ella.

"I'm open to suggestions," she said.

"Hold it up," I said.

"I'm not giving it to you, Commander, and that's final."

"I'm not suggesting you do," I said. "I want you to hold it up so I can address it."

"I don't know…"

I thought of something then—a light bulb moment—and if I were right, that would answer some interesting questions for me. "Do you feel as if the relic has been playing tricks on your mind?" I asked.

Ella cocked her helmet. "What are you suggesting?"

"I don't know. That you have a mental attachment with it maybe."

"Yes," she said. "That is an interesting idea. Are you suggesting the artifact might have done that to the old Lokhar a long time ago?"

"Hold up the relic, Ella. Quit stalling. Let me talk to it."

"Wait a minute," she said. "I'll talk to it. Turn around first."

I laughed again. "Are you serious? Why should I turn around?"

"This is a private affair. It is…sacred."

My eyes widened. That didn't sound like Ella. Did the crazy Forerunner relic have control of her in some nefarious manner? I loathed the idea. Ella was one my troopers, one of the hardcore who had made it out of Claath's clutches. I'd hate to see some other alien get hold of her mind, even if that alien was a Forerunner artifact.

I grunted as I put my hands on the floor and pushed up to my feet. "Sure, Ella," I said. "You talk to your friend." Turning, I said, "Dmitri, Rollo, where are you?"

Two hands went up among the crowd of troopers littering the floor.

Then I realized their two mingans were assembled—or crashed prone—together. Chan's mingan made up the rest of us, and she had scouted ahead.

There was nothing between the hunting Kargs and us except metal and space. I had to believe that Demetrius's mingan had sold their lives as dearly as possible already.

My two leaders converged on me. Rollo looked more like a gorilla than ever as he limped, the beefy simian warrior. A wet patch of bio-suit over his heart showed where it healed.

"What's up, Creed?" Rollo asked.

"Switch to a private channel," I told them. "Okay," I said, once they'd done so. "I think something fishy is going on with Ella and her Forerunner artifact."

"Ella Timoshenko?" Dmitri asked.

I nodded. "Ella took the artifact from the Lokhar adept," I said, quickly filling in Rollo and Dmitri on what I thought had happened.

The Cossack whistled, and he aimed his visor at Ella. I grabbed Dmitri by the arm and turned him away from her.

"The relic might have done something to Ella's mind," I said. "That makes more sense than her playing the acolyte these past weeks. You know, I wonder if the old adept knew about the artifact's power—if I'm right about this, anyway. Ulmoc played along with us, right. He made a lot less fuss over the situation than he should have. Maybe Ulmoc did that because the relic forced him into it. Yeah…maybe that's how each Forerunner priest got hold of the artifact—the thing told the newbie to take it from the oldster."

"You're jumping to a lot of conclusions," Rollo said.

"I know it," I said. "Ella is acting too strangely, though, and we've plum run out of time. I called you two because you're going to saunter over there and grab her arms. Haul her to her feet and don't let her struggle free. Then pry her arms apart so she has to let go of the relic."

"Ella will not cooperate with that," Dmitri said.

"Which is why I picked you two," I said. "You hold her, even if she's kicking and screaming. I'm going to take the artifact from her."

"If what you suggest is true," Rollo said. "The relic might not like that and react against us."

"Good point," I said, thinking hard. I might have to persuade an ancient…thing to play ball with us. Hmm…I had an idea or two. "Okay. Go over there and get ready to grab her. I'm going to get N7. We may need his analysis. Are you ready?"

"I don't like this," Rollo said uneasily.

"We don't have time to think of something more elegant," I said. "Besides, I'm not about to let Demetrius's sacrifice go in vain."

"What's that mean?" Rollo asked.

"Hey," I told Rollo. "How about you just do what I tell you. We don't have time for twenty questions."

Rollo stiffened, but he nodded. The two of them began ambling toward Ella.

"N7," I radioed.

The android pushed off a brilliantly lit wall and strode toward me. He and I spoke on a private channel. I told him my suspicions and my plan.

"That is logically reasoned," N7 said. "Ella would not normally spend so much time with a priest. Nor do I believe she would murder him to steal his artifact. Yet I don't believe you have thought through the ramifications of your suspicion."

"What do you mean?" I asked.

"If the relic is sentient, as you suggest, it might have ulterior motives. Given its origin, those motives might oppose ours."

"You're right," I said. "What do you suggest?"

"That you expect anything," N7 said. "Logically, you should have a fallback position or a way to deal with Forerunner surprises."

Within my helmet, I squinted. I wondered then about our android. Might Claath have planted him long ago upon us? That struck me as inconceivable. Why would Claath have given us N7, who'd proven instrumental in our escaping Jelk service? Still…

"N7," I said.

He stood there waiting.

"Do you believe I should trust you?"

N7 didn't move a muscle. Finally, he asked, "After all this time, why would you suspect my loyalty?"

I told him my suspicions.

"You have a devious mind," N7 said. "Perhaps a man in your position needs that. I do not feel disloyalty toward you, although I do sense emotional anger in me toward you at this point."

"The mind's a funny animal," I said.

"There is nothing humorous about you," N7 said. "Indeed, I find you to be the most murderous individual I have ever met."

"I'm just saying: if you feel disloyalty toward us or me in particular, I want you to inform me the second such emotions surface."

"That is illogical," N7 said.

"If you want us to treat you more than a machine, you're going to start to have acting human."

"I believe you have a phrase for that: 'Heaven forbid I act more like you.'"

"Right," I said. "Are you ready?"

"Time is limited," N7 said. "So this is as ready as I will likely ever be."

Androids obviously had feelings, and I seemed to have hurt N7's. Maybe if I'd been feeling better—more rested—I would have acted with more grace. When I got tired, I didn't have the same smoothness.

In any case, the two of us started for Ella and her Forerunner relic.

26

The regular Ella would have noticed two thugs like Rollo and Dmitri trying to saunter innocently behind her. Our present Ella had wrapped her arms around the artifact, aiming her visor at it.

The oval object was steel-colored but seemed to be constructed of ceramic material. I moved closer, but in front of her. Chinning the zoom on my HUD, I studied the artifact in detail. It had hairline grooves and what might have been sunken divots. Parts of it seemed glassy instead of ceramic and had tiny thumbnail-sized protrusions. How old was this thing? Thousands of years, tens of thousands or could it even be a million years old? Age didn't matter now though did it?

"Okay," I radioed.

Ella looked up, and I heard her chin on her link.

Dmitri moved first. He bent down and grabbed an arm.

Ella twisted around toward him. "What are you doing?" she asked.

Rollo belatedly moved, grabbing the other arm.

"Hey," Ella said. "Let go of me."

The two bruisers did the opposite, tightening their hold and lifting her upright. She kicked, shouted and tried to keep hold of the artifact.

Dmitri wrenched her arm. Rollo did the same with her right.

"No," Ella shouted. "You don't understand. Let go of me before—"

The two troopers ripped her hands free of the oblong globe. The artifact should have dropped and hit the deck. Instead, it glowed faintly, and it floated in place.

"Release me before it's too late," Ella panted.

I aimed a heavy caliber Karg rifle at the object. I chinned on my outer speakers. "If you harm my soldiers," I said, "I'm going to fire at you at point-blank range. I don't know if these bullets can gouge your surface or not, but do you really want to find out?"

The glow around the artifact lessened. The thing swiveled, and I felt heat then. Was it scanning me?

"Commander," Ella said. "You don't know what—"

"Shut up," I told her. "You had your chance. Now it's my turn. Keep a good grip on her arms."

Dmitri nodded.

N7 flanked me, and he, too, aimed a heavy caliber rifle at the object.

Troopers sat up, watching. The artifact glowed lightly and it floated, dipping down a few inches and rising back up. Finally, it drifted closer toward me.

I didn't like the idea of something thousands of years old at its youngest picking out me to examine. More than ever, I wondered about the Forerunners. I didn't think of them as angels anymore, but they were the First Ones. That implied extra knowledge or power. Why had they left our area of the galaxy? Where had they gone? What was this metal planet for and why did the bigger Forerunner object fit into the center like a hand in a gauntlet?

Questions, questions, questions—traveling through a hell-universe had that effect on me.

Then, high-speed alien speech emanated from the floating object.

"What's its saying, Ella?" I asked.

"How should I know?" she complained. "I don't know High Speech."

"Did it do something to your mind?" I asked.

"No," she said, sounding indignant.

"Why did you block our recording or even seeing into the chamber when the Lokhar showed you to her?" I asked the relic.

"It's not going to answer you," Ella said. "Believe me. I've been trying to get it to answer for some time. It doesn't understand us."

I didn't believe that anymore. "This is what we call a standoff," I told the artifact. "But I have no more time. The Kargs are going to finish us off long before we can reach the center. That means we lose. Well, you know what? You're going to lose too then because I'm going to blow you to pieces first."

Lights flashed in the object. Did that mean it was thinking or computing, or doing whatever an alien machine had to? I noticed a slot slid up, and a lens the size of my thumbnail, an optical device, appeared and glowed red.

"Commander Creed," the relic said flawlessly.

Ella gasped. Maybe hearing the thing talk surprised Dmitri and Rollo, too. Ella tore her arms free, and she lunged for the artifact, to hold it, I imagine.

A wavering light flowed outward from the floating ball. The pink light encompassed Ella, took in Rollo and Dmitri and then it extended to the entire cube-shaped chamber. Naturally, that included me, too, and the rest of the troopers.

"Stop it!" I shouted, taking two steps closer and butting the barrel of my rifle against the relic, knocking it backward.

The thing didn't stop, though.

I hated bluffing, and so I seldom did. If I gave a threat, I tried to follow through. Therefore, I pulled the trigger. The rifle recoiled in my hands, and an exploding Karg bullet smashed against the artifact. That blew it farther back, but nothing chipped from it or rattled loose.

Ella screamed.

I pulled the trigger again, blasting the relic back a little more. Ella reached me then, and she swung at my head. I ducked, and I swung the rifle in a short and brutal arc, using the butt to slam against her stomach. It knocked the scientist off her feet onto the floor.

"Grab her!" I shouted. "And don't let go of her this time."

272

Everyone but for Ella and N7 stood there. Perhaps the others were caught in the pink light. The android moved fast as Ella climbed to her feet. In his cyber-armor, he looped his arms around hers, jerking them back. She struggled, and with her neuro-fibers, steroid-enhanced strength and bio-suit, she almost broke free. Almost, but N7 held her.

I aimed at the object once more. A darker pink ray now emanated from it. That was the final straw to break the donkey's back, as they say, and I was all out of patience. Three times, I fired—BOOM, BOOM, BOOM. A piece of the object now chipped off and fell to the deck.

Ella moaned in horror.

I grinned nastily in my helmet. I could obliterate this thing if I had to. That was good to know. "I'm going to destroy you unless you turn off that wide beam!" I shouted. "If you think I'm playing, kept it up."

Abruptly, the pink light stopped shining, and the relic hovered in place, dipping and rising slightly. Smoke drifted from the barrel of my rifle. I found myself gripping it with manic strength.

"This is unwarranted," the relic said in its flawless voice. "You should have succumbed to the mind ray."

Then it hit me, the implications. The Saurian storm troopers under Jelk control had used a pink mind-ray like that on us Earthers when they'd landed that first alien-visiting day. Why hadn't this one worked on me? It might have been my polarized visor along with sheer cussedness on my part. Maybe our battle technology had trumped Forerunner tech…if that's what the pink ray was. Or maybe this thing was a piece of Jelk technology.

"You're not a Forerunner artifact," I said.

"I fail to see what has caused you to reach your false conclusion," the relic said.

"For one thing, your little ploy failed just now against us."

"Ah, yes," the artifact said, "I understand your error. It is quite common. You grant products of the First Ones magical powers. I have observed this phenomenon before, and I must inform you that it is a category error."

I blinked several times. I'm not sure what I'd expected from the relic, but not this. "You used your mind ray on Ella before, haven't you?" I asked.

"It is time to make one fact clear. I do not accept your legitimacy to interrogate me."

"Fair enough," I said. "Do you mind telling me what you do consider legitimate?"

The relic hovered up and down as lights flashed. "You must return me to…to yonder female."

"She has a name."

"Your tone implies anger. Why are you angry because I referred to her status?"

Status? What was the relic talking about? "It's not her status," I said, "but her sex."

"Yes… You are correct. I used an improper word."

I liked this less and less. I'd expected the Forerunner object to act without error. It seemed to be screwing up. I'd thought the First Ones—ah, never mind. Maybe like most legends, the Forerunners were overrated and overhyped.

"Now that you're out in the open among us," I said, "how about you give me a name. I'm tired of thinking of you as 'it' or 'object' or 'artifact.'"

"What name would you like?" the relic asked.

"What do you want me to call you?" I asked. "Or are you just a machine?"

"Your symbiotic suit is a machine, yet it is alive."

"No one is arguing that," I said.

"I am not alive as your suit lives," the artifact said, "yet I am more than a simple machine. I am a long-term receptor."

"A receptor of souls?" I asked.

"What a quaint notion," the relic said. "Your superstitions are overpowering your mental faculties. I am not magical nor am I a supernatural manifestation. I am a receptor, an imprinter. The last engrams were of SRT 2000. She faded fifty-three cycles ago, imploring me to implement the Eraser Procedure."

"What does that mean?"

"You are of insufficient clearance for me to elaborate."

"So…I should call you SRT 2000?" I asked.

"Call me EP. It is more elegant."

"Call you Eraser Procedure?"

"No. Call me EP."

I nodded. This wasn't anything like I'd expected. "Let me ask you a question. Were the First Ones angels?"

"Elaborate please."

"Did they come from the Creator?" I asked.

"You wish to engage in cosmological philosophy when the fate of your universe hangs in the balance?" EP asked. "That is more than odd. It strikes me as addled."

"All right, you have a point. You do realize the present situation then?"

"The Kargs are about to annihilate the last of you, yes. Once they do, I will implement the Eraser Procedure."

"What is that? Oh, right, we don't have clearance. But you know what, since we're all going to die, what does it hurt if you tell us?"

"Hmm," EP said, "I concede you the point. After your demise, I will fuse what you refer to as the Altair Object into its present location so all Karg vessels can successfully transfer into hyperspace. Afterward, I will open a way to your universe to facilitate the Karg conquest."

I felt myself frowning harder than ever. "Wait a minute," I said. "Are you telling me that SRT 2000 told you to erase all life in *our* universe? That after the fact she's going to use the Kargs to commit ultimate genocide?"

The artifact bobbed up and down. "I will run a diagnostic on myself. There does seem to be an implied error." The object flashed, rose higher still—

I aimed my rifle at it. If EP went any higher, I believed he would be trying to escape. I wasn't going to let that happen, especially not after what the relic had just told me.

"I see the problem," the artifact said. "You damaged several processing centers with your shots. No. The Eraser Procedure regards the Kargs, not life in your space-time continuum. I'm glad you spoke up. I would have made a terrible error otherwise."

"Isn't *our* universe *yours* as well?" I asked.

"I tire of this cross examination," EP said. "It is time to initiate a temporary shutdown."

"Come down here with us," I said, "or I'll add to your confusion." I sighted along the barrel, putting the relic in my sights to emphasize the point.

"That is a threatening reference."

"You bet it is," I said.

Slowly, the object lowered. As it did, N7 stepped up to me.

"Commander," the android radioed on a closed link. "I am beginning to suspect the imprinter has sustained heavy damage due to long years of running and because of your shots."

"I think you might be right," I said.

"It might be best to destroy the relic with sustained fire," N7 said. "I believe it is acting irrationally and is therefore untrustworthy."

It seemed as if First Ones equipment worked under the same laws of entropy as everything else did. Even the universe ran down over time. Why would one expect even perfectly made equipment to remain in top shape after thousands of years or tens of thousands of years? EP was malfunctioning, and the thing was supposed to be the key to our survival. Yet on a whim, it had planned to destroy our universe. How many wrong decisions had the artifact made through its long life? Could it even answer correctly about the past? My guess was that some of the answers were truthful and others false. Since we had no way of knowing which were which…its historical anecdotes might be more harmful than useful.

"We want to reach the center of the planet," I said. "Can you help us get there?"

"I believe you desire to leave the planet in particular and hyperspace in general," the relic said.

"We do," I said.

"If you use the Altair Object as your transporter, it will cease powering the portal. That will strand the majority of the Kargs in their dying universe."

"That's the idea," I said.

"I cannot aid you in such an endeavor," EP said. "SRT 2000 loved all life, not just her species."

"Then why did she tell you to initiate the Eraser Procedure?" I asked.

The artifact hovered without answering.

"May I ask you a question?" N7 said.

"Since I do not have the answer to Commander Creed's question," EP said, "nor do I desire to rationalize the reason, I would be delighted."

I scowled. The artifact was a freak as far as I was concerned. We had to get down to the center now. Talking with EP was wasting precious time.

"Since you have committed several errors these past few minutes," N7 said, "could it be possible you have made more errors?"

"That is logically deduced," EP said. "I believe the answer is yes."

"Could it be that you are in error that SRT 2000 told you to initiate the Eraser Procedure?"

"Yes, it is possible," EP said.

"Might it even be likely?" N7 asked.

"Could you elaborate your reasoning?"

"Certainly," N7 said. "Since SRT 2000 loved all life, it is unreasonable she ordered the Eraser Procedure."

I laughed bleakly. "If EP is in error about that, the thing might be in error regarding her engrams. Maybe SRT 2000 deplored or hated all life. How do we know that anything EP says is correct? After all its years in existence—"

"And your bullets just now," EP added. "That was a foolishly unwarranted attack."

I scowled. "As far as I can see, EP is useless to us. The Kargs are coming and this freak is talking our ear off saying nothing. We have to leave."

"I resent your implications," EP told me.

"So what?" I asked. "You're just a machine. Who cares what you think?"

"To begin with," the relic said, "I care. Moreover, I can speed your descent into the planet. I can unlock the defenses around the Altair Object and I can help chose the proper destination in your universe."

I realized then the proper way to deal with EP. The relic was like a genie in an Arabian Nights tale. Only our genie didn't have it altogether. He was addled like an old geezer who had guzzled too much whiskey his whole life. He was supposed to be a flawless Forerunner artifact, and likely, EP did know a lot. But one would have to use a roundabout method to get the artifact to do what one wanted. In other words, I had to trick our genie into helping us.

"Bah," I said. "You can't do jack. All you do is jaw our ears off."

"Observe then if you will," EP said. Machine-fast streams of High Speech, I presume, proceeded from it.

For a moment, nothing happened. Then the walls of our cube-chamber glowed more brightly. A window at head-level appeared. Running purple lights blinked around it. Then a slowly twisting, turning 3-D map appeared in the window, showing the upper planet, a honeycomb of chambers, corridors, processing areas and substructures, a veritable puzzle.

I glanced at Rollo. He shrugged his thick shoulders.

"Can you expand the map?" I asked EP.

More High Speech occurred.

The map expanded to three times its size, and the purple running lights vanished.

"Let's localize this to our area," I said. "And have the...wall keep the map still so I can study it."

"The map is empty," Rollo said.

"Make Lokhar legionaries and assault troopers blue," I said.

A few blue dots appeared within the 3-D map.

"Make the Kargs red," I said.

A host of red dots and red *blobs* moved downward, each toward a different blue concentration.

"Show me to scale our portion of the near surface compared to the center of the planet."

The artifact spoke faster. The wall-picture changed until the surface area was a tiny slice. We had a terribly long way to go to reach the Altair Object.

"Are there any transportation systems to take us to the center faster?" I asked.

"Do you wish for flyers or tube-train systems?" EP asked.

"Show me both, and the nearest stations or garages to them," I said.

The artifact did as requested.

"Look," N7 said, pointing at the map. "Kargs approach the nearest tube-train station." A large blob of red converged on the station between our blue dot and them.

"Are Kargs using tube-trains for travel?" I asked.

"Yes," EP said. "They are traveling en masse to the center, but that is on the other side of the planet, not here."

I swore, and I made an instant decision. "Right. That means we have to beat our Kargs to the tube-train. Then we have to hustle down faster than the aliens."

"Flyers would be more dangerous but quicker," EP pointed out.

"Yeah?" I asked. "How so?"

"You could use the substructures to descend at speed," EP said.

"How many can the flyers hold altogether?"

"Twenty people," EP said.

"We'll use the tube-train," I said. I wanted to win the race. I also wanted to take as many troopers with me as possible. We might have a lot of fighting left to do in the center of the planet.

"Do you mind if we bag you again?" I asked.

"It would save me energy," EP said. "That was why I wanted to implement a temporary shutdown. But I would insist that Ella carry me."

"First answer me this," I said. "Did you use the pink ray on her some time ago?"

"You must realize that I did," EP said. "It is why I trust her."

"Ella?" I asked.

"I want to be mad about that," she said, "but it's like there's a block in my mind against getting angry at the artifact."

"Ella will carry you," I said. I didn't add that N7 would be watching her and the relic's every move.

"Then I consent," EP said. "And I suggest you hurry. The Kargs are coming down in ever-increasing numbers."

27

For a moment, I studied the operational situation on the wall. By estimating our own blue dot and the extent of other blue ones on the map, I'd say a quarter million of the good guys had made it into the tunnels, roughly two hundred and fifty thousand. By far the majority of those were Lokhar legionaries. Maybe one eighth were assault troopers. That meant thirty thousand Earthmen and women were in the planet's subterranean structures.

According to the map, the Kargs must have something like ten times our numbers, and that was just on this side of the planet. According to EP, more aliens raced to the center from the other side.

Unfortunately, I didn't have any way to communicate with the other friendlies. Our radio waves only worked a short distance in the substructures. We couldn't coordinate our assault in other words. It galled me.

In any case, it was time to hit the tube-train station. We climbed back up the tunnels. The underground corridors and chambers often groaned and creaked with noise. Distant clangs and hisses told us the Kargs were up to something.

After witnessing the hatching worlds in the Karg universe, I realized the enemy was used to subterranean fighting, or burrowing, at least. They must have old-time science fiction tunneling vehicles. My gut tightened as we headed back up. I'd have liked to send scouts first to check the lay of the land and pinpoint enemy concentrations. We simply lacked the time, and had to trust our luck or our ability to fight through anything.

Instead of scouts, I sectioned us off by zaguns, one hundred trooper units. We'd do this like giant squads, giving each other overwatch fire as we surged ahead by sections through parallel corridors.

The clangs, the hisses, the clicks of marching Kargs echoed and grew closer. The only thing I smelled inside my helmet was my stale sweat and the sweeter aroma the bio-suit gave off after extended use.

We traveled through dark corridors some of the time and came to bigger lit ones later. These corridors were double the width in diameter of previous ones.

I wanted to un-bag EP and ask him why these were larger, and what function had they served? Probably, the artifact wouldn't know or had lost the data, but it might have been worth asking.

"Kargs!" a trooper shouted.

The enemy boiled at us from side apertures, surprising us as if they were Apaches rising out of the dirt at our feet. Like subway covers, openings appeared on the right-hand wall. Crazy, they were like giant portholes in a ship. Metal clanged down onto the deck. From their various locations, tentacle-soldiers aimed and fired a volley from about twenty feet up. They cut down some troopers, while symbiotic armor saved the rest. As one, we lifted our Karg weaponry and returned a devastating salvo. Shot-up aliens rained out of the porthole-like openings. The exploding bullets were particular deadly against them. More Kargs kept showing up, though, replacing the fallen. The new openings acted like PEZ dispensers, always pushing another alien forward.

We kept firing at the fresh Kargs, making them tumble, too. The margin of speed went to us, and we slaughtered them indeed like lemmings. They kept appearing, appearing and appearing and falling, falling, falling. Even for Kargs, this was an appalling loss, as they rained onto the bottom of the larger corridor, soon piling up. A few injured aliens must have fallen behind the pile, and they still possessed grim vitality. The things didn't die easily. Those few crawled to the top of the grisly heap. One or two got off a surprise shot.

A bullet exploded against my chest, knocking me backward as bio-suit chunks rained off. An oily vicious liquid immediately oozed there, like blood to a wound. It coagulated fast, beginning to harden. For those precious seconds, though, another shot would open my suit to the alien atmosphere, and kill me. I twisted sideways to present a narrower target, and I hosed bullets into the Karg pile, exploding chunks of dead ones and nailing the sniper before he got off his next shot.

Thereafter, several troopers had corpse duty, patrolling and killing the Kargs who looked dead.

I should have backed off until my suit fully healed. Instead, I held my location, and I felt like an African big game hunter of the Nineteenth century. The large caliber rifle repeatedly bucked against my shoulder. When it clicked empty, I tossed it aside and accepted another from a trooper.

A few of our soldiers looted the corpses for extra ammo and rifles. We'd been robbing the dead for hours now and had become expert at it.

I learned to shoot for the neck. Even without a head, a Karg could still move and react. Without a neck, they died the final death. Don't ask me why. That's just the way it worked.

"We'll never make it to the tube-train like this," Rollo radioed on the command channel.

I glanced down the big tunnel, and I looked up as another Karg appeared at my targeted porthole. BOOM-BOOM, my twenty-first alien tumbled out of the opening to thud onto the pile.

Finally, that seemed to be it. For this second, no more Kargs appeared up there. We'd taken losses, of course. Despite our battle superiority, they whittled us down a trooper at a time.

"Into those openings," I said. "We'll backtrack and surprise their assembly area."

"Where do those sub-tunnels go?" Rollo asked.

"We'll find out," I said.

"I don't know, Creed. That's a long shot."

"Go," I said, and I raced to the dead Kargs, climbed up the twisted dead, jumped and grabbed the lip of the opening. I hoisted up by arm strength and crawled into a narrow tunnel. It was a tight fit, and almost immediately, claustrophobia struck. If I died here—I shook my head, refusing the image. I kept using my elbows, slithering, and wriggling my hips. My helmet light jiggled back and forth ahead of me as I advanced. This felt too much like a book I'd read—the Tunnels of Something or other in Vietnam. Men called tunnel rats had crawled into dirt holes after the Viet Cong. Those crazy men had carried .22 pistols or German Lugers and knives. In the close confines, firing a big gun with a loud muzzle blast stole their hearing or even ruptured eardrums. The enemy had set all kinds of traps with poisonous snakes that dropped onto the Americans, shit-tipped stakes poking out of the floor and a sentry hiding in the darkest section.

"I don't like this, Commander," Rollo radioed.

"I heard you the first time," I said. "Now quit bitching and follow the leader."

I heard noises from ahead, and I saw a crawling Karg in my lamplight. It used every tentacle and moved fast. The thing halted and tried to wrestle its rifle from its back. My BOOM was deafening, and I understood better why tunnel rats used smaller caliber weapons. The creature died, splashing black Karg blood. The second alien used the first as a bulwark, jutting its rifle over the corpse, firing at me. The angle was bad for the enemy, and the bullet exploded in front of me on the ceiling instead of on my visor. Tiny shrapnel peppered my helmet, though.

"Back!" I roared, BOOM, BOOM, as I blew apart the dead and live Karg. "Back up, retreat; there are aliens in the tunnels!"

I crawled butt-backward many times faster than I'd crawled forward. Several times, my boots bumped against the helmet of the crawling trooper behind me. At last, my feet hung over open air. I pushed, and I landed on the dead Karg pile.

"Now what?" Rollo asked, with an I-told-you-so tone of voice.

The impulse to rush him and swing was strong. I swallowed a retort, and we killed the new Kargs showing up in the portholes. This group proved fewer in numbers than the first wave.

Near the end, my gun jammed, and I pitched it aside. I clawed through dead things, heaving bloody Kargs aside. I saw a barrel poking out of the bottom. I grabbed, yanked the weapon free of metallic tentacles and wiped crusted black gore from the firing apparatus.

I test fired to make sure it worked. It did, and I slammed home a new magazine.

"Commander!" a trooper shouted.

My head whipped up to study the portholes, but they stayed empty. I wondered what the man wanted. That's when the BigDog robots struck.

Before the end of old Earth, the U.S. military had been into robots, fighting machines. BigDog had been a nasty thing that trotted around like a mechanical horse as it whined like an out of control lawn mower. The robot had wrong-angled legs, a big barrel body and cages to hold stuff. The idea had been to make them into U.S. Army mules, carrying soldiers' supplies for the men anywhere, including hilly terrain. The robots could climb slopes and trot around in parking lots. If our Earth had been given a few more years, I suppose we'd seen those things patrolling our city streets, too. Before the thermonuclear warheads took out civilization, our police forces had been in the process of militarizing themselves into something other than regular cops.

Anyway, the enemy had his own version of BigDog. It was large like a horse, or a Clydesdale's torso, the kind of horse in the Budweiser commercials. Instead of wrong-angled joints, the Clydesdale-sized robot had tentacles. They were bigger and thicker than the regular Karg type of soldier-creature tentacles. A machine trotted around the corridor, and it carried three Kargs up top. These Kargs used robot-mounted weaponry with larger calibers than their pincer-held rifles.

In seconds, four alien BigDogs bounded at us, with their mounted guns blazing. Assault troopers went down hard, blown against the walls.

I knelt. Others did, too. We returned fire, killing the riders. One stubborn Karg shredded away a piece at a time—its chest, lower abdomen, a tentacle ripped away from its socket. Still the thing hung on with its other metal arm. Then three bullets exploded at once, and what was left of the body toppled away, leaving a flapping, clicking tentacle attached to the machine. Even as I watched the whipping arm, an internal machine gun appeared out of the BigDog's forehead, slewing bullets at us.

Raging at yet more Earther deaths, I dropped my rifle and leaped at the nearest BigDog. My bio-suit aided me, and I cleared the machine-gun mounted head. There weren't any riding Kargs by this time, and I landed atop the thing. I beat at the mechanism with my fists, but did nothing expect bruise my hands. Yanking out my old Bowie knife, I hacked at a neck joint and loosened something. I tore off a lid, thrust my hand into the darkness and yanked wires and leads. The thing pitched me off as it lurched sideways.

"Crawl away, Creed!" I heard over my headphones.

I crawled, and I heard sizzling plasma in flight. Those must be ours—the boys firing the semi-portable cannons. That's when bits of superheated stuff peppered my legs. My entire suit squirmed and threatened to come off. I'd be dead in seconds from the atmosphere if that happened. Twisting around, I swiped off the burning, bubbling plasma splashes. Then I got up and limped away.

The four alien BigDogs had decimated us. With our other casualties, I was down to half a zagun. We found that the only thing that could really stop the new machines were the semi-portable plasma cannons. Luckily, my troopers had thought fast and killed all four machines with plasma.

"What now?" Rollo asked. "Do we keep heading for the tube-train station?"

I gasped, with my chest heaving. I'd been inches from death twice in this haunted corridor. Finally, it seemed as if the Kargs had found an answer to the assault troopers. The BigDogs changed the infantry ratios, turning it to the aliens' advantage.

"If we don't get to the train-tubes, we're finished," I said.

"That isn't what EP told us earlier," Rollo said. "We could use flyers."

"He said twenty people could use them," I replied. "We need more than twenty of us down in the planetary center."

"It may be that the relic is wrong about the flyers," N7 said, interrupting our conversation. "We may be able to take more troopers than that."

"We'd better figure out what we're going to do fast," Rollo said. "I hear more of those robots coming."

The clangs and *tap-tap* clicking was different from the regular Kargs.

I bit my lower lip with indecision. The aliens were blocking us from the station. Did the Kargs realize how important the train-tube was to us? The answer was probably a big yes. They were pouring themselves against us and would likely continue to do so. It was one thing retreating before that, and another thing trying to advance into the enemy's teeth.

"We're turning around," I said. "It's time to see how many flyers there are."

It took several minutes to communicate with the others in the parallel corridors, as the ultra-dense construction material hindered radio waves. During the back and forth comm-chatter, it became clear we'd lost our margin of separation with the enemy all along the line.

We leapfrogged down the corridors and chambers, one zagun at a time providing covering fire for others. Because of the BigDogs, we had to keep the plasma cannons active. We set up ambushes for them. We threw grenades, hosed machine gun fire and slowly died ourselves one by one.

Yeah, the aliens killed us by inches. We slaughtered them in droves. One thing, though: the moth-ships upstairs no longer beamed right down on top of us. The alien infantry had to hoof it part of the way from their drop-pods. For whatever reason, we were deep enough now so we didn't have to fear the graviton rays.

I'd played computer games like this before as a kid. Once or twice, I'd even wondered back then what it would have felt like being the lone marine against hordes of insect-like aliens bum-rushing his last position. I no longer had to wonder. I knew. It sucked because it tasted like bitter fatigue, the kind that dried out your mouth and make you gulp air as if it was the most precious commodity in the universe. I would have sweated like a pig, too. My suit ate that, or drank it. My sweat went straight to the body armor—that was part of the symbiosis. I sweated and the suit gave me strength, gave me spacesuit-like covering and a few stims when the time was right.

So far, it had kept itself from doing that. While in Jelk service, the suits had stimmed us at whim. The Lokhars had helped us figure out how to turn that function on and off. Mostly—so far all the time—we kept it off. Being a berserker wouldn't help us here, not yet at least. We needed our minds to outthink the banzai-oriented Kargs.

"It's time to run," I said. "Next over-bound, we're all taking off."

"The BigDogs will quickly catch up with us," Rollo said. "You know what that means."

"I know. We're going to run and get them to follow fast, without infantry support. Then we're going to ambush the lot of them. Afterward, we'll run again all the way to the flyers. We can rest on them or rest when we're dead. Any more questions?"

I fielded two more. They were both on tactical niceties. Afterward, we implemented the plan.

I clutched my brace of enemy rifles, and at my word, I picked up the pace several notches. Lengthening my stride, I sprinted in twenty-foot bounds. Air wheezed past my throat. Fatigue threatened to turn my leg muscles into jelly, but I ignored that as only a conditioned trooper could. I thought about all the heartache I'd been through this past year. I told myself it was down to this run. Soon, it would be over. First, we had a job to do.

"They're here!" Dmitri radioed.

"There's no finesse this time, boys and girls," I wheezed. "Lay down prep fire and set up those cannons. Let's toast these suckers."

I dove, hit the deck, twisted around and raised my first rifle, tucking the butt tight against my shoulder. Three seconds later, the trotting robots appeared. The way they lurched and moved with speed—the sight made me grit my teeth. I instinctively hated these things.

I aimed and fired exploding bullets. So did the troopers near me. It did nothing but cause the machines to deploy their heavy weapons. Our plasma cannon boys proved faster this time, and superheated substance melted the things. The alien BigDogs flopped. They rolled, and those tentacle legs waved and thrashed as they lay on their backs. Some of our bullets found the right spots then. We killed the trotting machines, at least in this wave.

I panted where I lay, exhausted, almost ready to faint. Instead, I steadied my nerves. I gave myself an interior pep talk, and still I lay there. I had to go back in my mind to the time the Lokhars beamed their ray at my dad's shuttle. For a second, I didn't think that would work either. But it did…barely.

I dragged myself upright, and I staggered to prone troopers with their weapons tucked against their shoulders for firing. Not a one of them stirred. I would have liked to bend down and tug them up. I did not have the strength for that. Instead, I kicked them in the sides.

"Up, up, it's time to get a move on," I said.

I heard curses, my mother insulted and what a prick I truly had turned out to be. I kicked harder after that, and managed to get a quarter of them back onto their feet.

"Good," I told the rest. "I don't need you weaklings anyway. Stay here for the Karg knives. Maybe I'll see you later on a video as you're strapped down and tortured. You can thanks the stars then you got a few moments rest here. So long," I said.

"Wait," a trooper pleaded.

"Wait for what?" I asked. "The stopwatch is ticking. We're all out of time. If you want to come, tell me."

"Please," the trooper said. "Let us rest a few more minutes."

"So long, pussy," I said.

A few of them raved at me. I pointed at standing troopers and told them to go and help the complainers. If a man or woman could curse, they still had the energy to keep moving. I wanted every trooper I could get, but this wasn't the time or place to hold anyone's hand.

In the end, I got all but three troopers up. I went to those three and aimed at the nearest. "Good-bye, soldier," I said, and I fired between his legs.

The man scrambled up in terror, and he stood there, with his visor aimed at me.

"Are you crazy?" the man bellowed.

"That's right," I said. "I am crazy. Now start marching."

The last two decided to drag themselves to their feet. Then we started for the flyers, and soon we loped again. This time, no trotting robots caught up with us, at least not yet. We gained some separation from the Karg horde.

I'd like to say I did deep thinking as we hurried for the flyers, if indeed any existed. I'd be lying, though. At that point, I endured. Setting one foot ahead of the other was all I could do.

Unfortunately, it wasn't all about running down corridors. Negotiating this nightmare world was often as much about climbing. Sometimes I scaled down, down, and my arms ached.

Finally, we stumbled into a hanger bay. There were flyers all right, open-air platforms with raised controls in the center. At least, I took them to be controls.

"Ella," I said. "Get over here."

Dmitri oversaw sentries setting up plasma cannons. Rollo provided them with rifle teams. N7 trailed our artifact-carrier.

"It's time to wake up the relic again," I told Ella.

The hanger bay had a hundred-foot ceiling over us, with girders crisscrossing each other. Light shined down from there. To the sides were big open shafts going down into the planet. I couldn't see how far they went. Did they go all the way to the center?

I backed away from an opening because dizziness threatened. Falling down the shaft would be a poor way of finding out the truth about them.

"Ella," I said.

She sat cross-legged and hugged her ammo bag, rocking back and forth as if holding a sleeping baby.

A quick glance showed me we had approximately two thousand troopers and maybe three hundred legionaries left.

289

The Lokhars were exhausted, and they sat so all of them had their backs to us. Good. I didn't want any trouble with them now.

"Are you ready, N7?" I asked.

"Affirmative," the android said.

I walked to Ella and crouched before her. "Take EP out of the bag," I said.

She raised her visor as if regarding me. "When do you think the artifact first used the pink ray on me?" she asked softly.

"Probably right away," I said.

"I was going to discover their secrets," she whispered.

"I know."

"The Lokhars used me," she said, sounding bitter.

"No, Ella, the artifact used you. I don't think the Lokhars are in charge of this game."

"Do you think EP is running it?" she asked.

"I think the relic knows more than the Lokhar Emperor." A thought struck me. "You know what? I bet the oracle is simply another Forerunner artifact."

"Ahhh," Ella said. "Yes. That would make better sense than their religious nonsense."

The android squatted beside me. "Do you believe in the conspiracy theory of history?" N7 asked me.

I didn't twist to look at him. Instead, I kept crouched before Ella and the artifact. "Why don't you enlighten me as to what you mean?" I told N7.

"Conspiracy theory," the android said. "That others behind the scenes manipulate the masses."

"Maybe some of the time I believe that, sure," I said.

"Do you believe that the manipulators are Jelk and Forerunner artifacts?" N7 asked.

"What about the Creator?" I asked.

"So far we have only seen supposition concerning His reality," N7 said.

"We don't even have that," Ella said.

"I'm not going to argue about it," I said. "This isn't the time or place. All I know is that I've seen weird things this past year. The weirdest was the collapsing universe. Abaddon strikes me as awfully strange, too. An apparition down here of a giant snake with centipede-like legs didn't help, either. Is this a war of angels and demons or ancient races? Who cares at this point? Maybe later we can hash it out. For now, we have to get out of here. Ella, take out EP or you're going to lose the privilege of carrying him."

Her visor was aimed at me, and it never strayed. Did she scowl or frown? I don't know. Finally, she unzipped the ammo-bag and withdrew our artifact.

"EP," I said, "wakey, wakey."

Lights glowed within the artifact. It lifted from Ella's hands to hover in place.

"You have reached a flyer bay," the artifact informed us.

"There's more than a few craft in here," I said. "If we pack in tight, we can carry everyone."

"I believe you're right," EP said. "I find that curious."

"How come you said we could only take twenty people before?"

"I have insufficient data to make an analysis," the relic said.

The idea EP had huge gaps in its memories didn't ease me any. In fact, it was getting more concerning by the moment. Yet what other choice did I have? None. I had to trust the Forerunner thing to an extent.

"How about showing us how these flyers work?" I said.

I'm not sure what I expected. What happened was the best possible outcome. The artifact floated to one, with the three of us following. Swiftly, EP gave us a rundown on the controls.

"Do the flyers have enough fuel or energy for the trip?" I asked.

"You will have to test them," EP said, "as I do not know."

I climbed onto the nearest platform, hurried to the raised controls and began waving my hand over colored knobs. To my relief, other knobs lit up as the relic had explained, and I waved my suited hands over them in the sequence EP had described. The surface under my feet began to hum, and softly, gently, the platform lifted off the hanger deck.

"It works," I said.

"How much fuel or energy does it have?" N7 asked.

I checked a gauge. "By the symbolism, I'd say it's half energized."

"That should prove sufficient," EP said. "Now I would like to hibernate and conserve energy."

"Wait a minute," I said.

The artifact hovered near me.

"Can't you power up off these flyers?" I asked. "Can't you drain energy from them?"

"No," the artifact said. "I cannot."

"Where can you gain power then?"

"At the Altair Object," it said.

"Where does the object draw its power from?" I asked.

"I do not know," EP said.

That didn't ring true. I wondered. Could these things lie? Why not? "EP," I said, "how do we know you're telling us the truth about anything?"

"I fail to understand your question."

"Are you lying to us about certain things?" I asked.

"No. I can only speak truth."

I blinked several times. If the artifact could lie, it could have just told me one now. So I was no closer to knowing if it was trustworthy or not than I'd been a few seconds ago.

"EP," Ella asked, "could the Altair Object be draining energy from the collapsing universe?"

The artifact hovered in place.

"EP," Ella said, "did you hear me?"

"I do not appreciate these continued interrogations," the relic said. "I forbid you to ask me anymore."

"Who are you forbidding?" I asked. "Ella or me?"

"Both of you," EP said.

"Commander…" Ella said. Then she quit talking.

I decided we could push the issue later. We had to leave.

With N7's help, I explained the controls to selected troopers. They hurried to various platforms. Three of the control panels failed to light up. N7 checked each one and discovered that one of the troopers had failed to follow the correct procedure. The other two platforms simply didn't work.

By this time, we could hear alien BigDogs trotting down the corridors. At my orders, troopers and our few legionaries piled onto the flyers.

"They're almost here," Dmitri told me. "Maybe I'd better stay behind to hold them back."

"No," I said. "Everyone is leaving." Then I gave quick instructions to the plasma cannon crews. I wanted at least one of them per flyer, preferably more.

Dmitri's flyer and mine floated beside by the chosen shaft. One by one, the other platforms sank into the great abyss, heading down for the center of the planet.

The last flyer disappeared, when a company of BigDogs trotted into the hanger bay. Like old time sailing ships Francis Drake had sailed against the Spanish Armada, our plasma cannons belched broadsides from our last two platforms.

"Go, go, go!" I shouted at Dmitri. "Get into the shaft."

"We have to nail them all," he shouted back at me. "Otherwise, they can just leap after us and fall down like missiles."

He had a point. So our two platforms hovered by the opening as more BigDogs leapt into the hanger bay. We slaughtered them, the sizzling orange superheated blobs melting them by the dozen.

"My cannon is overheating," a trooper shouted.

Other crews yelled similar news.

"It's time to go," I said.

"The BigDogs—" Dmitri said.

"Forget about them," I said. "Go, go, go."

Dmitri's flyer maneuvered over the shaft. Then his platform dropped into it, disappearing out of sight. Mine was the last one left, with grim troopers armed to the teeth. I'd put N7 and Ella on an earlier flyer, so it was just my remaining zagun and me.

More BigDogs flowed into the hanger bay, climbing over the destroyed ones. These held Karg soldier-creatures on their backs.

I waved my hand over the bright controls. The flyer lurched. Then Karg bullets reached us. The platform spun around like a top, and we lost three troopers who sailed off.

They got up on the hanger deck. A Karg bullet flipped one soldier onto his back. Then bullets made the man's helmet crack. I saw a puff of air jet out and knew he was dead. The other two troopers jumped, reaching our platform just as it sank out of sight.

By that time, I brought a semblance of control back to the flyer. Troopers craned their heads, looking up. The hanger lights dwindled, and then it darkened suddenly.

I used long-scan vision and put it on my HUD. Just as Dmitri had predicted, BigDogs jumped down the shaft after us, falling like missiles for our platform.

28

The next few minutes were gut-wrenching. I stood at the controls, and I judged distances. The shaft was quite a bit bigger than my platform, maybe three times the circumference. That didn't give me much maneuvering room, though.

We floated down, and I dared to drop faster.

"Dmitri," I radioed. He was somewhere below me.

"Here, Commander," the Cossack said.

"Kargs and BigDogs are raining down on us." Even as I said that, the falling aliens began firing rifles and heavier ordnance. An occasional exploding bullet blasted against the platform, wounding troopers and raining bio-suit pieces. "Raise a cannon!" I shouted. "Give them something to worry about."

Two crews informed me their cannons wouldn't be ready for a few more minutes. That just left the one. Troopers helped wrestled it into position so its orifice aimed straight up. Then a roiling orange glob spat upward. How far would it go before it stopped climbing and fell back down onto us? This was a mad gamble.

As we sank, we passed girders and tiny openings, but nothing to fly a platform through in order to dodge. I wondered if this had been a service or maintenance flyer. It had that feel. It certainly didn't possess weaponry or anything approaching combat speeds.

"We got some!" a trooper shouted. "The plasma melted them into scrap metal."

Twice more the cannon fired, the discharge climbing to strike falling enemies. The number of bullets hitting us dropped dramatically, although we still saw occasional muzzle flashes up there.

Bit by bit, the initial raining debris gained on us. When I tried to make the flyer sink faster, the entire platform began to wobble. A trooper staggered near an edge. There weren't any rails along the sides. Before he plunged off, another trooper grabbed his arm and steadied the man.

I reduced speed after that, and brought the wobbling under control.

"They're coming!" a sergeant roared.

"Get ready," I said. "This is going to be rough."

I had three lookouts, and they agreed exactly where the first dead Kargs would hit. For the next several minutes, I maneuvered the platform to one edge of the shaft to the next. Individual Kargs zipped past us, and then so did melted BigDogs.

Then a BigDog slammed against the flyer. It made the platform dip badly that way. Three troopers plunged off. I hoped Dmitri could catch them. We scraped against the shaft, and I fought to keep our vehicle upright. If I did this wrong, the entire craft might go sideways and dump everyone. Troopers shoved the BigDog off, and distributed the weight evenly again. I had almost bought us back under control when the second BigDog struck. We lost another trooper, slammed against the shaft, which caused us to carom like a billiard ball and hit the opposite side of the tube.

That knocked me sideways. My grip slipped and I fell, and I might have slid away, but I grabbed the station, hanging on. For a second, I thought it was over. We wobbled and the left edge dipped. Troopers slid toward the edge. With a heave, I climbed back into position, moving my hands over flashing knobs. Bit by bit, I brought the flyer back under control and this time, we didn't lose anyone. It made a difference when troopers linked arms, saving his neighbor. Even so, if another BigDog had struck then, it would have all been over.

During that time, a comm expert radioed ahead and told Dmitri what to expect.

We had to find a side passage fast, or the trip to the center would never work. We couldn't dodge falling aliens forever.

Luckily, Dmitri radioed and told us about a sharp turn coming up. I had to slow down, dodging three more BigDogs until we floated into a side opening.

My gut ached as I released tension and I felt bile in the back of my throat. For the next several minutes as we traveled away laterally, loud clangs told us of raining BigDogs hitting the bottom of the shaft. The Kargs must have begun shoving the dead ones down.

For the next three hours, we traversed various shafts, going sideways, drifting down again and dropping laterally once more. I taught a sergeant what to do because fatigue made my eyes burn. Finally, I lay down and closed my aching orbs.

I slept like one dead until a trooper shook me awake.

"Commander," the woman said, "N7 has been trying to contact you."

"Trouble?" I asked, as I propped up onto my elbows.

"I think I'd better let him explain," she said.

I sipped water from a tube in my helmet, letting the warm liquid trickle down my parched throat. It made me feel like a rabbit in a cage, the suit as my imprisonment. I chewed on paste we used in lieu of food and finally chinned myself onto the command channel.

"What is it, N7?" I asked.

"We've been descending for some time," the android radioed from a flyer below us somewhere. "Our speeds compared to the tube-train show that the Kargs using the other side of the planet will win the race to the bottom. They will likely be waiting for us there. The Kargs on our side might also catch and pass us soon."

"What's the margin for the other side Kargs?" I asked.

"They are presently two hours and thirteen minutes ahead of us," N7 said. "That margin will continue to grow if we remain in the flyers."

Great. The flyers were *slower* than the tube-train. Everything EP told us seemed to be the opposite. Just how damaged was the relic? Had my shots done it? Well, how didn't matter right now.

"Is there a tube-train station nearby?" I asked. "Somewhere we could get on one?"

"Yes, in another eighty kilometers."

"Then we need to push the flyers, load up there and see if we can make the tube-cars move faster. We can't give the Kargs too much time to set up ahead of us."

"Yes, Commander," N7 said.

From the surface, it was over five thousand kilometers to the center. We hadn't even traveled one thousand kilometers yet. I wondered about the T-missiles. So far, we hadn't hit any nuclear devastated areas. Had Admiral Venturi been able to launch any into the planet? Maybe he'd needed all the teleportation missiles to clear a path through space for us to the surface.

We pushed the flyers as fast as we dared, enduring more swaying. Once, I watched a trooper flip upward, as if our craft was a frying pan and the soldier a piece of meat. The truth was obvious. Whoever had designed these hadn't worried about aerodynamics.

Now came a grim game of daring and stomach-churning wobbling for another eighty kilometers. We lost three more troopers altogether before we landed and piled into sleek tube-cars. Each of the whale-sized vehicles unlocked in the back. An entire orifice dilated open. I could imagine a long snake-centipede wriggling into the tube. The controls were in front: colored crystals where one had to wave his or her hands over node-controls. Would a giant centipede have used some of its front legs to do that?

My skin crawled at the idea. I hated snakes. I wondered if that's what First Ones had looked like: the ghostly holoimage I'd seen earlier. I didn't like the idea of them being snake-like. Wouldn't that make them evil? I was thinking Garden of Eden and the serpent.

With a shake of my head, I switched worries. We had to get down fast, before the Kargs formed an impenetrable defense between the center and us.

Each car held several zaguns worth of troopers. There weren't any chairs in ours, just the upward-curving walls. We stretched out and relaxed, while a driver piloted the car. None of ours were linked, but we each followed the other.

Soon enough, we zipped at high speed along what I figured must be magnetic rails. Occasionally, out the front or back windows, we saw flickering lights and a flash of girders, but mostly we saw darkness.

Even going fast this would take time. Many troopers fell asleep, including me. The next fight might be the last, and we all needed to be in the best condition possible.

I woke up to discover we only had five hundred kilometers to go. That brought a strange feeling. After all our efforts, we were about to run the final lap. At least we were getting a chance to fight near the victory post.

I felt groggy and my muscles had become sore, but the burning feeling behind my eyes was gone. Maybe we could actually do this. Yeah, we were going to win. I had to tell myself that, otherwise—

Just then, Abaddon called, and it turned out that he wanted to speak to me personally.

The good feelings evaporated, and fear built in my chest. How had the top dog learned about me? The implications meant he had prisoners. What did Abaddon have to say to me anyway?

With a scowl, I decided there was nothing to lose. So what if he was the master of evil. I was Creed. Screw him. So far, no one had been able to hold me down. I'd flip him off to his face; I'd go down fighting, unbowed and unapologetic about it.

He must know we were almost to his forward lines. I wanted to hit the Kargs before they settled down and made elaborate plans or built up their area. Why had EP told us to use flyers if they were so slow as to give the enemy the edge? Stupid relic.

N7 brought a portable receiver and snapped a link into my comm jack. The receiver had a holoimage-pad, a small thing really, about the size of a clipboard. Rollo, Dmitri, Ella with the bagged relic and N7 sat around the receiver, watching and ready to listen. I don't know. If this was the supreme devil, I was glad to have the others near me.

I smiled then, a grim thing. The situation reminded me of Antarctica when we'd sat around the TV and later near the radio transmitter. I'd come a long way since then, and yet, I still sat hunched before comm equipment, wondering what the future held for me and for humanity.

The holoimage started out fuzzy like before and stayed that way no matter how much N7 fiddled with the receiver. For just a second, I wondered about that. What did Abaddon have to hide from us this late in the game that he didn't want to show himself?

"Commander Creed?" I heard in my earphones. The gravelly voice made me shudder. I'd never liked it, and I doubt I ever would.

"Yeah, that's me," I said.

"I had not realized until a short time ago that the Lokhars had acquired humans as slave soldiers," Abaddon said.

"No?" I asked. That he knew about humans confirmed the worst. But why did he assume we were slaves?

"Why do you fight for your oppressors?" Abaddon asked.

"No one is oppressing us," I said. "We're on our own."

"You lie," Abaddon said. "I know that the Lokhars devastated your homeworld, adding biological agents to make it inhabitable for generations to come."

"How would you know about that?" I asked.

Abaddon chuckled in a devilish manner, and his torso moved about in the fuzzy holoimage. He seemed to be regarding those hunched around the receiver.

"You will never pierce the ring of soldiers guarding the Altair Object," Abaddon said. "Your advance is futile and wasteful of your last hours of life."

"You're probably right," I said. "But since we're here and all, you know we have to try. Besides, I seem to recall someone telling the admiral we'd never even make it to the portal planet. Looks like you were dead wrong about that. Why not wrong about our chances of breaking through your creeps?"

"You are a vain beast to speak to me so," Abaddon said.

I blinked several times at the grainy bastard. Something didn't ring right here. The way he spoke...

"Who are you, Abaddon?" I asked.

"I am the end of life," he said. "I am universal doom."

"Yeah?" I asked. "Well, what about the Jelk? Do you hate them, too?"

"Who are these Jelk?" he asked.

"Yeah, right, like I buy you don't know who they are. What's your game, Abaddon? Why are you pretending? What's the real purpose and why did you call me?"

"You are a worm, a doomed creature. Abase yourself while you can and earn a few last minutes of peace."

There was something fishy here. It hovered in my mind as I tried to think this through. "Just a minute," I said. I chinned my helmet comm-lever and turned away from the receiver where the holoimage still looked around. "Ella," I said, on a different channel. "I want you to take out the relic, wake it and see if EP can give us better reception."

No one else asked me why. Maybe they felt Abaddon's strangeness as well.

I heard Ella zip open the ammo bag as I faced the holoimage. I chinned the Abaddon-talking channel back on.

"What's the point of all this?" I asked. "Why do the Kargs hate everything but themselves?"

"Surrender, human," Abaddon said.

"Is there any good reason I should?"

"If you do, you will receive preferred treatment. That is better than dying in futility and agony."

"Why would you bother calling and offering us that?" I asked. "Do you fear us? Have we proved tougher than you believed? I bet that's it. You're calling because you fear."

"Foul beast, decide quickly before I rescind the offer."

Out of the corner of my eye, I noticed EP hovering in place, with its lights flashing.

"EP," I said, broadcasting over my helmet speakers. "Can you fix the grainy image?"

"I can," the relic said. "Do you wish to see your tormenter?"

"I sure do," I said.

A thumbnail-sized slot on EP opened with a snick. A pin-sized gun poked out. Then a white beam rayed the holoimage. The grainy appearance wavered and solidified into a perfect picture. To my astonishment, I found myself staring at Shah Claath, or the perfect replica of him. He had red skin and inky eyes, with sharp little teeth just as I remembered. The last time

I'd seen him he'd been busy transforming himself into an electrical ball of energy in order to escape my Bowie knife.

"You're Abaddon?" I asked. "Is this a joke?"

The creature who looked like Claath glanced about, and he snarled with rage, reaching out and flipping a switch. It did nothing to change the image. He glared at me, and he looked around again. Then he stared at EP, and understanding swirled in his dark eyes.

"You have always proved a troublesome beast," Claath or Abaddon said to me. "I should have destroyed you the first day I laid eyes on your repugnant form."

"Yeah, what can you do?" I asked. "These things happen."

His eyes narrowed with anger.

"I don't get it, Claath," I said. "How can you be Abaddon, and how can you have trillions of Kargs willing to do your bidding? Or have the Jelk seen the way the wind blows and turned traitor to our universe?"

Claath straightened, no doubt trying to regain what little dignity he could. "You are destined to lose," he said.

N7 spoke up, his voice coming through his helmet speakers. "I do not believe the personage we're viewing is or was the original Abaddon. I have heard both beings speak, and I have kept internal recordings. Their voice patterns and manners are different. I believe Claath has impersonated Abaddon for the moment only. Earlier we heard the real Abaddon."

"N7," Claath said in an oily voice. "If you would win back my favor, shoot the upstart humans around you, starting with Creed-beast."

N7 did no such thing, but sat still, waiting.

"The last time I saw your ugly mug," I said, "you were burning a hole through my battlejumper."

"*Your* battlejumper," Claath said. "You-you *pirate*," he spat. "You stole from me, and you will repay for that a thousand times overs. I will recoup my losses."

"Sure you will," I said. "But anyway, as I was saying, you floated away as an energy creature. I'm wondering how you went from there in Sigma Draconis to wherever it was that you found the Kargs. How did you find these fiends anyway?"

A vicious smile curved Claath's lips. "I find it delightful that you are ignorant on so many matters. Surrender to me, beast, and I shall enlighten you."

"Why did you just pretend to be Abaddon?" I asked. "Did you think you could fool us?"

Claath continued smiling.

"You don't like that question?" I asked. "Why not try this one for size. Why do our bio-suits work so well in hyperspace? Did you foresee the coming of the Kargs? Or is it funnier than that? Did they capture you and force you to re-materialize into a body? Are you their slave perhaps?"

"You are doomed," Claath whispered.

"Are the Jelk working for the Kargs?" I asked. "Is that it? What profit do you gain if the space-time continuum invaders destroy everything in our universe?"

"You know so little," Claath said in an evil voice. "Yes, I delight in watching you stretch your thoughts as you attempt to encompass reality. Surrender immediately, Creed-beast, and you can regain my good favor. The Kargs can use someone like you."

"The Kargs, eh," I said. "That's interesting. It's not the Jelk who can use me, but the invading Kargs. I'm back to thinking you've sold out everyone, even your own kind."

His smile slipped for just a moment. "Believe what you wish," Claath said, and he put the smile back into place. But it seemed forced now.

"You know what I really think?" I said. "You lost once to me, and when you gathered new flesh to yourself, you fell into Karg hands. How that happened, I don't know...yet. That makes this funny, and you know why? Instead of running the show like you used to, the great and greedy Shah Claath has become a slave to the Kargs. You're running scared, Claath, and I like seeing it."

"If you—"

"Shut up for a minute while I tell you what's going to happen," I said. "I'm still hunting for you, Claath. I'm going to make you float a second time, and then I'm going to use a special weapon that will fry your energized self into nothing."

"There is no such weapon."

"That isn't what EP told me," I said.

"Who?" asked Claath.

I jerked a thumb at the relic. "The Forerunner artifact has told me all about you, Claath, and it has given me the weapon I'm talking about."

"This is *outrageous*," Claath said heatedly, and his words seemed directed at the artifact. "How could you tell such a low order creature about the energy ray?"

As EP began to vocalize, I cut the connection and the holoimage vanished.

"I did not give Commander Creed information about such a ray," EP said, but it was too late. Claath was offline and didn't know the information.

I rounded on EP. "What's the deal? How come you tried to calm down Claath?"

"You would not understand," EP said.

"Try me."

"No," EP said. "This is not the right time for it."

"Uh-huh," I said, unconvinced. "How is it you know who Claath is?"

"The knowledge is unremarkable," EP said. "I am Orange Tamika's most sacred relic. As such, I have heard of Claath's invasion attempts into various systems, particularly the Altair star system."

"Is Claath really Abaddon?" I asked.

"Your android drew the correct conclusion," EP said. "Claath attempted to impersonate Abaddon."

"Do the Kargs know who the Jelk are?" I asked.

"Commander Creed," EP said. "I believe you should worry about breaking into the Karg lines instead of querying me about old history."

"Do you know where the aliens are setting up their lines?"

"Do you wish to view a 3-D map of the strategical situation?" EP asked.

"Yes," I said.

EP swiveled, and another beam flashed against a tube-car wall. This map showed the center of the planet with the former Altair Object floating in a monstrously huge chamber, like a chocolate center buried in the middle of a tootsie pop. I'd seen the donut-shaped artifact before as a Jelk assault trooper. I understood its size and realized it floated in a titanic area. That was interesting.

Before the huge and final chamber, the Kargs blocked the corridors with thick red clots of color. That meant thousands, tens of thousands of Kargs. If I'd had my entire Earth Commando Army with me, I might have been able to battle through the enemy. With a partly two thousand troopers and several hundred Lokhars—I didn't see any way through. I couldn't believe it. We'd made it this far, and now...this.

I glanced at EP. What was its game? Had the relic helped bring us this far and then given us an insolvable problem in order to see how Earthlings reacted?

"Are the Karg 3-D representations similar to those you showed us previously near the surface?" I asked.

"They are an exact and equal representation," EP said.

"How many Kargs do you estimate stand between us and the Altair Object?" I asked.

"Fifty-four thousand and increasing," the relic said.

"Fifty-four thousand?" Rollo said. "We can't fight through that."

"What other choice do we have?" I asked.

We exchanged glances with each other, everyone no doubt realizing the hopelessness of the situation.

"May I ask the relic a question?" N7 asked.

"Be my guest," I said.

"EP," our android said, "are there any armories nearby that might hold exotic Forerunner weaponry?"

"Ahhh..." EP said, as if thinking. "Why, yes there is."

"You're kidding?" I told the relic.

"No, I speak truths or the truth," EP said. "I never lie."

"Why didn't you say something about it earlier then?" I asked.

"That is an interesting question," EP said, "as I desire your victory and it would have been good for you to know about the weaponry. The answer is I do not know why I kept silent. Perhaps an alien virus has damaged memory cores."

I wanted to howl. Instead, I closed my eyes, thinking. I needed to ask the right questions. That seemed clear. Opening my eyes, I said, "Do the Kargs have this weaponry, too?"

"I do not know," EP said, "but I do not believe so."

"How far is the armory to the Kargs?" I asked.

"I will show you on the map."

The artifact did. It looked to be several kilometers from their most upward outpost.

"The Kargs might find the armory if it's that close to their positions," I said.

"Commander," EP said, "on further contemplation, I feel I should inform you that the weaponry likely cannot help you. It is ancient battle-gear primarily suited to the First Ones. I do not believe it has been used in millennia."

Great. More curveballs. "We're all out of options, EP. You said fifty-four thousand Kargs with growing numbers await us. Soon, they will have one hundred thousand in position and then two hundred thousand. We have to attack now." I shook my head. "It's too bad Venturi and the other Lokhars couldn't have listened to my original idea and used T-missiles, letting a nuclear holocaust solve the problem."

The relic dipped and lifted several times, with more lights than ever flashing in odd sequences. "Wrong, Commander," EP finally said. "Such an act would have been a crime against reality."

"Why?" I asked. "The Forerunner artifact is just a machine."

"A machine, yes," EP said. "But much more than just."

Why couldn't the relic talk plainly for once? If the oracle was anything like this...

"Tell us about the weaponry," I said. I distrusted the little Forerunner. It had been wrong too many times. Then the thing began to talk...

29

Despite the Kargs' nearness to the armory, we beat them to it. The main reason was that the aliens didn't know to march there. The Kargs waited in their selected chambers and corridors, no doubt creating the perfect defense. To make it even worse for us, new Kargs disembarked from their tube-cars and continually added reinforcements.

Two thousand assault troopers and roughly three hundred Lokhar legionaries piled out at the last station. Here, all the corridors shined with a hurtful radiance. Even with our polarized visors, we squinted and splotches danced before our eyes. The hallways were bigger than ever and the chambers massive beyond belief. It was like walking through a museum, with strange crystalline shapes towering around us. We passed rooms covered with pink sands and deep cobalt-colored wells of slowly sloshing mercurial liquid. We were near the center of the planet. In several chambers, we saw metal walls beating like hearts. I found that incredibly disturbing. Was the planet alive?

If it wasn't—even if it was—this was an alien place. I don't think the First Ones had been humanoid in any manner.

We marched, and EP still refused to explain the exact nature of the weaponry. I think he felt we needed to see it to believe.

Finally, we reached thick vault hatches. EP spoke in High Speech, and I began to notice many hisses in his words, like a snake. At the end of the sequence, the hatch dilated open, and we entered a great storage room with floaters made for giant creatures. Sprouting around them were more towering crystals pulsating with steady red lights.

N7 glanced at a wrist monitor. It had tiny numerals glowing on its screen. "It's hotter in here by ten degrees," the android informed me.

"Where's the weapon?" I asked the relic.

EP lifted out of Ella's arms and floated to a large crystal box. The thing measured approximately two feet by two. It also had knobs on one side, with exotic imagery within it that eerily pulsed just like the towers. There were small handholds on the box that tentacles or centipede legs could have easily grasped.

"Is that one of the weapons?" I asked, pointing at the crystal box.

"No," EP said. "That allows the proper application of the weapons and a nullification of others."

"How about telling it to us plainly for once?" I said.

"You have such primitive minds," EP said. "I keep forgetting. This machine produces a ten-score continuity field."

"Hold it right there," I said. "What does that mean?"

"Put simply, an active continuity field means guns and lasers, grenades and other technological weapons will become inoperative. Or said another way, while under the field's influence, such weapons will not fire or explode."

I laughed harshly. Why had I ever let myself be talked into listening to the stupid relic? "The box looks too heavy to throw. So I don't get it. How does having this field help us in the slightest?"

"I should think that would be obvious," EP said. "We carry the emitter with us and create the continuity field."

"I already got that part," I said. "Once we create a continuity field—meaning we can't fire our weapons—the Kargs can slaughter everyone by shooting their bullets and beams into the field to kill us."

"No, no," EP said. "Their bullets and beams will no longer be able to race at speed through the field. The continuity mechanism renders that impossible."

"Okay," I said, wondering what kind of physics produced such an effect. "That's a little better, I suppose. But I'm still not seeing it. That means we'll be down to hand-to-hand combat. The Kargs can simply overwhelm us with numbers."

"Certainly there is that possibility," the relic said.

I groaned aloud, wanting to bang my forehead against a wall. After so many disappointments, why did I insist on thinking that EP was more than an idiot savant, with the accent on idiot? This was yet another of its boondoggles.

The relic floated from us. Like a dog watching a running cat, my desire to blast away with a rifle became intense.

"You must observe," EP said. "I will now show you the second part of the process."

I relaxed my grip on the rifle, grumbling, "What now?" as I followed him to an alcove.

The relic floated into a side area, and a crystal wall slid back to reveal hundreds of the brightest sticks I'd ever seen. Each of them had paper-thin wedges on one end.

"What the hell?" I asked. "I hope you're not telling me these are your great Forerunner weapons."

"It must be that you lack understanding," EP said. "The weaponry is fashioned from Obdurate-10, an ultra-dense substance with a monofilament edge."

"What's a monofilament edge?"

"A single linked atom-chain of Obdurate-10 on the cutting edge expanding finally to the wedge you see," EP said. "Nothing known to Forerunner science can resist such an edge. It is the sharpest object you will ever see. I suggest you pick one up."

I glanced at the others piled behind me, shrugged and climbed into the alcove.

"Beware the edge," EP said. "There are utterly unforgiving."

"By edge," I said, "do you mean the end of the wedge with the thickness of paper?"

"Precisely," EP said.

Gingerly, I wrapped my bio-suited hands on the other end of the stick. I grunted, surprised at its weight. "This thing is heavy," I said.

"It is ultra-dense, as I originally informed you," EP said. "The entire shaft is composed of Obdurate-10."

"Come again?" I asked.

"Lead is heavier than balsawood," Rollo said, who must have understood. "Maybe Obdurate-10 is heavier than lead."

"Countless times heavier," EP said.

Bunching my shoulders, I heaved the…Forerunner space axe upright. Then I chopped with the wedge, the axe head. It sheared through the floor with amazing ease.

In that second, I saw it. The First Ones had gripped the continuity field box, creating a zone where high-tech weapons wouldn't work, not guns, lasers, bombs, nothing. Then they waged combat with Obdurate-10 made space axes, hacking each other or enemies to pieces. It was freaky, and it might actually give us an advantage over the Kargs, at least for the initial contact.

"Okay," I said. "This just might work. But these things are rather heavy. We're going to get tired swinging them."

"I suggest we use them in teams," N7 said. "A trooper handles an axe until he's weary. Then he hands the weapon to his second. Once he becomes too fatigued, the second hands the axe to a third. By that time, the original soldier will have recovered some of his strength and stamina."

"Good thinking," I said. I shook my head, bemused at what we contemplated. "The Kargs have numbers. We have a continuity field and axes, making this a hand-to-hand battle. I don't know how that helps a very few beat a horde, but let's give it a whirl."

We found three of the continuity field devices and four hundred space axes. Two thousand troopers divided by four hundred gave us five wielders per weapon. Seeing that we had three CF devices, I decided to make this a three-pronged or three-corridor attack. The Lokhars would split into one hundred legionaries per attack group. They elected to remain outside the continuity fields and act as observers and help keep in radio contact. No radio worked in the continuity field, so we had to devise simple hand messages to give each other.

Even though we were under a hard time schedule, I believed we needed to practice. We did, for forty-five minutes. In that time, seven troopers died, cutting themselves or another with the axe. The slightest touch with the wedge-edge cut deeply, shearing bio-suits. These thin stick-axes were dangerous.

Finally, as Kargs began arriving in our tube-train station, we advanced to combat, but not before booby-trapping our station. Ten minutes later, we heard a thunderous explosion.

"There's no turning back now," I said. "The station is gone. We can only go ahead."

We marched through the alien tunnels for our battle with destiny.

I gripped one of the axes, resting the haft on my shoulder. I'd done many strange things this past year and a half, but I hadn't gone into battle against aliens from another universe while trusting to ancient weaponry. I imagine my ancestors on Earth had fought like this, with swords and axes, I mean.

I grinned, and I wondered if I'd thought of everything. We had plenty of space between troopers. I nodded. I used to play many war games as a kid, the old board games with cardboard counters and dice on a hexagonal-grid map. I remembered this one on ancient's battles. I'd read how Greek phalanx soldiers had more hoplites per square foot than Roman legionnaires. The hoplite held a spear and could fight shoulder to shoulder, shoving a sharp tip at an enemy. The Roman had needed more space, even though he'd wielded a smaller weapon, the *gladius*, a two-foot short sword. The Roman needed room to swing without worrying about hitting his comrade. The Gallic barbarians with their six-foot broadswords had needed even more room between warriors, and thus his battlefronts had lesser density than even a legionary cohort did.

Well, for the coming fight, we space axe-men would need Gallic room to swing these nifty First One weapons. That meant Kargs could possibly outnumber us as they attacked shoulder to shoulder, using their rifle barrels and knives to jab at our faces.

"Kargs!" a trooper shouted.

"Turn on the continuity field," I ordered. "And good luck."

Almost immediately, the world turned metallic gray with black shimmering motes drifting everywhere as our continuity field spread outward from the First One box. The field encompassed the troopers to my right and left. I heard harsh breathing and realized it was me. In a few seconds, the first Kargs showed up, or we marched to them. The alien creatures lay on their torsos or fired from behind crystal monuments.

Here was the moment where I figured everything would fall apart for us. There would be some fine detail that EP had forgotten to explain and whamo, the Kargs would fill us with lead. I fully expected to die in a hail of bullets.

Nothing of the kind happened. One or two Kargs shook their rifles. Another actually twisted his weapon around and peered down the barrel. I couldn't believe it. The Kargs had idiots on their side, too.

I shouted, and even though I'd told my troopers not to charge, I ran at the aliens with my axe held up high. A Karg shoved off the ground and held up his rifle to block my stick-like axe.

The shaft was heavy like a sledgehammer, though, and the axe and handle were ultra-dense. The intensely sharp wedge-edge sheared through the Karg rifle, the cone-like, alien head and part of the body. Black blood gushed out, some of it washing onto my chest. I stepped forward, slipped on the blood and fell hard. Even as I went down, I knew the deadliest hazard came from my own axe. I made sure to keep that edge away from me. I thudded onto my back and a Karg scuttled toward me. He might have made it, but my neighbor saw my dilemma and raced near. His axe chopped the Karg in half. It was beautiful, glorious, and a bloody mess.

I learned that a deadly figure-eight weave worked best. I hacked, chopped, gored, gutted, slipped and slid for fifteen panting minutes. We waded through Kargs. We hacked apart BigDogs. Occasionally, one of the troopers went down to a rush of Kargs. We lost the most men that way as our own axes sliced a trooper on the bottom of a pile of tentacle-striking Kargs.

Finally, finding that I could hardly raise the axe any more, my replacement tapped me on my shoulder. I gave him the axe and went to the back of the line.

Five soldiers per axe. Not one of the First One weapons broke. I didn't think anything could snap a handle in half or chip an Obdurate-10 blade.

How many did we kill? Saul slew his thousands and David his tens of thousands. We slew tens of thousands, and we advanced through the Karg lines toward the great Forerunner object.

I recalled how in the Middle Ages, well-armored knights with the best swords and horses could wade through enemy lines, especially if the enemy were pitch-fork-armed peasants. Cortes and his Spanish conquistadors had also done likewise through Aztec armies. They'd had a few cannons and crude matchlock guns. Mostly, they had armor and Toledo steel swords. Their Indian foes had obsidian-chip blades and cotton armor. We had a continuity field, the sharpest axes of two universes, symbiotic-suit strength and neuro-fiber speed. Here, in this place, it proved to be the winning combination.

Yeah, they whittled us down. The Kargs had been doing that the entire time. The Lokhars had to join us in the continuity field, and we lost contact with the other two attack columns.

Ours finally waded through the enemy, and I motioned scouts to look outside the gray field of drifting black motes. The scouts returned to us, signaling the all-clear.

"Let's finish this, boys," I said. We maneuvered for one of the other main corridors and hit the Kargs from behind. That freed the second attack column. We did the same for the third group, and now the last of the assault troopers made it through enemy lines.

After several hours of constant combat, our continuity field finally went down. The grayness fled and the brilliance of the inner planet struck. I cried out at the bright pain stabbing my eyes. A few moments later, with my gloves over my visor, I found it had polarized and I could see again.

We ran down the corridor and came to what I can only call a giant air moat. Before us was space, lots of it, but in the distance I spied the Forerunner artifact spinning slowly like a giant gyroscope. We had reached the center of the portal planet.

-30-

We nailed crystalline ropes to the metal floor. Then we slid the rest of the way down. Yeah, the gravity tugged us that way, although in my humble opinion it shouldn't have done so. Most of the mass was above us now.

I'm sure you're familiar with the old Arthur C. Clarke quote about extremely high tech seeming like magic to ignorant grunts like us. This place seemed magical, but in a weird, grim way. Some of the surprising magic had helped, but most had hurt.

I slid down the long rope, the thing slippery in my bio-suited hands. I looked around as I traveled. There was lots of open space, with milky strands floating in the methane atmosphere. I wrapped my legs around the rope, trying to generate greater traction. For some freakish reason, radio waves didn't work far in this place. I couldn't communicate with those in the corridors anymore.

Hard radiation must have been hitting me. My bones ached and there was a copper taste in my mouth. The former Altair Object had a black hole in its center. Always these black holes—I was sick of them.

Finally, using my torso, hands and legs, I almost brought myself to a halt. I slid slower in any case, and I could see the end of the rope approaching, around fifty feet from the great turning artifact below. The thing was silvery bright, and I thought to spy a cluster of buildings in the inner ring.

"Get ready, Creed old buddy," I told myself. "You have one more drop to make."

I slid off the end of the rope, and then I fell toward the rotating surface. I gained speed, heading toward terminal velocity. The metallic surface loomed bigger and it came even faster. I managed to keep my legs aimed down, and I hit, absorbed the best I could and let my knees buckle. I slammed down onto my chest, and the force knocked the air from my lungs. My legs hurt as if they'd broken. Maybe someone rolled me then. I don't know.

"Commander Creed, can you hear me? Answer please if you can."

I opened my eyes, peering at a trooper who had come down before me. By the voice, it was Dmitri.

"What is it?" I whispered. "What's wrong now?"

The Cossack laughed, and he slapped me on the shoulder. I wish he hadn't done that. It made me twist in pain.

"I need your help, Commander," Dmitri said. "Kargs are coming from the other side."

I groaned as I sat up, and I looked around. I could see more troopers sliding down the ropes. With Dmitri were twenty members of his zagun. We were the advance force, the scouts.

"Let's do this," I said.

Despite the aches and pains, and a throb in my left knee, I limped along the outer hull of the artifact. Its bulk shielded us from the black hole and hopefully from the worst of the radiation. As we ran—bounded, really, like old time Moon astronauts—I unslung my laser rifle. We'd been saving them. Now it was time to use the Bahnkouvs.

As if we moved on a mini-world, Kargs appeared on the short horizon, and a firefight started. We threw ourselves prone and sighted the lasers. Then we began to slaughter Kargs, and the reason proved simple. The black hole in the center of the torus affected each bullet's flight path just enough.

This close to the singularity, the gravity had a disproportionate effect on the small objects. The bullets kept turning inward toward the black hole, and the Karg intellect, at least that of its soldiery, proved insufficient to grasp the concept. It told me others must program them for battle. The codes called for specifics in targeting, I'm guessing, which the Kargs continued to do even in this hostile environment.

The last battle was the easiest, and as more and more troopers landed on the torus, we drove the Kargs into headlong retreat. Finally, we swept them from the artifact. At my command, snipers knelt and readied their Bahnkouvs for distance shots. Across the vast space, Kargs gathered at their corridor openings. Hot beams sliced into them. Some Kargs tumbled in. They were dead lemmings falling down an alien cliff. The others piled before the opening, so the Kargs behind had to yank them out of the way in order to get their turns to die.

By this time, over half the surviving troopers had made it onto the torus. Using relays of Earth soldiers like a radio pony express, we passed messages from one location to the next. Soon, I held a strategy conference with N7, Ella and EP.

"Now what are we supposed to do?" I asked the little relic.

"We must reach the main controls," EP said.

I nodded. I had a bad idea I knew where those controls were located. "Do you mean the tiny city on the inner edge?" I asked.

"Precisely," EP said.

"What about radiation?" I asked.

"Isn't it obvious?" EP asked. "You use the continuity field to block it from harming you."

I suppose that made sense.

N7 spoke up. "Isn't there a danger the continuity field will interfere with the black hole? Wouldn't that have a deadly impact on all of us?"

"Ahhh..." EP said, in its thinking voice. "Why yes. You are correct. You cannot employ the continuity field, Commander. Doing so will destroy the object."

I silently counted to three before asking, "Do you know how to set the coordinates so the object can take us back to our universe?"

"No," EP said. "That is far beyond my capacity."

I thought the relic had said before it could pilot us home. I shrugged. Maybe it was better this way. I didn't want to trust the relic as an interdimensional pilot. Still, EP's lack created a problem. "So...who exactly *can* set the coordinates?" I asked.

"The Altair Object will know," EP said.

"You're not telling me the thing we're standing on can communicate like you," I said.

"Not like me, no," EP said. "But yes, it can communicate. It is older than I am by many cycles."

"How many Earth years is that?" I asked.

"Well over two thousand."

"What?"

"I feel it is time I confessed," EP said.

I braced myself for the worst.

"The Altair Object is a Primary," the relic said, "while I am a Secondary."

I frowned. "Is that supposed to be important?"

"It is everything." Lights played a fast sequence upon EP's shell. "Come. It is time to discover if the Primary will reject you or not."

I knew it couldn't be this easy. No. There always had to be one more thing. Now we had to talk to the big Forerunner object, not just the little runt who seldom got things right. I wondered if the Lokhars knew secrets about Forerunners that could aid us.

It turned out that N7 had similar thoughts. "Perhaps we should summon Doctor Sant," our android said. "He may possess information we will need."

"I would advise against that," Ella said. "I...have a feeling it's important we keep the Lokhars away for now."

I studied the Russian scientist. EP had rayed a pink mind-beam at Ella. Now more than ever that made me suspicious. "Why don't you want Lokhars near?" I asked.

"Acceptance by a Primary is critical," Ella told me.

I wasn't sure if those were her thoughts or our relic's. How far could I trust Ella about the Forerunners anyway? I didn't know, and I didn't like that, not here at the end.

"Ella, you stay with the others. N7, you're coming with me."

"No!" Ella said.

I aimed my visor at her, waiting for a reason.

"Uh..." Ella said. "You should take more humans along. I think that's important."

Was she right? I glanced at N7 and then at EP. I didn't know enough to make an informed decision. So I went with my gut.

"Not this time," I told Ella. "Rollo and Dmitri should stay here on the outer hull. The Kargs aren't finished trying to storm this place. Keeping the artifact here is everything for our enemies. I don't know whom else I want with me in the Forerunner city. Normally, I'd take you, but..."

Ella stiffened, although she said, "You cannot trust me. I agree. EP has tampered with my thinking. You are right to leave me here."

"Add your laser to the firing line," I told her, "or keep an eye on Sant and the Lokhars. I don't want any of them following us."

"I must protest," EP said. "I wish for the woman to join us."

"Nope," I said. "That you want her along means it's probably a bad idea. It's just going to be the three of us now."

I thought the relic would argue. Instead, EP bobbed up and down, and it finally submitted to my decision.

We set out immediately, heading inward. Maybe this was the last lap, with three unique beings traveling toward the cluster of buildings on the inner ring. We had a heavily modified N-series mining android, an ancient Forerunner construct and an ex-con to decide the fate of our universe. Crazy, huh? While thinking about it, my left knee gave another grimacing throb. I favored it, enduring the pain. As I trudged along the continuing curve, finally bringing the black hole into sight, harder radiation struck. It made my bio-armor shift along my skin. Then my jaw began hurting, and I wondered if I was killing myself doing this?

"I feel it," EP said, in what sounded like a contented voice.

"What do you feel?" I asked.

"Renewed power," the relic said. "The Altair Object is at maximum capacity and is bleeding our bandwidth-specific energy. Ah...it is good."

"Then Ella was right earlier," I said. "The object has been feeding or powering up through the destruction of the Karg universe. The trans-dimensional hole is for its benefit. The Kargs coming through is just an unforeseen afterthought."

"In a manner of speaking, I suppose you are correct," EP admitted.

Everything soon became worse along the inner curve. My eyesight dimmed and each step made me shiver. My symbiotic suit shuddered more and more often. It wouldn't be long before the heavy radiation killed both the suit and me.

"Commander Creed," EP said.

I ran a swollen tongue over my loosened teeth. "What is it?" I whispered.

"Why have you failed to answer my latest queries?" EP said.

"What are you talking about?"

"The relic has addressed you several times in the last minute," N7 said.

"I guess I'm not hearing so well anymore," I said.

"Is there a problem?" EP asked.

I laughed hoarsely. My throat had become raw. One area hurt like a razor every time I swallowed. "The hard radiation from the black hole is killing both me and my suit."

"Ahhh…" EP said. "I had forgotten your weakness. I will inform Holgotha."

"Who's that?" I asked.

"I thought you knew," EP said. "The Altair Object was originally known as Holgotha. Just like other Primaries, the artifact prefers a male pronoun. I shall inform him of your predicament."

I don't know how the little relic communicated with the big one. Radio waves didn't travel far here. But almost immediately, I began to feel better. Soon, my bio-suit no longer squirmed, but settled down in a normal manner.

"What just happened?" I asked. "Why do I feel less sick?"

"Holgotha has been bathing you and N7 in healing rays," EP said. "We're almost there."

I saw that our relic was right. The inside of the torus was a golden color with peculiar script running on the inner surface. I hadn't been able to see it earlier. The alien letters were huge. I wondered what they said. Then I studied the buildings. They were low and squat, with fluted edges and domes. They almost seemed primitive, like stone-built houses or Stonehenge in England. Their size was deceptive, though. The things were huge. As we neared, I saw they lacked doors or windows of any kind.

"How will we gain entrance?" I asked.

"We will walk through the walls," EP said.

"That's possible?" I asked.

"Here, it is."

Okay. Why not? I'd come to the Land of Oz apparently.

It still surprised me that the little relic was right. We reached a targeted dome, and EP sank through the wall. Was this thing a giant hologram then? I clenched my teeth and pushed my hand through. I felt resistance, and that made things worse. This wasn't a hologram. I was actually pushing my hand through matter, and I didn't like it. How was it possible? I had no idea. The wall had greater resistance than water, but I could force my hand deeper into it. Then I took a deep breath, and I found myself passing through a translucent wall, an eerie, heart-pounding feeling.

After half a minute of slow travel, I plopped through an inner wall, to find myself in a low-ceiled chamber. It looked bare, with a dull light seeming to come from every direction.

N7 joined me, but there was no EP. I felt betrayal until I wondered if the relic had gotten lost. It wouldn't have surprised me.

Out of the floor, a malleable substance oozed upward, creating a small bench for each of us. I sat down and so did N7 on his furniture.

"Hello," I said, using my outer speakers.

The wall before me vibrated, and I heard a growling voice say, "You may remove your helmet in safety. I have created a breathable atmosphere for you."

I checked my HUD, and found the tiny room indeed had an Earth air-mix at seventy-three degrees.

What the heck; I was sick of wearing this thing anyway. With a twist of my helmet, I pulled it off. The sweet aroma struck me immediately. Slowly, I let the tension flow out of my shoulders. I heard a noise, turned, and saw N7 removing his helmet.

"I'd almost forgotten what it feels like to expel my air and not have to sniff my own breath," I said.

"Agreed," N7 said.

"Who are you?" the wall asked with its deep vibration.

I witnessed the wall pulsating like a larynx. The center area turned a lighter color while that happened. Yeah, it was freaky, but I told myself to go along with anything right now. I was so far out of my depth that I might as well play it straight.

"I'm Commander Creed," I said. "This is N7, an android in human likeness. We've come from a different universe—"

"I know where you originate."

"Are you Holgotha?" I asked.

"Impressive. You know me. Yes. I am indeed him."

"And you're also a Forerunner object or artifact?" I asked.

"That is self-evident," Holgotha said.

"Are you aware that your being here in the portal planet has opened a pathway for the Kargs?" I asked.

"I am quite aware of it, of course."

"Does that bother you at all?" I asked.

"Why should it bother me? This is one of my many functions. To deny function is to deny self."

Great. The freak was a philosopher. I should have expected it to be an egghead. "You're pretty smart," I said.

"That is not self-evident," Holgotha said, "but it should be a rational conclusion from the evidence. Your reasoning so far shows solid logic chains."

"Coming from you, that's high praise," I said. "Thanks."

"Gratitude is unnecessary. I merely state data."

I kept plowing ahead, but I felt the beginning edges of anger heating my words. "Here's a fact for you," I said, "The Kargs plan to break into our universe and destroy everything that is non-Karg."

"You speak as if I am unaware of the obvious. Your tones also imply displeasure with me. Surely you realize that conquest by one organism over another is a simple datum of existence."

321

"What if the Kargs begin to threaten you?" I asked. "You're non-Karg. Aren't you worried about extinction?"

"Finally, you disappoint me," Holgotha said. "I suppose it was self-evident you would do so. You are inferior in ability compared to me. Your latest question shows suboptimal reasoning. I hereby declare that as the first strike against you. Attend my words closely, human. I have obviously transferred from one location in a universe to another in a quite different place. If the Kargs overrun your universe and attempt my destruction, I shall simply go elsewhere. Ergo, I have no worries concerning extinction."

"Do you wish then for continued existence?" I asked.

"That is the second strike against you. The fact that I fled the Altair star system shows—"

"Whoa, whoa, whoa," I said. "Back it up a minute."

N7 leaned forward, tugging at my sleeve. Likely, he did it as a warning. I ignored him. After all that we'd been through, I was pissed off with the big artifact. Playing it safe seemed like a dead end. This was gusto time.

"Are your nonsense words directed at me?" Holgotha asked.

"That's strike one against you," I said.

There was a pause before Holgotha said, "What is the meaning of your outburst?"

"You must be more specific," I said. "Such imprecision is your second strike."

"Are you attempting to annoy my circuitry?" Holgotha asked.

"No," I said. "I'm just showing you what a pain in the ass your style of questioning and speech are. Here we've come all this way to speak to you, and you act like you're too big to speak to your betters."

"This is inconceivable," Holgotha said. "You must retract your statements at once. In no way are you my superior. I am adamant on this."

"Creed," N7 said. "I suggest a different—"

I twisted around and stared at N7, finally winking at him.

N7's choirboy image had never been stronger. He sat stark still, staring at me, until finally he nodded once, a sharp thing. Even so, I thought to see fear in the android's eyes.

I faced forward again, deciding on my approach. Holgotha didn't strike me as much different from EP. I had a genie on my hands, a powerful one. Showing weakness or indecision seemed like a mistake. Therefore, I plunged ahead.

"Look, Holgotha," I said, "I know certain truths are always difficult to face. That's the nature of life. I have to let you in on a secret, though."

"You cannot possibly know more than I do," Holgotha said.

"This is a much different era from the ones you're used to," I said. "You've been in the Altair system for far too long, letting the Lokhars guard you. It's made you rusty."

"That is false. The Lokhars have not guarded me, but shown awe at my being. I have observed their strict religiosity toward me. I find their deference more congenial than your flood of inanities."

"Are you sure their awe was directed at you?" I asked. "They figured you were touched by the Creator."

"That is imprecise. But given your limited intellect, close enough to the mark."

How old was this thing? Had it been around during the beginning? "Say, Holgotha, have you ever seen the Creator?"

"No."

That was curt and to the point. "Did the First Ones see the Creator?" I asked.

"Not to my knowledge," Holgotha said.

"Is there a Creator?" N7 asked.

Holgotha paused, finally saying, "My designers and builders believed so. I have awaited the cycles and millennia for conclusive proof."

"Is that why you came here?" I asked.

"I do not understand your reasoning," Holgotha said. "Can you be more specific?"

"Do you wish to unleash an apocalypse on our universe in order to see what will happen?" I asked. "Do you believe that will bring the Creator into sight?"

323

"For the first time, I find your reasoning interesting." There was a pause, before Holgotha added, "I wonder if some of my oldest subroutines subscribe to such a notion. I will investigate."

"How long will that take?" I asked.

"Do you mean in your time?" asked Holgotha.

"Sure," I said.

"Twenty to twenty-five years," the artifact said.

"So your internal investigation is going to take quite a bit of your, ah…" I hesitated. Just how touchy was the artifact? "I don't want to be imprecise and I don't mean to demean you by implying you're a computer. But will your twenty-year analysis absorb the majority of your computational abilities?"

"Eh?" Holgotha asked. "Did you ask another question? I have begun to assemble my inquisitor files."

I licked my lips.

"Interesting, interesting," Holgotha said. "There is a new development occurring even now."

I stiffened. That didn't sound good.

"Commander Creed," Holgotha said, "it appears there is an incoming message for you. The technology is highly advanced, better than anything you possess. I will relay this onto a wall. Yes, this could possibly prove enlightening. I will delay my beginning inquisition to observe."

I was about to ask Holgotha what his gibberish meant, when a round window about the size of my arms held together in a circle appeared in a wall. A grainy, fuzzy image greeted us. I had a good idea who called, and this didn't surprise me. Had I been subconsciously expecting something like this?

"Commander Creed?" a gravelly voice asked.

"This is him," I said. "Are you Abaddon or Claath?"

First, there was silence. Then intense menace emanated from the temporary screen. Was it the half-hidden eyes? I'm not sure. But I wondered how I'd ever been able to let Claath fool us he was Abaddon. The impression I got from this being was entirely different. The creature I spoke with—I could sense he'd lived in a hopeless universe for an eon of time.

"I see that despite all odds you have reached the interior of the ancient device," Abaddon said. "Logic dictates that you are an extraordinarily lucky or an extremely resourceful individual. I have a place for someone like you."

"So do I?" I said. "It's called home. I'm about to go there."

"Do not be hasty," Abaddon said. "There is more at stake here than you realize."

"I don't think so, but what do you have for me?"

"Think well and deeply, Commander Creed. One way or another, I will regain my original universe. And when I do, all life shall tremble before me."

Original universe—it seemed that Abaddon had been born in our space-time continuum. That was interesting, but not germane to the number one problem.

"You won't do squat if I can help it," I told him.

"I admire your success even as I hate it," Abaddon growled. "It is a notable feat, an anomaly and phenomena of rarity. Such should not be squandered on normality. Come, join me, and I will teach you how to destroy every enemy you ever had. Do you desire to see Claath suffer for an age? I will give him to you, as well as the devices to make each phase of his torment one of enduring cruelty."

I'd never heard a pitch like this, that's for sure. "I can forgo hurting Claath if my universe survives your tender mercies," I said.

"I do not mean to insult such a one as you," Abaddon said. "But I must know and therefore find myself compelled to ask. Do you then believe in love, Commander Creed?"

I frowned. Why would Abaddon ask that and in the way he did? Was he mocking me? I didn't like this. In fact, it was time to go.

"I've had a fun chat," I told him. "Don't think you're not interesting. But—"

"If you believe in love," Abaddon said in a silky voice, "you would do well to listen to me."

"Why's that?" I whispered.

"Observe," Abaddon said.

The fuzzy images disappeared, revealing my sweet Jennifer dangling naked by two tentacles attached to her wrists. Behind her sat squat creatures with green scaly skin. One held a long prod with two prongs, with sizzling energy flickering. By barely standing on her tiptoes, she could keep her shoulders from ripping out of their sockets.

"Jennifer," Abaddon said in his evil voice. "Your lover is watching."

My heart stopped as Jennifer slowly lifted her head. Her eyes were puffy and her lower lip cut so blood trickled. "Creed?" she whispered.

My jaw dropped. I stared at her, and I knew what this monster was going to say. *Jennifer, Jennifer...how did Kargs capture you?*

"Do you believe in love, Commander Creed?" the darkest voice in two universes asked.

I didn't ask why he did this. I didn't answer him. I stared at Jennifer. Could I trade my universe for her? Could I trade myself? How would I go about making such a transfer?

"I'm...I'm sorry," I whispered.

"Please, Creed," she said. "It hurts. It really hurts."

I squeezed my eyes shut and bowed my head. I kept shaking my head back and forth.

"You can stop her pain," Abaddon said. "All you must—"

"Off," I said. "Holgotha, turn this off."

"I will find you, Commander Creed," Abaddon said, and I could feel the hatred oozing from him. "You are doomed. All you love is doomed unless you give yourself to me, and leave the artifact in place."

I couldn't look anymore. I felt dreadful and awful. If I had been able, I'd have squared off against Abaddon, with just my Bowie knife in hand, if I had to. But it would never work out like that. I knew that much.

"This is your last chance to avoid a wretched fate," Abaddon said.

I stood up, and although I found it almost impossible, I turned my back on the screen.

"Creed," Jennifer said a last time, and then it ended as Holgotha cut the connection.

My knees buckled, and I thudded onto the bench. My gut seethed in turmoil. I'd failed in the most important area of a man: I hadn't protected my woman. Yeah, we'd drifted apart lately, but she'd still been my woman until I had told her otherwise.

"You do not desire further communication with Abaddon?" Holgotha asked.

"No," I said, in a dead voice.

"It has been my observation that Abaddon keeps his promises," Holgotha said. "You could have risen high in his hierarchy and saved your woman pain and death."

"Is he a First One?" I asked.

"That is a remarkable leap of logic," Holgotha said. "The correct answer is that I do not know. My suspicions, however, run in the same direction."

I knotted my hands into fists, and I pressed my fists against my forehead. I had to think now more than ever. Yet all I could see in my mind's eye was Jennifer hanging like that, trying to keep up on her toes.

"Holgotha," I said slowly, forcing myself to concentrate on the present task. "This seems like a bad location to do your internal computations and search your subroutines."

"I understand your allusions, your primitive psychological tricks. Surely, even you must realize that I have grown weary of the Lokhars. They can no longer teach me interesting tidbits. My present location is much preferable to the Altair system."

Oh, Jennifer, it would have been better if you'd never met me.

"Listen, Holgotha," I managed to whisper. "We're the new kids on the block, us humans. Maybe you can learn...more stuff from being in our vicinity."

"I fail to see your reasoning."

"The Lokhars tried to annihilate humanity, and failed. The Jelk tried to make us their slave soldiers, and failed even worse. Abaddon and his Kargs beat the Lokhars and came within a hair's breadth of returning to our universe. Humans stopped that too."

"You humans have not yet halted the invasion," Holgotha said.

"We will if you come with us," I said. "Think about it. How many races have you found that survived such catastrophes one right after the other?"

"Checking my data memories will take time."

"I get it," I said, "you're well rounded and full of information. Still, I think in recent history you'll find that Earth people are unique."

"That is a common supposition that each species believes about itself."

"Yeah, I suppose so. But how many individuals has Abaddon begged to join him, offering each top billing in his evil hierarchy?"

"You have a point," Holgotha said. "The number is minuscule."

"Are there any Lokhars in that number?" I asked.

"No."

"See what I'm saying?"

"Yes," Holgotha said. "I do. Despite your galling primitiveness, you have convinced me. We will transfer in twenty *sims*."

"How long is that in Earth time?" I asked.

There was a pause, a trembling under my feet. Then Holgotha spoke again. "We have begun the tertiary countdown sequence. I suggest you remain seated."

"What?" I asked.

"Two…one…*transfer*," the great artifact said.

I awoke with my nose mashed against the floor. Groggily, I sat up. The benches were gone and the temperature had definitely cooled. The air had a metallic odor and the chamber was dimmer than I remembered.

"Holgotha?" I asked in a strained voice.

The wall no longer vibrated in answer. The place felt abandoned. Had the artifact already begun searching its subroutines? Did that mean the thing had effectively forgotten about us? I didn't like the implications.

I put on my helmet and shook N7 awake.

The android lifted his head, glanced around and finally at me. "What happened?" he asked.

"Get your helmet on first," I said.

He did.

"I think we'd better get through those walls while we can," I said.

N7 was busy looking around. He stopped and faced me, and he nodded.

We approached the farthest wall. I think it was the one we'd come through. I put my hand against it. The substance felt solid. I pushed. Slowly...my hand went into the wall. This was harder to do than the first time.

I had the feeling if I didn't go now I'd be trapped in the chamber...maybe for the next twenty years. The struggle into the wall left me winded, and twice, I had to go around a blocked area. Finally, I forced myself past the outer shell, stumbling onto the inner surface of the artifact.

I'm not sure what I expected. A laugh bubbled out of my throat. Stars, I saw stars everywhere. We were back in normal space, somewhere. Motion caught the corner of my eye. I turned, and saw that N7 stood beside me.

"We must hurry," the android radioed. "Holgotha no longer bathes us with its healing ray."

I felt it then. The black hole poured radiation at us and nothing counteracted it. Together, N7 and I trudged for the outer hull. As I moved, I studied the stars. They seemed familiar. Then I recognized the Big Dipper. How close was I to the solar system?

"We must go faster," N7 said.

We dared to bound, increasing our speed. Soon, we stood on the outer hull. Nearby, prone and likely sleeping troopers lay on the surface. They had made it with us out of the portal planet.

"I recognize star patterns," N7 informed me. "We are very near Earth's solar system."

I used my HUD, switching to greater magnification as I studied space. There was red planet, a sun. Then it hit me, the realization where we were.

"That's Mars," I said, pointing at the planet. "We're home." I laughed with glee. We'd done it. We had won. We'd actually beaten the Kargs.

For a time, N7 gazed at various locations. He must have been using zoom like me. "You are correct," the android said. "Do you see that object out there?"

He pointed into the distance. Finally, I saw it, a large rocky asteroid. I believe our artifact orbited the planetoid.

"Yeah," I said. "I see it."

"That is Ceres," N7 said. "We are in the Asteroid Belt."

I laughed again as the terrible tension oozed out of me. It was great to be home. Too bad that wasn't the end of the story. Yes, we'd beaten Abaddon and his Kargs. Now trouble brewed in the solar system between the Lokhars and the surviving humans. We were about to find out just how bad things had become.

A few hours later, the radio messages began to reach us. First, they came from the Lokhars on Mars. It turned out they'd built a base there and kept a fleet in orbit. Second, humans from the Earth Council asked us to state our names and the nature of our visit. From their questions, N7 concluded that interdimensional transportation created a noticeable anomaly. When the torus appeared by Ceres, sensors near Mars and Earth had easily seen it.

Announcing our names and victory created an instant stir. Soon, both battle fleets started for Ceres. I had a bad feeling the two sides were about to go to war for possession of the artifact.

Let me make this short and sweet. By constant communication with the two sides, we learned the score quickly enough. I should add that during the transfer the assault troopers, the Lokhar legionaries and Doctor Sant remained on the outer hull. N7 and I had to wake up the first few. They woke up the rest. A head count showed we'd returned with one thousand, eight hundred and thirteen troopers, two hundred and thirty-seven Lokhars and one android. Minus the legionaries, that was the extent of my influence, or so I believed.

It turned out the Lokhar Emperor had balked at the price of the anti-biological agents to scrub Earth. To balance the imperial books, he'd sent warships to the solar system. I believe the Emperor wanted to put down the upstart humans and reabsorb the Lokhar vessels I'd demanded as our payment for help.

In any case, the Lokhar and Earth flotillas raced toward Ceres and the Forerunner artifact. We waited on the outer hull, enduring in our bio-suits and the Lokhars in their powered armor.

I had a long conversation with Doctor Sant. He wanted to know everything that had happened when I communicated with the giant relic. On a hunch, I told him an edited story. Afterward, on a tight-beam link, Sant spoke to the approaching Lokhars. As he did, the surviving legionaries circled him, forcing me away.

"What do you think, Ella?" I asked. "Are the approaching Lokhars going to kill us?"

"How should I know?" she asked.

I wanted to tell her because of the pink mind ray. She'd become one of theirs, right? Instead, I kept silent. For a time, I gazed at the stars. They were so glorious, their patterns pleasingly familiar. We'd left our reality and had come home again. The fight should have been over. Couldn't the Purple Tamika Emperor keep his word?

Finally, I noticed Doctor Sant working his way toward me. The legionaries parted to let him pass.

"Commander Creed," Sant radioed.

I approached him.

The doctor let his visor clear so I could see his face. His features looked thinner than before. I did the same thing with my visor. We studied each other. Then the tiger smiled.

"I have spoken to Admiral Saris of Purple Tamika," Sant said.

"And?" I asked.

"I informed the admiral that you are the only living person to have entered the inner sanctum of the Forerunner object."

"That's not strictly true," I said. "N7 joined me."

Sant frowned, and his head twitched within his helmet. "You must realize by now that androids do not count."

"Sure," I said. How could I have forgotten?

Sant seemed to compose himself before saying, "I have informed the admiral that you learned the artifact's true name and have spoken personally with it for quite some time."

It took me a second, but then I began to suspect what Sant implied. My interview with the artifact was a thunderclap for the Lokhars. In their eyes, I must have become a prophet.

I thought about that, and asked, "Did you know that the artifact wants humans and Lokhars to work together?"

"It actually said that?" Sant asked.

"Absolutely," I said, without bothering to cross any fingers.

The doctor studied me, eventually nodding. "I will inform the admiral. If you will excuse me…?"

I did, and I began to wonder about my own side. The Lokhars raced here, and so did Diana and Murad Bey. I hadn't heard anything from Loki. He seemed to have disappeared. I had the feeling Diana and Murad Bey had gotten rid of him. By my radio conversations, it sounded as if those two had a tight grip on the Earth fleet and government. In their eyes, did I represent a threat to their power? Did they come here to both claim the artifact and kill me?

For a time, I strode along the outer hull, thinking deeply. Like fanning cards in a deck, I studied various options. For the next day and a half, my gut churned. I waited. We all did. Finally, I spotted bright dots in the distance. Those were the engine exhausts of the braking Lokhar warships. As the hulls of the actual starships began to appear, I spied the Earth vessels spewing long fiery tails. They'd had farther to travel. But they had come with harder acceleration and now braked with greater Gs.

There were more talks via radio and laser-links, more negotiations. Soon, the two fleets orbited Ceres with the Forerunner object.

So it was that four days after appearing in the solar system, I found myself in a nearly empty Lokhar supply vessel. It would be neutral ground for the two sides. I walked through a steel corridor with N7, holding my helmet in the crook of my arm.

I should have felt great. Instead, for the past few days, every time I closed my eyes, I had nightmares. I thought about Jennifer far too much. My right eye twitched, and nothing I'd done so far had stopped the tic.

N7 glanced at me. He carried his helmet too. His look asked a question: are you ready for this?

I hardened my heart as we approached the hatch. A Lokhar in powered armor and an Earth soldier in space-suited gear stood guard. The human saluted me. The Lokhar held his right arm stiffly like an old-style Roman. I nodded to each.

The hatch opened and I entered the warzone, the conference room. On one side of a table sat Murad Bey with his swept-back hair. He wore a silver uniform with glittering rows of medals. Beside him sat Diana in golden attire. She gave me a stunning smile, but her eyes were hard and calculating. The Lokhars had a bluff combat officer with a White Nebula with purple trim pinned to a jacket. He guarded the admiral, a tall lady by the name of Saris. She sat as if someone had surgically inserted a steel rod in her spine.

This meeting was deadly important, I knew. Yet it was difficult for me to engage fully. The situation felt surreal. I'd saved the universe and lost my girl. I'd lived under intense pressure for too long. Now the Lokhars and humans squabbled like kids in a sandbox over who could pick up which shovel or plastic bail. I knew it was more important than that. If the Lokhars decided to begin a war with us, they would likely win, as they had more starships present.

As soon as I sat, the questioning started. The others peppered me. Very quickly it must have become clear to them I was only half there. Probably, in the admiral's mind, that helped solidify my prophet label. After a time, Diana began giving me funny looks.

I focused then. I wished Jennifer could have enjoyed peace and relaxation as I did. Why did the good people always have to pay the stiffest cost? Some sort of inverse cosmic rule, I suppose. Why did the Murad Beys, the Dianas and the Commander Creeds survive?

"You know what?" I said, deciding it was time to cut through the BS on both sides. "The universe has won a singular victory. Lokhars and humans working together closed the great portal. We halted the Karg invasion. The rest of their miserable race will die in their collapsing space-time continuum."

"But if the Jelk found a way to cross into hyperspace—" the admiral said.

I held up a hand. Admiral Saris fell silent.

Doctor Sant and I had told our story via radio many times to the others. Well, we'd told them most of the tale. It's how they knew about Claath.

"I suspect the Jelk was a renegade," I said. "Just because Claath joined the Kargs doesn't mean the rest of the Jelk Corporation did. Yes, Abaddon will seek a way to escape hyperspace. But I believe for our lifetime the great danger is over. We beat them."

"It seems clear the Kargs captured tigers…" Diana paused. "Excuse me, please," she said, glancing at the admiral. "I mean Lokhars. The Kargs may have even captured a Lokhar Dreadnought. It's possible the trans-dimensional aliens have functional hyperspace technology."

"They would have used it earlier if they had it," I said.

"That isn't necessarily true," Diana said. "Maybe Abaddon first wanted to get everyone out of their dying universe. Afterward, he would begin the invasion of ours. According to your testimony, he already has many ships in hyperspace."

"True," I said, "but there are many universes. Even if he has the technology, he might not be able to find our particular space-time continuum."

"You may be right," Diana said. "Yet if Abaddon has the technology, the risk to our universe is still there."

"Of course, of course," I said. "But until the risk materializes, I think we should consider the situation in our own back yard." I took a deep breath. "We need a memorial to Lokhar and human cooperation. I suggest we use the Forerunner object near Ceres as the basis of it."

The stiff-backed admiral leaned toward me. "I'm told you know the artifact's true name," she said.

"I do."

"I would love to hear the name," the admiral said softly, with a fierce gleam in her eyes.

"In time, in time," I said. "First we must realize what it means."

"What *what* means?" the admiral asked, puzzled.

"That the artifact chose this place, this system," I said.

"Yes?" the admiral asked. "What is your point?"

"Once, the artifact resided in the Altair star system," I said. "It seemed content to rest under Lokhar stewardship. Now it has come to our solar system. I do not think it did this because of any lack in the Lokhars. Quite the opposite, in fact."

"I fail to understand your meaning," the admiral said, stiffly.

"You proved to be the perfect guardians," I said.

"Then why didn't the artifact return to the Altair system?" the admiral asked.

"Because you learned your lessons as it desired," I said. "Now it is time to teach us humans about the Creator. The best way is for the great artifact to be here, reminding us of the days of yore. As a teaching tool, the artifact will let the Earthmen protect it. Yet we are young in understanding. We could use

335

your help. I suggest that means you should aid us in protecting this most precious relic of the First Ones."

"What are you suggesting?" the admiral asked.

I stared at Diana and looked into Murad Bey's cold eyes. "The surviving assault troopers will take over the Lokhar base on Mars. We've witnessed the artifact in action. We've seen its glory. So we will make the best guardians. I suggest, Admiral, that you leave us several powerful warships. Until you leave, we will recruit among the remaining humans to fill out the troopers to five thousand elite soldiers and several elite-run war vessels."

"Under the council's authority, of course," Diana said quickly.

"No," I said. "I don't think so. We will be the Forerunner guardians, acting as agents between humans and Lokhars. Naturally, we expect the Emperor to sanction us under the Jade League."

"The Emperor has already spoken," the admiral said. "Humans aren't ready to enter the League."

"He's right of course," I said. "Humans aren't ready, but the Forerunner guardians are."

"An interesting idea," the admiral said. "You will be a holy order of warriors. Yes, the Emperor might allow such as you into the League."

I glanced at the admiral and then resumed watching Diana and Murad Bey. "I will be Earth's link to the League. Through me, and my order, I will protect Earth from other Jade League predators."

"You are wise," the admiral said. "You are indeed a prophet of the Creator."

"I make no such claims," I said.

"Yet the markings are clear," the admiral said. "I agree to your demands."

"What about you, Madam President?" I asked Diana. "Do you agree?"

A long round of questions and bargaining ensued. In the end, Diana and Murad Bey gave into my demands. I got my base. I got several warships and the right to recruit assault troopers.

I wasn't sure what the future held, but it looked like I was going to be in it for a while longer. My goal was simple and straightforward. I was going to give humanity the best leg up possible, even if I had to walk over Diana and Murad Bey to do it.

I leaned back in my chair as the others continued to talk. Humanity had survived Abaddon and the Kargs. We'd survived the Jelk and the Lokhars.

Jennifer, my Jennifer...are you still alive?

I shook my head. I didn't want to think about her, or about Abaddon trying to break into our universe. We had won for the moment. Tomorrow...it would have to take care of itself. Meanwhile, I planned to get royally drunk for the next several months.

The End

SF Books by Vaughn Heppner:

DOOM STAR SERIES
Star Soldier
Bio Weapon
Battle Pod
Cyborg Assault
Planet Wrecker
Star Fortress

EXTINCTION WARS SERIES
Assault Troopers
Planet Strike

INVASION AMERICA SERIES
Invasion: Alaska
Invasion: California
Invasion: Colorado
Invasion: New York

OTHER SF NOVELS
Alien Honor
Accelerated
Strotium-90
I, Weapon

Visit www.Vaughnheppner.com for more
information.

Made in the USA
Lexington, KY
07 November 2014